Nuclear JELLYFISH

TIM DORSEY

Nuclear JELLYFISH

wm

WILLIAM MORROW

An Imprint of HarperCollins*Publishers*

NUCLEAR JELLYFISH. Copyright © 2009 by Tim Dorsey. All rights reserved. Printed in the United States of America. No part of this book may be used or reproduced in any manner whatsoever without written permission except in the case of brief quotations embodied in critical articles and reviews. For information address HarperCollins Publishers, 10 East 53rd Street, New York, NY 10022.

HarperCollins books may be purchased for educational, business, or sales promotional use. For information please write: Special Markets Department, HarperCollins Publishers, 10 East 53rd Street, New York, NY 10022.

FIRST EDITION

Design by Daniel Lagin

Library of Congress Cataloging-in-Publication Data has been applied for.

ISBN 978-0-06-143266-8

09 10 11 12 13   OV/RRD   10 9 8 7 6 5 4 3 2 1

For Erin

Money doesn't talk—it swears.
—**BOB DYLAN**

Nuclear
JELLYFISH

PROLOGUE

SOMEWHERE IN CYBERSPACE

Serge's Blog. Star date 485.328.

First off, fuck the word *blog*. I hate it and all who use it. "Lol," "imo," "Today's mood: Introspective yet spunky." Shut up. The Internet was supposed to become the ultimate democratic forum. It did: Now everyone can be a porn star. Then there are those retarded blogs. It's been said that inside every life is a fascinating book, or at least a chapter. Wrong. Some people don't have a freakin' semicolon, like that woman in Delray who blogs everything her cat does, and her cat even has a blog and every word is meow. But you have to play the hand you're dealt, and I can't exactly stand on street corners with a megaphone sharing Big Answers on Everything. That was my first choice, but a monkey wrench hit the works: a few itsy-bitsy little incidents. *Murder* is such a charged word. You know how some people fixate and won't let things go? They're called cops.

So I guess I should be thankful for the Internet. Especially since my newly launched travel advisory service demands the latest cutting-edge communication technology! Who better to guide you around my fine state? Right, I know what you're thinking: "Serge, without delay, give me an example chocked with more value than I could expect to find elsewhere!" Okay, if you're staying at a budget motel that has *mandatory* daily maid service, they have a meth lab problem. Or I can tell you how to extract yourself from the wrong bar with only a paper clip and a ballpoint pen. And if you've ever seen a motel room scanned with one of those ultraviolet semen cams, your head would never hit another pillow. Does William Shatner provide this kind of biting insight? I think we both know the answer. Before I debuted this blog, I applied to all the big established Internet travel sites, but they said they didn't think their clients were interested in how to choose hookers who wouldn't take all their credit cards. I said, "Look, you can spend the rest of your days shuffling through the website ghetto, or you can make the roaming gnome your bitch." I think there's something wrong with my phone because the line keeps going dead. So until I get proper sponsorship, I'm forced to put up my own wildcat site. Did I mention it's totally free? What a bargain! Let's get to it!

Serge's definition of total happiness: Florida, a full tank of gas and no appointments.

Except all the jerks down here keep making appointments *with me*. What are you gonna do? Someone has to instruct them. But as I always say, if you love your work, it's not really work. My psychiatrist disagrees of course, because she wants to medicate my ADD and OCD. I said, but those are the most important selling points on a travel writer's résumé. We notice *everything*: bridge weight limits, discarded rolls of carpet padding, bleached livestock skulls, plywood signs for pond demolition, bus stop benches advertising discount vasectomies, billboards for laser hair removal featuring chicks with mustaches, witty country church marquees where Jesus battles Satan with puns, dilapidated rural homes with a baffling number of disabled schoolbuses in the backyard, and malfunctioning brake lights on the car up ahead where the hostage in the trunk ripped out wiring. Then my shrink asks about manic depression. I say I'm never depressed. She says, what about when you beat up jerks? I say I'm happy then, too.

I decided to start this service because everyone is always coming up to me and saying, "Serge, you should start a travel service." They actually say, "What the fuck's your problem?" But I can read between the lines. I'm constantly seeing clueless Europeans with pasty legs stumbling around the wrong motels, and I shake my head. Yep, they're going to get robbed. So I run up to them and say they're going to get robbed. Then I say, not by me, put your hands down. Now they're not thinking straight and don't listen when I explain how to cut their homicide rate in half. But they'd already know that if they subscribed to Serge's Florida Experience! (Free!)

From the Mailbag: "Hey, Serge, how did Florida become Dirtbag Central?" Because if you pass out in the snow, you die.

Hold the phone. Speaking of passing out, Coleman wants to give a travel tip. "Don't buy any coke from Rico. It's stomped on." Coleman, that's not a travel tip . . . No, it's not . . . No, I won't help you get your money back . . . Anyhoo, where was I? Weirdness. Florida has such a rarefied per capita concentration that CNN might as well be the local news. Some guy shoots a Wendy's manager over their three sauce-packet limit; alligator attacks naked guy on crack doing backstrokes in retention culvert; driver falls out of car at forty-five miles an hour opening door to spit; smuggler makes it through airport security with monkey under his hat. And if something *does* happen in another state, it's just a matter of time for the Florida shoe to drop. You say some criminal Rhodes scholar stole Crystal Gayle's tour bus in Tennessee? Gee, where on earth might he head next?

Today's Tip: A three sauce-packet limit is wrong. But pulling a gun is just as wrong. Go to Arby's instead. They understand packet dynamics.

Back to the Mailbag! . . . Uh-oh. It's Agent Mahoney. "I'm going to get you." What a broken record. Mahoney blames me for *everything,* especially the stuff I've done. To compound it, there's been a recent spike in businessmen mugged at hotels by highly organized crews. And now someone's going after the robbers. So Mahoney naturally thinks it's me, just because I happened to be at all the same places at the same time. I wish it *was* me (lol).

Mahoney, Mahoney, Mahoney . . . maybe that explains this nagging sensation I've been having lately, like something really bad's about to happen. Can't quite put my finger on it. And I'm not the superstitious type, which is why I don't like superstitious people. They're bad luck. But everyone's number eventually comes up, and I've already skated through more than my share of tough jams. So just block it out. Enough negative thoughts! I hate them. They suck. They piss me off. If they were people, I'd get a chainsaw and . . . You're still doing it. Have to bear down. Concentrate: Appreciate God's gift of this beautiful day where the Florida sun is shining and my gas tank's full. Now I'm so happy I could burst! Off we go!

Part One

THE PRESENT

CHAPTER 1

*M*idnight.

Two young men walked along the bank of the St. Johns River, sporting shaved heads, sleeveless T-shirts and bituminous eyes that proudly announced: MINIMUM WAGE 4 LIFE. They gripped baseball bats halfway up the barrels.

"I hate fuckin' bums."

"So where are they?"

"Supposed to be a bunch of them right around here."

"Just like fuckin' bums."

There had been a light rain, and warm mist rose from the road. Work boots slapped across glistening tar and splashed through moon-lit puddles. They approached the underpass of the Fuller Warren Bridge.

"Where the hell are those damn bums?"

"Hold up."

"What is it?"

"Over there."

"Where?"

"Shhhhh. Get your camcorder ready . . ."

A two-tone 1971 AMC Javelin with split upholstery sat in darkness and trash beneath a downtown bridge over the St. Johns River.

"Theories abound concerning the phenomenon of the nation's

trash elite inexorably percolating down to Florida like industrial toxins reaching our aquifers . . ."

A beer can popped. "You're doing it again."

Serge wrote furiously in his notebook. "Doing what?"

"Talking to yourself."

"No I wasn't." More writing. ". . . This travel writer places his money on time-release scumbag DNA . . ."

Coleman burped. "You always talk to yourself and then say you're not."

"I am? Really? That's embarrassing." He leaned over his notebook. ". . . The scumbag genetic factor is like hereditary blood disease or male-pattern baldness. At progressive age milestones, a series of rusty, chain-link twists in the double helix trigger a sequence of social tumors: Buy a pit bull, buy an all-terrain vehicle, get a DUI, sponsor a series of blue-ribbon slapping matches with your wife in the middle of the street, discharge a gun indoors, fail to appear in court, discharge fireworks indoors, get a DUI, forget where you put your Oxycontin, crash your all-terrain vehicle into your pit bull, spend money to replace missing front teeth on large-mouth-bass mailbox, get stretchered away by ambulance for reasons you don't remember, appear on *COPS* for a DUI, run out the back door when warrants are served and, in a trademark spasm of late-stage dirtball-ism, move to Florida . . ."

Serge finished the transcription and turned to a fresh page. There was a period of silence in the two-tone Javelin (orange and green) sitting under the Fuller Warren Bridge. Then, a crunching of wax paper. A soggy tuna sandwich appeared. A travel mug of cold coffee came off the dashboard.

"Serge," said Coleman. "What did you mean before, 'We're on stakeout'? We're not police."

"Common mistake everyone makes, like the Constitution's reserve clause for states' rights. Just because cops do it, doesn't mean we can't." Serge took a sip from the mug. "This is our new job."

Coleman finished unwrapping the sandwich. "I thought our new job was visiting hotels to fill out checklists for that travel website."

"And on every hotel listing, there's a section called 'local things to do.'"

"I'm not sure the websites want to send their customers under bridges at night in dicey parts of town."

"That's my offbeat niche: I give the people what they want before they know they want it."

"But your new boss specifically said no more offbeat reports."

"Everyone does what their bosses ask, and that's precisely why you need to distinguish yourself from the herd." Serge killed the coffee. "I stun them into paralyzed respect with my withering insubordination. First impressions are important."

"They usually call security."

"Because I made an impression."

Coleman checked one of his pants pockets, then another. He pulled out his hand and raised the twisted corner of a Baggie to his eyes. "Where'd it all go? Did mice chew through here? Oh well . . ." He bent over.

"Thought you'd outgrown that."

"What do you mean?"

"Everyone now knows coke is fucked up. You had an excuse for a while, because our hypocritical government lost all credibility by lumping pot in with crack to court the weed-bigot vote. Meanwhile, congressmen crammed all orifices with huge wads of cash from tobacco and liquor lobbies. But who would have guessed they were actually right about that stupid white shit?"

Coleman raised his head and sniffled. "I just do a little bump now and then so I can stay up and keep drinking beer."

"For a second I thought you weren't being productive."

Coleman's head suddenly snapped to the side. He pointed out Serge's window. "What was that?"

Serge turned. "What?"

"Something moved under the bridge."

Serge returned to his notebook. "Nothing's there. You're hallucinating again."

Coleman squinted a few more seconds, then shrugged. He stuck his tongue inside the empty bag and reached under the seat for another Schlitz. "We need to make some money."

"That's what I'm doing now." Serge flipped a notebook page, stopped and tapped his chin with a pen. "I need travel-writing tunes."

He reached for his iPod, synched it with an RF transmitter to the Javelin's radio and cranked the volume.

" . . . *Fly high, oh, Freebird, yeah! . . .*"

Coleman rewrapped his tuna sandwich. "You've been listening to Skynyrd all day."

"We're in Jacksonville. I'm required to listen to Skynyrd."

"Why? Skynyrd's from Alabama."

Serge began punching the steering wheel like a speed bag. "Everyone thinks they're from Alabama! They're Floridians! Apocryphal motherfuckers . . ."

"Okay, okay, they're from Florida." Coleman set a wax ball on the dashboard. "I don't know this stuff like you."

Serge pointed at the ball. "You're messing up my horizon."

"The sandwich is soggy."

"Soggy's better."

"Fuck that shit."

"Your little chestnuts complete my life."

"So Skynyrd's really from Florida?"

"Too many of our state's native accomplishments are credited elsewhere. First Skynyrd and Alabama, then everyone thinks the Allman Brothers are from Georgia."

"They're not?"

"South Daytona Beach." Serge flipped down the sun visor and gazed up at a photo attached with rubber bands.

"You sure keep looking at that picture a lot."

"I think I'm in love for the first time in my life."

Coleman leaned for a closer view of a smiling woman in a NASA pressure suit. "But it's just that crazy astronaut."

"So?"

"So she's a basket case. Got obsessed with some rival babe, filled a tote bag with tools, and drove like twelve hours straight through the night to kidnap her at the Orlando airport."

"Exactly." Serge took the photo down and kissed it. "This chick's focused."

A dark form stepped out from behind a bridge pylon. It slowly approached the Javelin from the driver's blind spot.

Coleman looked down at his lap. "Serge?"

"What?"

"I don't want to wear a diaper anymore."

"Then don't drink so much beer. We always have to pull over while I'm doing research."

"Ever since you heard of that batty astronaut—"

"Don't talk about my woman!" Serge replaced the photo and flipped the visor back up. "Besides, if I can wear a diaper, so can you."

"But why are *you* wearing a diaper?"

"Maturity," said Serge. "I've always wanted to be an astronaut, but my psychiatrist taught me to accept things I cannot change." He wiggled into the driver's seat with a plastic crinkling sound, then looked out the window at the stars and smiled. "This may be the closest I get to going into space."

INTERSTATE 10 CORRIDOR

Toby Keith on the juke. Expense-account martinis covered several cocktail tables that businessmen had pushed together in a smoky motel lounge called the Pirate's Cove. The decor was saddles and spurs and branding irons. The sign remained a lasting testimony that pirates don't sell drinks in north Florida, and cowboys don't sell enough for a new sign.

Swinging saloon doors creaked; a familiar face rolled luggage into the cove.

"Steve! Get over here, we saved you a seat!"

"It's now *Sh*-teve."

"*Sh*-teve?"

The adjoining tables were inhabited by a race of subterranean, combed-over business travelers with the physiques of water balloons resting on something flat. They racked up massive 41-cent miles and a gold-card number of hotel nights due to very good or very bad marriages. The chair they'd saved was at the head of the first table because the rest of the gang lived vicariously through Steve's sex stories. They were all false, of course, but the guys believed him since he was the youngest and the best looking of the bunch, which was beyond relative and little coin in the realm of getting any.

"Why '*Sh*-teve'?"

"Babes dig it. Still spelled the same." He plopped down and looked back toward the swinging doors. "Did you check out that piece of ass at the reception desk?"

"Couldn't miss. Looks like she's still in high school."

Steve leaned back arrogantly.

"Don't tell me you did her."

"A gentleman doesn't talk."

"Come on!"

"Okay, first I grabbed her ears . . ."

They were an hour east of Tallahassee, just off I-10, in the state's Spanish-moss belt girding the Georgia line. The nearest dots on the map were Live Oak, Madison and Shady Grove. It was a modest but sanitary motel, kept to chain standards, that went up quickly when economy at the exit ramp exploded with a convenience store and fast-food franchise that did morning biscuits right.

The lounge side of the property sat in the shadow of the highway overpass, and long-haul truckers rumbled by at such an acute angle as to suggest landing aircraft. Beneath the bridge's eastern berm stood the lighted motel marquee—WELCOME DIVERSIFIED CONSOLIDATORS—and below that, someone in a dishwashing hairnet manipulated a twelve-foot telescoping aluminum pole to capture black plastic letters. He left the WELCOME up and changed the rest to DATA IMPLEMENTERS. The WELCOME had an off-putting slant in the middle because they were short on *L*'s and flipped over a 7. The largest conference room had a fire-marshal capacity of eighteen.

The gang in the hotel bar—like all gangs in all hotel bars—had a universal familiarity. Some was the result of actually knowing each other, traveling identical job circuits and enrolling in the same reward-points program. The rest had never met but recognized their own kind. Like Darin and Frank.

"I'm Darin, he's Frank. Join you?"

Another table slid over.

"What's your line?"

Frank removed a plastic straw convention hat. "World Congress of Data Implementers."

Someone pointed at the military ribbons on Darin's jacket. "What are those?"

"Seven straight quarters, most data implemented."

"Nobody can touch Darin," said Frank. "They call him the terminator."

Beer bottles clinked. A toast to data.

Frank turned to Steve. "Who are you with?"

"Southeast Rare Coins. Finished a show in Tallahassee, getting a leg up on Jacksonville tomorrow. I'm *Sh*-teve. This is Ted and Henry."

"Nice to meet . . ."

"Saw the billboards," Frank said respectfully. "That big expo with the stamp collectors."

Ted winced.

Henry made a silent, slashing gesture across his throat with a finger.

"I say something wrong?"

Steve stared down into his cocktail. "Stamps guys are faggots."

Ted crouched and lowered his voice. "Some exhibitors pulled out of the tour. Forced to let philatelists in or we'd get creamed on the hall deposits."

"Speaking of exhibitors . . ." Ted looked around the room. "Where's Ralph?"

"Stayed back at the conference," said Steve.

"What? The hotel where we had the show?"

Steve nodded curtly, biting an olive off a plastic spear.

"But Ralph should know better. You never stay at the show hotel."

"He's an adult."

"So was Buffalo Nickel Bill."

"How's he doing?" asked Henry.

"Getting out of the hospital next week."

"Who would have thought he'd be hit in Panama City?"

"Whole state's gone crazy."

"Police think it's one of the new professional gangs."

"Good," said Steve.

"How's that good?"

"Because pros only hit when they're absolutely sure you're out of the room. And we're insured."

"Then why'd they jump Bill?"

"Must have varied his routine and come back at the wrong time."

"I'm worried," said Henry.

"You *all* worry too much," said Steve. "It's an isolated incident . . ."

". . . That required sixty stitches."

"Listen," said Steve. "Bill got sloppy."

"And some punks got lucky," said Henry. "Police found a few loose gems in the carpet that were scattered in the attack. How'd they know there'd be such a score?"

"Back up," said Ted. "What was Bill doing with stones? He's a coin guy. Not even good coins. Warned him about loading up on buffalo nickels."

"Do you have to talk about him like that while he's still got tubes?" said Henry. "We all took a beating when the buffalo bubble burst."

"But what was Bill doing with stones?"

"Police said they were definitely pros who knew exactly what they were looking for. Didn't even touch the nickels."

"Screw the nickels already! What the hell was Bill doing with stones?"

"Just telling you what I heard."

"Makes perfect sense now," Steve said with authority. "Read all about it in the paper: the latest thing . . ."

Everyone turned and waited.

". . . Traveling businessmen secretly moonlighting as diamond couriers."

"Diamond couriers?" said Henry.

"Little-known fact, but secret networks of highly trained couriers are crisscrossing Florida at all times. With the state's insane growth, there's more than enough work to go around, and they've started recruiting part-timers."

"Don't they use armored cars?" asked Ted.

"Sometimes." Steve opened his wallet, removing an iridescent plastic card. "But you do the math: too many jewelry stores and not enough vehicles. Plus, those trucks are neon advertisements. So couriers go under the radar, no security, dressing down, the last people you'd ever expect, like Bill. Unfortunately, there's also a secret network of professional robbery crews who know the deal, and it's become a high-stakes game of cat and mouse from Pensacola to Key West."

"But if couriers are undercover, how do the gangs find out?"

"Police theorize paid informants . . ." Steve tilted the shiny card back and forth in the light. ". . . People *very* close to the couriers, possibly the same line of work. Maybe even staying at the same hotels . . ."

Everyone at the tables hushed and leaned back. In their minds, Vincent Price played the pipe organ. Eyes darted from person to person in a round-robin of suspicion. Steve's card found the perfect angle; a hologram appeared.

"When did you reach platinum?" asked Henry.

"Last week." He began sliding it back into his wallet.

"Can I touch?"

"No."

CHAPTER 2

erge grabbed a briefcase from the Javelin's backseat and opened it in his lap. Pockets brimmed with tourist pamphlets aggressively harvested from hotel-lobby racks, then alphabetized. Florida Theater, Fort Caroline, the symphony, the zoo . . .

Coleman cracked another beer. "When do we get to the part about making money?"

"We're already there." Serge pawed through flyers. "This is the perfect spot to take in all the bridges." A digital camera sat on the dash, and Serge rotated it ten degrees at half-minute intervals for an overlapping panorama of time-lapse night shots. "I love bridges, and Jacksonville loves me! Hard to find more spans in one spot except Pittsburgh, but then you're in Pittsburgh. Here we have seven bridges downtown alone, because of the mighty St. Johns, and even more downstream."

"What about tunnels?"

"Love them too, but in the current climate of homeland security, authorities now frown on my tunnel routine of taking twenty photos while standing in the moon roof steering with my knees. I think they frowned on it before as well." Serge hit the recline lever on the driver's seat for the required bridge-appreciation angle, smiling as he scanned sparse evening traffic crossing respective west-to-east spans: Corporate climbers from skyline insurance buildings heading south to the suburbs after another late night at the office, rental cars and hotel shuttles driving down from the northside airport, Disney-bound families in minivans with New York and New England plates getting some last miles under their belts before putting up, a stretch limo full of non-limo people who'd pooled money for a birthday party, a windowless white van with ladders on top and magnetic licensed-contractor signs on the side.

Outside the Javelin, in Serge's blind spot, an ominous shadow grew larger.

Serge raised his eyes toward old girders of the bridge they were beneath. He grabbed his travel mug off the dash and refilled from a thermos. "Now I'm milking the last few moments of simple pleasure."

Coleman crumpled a beer can. "From what?"

"Lightbulbs. I can't get enough of the bulbs."

"Bulbs?"

"Blue. All along this bridge as well as the neighboring John T. Alsop built in 1941. Rare remaining treasure of a center-steel sensibility."

"Why blue lightbulbs?"

"*Monday Night Football.*" Serge chugged his travel mug. "Jacksonville now has the Jaguars, and network people are always broadcasting nightscapes of whatever city they're in before cutting to commercials. But downtown Jacksonville was about as hopping as the *Andromeda Strain* when everyone's dead from an extraterrestrial virus. TV cameras might as well have been panning the dark side of the moon. A PR windfall from professional football was about to turn into national disgrace."

"Dear Jesus," said Coleman. "What happened next?"

"Genius struck!" Serge took another long pull of coffee. "Someone who will forever go unrecognized said, 'Let's put blue lightbulbs all over the bridges.' It's dark; they won't see the rest of the shit. Shazam! For pennies on the dollar, they created the illusion of a modern civilization."

"Wow," said Coleman. "And all because of *Monday Night Football*?"

"Just a guess, but fuck it: I'm going with that anyway!"

"You're at the party!"

"Damn straight!" Serge stared down at his wristwatch, counting along with the sweep-second hand. He looked back up at the bridge. "Aren't those lights absolutely beautiful? I feel drunk just looking at them. My soul wants to devour it all so badly that it makes me want to weep. Those lights scream Jacksonville to me. More Skynyrd for everyone!" He clicked the iPod and looked back at his watch. "Ten, nine, eight . . ."

". . . *Seven years of hard luck* . . ."

"What are you counting down?"

". . . *from the Florida border* . . ."

"They turn off the lights this time each night to save money . . . three, two, one . . ." Serge looked up. The bridge went dark. The shadow behind the car grew closer. "Damn. Now I'm depressed. All life eventually dies. How could God have allowed Hitler to be born?"

"Remember your psychiatrist?" said Coleman. "Accept what you can't change."

"Good thinking." Serge closed his eyes and smiled. "The bulbs are still on in my mind."

A sharp knock on the driver's window.

Serge and Coleman jumped.

A bearded man stood outside making a vigorous twirling signal with his hand.

Serge rolled down the window. "My name's Serge. I'm wearing a diaper for the space race."

"Have any money?"

"Yes, but you're only going to buy beer."

Coleman leaned across and handed him a Schlitz.

"Thanks."

"Coleman!"

The man pointed at the wax ball on the dashboard. "Food?"

"Tuna salad," said Serge.

"Soggy," said Coleman.

"Soggy's better," said the man.

"Right-o." Serge tossed the ball out the window.

The man peeled paper and took a bite. "Is that Skynyrd?"

"We're in Jacksonville," said Serge. "I just drank a lot of coffee."

"I love Skynyrd."

"The lightbulbs are still on in my mind."

The man pointed beneath the underpass. "I need to get back to my cardboard box."

"Have a pamphlet."

"The zoo?"

"Who's to say?"

"Later."

Serge rolled up the window.

Coleman pulled a joint from over his ear. "What now?"

"Next bridge." He reached for the ignition. Something caught the corner of his eye. "What was that?" He turned quickly. Two more dark forms appeared and moved fleetly toward the underpass.

"Who are they?" asked Coleman.

"Skinheads with baseball bats and a camcorder," said Serge. "In certain societies, that's a sign of bad luck."

"What are they doing?" asked Coleman.

"Oh my God!" said Serge. "They're beating the shit out of that cardboard box!"

"They're attacking a Skynyrd fan!" said Coleman.

Serge was out of the car in a flash, followed by Coleman at a lesser marijuana rate.

The bearded man spilled from his box and curled defensively on the ground. "Don't hurt me!"

A Louisville slugger came down hard in his ribs. "Fuckin' bum!"

A second bat found a kneecap with a nauseating clack. "You make us want to puke!"

The man screamed like a child.

The first skinhead turned on the camcorder and held the glowing viewfinder to his face. "Hit him again!" The camera kept filming, but there was no swing.

"What are you waiting for?"

The answer came in the sound of a baseball bat bouncing impotently on the pavement.

The first skinhead lowered the camcorder to see his partner with a knife at his throat. "Who the hell are you?"

"The Lone Road Ranger," said Serge. "We've had complaints of aggravated stupidity. I'm afraid I'll have to ask you to come with us."

"Fuck you!" said the one at knifepoint. "We're not going anywhere!"

"You're a traitor to your race!" shouted the other. He began pumping a fist in the air. *"White pride! White pride! . . ."*

"White pride?" asked Coleman. "What's that?"

"You've heard the joke," said Serge. "White pride is rotating the tires on your house."

100 MILES AWAY

A young woman took a sip of Diet Coke on the rocks. Slender, freckles, sandy-blond. Severely sexy, but dressed down in a way that was deliberately trying to hide it, which only made her more so. A purse sat next to a small backpack with the name of a community college. She turned the page in a history textbook and asked for a refill.

The woman escaped notice of not a single businessman in the hotel lounge, staring shamelessly at her tight bottom on a stool at the bar.

The gang had already nominated their designated hitter.

Someone elbowed Steve again. "Go for it."

"I am."

"You've been saying that for the last hour."

"Leave him alone," said another voice. "He knows what he's doing. Don't you, *Sh*-teve?"

"These things need to be handled very delicately."

"Someone buy him another drink . . ."

New guys came through the lounge entrance, rolling a pair of styrene expo-booth organizers. "Jerry, Tom, National Association of Trade Shows . . ."

No hellos.

Jerry looked at Tom, then back at the tables. "Something wrong?"

A data implementer nodded toward the bar.

"Holy mother," said Jerry. "Where'd she come from?"

"*Sh*-teve's about to make his move."

Steve, already sloshed, fortified himself with a final drink and stood up. The rest of the gang scooted chairs around in stadium configuration as he staggered toward the bar and grabbed a stool on the woman's left. "You live around here often?... Ha! I got a million of 'em!"

No answer.

"My name's *Sh*-teve. What's yours?"

Still staring down at the textbook. "Story."

"Story? What kind of name is that?"

"Like Musgrave, the astronaut."

"You have a man's name?"

She highlighted something with a yellow marker.

"That's okay," said Steve. "Lots of two-way names now. Alex, Mickey . . ." He extended a hand to shake.

She gave it a look like it was covered with raw sewage.

Steve changed tactics and opened his wallet. "Let me buy you a drink." He set a twenty on the counter and raised a finger. "Bartender!"

She grabbed the bill and stuck it in her pocket.

The barkeep came over. "What can I get you?"

"Uh, nothing." Steve turned. "What brings you to town?"

"Meeting my brother."

"What are you reading?"

She sighed deeply and closed her eyes.

"Something bothering you?"

"An asshole sat down next to me."

"Look," said Steve. "If you don't want company, just say so."

"I don't want company."

"That means you're lonely." He grinned. "And there's only one cure for what ails you: *Sh*-teve!"

"Go away."

"I got coke."

"I'm not going to ask you again."

"Can I have my twenty back?"

"No."

Steve bit his lip in thought. Then under his breath: "Bitch."

Story slowly raised her head, eyes boring holes in a blank spot on the wall. Blood pressure zoomed into the red zone. The bartender was looking at them. He smiled. She smiled back until he turned around

to run an American Express card. Like lightning, her left hand shot out, seized the hair on the back of Steve's head, and smashed his face down into the bar. It happened so fast, the guys in the cheap seats weren't exactly sure what they'd seen. Then, just as quickly, her hand withdrew before the bartender could spin around at the sound of the attack.

"Good God!"

Story looked up from her textbook. "What?"

The bartender ran over with a thick stack of napkins and handed them to Steve, blood pouring from his nose all over the counter. "You okay, fella? What happened?"

Between booze and kissing the bar, Steve could only manage incomprehensible slurring.

"I think he's drunk," said Story, turning a page.

AN HOUR LATER

Two young men with shaved heads couldn't move. They lay crammed in the trunk of a 1971 Javelin. The hood opened. Serge stood back-lit by an energy-saving streetlight. The pair glanced up with puzzled faces.

"You'll absolutely love it!" said Serge, panning the camcorder from one skinhead to the other. "I'm filming the perfect ending to your movie."

"What are you going to do with us?"

"First I'll tape your mouths, because I don't like interruptions when I'm teaching class."

On the side of the road, Coleman pushed himself up from where he'd lost another dance with gravity. "Serge, what gave you this idea?"

"Back when we were renting on Triggerfish Lane." Serge set the camcorder on the ground and tore off long stretches of duct tape. "Had that embarrassing near-fatal accident in the front yard performing my one-man interpretive dance honoring those natives in *National Geographic* with the big neck hoops."

"That's right. I saved your life with just seconds to go by turning off the hose."

"And don't think I haven't forgotten," said Serge. "Sixty more times and we'll be even. After the blood returned to my brain, I said to myself, I may have just tripped over a major advancement in my chosen field. Let's take it to the next level! But until today I never had the right dick-wads."

Serge finished with the tape, stood back up and smiled proudly with arms outstretched in an encompassing gesture. "Welcome to the First Coast! The chambers of commerce name them all: Space Coast, Treasure Coast, Gold Coast, Nature Coast, Emerald Coast. But you're at the First! Florida is a paradox that way, one of the youngest states, yet with some of the oldest European settlements. And this particular section of the northeast shore was home to a couple of the earliest sixteenth-century Spanish and French fortifications. You mentioned before your admirable devotion to pride, so I can tell by your buggy eyes that you're overwhelmed being bound and gagged at a seminal site of Euro-centrism in the New World. I built that into tonight's program just for you! . . . Coleman, give me a hand."

Coleman grabbed a pair of wrists. "What about the neighbors?"

"What neighbors?" said Serge, gripping ankles. "It's the only house at this end of the new development. And there's extra newspapers in the driveway, which means they're on vacation. That's why I picked it."

They hoisted the skinheads out of the trunk. Legs tied tightly together with rope; more coils secured arms against their sides. Serge pulled one by the feet and dragged him across a lush lawn. "We're heading down to St. Augustine next. Well, you won't. Sorry, those are the rules. But get this: It's St. Augustine grass I'm dragging you over! What a coincidence! America's oldest continuous city *and* name of the grass. I'm getting dizzy. St. Augustine is my favorite lawn, reeks of childhood. But it need lots of watering, which means these home-owners were more likely to have an automatic sprinkler system that is essential for converting my accidental discovery a decade ago into practical, everyday use. There's the timer on the side of the house. I reset it to twenty minutes before opening the trunk. And that's the pump and main PVC line aesthetically hidden in those bushes . . . Stay put. Just be a sec . . ." He left them in the middle of the yard and ran back toward the car.

Coleman swayed with a beer and smiled down at the captives. "You guys really bald?"

Serge quickly returned from the Javelin, got on his knees and began emptying shopping bags. "I love Home Depot! Especially the locations open twenty-four hours, when I need them most . . ." He ambitiously went to the task, starting at their toes and meticulously working his way up with the recent purchases. "Don't look so bored. Almost done . . ."

Serge finally stood and pulled a small, threaded adapter from his pocket. "Excuse me again . . ."

Another quick trip, this time to the sprinkler pump, and he was back, gleefully clapping his hands. "The show's about to start!" He picked up the camcorder and aimed it at the side of the house. "That PVC junction has a tie-in for auxiliary manual-watering flow, which I utilized with my adapter. More specifically a Y-adapter. Splits into two additional lines, one for each of you. The adapter has a little plastic lever on the front. Right now it's in the middle, which means both your lines will get water. But push the lever to either side, and the ball valve in the adapter will cut flow to one line and provides extra pressure to the other."

They stared in confusion. So did Coleman.

"Still no idea?" said Serge. "One lives, one dies—you make the call!" He panned the camcorder down to ashen faces. "I should have my own reality show."

"But Serge," said Coleman. "How can a sprinkler system kill?"

"Easier than you'd think." Serge lowered his eyes toward the contestants. "You're a couple of worms, so we're going to have a worm race. If one of you can get to the valve . . ."—he checked his watch—". . . in the next five minutes, and switch it with your nose, you live and your pal dies. If both of you get there at the same time, I guess you'll be smashing your faces together in a desperate bid for survival." Serge zoomed in with the camcorder. "If this doesn't get a million hits on YouTube, we're lost as a people."

The skinheads desperately thrashed across the grass, but progress was less than modest.

"Forgot to mention," Serge called after them. "You're on an advanced strain of St. Augustine called Floratam. Fun fact: got its name when cross-bred in 1972 by a joint research project from the University of Florida and Texas A&M. Get it? *Flora-tam*. Genetically engineered it to be extra chinch-bug resistant, in case you're planning on sodding anytime soon."

"Serge," said Coleman. "I don't think they care about chinch bugs."

"They should. Fuck up your yard something fierce."

"I doubt they're going to make it to the lever."

"Oh, they'll make it to the lever all right," said Serge. "Just won't do them any good."

"Why not?"

"I removed the ball valve from the adapter. No way to cut the flow."

"Then why'd you tell them they had a chance?"

"Because some types are prone to panic when faced with certain doom." He fiddled with the camera's focus. "I like to give the people hope."

"Still don't understand how . . . whatever it is you've done here is going to work."

"Neither will the authorities after I've removed my yard-care products of death."

"I thought you liked to get credit for your projects."

"I do."

"But that won't happen if they can't figure it out."

"They'll eventually figure it out."

"How?"

Serge pressed an eye to the viewfinder. "Stay tuned for shocking footage at eleven!"

CHAPTER 3

NEXT DAY

*T*he conference room was cavernous and perfectly square, half the size of a football field, far too large for the current function, making its lack of attendance seem even more so. Exhibitors tended merchandise at folding tables along the walls. The middle of the room was no-man's-land, an expanse of high-durability carpet that remained empty except for the occasional customer cutting diagonally across for the exit. Droning ducts in the twenty-foot ceiling over-pumped air at a perky sixty-eight degrees.

Three tables sat in the back of the hall by the service exit, the worst possible retail location. Behind them, Steve, Ted and Henry stood silent and idle in an unintentional line. Their tables supported a series of locked glass display cases that nobody was looking into. Mercury dimes, Indian-head pennies, Franklin half-dollars. The trio's arms stayed firmly folded as they glared across the room at a cluster of customers gathered around prime real-estate tables near the entrance.

"Stamp-collecting fucks."

"Look at 'em all smug with their pussy first-day covers and upside-down airplane misprint cocksucking—"

"Shut up," said Steve. "This is all your fault."

"Why's it my fault?"

"Those were supposed to be *our* tables," said Steve. "How'd you let this happen?"

"They were there when I arrived."

"The tables had reserved numbers."

"They just grabbed 'em."

"And you let them?"

"Already had their supplies set up."

"So shove those adhesive hinges up their ass!"

Ted looked at his watch. "Thought about lunch?"

"Cafeteria here stinks."

"Your turn to make the take-out run. I'll watch the dimes."

"Oh, Jesus."

"What?"

"Don't look now."

A gloating man savored his stroll across the middle of the carpet. His tropical shirt had a pattern of airmail postage through the ages. He arrived at the tables and smiled. "I hear it's *Sh*-teve now."

Steve reluctantly returned a nod. "Gary."

"When's the nose bandage come off?"

Steve just stared.

Gary solemnly shook his head. "Terrible. Absolutely terrible. What's happening to this country? That's what I told the guys when I first heard. It was a woman, right?"

"You have any business here, or are we just wasting oxygen?"

"What's the matter? I can't come and say hello?"

"You just did, so why don't you go—"

Gary looked down. "Nice threads."

Steve winced. He knew he shouldn't have worn his buffalo-nickel shirt.

"So," said Gary. "How are nickels moving these days?"

"I wouldn't know."

"That's not what I heard."

"You've obviously been out of the loop. We don't do buffalo nickels anymore. But I guess they didn't get the word to you over in pretend collecting land."

"What's that supposed to mean?"

"I think you know what it means." Steve walked out from behind the tables.

Gary stepped up to his face. "Why don't you tell me what it means?"

Dugouts cleared. The rest of the coin and stamp vendors poured in from around the hall, encircling the two.

"Maybe I will tell you."

"Then tell me."

"Make me."

"What if I don't feel like it?"

"I'll bet you jerk off in that stamp shirt, don't you?"

"Motherfucker!"

Ted jumped between them. "Guys! Guys! . . ."

The glass facade of a massive downtown convention center sparkled in the midday Jacksonville sun. Two men approached the front entrance. The plumper one sipped a quart beer from a brown paper bag, and the taller read a computer printout: INTERNET JOB FAIR. Serge opened the door and stepped into air-conditioning.

"Whoa," said Coleman. "Check the size of this place! I didn't realize the Internet had so many work-at-home jobs."

"Better than my wildest dreams," said Serge. "We're guaranteed to find super-high-paying gigs in a place this huge."

They headed across the lobby for the main exhibit hall. A registration desk sat just inside. A woman dressed entirely in tight leather with shiny rivets looked up from a sea of carefully arranged name tags. "Can I help you?"

"More like, 'Can I help *you*!'" said Serge. "We're ready to start immediately. I bring to the table alarming sleep patterns, world-class daydreams, an unwilting tolerance of lawn statuary, and sensible shoes. We'd like something in the six-figure range please."

"I don't . . . understand—"

"Our new jobs!" said Serge. "When I heard about your show, I told Coleman, 'These are our kind of people!' Not like the others who call police when the first little buffet table tips over on the outgoing president. Not my fault the water in those steam trays was too hot."

"Sure you have the right show?"

"More than ever!" Serge energetically flapped his computer printout in the air. Then he stopped to appraise the woman's leather ensemble and gothic tattoos crawling up her neck. He leaned forward, placing his palms on the edge of the desk. "Say, is this one of those porn sites where we have to install twenty-four/seven cameras throughout our house with no blind spots so fringe players can watch Coleman take a dump?"

"What are you talking about?"

"The Internet Job Fair!"

"Internet?"

"I'm sure you've heard about it. Very big."

"This isn't the Internet Job Fair."

"It isn't?" Serge looked around the hall, velvet ropes surrounding dozens of stunning motorcycles. Gleaming chrome forks and gas tanks airbrushed with flames and winged skulls. First-place ribbons, gold trophies. He turned back around. "Then what strange existence is this?"

"Southeast Regional Chopper Expo."

"I thought it was just the motorcycle section of the Internet." He showed her his printout. "Says today's date and the convention center."

"It's a big building. Maybe down at the other end."

"Thanks. And I meant no offense about the porn. Just the leather and all those tats, but I'm sure you did what you had to in prison."

"What?"

They were already trotting down the corridor. Serge grabbed the handle of a massive door. It creaked open. Another conference room, long tables with white linen, metal ice-water carafes dripping condensate. Hundreds of people in leather jackets with affiliate patches taking notes from an overhead projector.

Serge closed the door. They ran to the next room and peeked inside: a potbellied man in a Harley shirt delivering a PowerPoint presentation. Next room, and the next. Just more bikers. Serge's trot broke into a run. He passed an open door. A large, hair-pulling pile of coin and stamp dealers in the middle of the floor.

Serge finally reached the last door at the end of the hall. Coleman caught up, panting. "Is this where they give us lots of cash?"

"We'll soon find out." They went inside a room the size of a small hotel suite. Another reception desk by the door. The man behind it had a fifty-dollar haircut, a stockbroker smile and a résumé of rolling back odometers. He looked up from paperwork. Serge grinned. "Can you point me toward the Internet Job Fair?"

The man smiled back. "You're standing in it."

Serge looked around. "No, not the sign-up room. The main hall."

"This is the main hall. Welcome!"

"You're kidding, right?"

"That's the beauty of the Internet. It's all virtual reality: very low brick-and-mortar overhead. Why don't you start at that table over there and work your way around the room. You'll have trouble choosing from all the marvelous new careers that await. Seize the day! Opportunity knocks!"

Serge eyed him skeptically, then began making the rounds.

The man at the reception desk filled out forms for the next job fair at the Jensen Beach Econo-Inn. Someone cleared his throat. The man looked up.

Serge leaned in and lowered his voice to a whisper. "I think there's some kind of problem you need to be aware of."

"What's that?"

"These so-called job people? They each want me to give them several thousand dollars."

"And?"

"All the jobs I've ever had, the money comes the other direction."

The man chuckled and shook his head. "That's the beauty of the Internet. In this new economy, you control your own destiny. So when you give them start-up money, you're actually believing in yourself." The man stood and placed a hand on Serge's shoulder. "You do believe in yourself, don't you?"

"But I'm not—"

The man squeezed Serge's shoulder. "Believe!"

"I believe!"

"You're believing!"

"Can I get a witness!"

"That's the spirit! Now get over there and— What are you looking at?"

"The little stand in the corner. Is it what I think?"

"What?"

"Free *coffee*?"

"Uh, sure. Listen—"

"Don't move!" Serge ran off.

The man looked questioningly at Coleman, who grinned and took a swig from a brown paper bag. "Know where there's any weed?"

"What?"

Serge ran back with a tall, white Styrofoam cup. "It's cold."

"Been meaning to make a new pot."

"No, I mean that's good. I can drink it faster." Serge chugged half in one long gulp. "And you got the giant twenty-four-ounce cups! Usually when it's free coffee, they're these little thimbles." He took another big chug. "Bullshit on thimbles! I can't resist free coffee, like when I was at that funeral chapel. I wasn't really at the chapel, just walking by. The door was open, and so was the casket. People crying. Bunch of folding chairs. Guess it was a viewing. Then I see the big silver coffee urn in back. Next thing I know: 'What the hell are you doing?' I say: 'Drinking free coffee.' 'Did you know the deceased?' 'Not remotely.' 'I want you to leave.' 'Right after I get a refill.' 'No! Get the fuck out now!' I said, 'Have some respect: There's an old dead guy up there.' 'That's my mother!' 'Then you have a refund coming. They did a messed-up job. Of course I didn't know what she looked like before, so maybe it's a great job.' 'Why you—!' Then all these guys attacked me. Well, tried to, but they didn't anticipate my triple-threat martial-arts weapons training. I can handle a folding chair like nunchakus. Except I lost my grip and the thing went flying. I tried to explain that the old woman was already dead so it didn't matter that the Samsonite hit her in the coffin. Things like that always seem to happen when I drink coffee. It's weird." Serge looked toward the corner. "I need more coffee. Wait here . . ."

The man stared with open mouth.

Serge jogged back and chugged. Then he placed his own hand on the man's shoulder. "I believe in myself all right! In fact, I believe I have a great new business venture that isn't represented at your fair!"

No answer.

"Don't you want to hear it?"

Nothing.

"I track down Internet Job Fair scam artists, break into their bedrooms in the middle of the night and shatter their shins with a pipe wrench. I'll only require a ten-thousand-dollar investment to join your traveling expo. Exceptional bargain if you believe in yourself. You *do* believe in yourself?"

The man's mouth stayed open, but nothing came out.

"If you can't give me the cash, no problem. I'll just go to a rival job fair, but then of course I won't be able to guarantee *your* safety . . . Jesus, Coleman, look: He's white as a sheet. Get him some water!"

The man nervously rustling papers. "I-I-I think I can find something in here that pays from the start."

"Really?" Serge pulled up a chair. "I'm all ears!"

"Internet map sites." He handed a clipboard across the table. "Here's one that's hiring."

"Map sites?" asked Serge.

"Yeah," said Coleman, standing over him with his paper bag. "Like Google Earth. I zoomed in on nude beaches at the library, but the boobs were still fuzzy."

"Coleman, that's an aerial image site," said Serge. "I think he means those mapping services that give wrong directions."

The man behind the desk nodded. "They need street checkers."

"What's that?"

"You drive all day with a GPS-laptop and maps, working your way around the state, going up and down every street to check for accuracy and new highway construction."

Serge looked up from the clipboard. "But I do that anyway."

"Gas and two hundred bucks a week."

"They actually pay?" said Serge. "I had no idea this was going on."

"Most people don't. But between the big three map sites, there's at least a thousand people canvassing the country at any moment."

Serge killed the rest of his coffee and slammed the cup on the desk. "Two hundred isn't enough. I'll take the Internet cheat job instead. Just got my concealed weapons permit. Looks pretty real if you don't know what the real ones look like . . . '*Mr. Saturday Night Special!*' . . . Sorry, been hung up on Skynyrd since I got to town. *Brrrrowwwow-wow-wow-wow-wow!* Good coffee! *Monday Night Football,* blue lightbulbs, brick and mortar, thimbles, pipe wrench. Please proceed . . ."

A bead of perspiration formed on the man's left temple and trickled down his cheek. He conducted another rapid search under stacks of paper. "Here's something else. Hotel evaluator for travel-discount website."

"Perfect!" said Serge. "Already doing that, too. Got fired from a couple of the big outfits last month, so I had to start my own site for free. Have you seen it? Revolutionary features, like rows of cute little icons to grade hotels on a scale of zero to five. Anything over two-and-a-half cartoon hookers, syringes or Lyme-disease ticks, keep driving . . . See, Coleman? Told you I knew what I was doing. Now we get to cash in on all that hard work." He turned back to the man. "How much to buy out my site? Bidding starts at a million."

"Doesn't work that way. You'll need to use new lists of hotels chosen by the website and fill out a special checklist they supply. Pays twenty dollars a property and a free room."

"Twenty bucks a day!" said Serge. "How are we supposed to live on that?"

"Oh no, you don't just do the one hotel you're staying at. Most of the guys hit five or six others during the day, maybe seven if you're fast. Are you good with time management?"

"You kidding?" said Serge. "I fuck Time's mother."

"What?"

"I used to say Time's wife, but it didn't sound as good. What do you think?"

The man trembled with paperwork. "So you want the hotel job?"

"And the map thing."

"Both? But that's too much for anybody."

"Not me. Probably even have time left over for the job-fair cheat thing."

"Let me start filling out these forms for you."

"I'll be over at the coffee."

CHAPTER 4

*A*n ad-hoc convoy of independent truckers rumbled south through Georgia. Dixie mudflaps, CB antennas. The lead Kenworth had running lights arranged in a cross on the front grill. Black diesel smoke puffed in military rhythm as the setting sun flickered through distant pines and oak. The Florida state line went under the first tires.

They continued down the highway, passing pockets of chain and off-brand budget motels nestled around each exit. One motel had a tiny discolored swimming pool just over the pushed-down interstate fence, where a theme-park-or-bust Ohio family wrung low-expectation joy from the diving board. Children did cannonballs and splashed and shrieked in high-pitched counterpoint to the background drone of eighteen-wheelers. They used to tap trees for turpentine in these parts.

The Sand Flea Motel was popular among economy tourists who fell for a scam from the newspaper-quality pages of coupon booklets distributed at official state welcome centers. The booklets promised twenty-five percent discounts for a double-bed regular. Then the coupon was presented, and management wagered on parents being too drained to object when informed that all the discount rooms were full—but they still had plenty exactly like them at standard rate.

It was a flat, two-story motel, with faded concrete stairs leading to the balcony and a long steel railing encased by six simultaneously chipping layers of paint. One of the second-floor rooms had its curtains pulled tight. Outside the door were four muscular men with shoulder-length, shampoo-resistant hair. They stood in a line at the railing, like bodyguards on lookout, which they were. Inside the room, a pert young brunette from Macon hopped next to the dresser, wiggling panties off her ankles and flinging them over a lamp with her foot. Across the bed: an already naked man, strapping strong like the others outside, but in a different way. Trim at the waist, then broadening toward the chest and shoulders from the kind of workout regimen that only takes place in lockdown. He couldn't have been a day over twenty-five, with short, dyed-blond hair, a reddish tan, and a giant dagger tattoo running navel to sternum. The knife's handle was . . . well, it was kind of hard to tell. The man had told the tattoo artist to surprise him with something scary, but the artist was ripped on crank and kept messing up. A spitting cobra became a flying lizard, then a gargoyle, then a tarantula —"Wait, I can fix it!"—vampire bat, horned toad, mud dauber wasp, Gila monster—the customer's face growing increasingly crimson with silent rage—coyote, *T. rex,* briefly a badger, space robot, Chinese symbol, daisy chain of swastikas, and the head of Mamie Eisenhower, until it was finally one big, irreversible blob. The customer was about to explode . . . "Hold on, I got an idea!" The tattoo parlor doubled as a screen printing shop, and the artist quickly retrieved a squeeze bottle. He fired up the needle again and incorporated the bottle's contents into the design. Finally, he was finished and looked up with a smile. "There! How do you like it?"

The young man stared down. "What the fuck is it?"

"A jellyfish. Pretty scary, eh?"

"What's scary about a jellyfish?"

"Wait . . ." The artist ran to a wall and turned off the lights.

"What the hell did you do to me?"

"I added some of the luminous fluid we use to make glow-in-the-dark T-shirts."

"Now it's just a blob that glows."

"Glowing is scary."

The artist was paid for his work with a free burial at sea.

That was two years ago, when the "Jellyfish" nickname started. Of course no one ever said it to his face. At least not twice. Instead, he demanded being called the "Eel," because that's what he insisted the tattoo looked like. Terrified subordinates studied the unrecognizable, glowing splotch and swore they saw an eel. "It's fantastic, Eel!" Until his back was turned, then it was the forbidden sobriquet again . . .

And now the Eel stood in a second-floor budget motel room near the Florida line with a young nymph from Macon. He grabbed a drawstring leather pouch from his suitcase, loosened the neck and dumped the contents on the bed.

The woman gasped. Sheets sparkled with what looked like tiny shards of ice. "Are those real diamonds?"

The man made a silent motion.

The woman climbed into bed. "You don't talk much, do you?" She leaned back slowly on top of the gems. Some of the larger stones stung slightly. And she liked it.

He turned off the lights.

"Holy shit! What's that thing on your chest?"

The man pounced. More attack than liaison, headboard pounding so violently that asbestos dust fell from drop-ceiling tiles. The woman shrieked with ankles pinned to her ears. Eyes closed, chin thrust up. "What a turn on! Fuck me on the diamonds! Fuck me on the diamonds! Oh God, I'm going to come so hard! Fuck me on the diamonds! How much do you think they're worth?"

The answer was stillness. She opened her eyes. All over before the fifty-second mark. At two minutes, the man zipped his jeans.

The woman sat up extra carefully so as not to scatter the gems sticking to her back. "You don't waste time either." She reached a hand behind her shoulder blades and slowly brushed them off, making sure they stayed in the middle of the sheet. Then she knelt next to the bed and scooped them into a pile. "We still have a deal, right? I get to keep 'em?"

The man slipped into a faded Biketoberfest T-shirt.

She shook her head. "Whatever . . ."—resuming the gathering process—". . . feel free to jump into the conversation anytime . . ."

The man walked to his suitcase.

She grabbed the drawstring pouch off the nightstand and began filling it.

He removed something from his luggage.

She finished and pulled the bag's string, then reached for her clothes. "Been fun, but I gotta run."

The man turned to face her.

She dropped the pouch. "What's that for?"

He stepped forward.

She stepped back. "Stop fooling around. This isn't funny."

JACKSONVILLE

"A two-tone Javelin sat in front of a long line of traffic on the John T. Alsop Jr. Bridge—named after the city's Depression-era mayor—but natives all call it the Main Street Bridge."

"You're doing it again," said Coleman.

Serge looked up from his clipboard. "What?"

"Talking to yourself."

"No I wasn't."

Coleman pulled something out from under the seat. "Serge?"

"Yes, Tonto?"

He waved a wooden object in front of Serge's nose. "Why do motels always have clothes hangers that don't work anywhere else."

"So people won't steal them."

"Who would do that?"

Serge checked the idling Javelin's temperature gauge. "How many beers have you had?"

"I don't know. Eleven-teen? . . . What am I supposed to do with the hanger?"

Serge took pictures.

"Hey, check this!" said Coleman. "I'll bet I can wing it clear off the bridge!"

"Wait! Don't!—"

He whipped the hanger hard out the passenger window.

Crash.

"Ow! Jesus!" Coleman grabbed his forehead, then checked his hands for blood. "What the fuck just happened? . . . And why is the hanger back in my lap?"

"Okay, first, you just tried to litter. Second, the window was closed."

Coleman stuck an arm through the top of his door. "No, it's not."

"It *was* closed. Now it's broken."

"That's the noise I heard?"

"You might have learned something if you paid closer attention to our in-room movie last night."

Coleman swept broken glass off his pants. "*Leaving Las Vegas?*"

"Excellent road-trip movie if it wasn't so incredibly tragic."

"What do you mean 'tragic'?"

"Coleman, that was one of the saddest films I've seen in my entire life. What did *you* think it was?"

"An option." Coleman stuck his head out the window and looked down at the St. Johns River. He came back inside and pointed toward the windshield with a joint. "I've never seen a drawbridge like that."

"Will you keep the drugs below window level?"

"Sorry. It's just a cool bridge."

"The coolest. And I know a lot of bridges personally. Instead of how the regular ones open with two segments parting and arcing back, the center span on this baby stays level and goes straight up on those two humongous lifts. I can never get enough of that."

"Is that why we just drove back and forth over it ten times?"

"Synchronizing our pass so we'd be at the front of the line for the show. I was actually hoping to sneak our car onto the center span and ride it to the top, but the bridge tender was paying attention and not drunk like the one in Miami who sent those people into the water."

"I thought we were just lost."

"I never, ever get lost in Florida. Except when I deliberately get lost to appreciate not being lost."

"So we're still going to that bar like you promised?"

"I gave my word."

The top of a sailboat mast passed in front of the motionless traffic. Gears and cables shuddered to life; the center span began coming back down. Serge grabbed his digital camera and let loose a sequential burst. Cars moved again; the Javelin reached the north bank of the river, winding through downtown skyscrapers. Serge parked on Duval near the main Jacksonville Library. They entered the granite building, and Serge made a beeline for special collections.

Coleman followed him down a narrow aisle. "You promised we were going to that bar."

"We are. This is the way." Serge threaded between rows of shelves, running an index finger along large, musty volumes at eye level. The books had descending years on their spines: 1980, 1979, 1978 . . .

"How are we supposed to get to the bar from inside a library?"

"Time travel."

"But time travel's impossible."

"Usually." Serge pulled a book off the shelf. "Unless you're at a library. I'm already in the time pod."

Coleman looked around. "I don't see anything."

"Children have it all over adults, possessing magical powers of imagination. Then they grow into cynical tall people. That's the whole problem with the human race: reverse metamorphosis. We turn from butterflies into caterpillars. The key to keeping your wings is regular exercise of your kindergarten muscles of make-believe." Serge grabbed another book off the shelf and flipped pages. "Wait here. I'll be right back." Serge stood perfectly still.

"But I thought I was coming with you," said Coleman.

"It's just a one-man pod."

"If the time pod's make-believe, can't you add an extra seat?"

"Pretty dangerous," said Serge. "Could put too much stress on the dilythium flux capacitor."

"I'll take the risk."

"Okay." Serge closed his eyes. He opened them. "Time pod, Mark II, with more leg room, extra seating and a killer sound system."

"Shotgun!"

"Don't forget your seatbelt."

Coleman made a phantom motion across his chest.

"Stop farting around in the time pod. The strap's on the other side."

"Sorry. Got it now. Click . . . Where are we headed?"

"Early seventies. Look here . . ." Serge tapped a page in the W section of a thirty-eight-year-old greater Jacksonville phone book. "For the Local Attractions section of my first hotel report, I need to locate the most excellent Skynyrd pilgrimage site. And here it is!"

Coleman squinted at the page. "'West Tavern'?"

"Know the song 'Gimme Three Steps'?"

"Who doesn't?"

"Guy's dancing with Linda Lu," said Serge. "Then her boyfriend threatens him with a gun, and he begs for a three-step head start out of the bar before the dude starts shooting."

"Great tune. Crank it up in the time pod."

Serge reached out and turned an invisible dial.

"Louder," said Coleman.

"It's all the way up to eleven." Serge produced his digital camera. "Last month I read an interview with founding guitarist Gary Rossington, who said 'Three Steps' was a true story. They wrote the song while speeding away from this down-and-dirty roadhouse called the West Tavern, right after Ronnie Van Zant had a pistol waved in his face." Serge snapped macro photos of an address on the page: 5301 LENOX AVENUE. "Hoping against hope, I tried looking it up in a current phone book, but no luck. Like most historic places I seek, it's obviously been demolished. That's why we had to come to the library and find a period phone book. And now I have the address."

"But I wanted to party. What are we going to do at a demolished bar?"

"What children do." Serge replaced the book on a shelf. "Stand in an empty lot and make-believe."

CHAPTER 5

THE SAND FLEA MOTEL

*O*ut of the pool!"

"Fifteen more minutes. *Please!*"

"I just gave you another fifteen—twenty minutes ago."

"Let 'em stay," said the mom. "They only know above-ground pools in Ohio."

"Okay," said Dad, turning to the pool and raising his voice. "But only fifteen!"

The couple headed up the stairs to their motel room overlooking Interstate 75 and the lighted yellow-block letters that alerted traffic to upcoming Waffle House fulfillment. They reached the balcony and stopped in front of room 231, registered to the Montpeliers of Sandusky.

The Montpeliers had chosen their motel based on value. Three hours earlier at the state line, they pulled into the official welcome center, featuring vending machines for all needs, cheerful tourism pamphlets announcing they were now in paradise, and flyer-covered bulletin boards of people who'd gone missing near the rest stop. Mr. Montpelier grabbed a coupon book from a fake-wood display and, an hour after that, presented a jaggedly torn square of paper at the front desk of the Sand Flea Motel.

"Sorry," said the whiskered manager. "Sold out of those rooms."

"You have no more double-bed regulars?"

"Yes. Would you like one?"

"You just said they were sold out."

"At that price."

"I don't understand."

"We set aside a block of rooms for those coupons. They're taken."

"It doesn't say that on the coupon."

"They're taken."

"Let me see if I have this straight," said Mr. Montpelier. "The coupon is good for a double-bed regular."

"That's right."

"And you have some available?"

"Dozens. It's a slow night."

"Can I use the coupon?"

"We're sold out."

Mr. Montpelier's face reddened. "Essentially there's nothing stopping you from telling *everyone* you're sold out. How do I know you had any discount rooms to begin with?"

"You're holding the coupon."

"And?"

"It says so. Pretty good deal, too."

"Will I be able to experience it?"

"Not really."

"Honey," said Mrs. Montpelier. "We're all tired. Let's just get a room."

And now it was after dark as their kids screamed below in the pool. A chlorine drip trail led along the second-floor balcony and up to the towel-wrapped couple standing outside the door of room 231. Mr. Montpelier stopped a second to eye the four dubious men standing quietly at the railing in front of the next room. Then he produced a magnetic card, and they went inside. Wet clothes hit the bathroom floor. Mrs. Montpelier reorganized suitcase belongings that had been scattered like a mortar strike when the family first hit the room. Mr. Montpelier went on Safety-Dad sweep, checking the closet, under the bed, making sure the window latch wasn't too broken.

The Montpeliers were in one of those rooms with a side door that led to the next unit, in case a large family wanted to book both. The Sand Flea called the arrangement a "suite."

"Honey . . ." He gave the window latch a final test tug. "Is the pass-through door locked?"

She stopped folding socks and looked up: "The what?"

"Right behind you. That door connecting to the next room. There should be a second door on the other side for that person to lock."

"Looks locked."

"I'll double-check."

"No, I've got it, dear."

They arrived in front of the door at the same time. Mrs. Montpelier turned the knob. Good thing they decided to check; it wasn't locked. Neither was the other room's door. Sometimes you just do things and don't know why. That was Mrs. Montpelier, when she turned the second knob.

A sunburned man with an amorphous, glowing tattoo stood beside a bed in room 232. A wide, hollow-point blast pattern of blood covered the wall behind the headboard. A 9mm Ruger automatic and silencer hung by his side. He was leaning over the bed, staring detached at the lifeless woman with a pair of entry wounds, one for each eye. Behind him, the sound of a door creaking open.

He turned to find a pair of tourists from Ohio, neutral expressions turning to horror. Mr. Montpelier grabbed the knob and yanked the door shut.

The sunburned man quickly braced his shooting arm across the other and fired a silent fusillade. Door splinters flew from a chest-high row of bullet holes, left to right, at precise, six-inch intervals. Then he stopped in a haze of ammunition smoke and listened.

On the other side of the door: two heavy thuds.

JACKSONVILLE

Rush-hour traffic out of downtown was thick and slow on westbound I-10. Horns honked. Off-key singing inside a two-tone AMC Javelin.

Serge: "'Gimme three steps . . .'"

Coleman: "'Gimme three steps, mister . . .'"

"'Gimme three steps toward the door' . . . Here's our exit . . ."

They took the ramp at mile 358, drove a block south and turned right on Lenox. "Start checking numbers. It's 5301."

"Here's 55-something. Now a 54."

"We're getting close. It's at the crossroads with Verna Boulevard."

Coleman nodded up the street. "There's a traffic light."

"Must be the crossroads."

The Javelin slowed. Their jaws fell. The car pulled onto a dirt shoulder. Its occupants turned and looked at each other in wide-eyed astonishment. The heads rotated back, staring out the windshield at a plain, gray concrete blockhouse. Harley and an old pickup. Neon Budweiser signs and a small notice in the window: BIKE PARKING ONLY. The front door remained open to the bright, sunlight world outside; shadows in the dim interior silhouetted by more lighted beer advertising. Four numbers above the entrance: 5301.

Serge grabbed Coleman's arm. "Tell me it's not a mirage."

"No, it's here all right. But you said it had been torn down."

"They just changed the name." He pointed up at wooden, Old West-style letters. PASTIME. "I simply assumed because of all the other empty lots I've stood in." Serge grabbed a tall Styrofoam 7-Eleven cup of coffee from its window holder, and they exited the Javelin.

Coleman was almost to the door when Serge grabbed his arm again.

"What's the matter?"

"You can't just bluster into a place like this," said Serge.

"Why not?"

"Any joint that chased off a man's man like Ronnie Van Zant is no place to be trifled with."

"But you're not afraid of anything."

"*Respect* is more the word." He turned sideways and checked the pistol in his waistband. "Regulars in dives like this smell fear as sure as Dobermans. Before we go in, we have to get our shit wired tight and project insane confidence. And whatever you do, under no circumstance are you to mention that song. Then they'll think we're goofy tourists and pick our bones clean."

"Can I go in and get a beer now?"

"One more second." Serge ran his fingertips over a bas-relief metal plaque just outside the door. Established 1948. He looked up at the American flag flapping above the building, then took a deep breath and drained his Styrofoam cup. "Ready."

They walked inside to nobody's notice. Serge took three steps and threw up his arms. "God*damn*, I'm in the bar from that freakin' Skynyrd song!"

Everyone turned.

Serge grinned awkwardly. "Shit . . . I mean, *shit!* Do I feel confident! If you think you smell something, it's my No Fear hormones marking territory with their musk." He bellied up to the venerable bar. "I'm all about Dixie, yessiree. Love 'Sweet Home Alabama' in those KFC ads. Keepin' it finger-lickin' real! Unlike Yankee ad jingles for processed cheese: 'You're crumb-believable.' Fuck those assholes."

A female bartender strolled over. "What can I get you?"

"Bottled water . . ."

The regulars glared.

". . . And a dirty glass!"

"Boilermaker," said Coleman.

The others nodded approval and returned to private discussions.

"Serge," said Coleman. "What are you doing?"

Serge's back was to the bar. He held a digital camera inconspicuously below hip level. "Got the flash turned off. I'm taking a three-dimensional grid-sequence of spy photos for future forensic study. There are certain places it's far too dangerous to openly take pictures. I perfected my technique based on CIA surveillance protocol so there's no possible way anyone can detect what I'm doing."

The barkeep returned with their drinks. "Nice camera."

Serge spun around. "I'm not taking pictures!" He slipped the camera back in his pocket. "Not many."

"You guys here on business?"

Serge uncapped his water. "I'm a travel expert. Thinking of writing a big spread about your fabulous place here. The whole Skynyrd mystique."

"Really?" said the bartender. "Wait here. Someone will want to meet you." She disappeared out the back of the bar.

"Uh-oh." Serge cautiously slid off his stool, eyes shifting side to side.

Coleman dropped the shot glass in his beer. "What's the matter?"

"Shit's on boil. We've been radar-pinged in the 'Gimme Three

Steps' bar, the most bad-ass honky tonk in all America." He walked over to the wall and grabbed a cue stick. "The end is near. There's no way both of us can make it, so as soon as the bloodbath begins, you make a break for the door. The best I can hope for is a valiant fight to be immortalized in song."

"Serge, I think you should live." Coleman killed the boilermaker. "I've had a full life."

"Not a chance. The end will be slow and unspeakable. When they swarm us, I'll charge and take out the biggest with my patented pirouette of death. That should give you time to reach the door in three steps."

"But I don't want you to die."

Serge shook his head. "Too late. And whatever you do, don't look back no matter how loud I scream."

Coleman began to sniffle. "But Serge—"

A deep southern accent from behind the bar: "Hey! You fellas!"

TALLAHASSEE

A uniformed police officer stood guard outside a hospital room door. Two detectives returned from lunch and peeked inside. An unconscious young man, IV tubes, wires, electronic monitors. A nurse wheeled a ventilator out the door.

One of the investigators touched her arm. "Still improving?"

"Doctor said a complete recovery."

"When can we talk to him?"

"He's heavily sedated."

"But it's important."

"So is his rest." She pushed the medical cart down the waxed hall.

The detective looked at his partner. "We don't have the luxury of time."

"Three hotel robberies in one week."

"That other guy, Ralph—what a worthless witness."

"And the third is dead."

"This kid's the only one who got a good look."

"We better double the guard. Once they killed that last guy, our patient here became their ticket to death row."

"But we already moved him from the other hospital and registered him under a fake name."

"Can't hurt to be safe."

"Why don't they use armored cars anyway?"

"I don't know shit about the diamond business. Guess these couriers try to blend in as the last people you'd suspect to be carrying a fortune in stones."

"They're right in this case. Just look at the guy."

"Same as the other two victims: unassuming faces, low-key attire, fake business covers that would throw anyone off."

"So how did the gang nail three in a row?"

"Only one possible answer. Someone on the inside's feeding information."

CHAPTER 6

THE PASTIME

erge stood in the middle of the empty dance floor with a pool cue at the ready.

A tall, rugged southern man in a black T-shirt came out from behind the bar, wallet chained to his jeans. "You a travel writer?"

"One second," said Serge. He gave Coleman a good-bye hug. "It'll be okay. If they resort to torture, I'll bang my head on the floor and knock myself unconscious." Serge turned back toward the voice. "I'm ready to face my fate."

The man broke into a warm smile and extended a hand. "I'm the owner, Billy Bob. This is my wife, Vicki."

Serge warily shook the hand.

"Heard you're a Skynyrd fan," said Billy Bob.

"Big-time, but not in a tourist way."

"Let me show you something." The owner headed past a pool table. Serge glanced back at Coleman, shrugged and followed.

Billy Bob reached the southwest corner of the bar and pointed up at a locked glass case near the ceiling.

"What's that?" asked Serge.

"Old Skynyrd drum cover signed by Artimus Pyle."

Serge's heart pounded. "Do you think . . . maybe . . . I could . . . you know . . . take photos of the bar?"

"Be my guest."

Serge began shooting with the drum cover and worked clockwise, covering every inch like he was mapping a threatened rain forest.

The enthusiasm impressed Billy Bob. "Say, why don't we take a ride in my truck? I know the families. Give you the Skynyrd tour of west Jacksonville."

Serge stopped and looked at Coleman. "This is it."

"This is what?"

"They lull you with southern hospitality while plunging the knife. We're no doubt going to be driven to a pair of pre-dug graves behind a catfish farm."

"So let's not go."

"But it's the Skynyrd tour."

Soon they were all packed tight in Billy Bob's red pickup with a number eight Dale Earnhardt Jr. license plate on the front. The truck whipped through working neighborhoods, from the band's boyhood homes, to the high school, the old store from the "Ballad of Curtis Lowe," and finally the cemetery where the lead singer had to be secretly reburied after his first grave was vandalized under mysterious circumstances. Serge knelt in reverence at a modest marble marker: RONALD WAYNE VAN ZANT, 1948–1977. He lifted glassy eyes toward Billy Bob. "I'd heard about this, but never would have found it without you . . ."

Fifteen minutes later, the pickup arrived back at the bar. Serge slowly climbed down from the passenger seat and studied his outstretched arms. "I'm not dead."

Billy Bob laughed. "Of course you're not dead."

Serge had never made a friend so fast. He gave the owner a big bear hug, briefly lifting him a couple of inches off the ground. "Oh, thank you! Thank you! Thank you! . . ."

"Are you okay?"

"More than okay! This is the best day of my entire life!" Serge sprinted back inside the bar and leaped onto a stool like it was a pommel horse. The corner TV had local news: "*. . . Police continue to investigate what they believe is an organized gang or gangs targeting traveling businessmen for robberies at local hotels. The latest victim, a positive-thinking seminar teacher, remains in critical condition after attempting suicide . . . Meanwhile, another shocking development in the case of two so-called skinheads found executed in what authorities have described as the most bizarre and nauseating crime scene they've ever encountered. The cause of death had investigators*

completely stumped, and an unnamed source inside the medical ex-
aminer's office said the fatal injuries most closely resembled being
crushed by Burmese pythons, except their faces had also been
smashed beyond recognition. But a major break came within the last
hour when a video of the victims' final minutes was discovered posted
on the popular website YouTube . . ."

Someone changed the channel: ". . . *This revolutionary spin-*
ning lure is the magic bullet if you want to put a heap of fish in the
boat . . ."

Billy Bob walked around to the business side of the bar. "Drinks
on me. What are you having?"

"Three boilermakers," said Coleman.

"Water."

"Never had anyone ask for water when drinks are on the house,"
said Billy Bob. "Sure you don't want something with a little more
kick?"

"Coffee."

"I guess that's got a little kick."

"You have no idea," said Coleman.

The coffee arrived first. Serge burned his mouth chugging. "So tell
me about the bar!"

"Let's see . . ." Billy Bob began lining up Coleman's drinks. "Probably know it used to be the West Tavern, but a lot of people think that
was because this is west Jacksonville when actually one of the old
owners was named West . . ."

"Preach!"

". . . Me and Vicki picked up the place a few years back. I mean,
who could resist the history?"

Serge pounded a fist on the bar. "Who could!"

"Skynyrd even played a few early gigs out back where we barbecue.
If this place wasn't so small, the song might have been 'Gimme Five
Steps,' because three's literally all you need to hit the parking lot."

Serge manically waved his empty cup. "Java me!"

Billy Bob laughed again as he poured. "Am I going to have to cut
you off from coffee?"

"It's happened before. You know the old tourist observation tower
in Lake Placid? Not the New York Lake Placid; the one below Sebring,

whose town name was suggested by none other than Melvil Dewey of Dewey Decimal System fame, who changed life as I know it, and not for the better. Can't tell you how many times I've been hot on the trail of a book, and the library's aisles run out before I get to the number and I go, 'What the fuck?' Anyway, U.S. Highway 27 runs down the spine of central Florida where three curious towers rise like bulb-less lighthouses: the Citrus Tower in Clermont, Bok Tower in Lake Wales and Lake Placid's tower, whose viewing deck is now closed because of some risk from telecommunication microwaves, and there's a coffee shop on the bottom floor, where I was on my fourth cup, strip-mining the waitress for trivia, and she said, well, a few years back one of those self-appointed spidermen free-climbed up the side all the way to the observation platform. And I said, of course! They won't let me take the elevator, so I'm forced to chart my own route up the north face. Ran outside and prepared for the big climb. Said another precautionary good-bye to Coleman, because I swore I would reach the summit or die trying, and after three hours I'd drawn a pretty good-sized crowd, including the restaurant staff and a couple off-duty cops, and Coleman's shouting encouragement up at me, my fingers wearing raw as I clung desperately to the side of the building. Held on as long as I could, but at the five-hour mark, my body finally betrayed me and I lost my grip. Luckily I'd only made it two feet off the ground and was able to escape lasting disfigurement by going into a paratrooper's tuck-and-roll, but they still wouldn't let me have any more coffee." Serge held out his empty cup again.

Billy Bob poured. "Where you headed?"

"Points south. First, the Martin Luther King Jr. lunch-counter site in St. Augustine that triggered an act of Congress, then the Aileen Wuornos walking tour of Port Orange. Got a lengthy scavenger list." Serge pulled a lengthy scavenger list from his pocket and spread it across the bar. An item near the top reminded him of something, and he looked around. "Thought you'd have a jukebox."

"We do," said Billy Bob. "Over there."

"What? That little thing?"

"One of those new touch-screen jobs connected to the Internet. Got almost every song ever recorded."

Serge sprang off the stool and fumbled for his wallet. "Please, dear God, let it be so . . ."

DOWNTOWN FLOPHOUSE NEAR
THE OLD FLORIDA THEATRE

Serge's trail had grown icicles. And Agent Mahoney, former ace profiler for Florida's counterpart to the FBI, was slowly rebounding from another involuntary mental commitment and back to a world where the color of the sky is blue. Nobody had ever come remotely as close as Mahoney to catching Serge. Because nobody had ever gotten so far inside Serge's head. Mahoney was ideally suited to the task, sharing the same passion for nostalgia, geography and arcane tidbits. But it came with a hefty price tag. Nearly a decade had passed since the first of Mahoney's six paid medical leaves, and he was now under strict doctor's orders to "drop this Serge thing."

Recovery progress was steady. Until Mahoney walked back into the lobby of his by-the-hour Jacksonville motel, and the varicose woman behind the desk reached into a wooden cubbyhole.

"Got a message for you . . ."

CHAPTER 7

PASTIME

Serge swiftly navigated the Internet jukebox's on-screen menu. Soon, unmistakable guitar chords filled the tavern. Serge raced back to the far end of the bar, where an attractive young blonde in Daisy Duke cutoffs idly peeled the wet label off a cold tallboy.

"*. . . I was cutting a rug . . .*"

Serge tapped her shoulder. "Would you like to dance?"

Her female-barroom-defense-wall went up before she even turned around. But then she caught Serge's smile and piercing ice-blue eyes. The wall crumbled. "Sure."

He led her to the middle of the tiny dance floor and waved Coleman over. "Dance with him."

The woman stopped. "I thought you were asking me to dance with *you*?"

"That part's coming up. I'll cut in."

"When?"

"Don't worry. You won't miss it."

She reluctantly began dancing, but had to avert her eyes to stomach it. Coleman held a beer to his chest and did the drunk-white-guy shuffle.

A minute into the song, "Hey!" Serge leveled a gun at Coleman. "What are you trying to prove?"

Coleman began shaking. "But you told me to dance with her."

Serge leaned and whispered: "Work with me."

Eyes grew large around the bar. Everyone eased off stools and began backing away. Someone dialed 911.

Serge waved the gun wildly. "This might be it for you!"

"You're scaring me," said Coleman. "Be careful with that thing."

Serge cupped his mouth and whispered again. "Say the words."

"What words?"

"Serge!" Billy Bob yelled from behind the bar. "What the hell do you think you're doing?"

"Putting the cherry on the best day of my entire life!"

"Get rid of that gun! Now!"

"It's not loaded, see?" Serge pointed the pistol out the open door and squeezed.

Bang.

"Serge!"

"Demonstrating firearm safety: No such thing as an unloaded gun."

Someone ran in the door. "What just happened to my windshield?" He saw Serge's pistol and dashed back out.

"Coleman! Say the words!"

"What words?"

Serge whispered in his ear.

Coleman looked at him oddly. "Gimme three steps?"

"Run!"

"I'm running!"

Coleman darted out the door with Serge on his heels. They raced across the gravel lot and jumped in the Javelin.

An unexpected voice from behind: "Hold up!"

The woman in the Daisy Dukes ran toward the car with a small duffel bag. "Can I get a lift?"

Without waiting for an answer, she opened Coleman's door and pushed his bucket seat forward, throwing him into the dash. Then she dove in back with her bag. "Might want to start driving. Those are police sirens."

Serge patched out in a dusty, white cloud and sped for the I-10 ramp. They snaked east on elevated lanes and merged with downtown rush hour. Sirens faded. Serge eased off the gas and looked in the rearview: "What's your status?"

The woman calmly applied blush. "Heard in the bar you were headed south. I need a ride."

Serge hit his blinker for the 95 bridge. "But back there . . . the gun and everything . . . I mean, you're not afraid of us?"

"*Please!*" She snapped her compact closed. "After all the other men in my life, you two are pussycats."

Coleman giggled. "She said 'pussy' . . . Ow! Serge, she just smacked me in the back of the head!"

Serge glanced in the mirror again. "I'm Serge, this is Beavis. What's your name?"

"Candy."

"Candy?" said Serge. "What are you, a stripper? . . . Ow!" He rubbed the back of his head.

"I am *not* a stripper! I'm a dancer."

"Do you take your clothes off?"

"Of course." She pulled a date book from her purse. "You stupid or something?"

"Then you're a stripper . . . Ow!"

"Stop saying 'stripper.'"

"Deal."

She opened the date book in her lap. "Look, everyone thinks strippers are dumb slut pieces of trash who curse and smoke and drink and do drugs all the time." She reached over Coleman's shoulder and grabbed his beer.

"You're drinking," said Serge.

"I don't smoke. Or do drugs. On weekdays."

"'A foolish consistency . . .'" Serge said sarcastically.

"'. . . is the hobgoblin,' blah, blah, blah," said Candy. "Don't condescend to quote Emerson at me."

Serge's eyes snapped toward the rearview mirror. "You know Emerson?"

"Who the fuck doesn't?"

Coleman cheerfully raised his hand.

"But how do you know Emerson?" said Serge.

"English lit. That's why I need a lift. Just came home to Jacksonville during break to dance for next semester's rent because money's better up here."

"You're a lit major?"

She shook her head. "Florida history."

Serge placed a hand over his heart. "What's your real, nonprofessional name?"

"Story."

"Story?" Serge flipped down his sun visor for a quick peek at the photo, then flipping it back up. "Like Musgrave? The astronaut?"

"Duh."

"What's your last name?"

"Long."

"Story Long. Story Long. Where have I heard that name before?" said Serge. "Story Long . . . Wait, I remember now." He glanced over his shoulder. "You were in the newspaper, weren't you?"

She just reached into her bag for a textbook.

"It *was* you." Serge slapped the steering wheel. "I knew it! You're like my hero."

"What'd she do?" asked Coleman.

"Oh, it was so cool!" said Serge. "The police raided this strip . . . I mean dance club north of St. Petersburg, trying to shut it down for obscenity. But Story was smarter than the cops. American obscenity laws are delightfully quirky. First, the offense has to be of a sexual nature. You can stand onstage with two handfuls of shit, and it's not obscene, just gross. Second, even if it is sexual, it's not obscene if the act contains material of a scientific, political or artistic nature. So the night after the raid, Story organized the other girls. Instead of dancing, they performed Shakespeare in the nude."

"And they didn't get busted?" said Coleman.

"No, they got busted all right," said Serge. "That was even better. She showed up the cops, understanding the law better than the people whose careers are *law* enforcement. One of the top police officials went on TV to explain that even though it was a famous play, they were still arrested because none of the girls had formal acting training and their performances stunk. The statutory ignorance was so monumentally obvious that Lenny Bruce was making jokes about it more than forty years ago. For something to pass the non-obscenity test, it's just a question of whether it *contains* art, not whether the art's any good."

"How's that cool?" asked Coleman.

"She got that police official to unwittingly admit they went to jail for bad acting." He looked in the rearview again and detected traces of a faint smile. "Coleman, this is a special day. We're sitting in the presence of the smartest stripper in Florida—" Serge ducked.

Story's hand swished empty air.

"Don't get me wrong," said Serge. "I *love* history, but what can you do with a degree besides teach?"

"I'm actually going to graduate school to be a vet."

Serge reached up and snuck another quick glimpse of the visor photo. "Tell me . . ."—he crossed his fingers—". . . did you ever want to be anything else besides a vet?"

"Well, when I was real young, before I got practical, I wanted to be an astronaut—"

"Yesssss!" Serge flipped down the sun visor, tore out the picture and crumpled it into a ball.

Coleman pointed at the empty visor. "Does that mean we can stop wearing diapers?"

"You guys are wearing diapers?" asked Story.

"For the space race," said Serge.

"Changed my mind." Story stuck her textbook back in the duffel bag. "I'd like to get out of the car now."

"But we just started having fun."

"This has gotten way too weird. You're no travel writer."

"Yes I am."

"You're a psycho in a diaper."

"I'm . . . multi-tasking." Serge opened his cell phone and punched numbers. "Just get to know me a little better." Serge listened a moment, then began beating the phone on the dashboard.

"What are you doing?" asked Story.

Bam, bam, bam. "Making a hotel reservation."

"Having problems?"

"Those goddamn endless phone menus. And they always finish with: 'Rotary callers please stay on the line.' That last part only takes a few seconds, but over a lifetime it adds up to days of lost existence. And all because one guy won't get with the century. Who the hell out there is still using a rotary phone?"

Twenty miles away, a thick, callused index finger dialed a rotary phone. The heavy black receiver went to an ear.

"This is Agent Mahoney. You left a message for me at the motel? . . . Of course I'm still interested in Serge . . . No, not over the phone . . . The usual place . . ."

Mahoney headed north in a late-model Crown Vic with blackwall tires, but to Mahoney it looked like Broderick Crawford's highway patrol car with vintage bubbletop police light. He pulled into a dim parking garage and stopped next to the elevators.

The agent entered the Jacksonville airport in a frayed tweed jacket and rumpled fedora. He strolled past the men's room and climbed onto a small platform, taking a seat in a comfortable, padded chair. His feet went onto metal rests. A toothpick wiggled in his teeth.

"Sparky, give me the works."

"The name's Luke."

"It should be Sparky."

Below him knelt a short, thin man with white hair and drooping, blotched cheeks. A shoeshine box opened. Mahoney's eyes swept the terminal for nosy eavesdroppers. The shine man was old school, working the buffing rag in a furious 1940s Times Square subway choreography.

Mahoney lowered his gaze. "Sparky, what's Serge's twenty?"

"Huh?"

"Location."

The man's eyes stayed on the agent's wingtips.

Mahoney pulled a fin from his wallet and handed it down.

The man slipped the five-spot in his shirt pocket. "I don't know where Serge is."

"You mumbled on the blower about the bona fide."

"That's right."

"Canary."

Buffing resumed in silence. Mahoney passed down another fiver.

"Someone's on Serge's trail. And I don't think he wants to catch up on old times."

"Don't shine me on. Everyone's snooping for Serge."

Luke shook his head. "This is different. He's got a target on his back."

"The big sleep?"

"That's how it looks from here."

Mahoney ruefully removed his toothpick. "Where'd you score the dope?"

"Talk's on the street."

"Sing."

The shoes got more polish. Luke got another five.

"Couple of guys came poking around."

"Solid they weren't shields?"

"I'd know if they were cops. I just got this vibe. Not warm and fuzzy."

"Chin?"

"Huh?"

"What'd they say?"

"Same thing you always do: just wanted to know if I'd seen Serge. Said they were old friends, but I wasn't buying. Actually only one talked while I did his shoes; think the other was the lookout—hung back by the ticket counter."

"Strapping iron?"

"The talker had a bulge in his shirt. Both gave me the creeps."

"Reruns?"

"Never seen them before in my life. That's what doesn't add up: I don't even know Serge. Why'd they come to me?"

Mahoney removed the toothpick. "History."

"Don't follow."

"Someone yodeled up a pair of zippers to close Serge's eyes. Did their homework on the mark. Serge is all about tradition, and you're the end of a dying breed, the best shine in the state. If they heard Serge was in J-ville, it's just a matter of time before he lands in your chair."

A narrow brush scraped leather above the sole. "But it's a big state. Why do they think Serge came to Jax?"

"He's fobbing the tourists a bent travel angle. After getting your Western Union, I found a blog with photos under the Fuller Warren Bridge from Monday Night, and nobody was playing football if you catch my drift."

Luke stood and gave the agent's shoes a last theatrical snap of his towel. "How'd you hear about this blog?"

"Dropped a dime to the hundredth power."

"What?"

"I Googled him."

CHAPTER 8

ELVIS

$\mathcal{S}$erge looked over his shoulder as the Javelin raced east toward downtown Jacksonville. "Make you a deal, Story. I'll prove I'm a Florida travel writer."

"How are you going to do that?"

"State trivia."

"You're nuts."

"Fair enough. But it works both ways. All I see back there is a dancer. How do I know you're really a history major?"

"I am so a history major!"

The Javelin crossed back over the St. Johns. "Then you won't mind a spirited little competition."

She stewed with folded arms. "You're on. What's the category?"

"Elvis."

"Elvis?" said Story. "That's not history or travel."

Serge paused. "Can be."

"No, it can't. Pick something germane, like Ponce de León's burial site or Andrew Jackson's controversial execution of British subjects during the Seminole conflict."

"Old San Juan Cathedral, Puerto Rico; Armbrister and Arbuthnot." Serge sighed. "I want it to be challenging. But if you're afraid . . ."

"I'm not afraid."

"Then what's your problem with a little pop culture?"

Story folded her arms in defiance. "Question!"

"That's more like it," said Serge. "Elvis's first indoor concert in America."

Story grinned malevolently. "Nice touch. Jacksonville, August 10, 1956. Florida Theatre . . . My turn."

"Fire away."

"Why did the appearance make *Life* magazine?"

"A judge sat through the show, threatening arrest if offended by his pelvis," said Serge. "Who was that judge?"

"Marion Gooding. Name one of the opening acts."

"Shit, you're not bad." Serge stared up at the ceiling for a dramatic period, then raised an index finger. "Jordonaires."

"Damn!"

"Back to your side," said Serge. "Elvis's favorite hotel room in Jacksonville?"

"You mean hotel?"

"No, room."

"I . . . don't know."

"Serge wins!"

The Javelin angled up a private drive.

Story leaned out her side window. "The Riverfront?"

"Used to be the Hilton, now the Crowne Plaza."

"Wow, we're staying here?"

"Not exactly."

"What's that mean?"

"Just follow my lead."

The trio marched through automatic doors and into a finely paneled elevator with brass accents.

Five minutes later: "We're still in the elevator," said Story. "We've just been riding up and down over and over."

"There's a good reason for that." Serge pointed toward a special slot in the elevator's control panel, which required a magnet key to access the executive level.

The elevator reached the lobby again; Serge fumbled for his wallet as the doors opened. An older couple in formal evening attire got on and smiled. Serge returned the greeting and resumed his wallet search. The man in the tux pressed the button for the executive level. "What floor?"

"Same," said Serge, still going through his billfold. "That key has to be in here somewhere."

"Allow me," the man said cordially, producing his own magnetic card and inserting it in the control panel.

After a quick ascent, doors opened, and the man nodded at Serge with a slight smile. "Have a nice evening." He took his wife by the arm and headed down the hallway until they reached the last room on the western end. There was a small plaque next to the door with the name of the suite: SAN CARLOS. The couple went inside.

Seconds later: Knock-knock.

The woman stood at the room safe, removing dangling diamond earrings. "Who can it be at this hour?"

"Don't know." The husband walked over and put his eye to the wood. "Something's wrong with the peephole." He opened the door on the chain.

Serge's grinning face pressed right up against the gap. "Hello! We just met in the elevator!"

"How can I help you?"

"Spot check."

"For what?"

"Quality assurance. Won't take long. And you get a free gift."

"So late?"

"Best time to catch the staff with its pants down. Want to make sure you're receiving the absolutely finest hospitality value. We won't accept anything less."

"But everything's okay."

"You'd be surprised."

A woman's voice from behind. "Who is it?"

"Hotel inspection."

"This late? What kind of inspection?"

"We get a free gift."

"Tell him to come back in the morning."

"Wish I could," said Serge. "But then I'd be breaking the rules and the terrorists win." He slipped something flat through the still-chained opening. "I have a clipboard."

"He has a clipboard," the man said over his shoulder, unlatching the chain. Three people filed into the room. Serge made a quick sweep of the suite, jotting notes, then pacing off from the walls until he was satisfied he had located the exact center of the room. He reached into his pocket.

The man walked over in a hail of camera flashes. "You guys with the hotel?"

"Heck no." Serge slowly rotated in place, capturing another photographic panorama.

The man glanced dubiously at his wife, then back at Serge. "But if you're not with the hotel . . ."

Flash, flash, flash. "Familiar with the roaming gnome?"

"You're with *them*?"

"Used to be." Flash, flash. "But they rejected my hotel photos just because they all had crime tape. The roaming gnome is dead to me."

"But—"

Serge stuck out his arm. "Please stand back. Insurance reasons. Mainly a formality, but I wouldn't want you to end up like the last couple."

"Serge," said Coleman, crouched in front of a small door. "Check it out: They left the key in the minibar."

"Richard," whispered the woman. "What's going on?"

"Something's not right."

Story sat at the end of the couch and rolled her eyes. "You can say that again."

The woman grabbed her husband's arm. "Maybe we should check with the front desk."

Serge held up the clipboard. "That's also against the rules."

"Sir," said the husband. "I can assure you everything is in order. Now if you wouldn't mind—"

Serge produced a plastic DVD case from the waistband under his tropical shirt. "Your free gift!" He walked to the suite's entertainment center and inserted the disk.

"What the hell are you doing now?" asked Richard.

Serge clicked the remote control. "You think I chose this room by accident?"

"I don't know and I don't care—"

"You're in the Elvis suite!"

"What?"

Serge removed a pair of tweezers from his pocket as a movie began. "This was Elvis's favorite room in Jacksonville." He got down on hands and knees. "Stayed here so often there used to be gold records all over the walls."

On TV, a young Elvis stood on a sunny beach and picked a guitar.

"... *You gotta follow that dream!* ..."

Serge tweezered strands of carpet fiber into a small, glassine envelope— "Elvis's skin molecules"—and stood back up. "You've been incredibly cooperative, unlike that Miami couple in the Lucille Ball room."

"Richard," said his wife. "I want them to leave immediately!"

"Already on my way," said Serge. "Sorry for taking up your time. And I have to say I really admire everything about you."

"You're— ... What?" said Richard.

"Wanted to see the inside of the Elvis suite my whole life—and all the other celebrity rooms in Florida—but the only opportunity on my budget is by working for a travel service. Smile! ..." The flash caught Richard off-guard. "You, on the other hand, must be supersuccessful in your chosen field to afford Elvis-level pampering. Bet you were on magazine covers."

"Well, once. *Southern Sheds Quarterly.*"

"I knew it!" said Serge.

"Richard!" said his wife.

"Plus, your obvious taste," Serge continued, "picking this suite without even realizing it was the King's choice." He went over to the desk and scribbled an address on a sheet of hotel stationery, then added his signature. "In addition to the DVD, this will get you free admission to the best nightspot in town." He handed the page to Richard. "But only the *right* people know about it." Wink.

"That exclusive?"

"You kidding?" Serge tucked the digital camera back in his pocket. "I only know about it because I'm a travel expert, but it's going up on our website soon. Tonight may be your last chance to experience its historic state before the social register descends. I can't imagine visiting Jacksonville and never seeing this place."

"Sophia ..." said Richard.

"You're not actually thinking of going."

"He said it might be our last chance."

"Look at the hour."

"It's not *that* late." Richard turned back to Serge and smoothed out the front of his jacket. "Am I dressed appropriately?"

"The tux is perfect . . ." Serge turned. ". . . And ma'am, may I say your evening gown is absolutely stunning. Everyone in the club won't be able to take their eyes off you."

"Really think so?"

"Trust me: You'll be the center of attention."

"It's our last night in town," Richard told his wife. "We should take advantage of it."

"If you're sure that's what you want," said Sophia.

"One last question," said Serge. "How's hotel security?"

"Everything seems fine."

"That's no surprise. This place has a great reputation, but I'd advise you never to open your door to strangers, even if they have a clipboard. One of the newest scams."

"Really?"

Serge nodded hard. "Well, that concludes my mission here . . . Oh, almost forgot . . ." He took back the piece of stationery from Richard and jotted something on the bottom. "I know the owner of the club personally. Mention my name and he'll give you the VIP tour." He handed the page to Richard. "Just ask for Billy Bob."

CHAPTER 9

NEXT AFTERNOON

A white van with no side windows sat on the far edge of a convention center parking lot. Magnetic signs on side panels advertised affordable electrical repairs for home and office. The two men sitting up front wore overly dark sunglasses and plain baseball caps. An unseen number of additional passengers sat on boxes in the stripped-down cargo area. Gym bags at their feet. The plates were Illinois.

Two hours passed quietly. The van idled for air-conditioning in the Jacksonville heat. The driver stared off without objective as the center span of a bridge rose to block the sun.

The vehicle strategically faced the convention center's entrance. Toward the end of the day, small groups left the facility in spurts. Then a lull.

The building's double glass doors opened again. The van's front passenger checked Xeroxed black-and-white photos in his lap. He looked up toward the front walkway. "That's him."

The driver waited with silent discipline. At the instinctive moment, he threw the van in drive and followed a five-year-old Nissan Altima out of the parking lot. The van remained under the speed limit as it picked up Interstate 95 southbound, keeping a minimum three-vehicle separation with the target car.

The Nissan got over in the right lane for exit 341, then headed east on Baymeadows Road. It pulled up the driveway of an architecturally sterile extended-stay hotel and stopped under an overhang in front of the lobby.

A half minute later, a white van entered the lot and slowed as it passed a short line of cars parked temporarily for registration. It sped up again, turned the corner of the building and backed into an isolated parking space against the rear of the hotel. The van's side door opened. Someone in maintenance overalls climbed down and swapped the magnetic signs with ones promising longer septic tank life. The person got back in and closed the door. The van was still.

A 1971 Javelin sped south on I-95, through the underside of Jacksonville, characterized by viral suburban growth and distracted-driving accidents. It exited at Baymeadows and entered the parking lot of an extended-stay hotel. Serge leaned as far as he could over the steering wheel as they rolled past rows of empty cars.

Coleman exhaled pot smoke out the window. "Why are you driving so slow?"

"Hunting down the perfect parking space," said Serge. "The perfect space is absolutely essential. Sets the whole tone for your visit. But it looks like everyone else already grabbed the perfect tone, and *this* inconsiderate asshole parked too far over the line for me to fit, so I'll have to come back and deflate his tires to downgrade his tone."

The joint pointed out the window. "There's a great spot."

"I see it," said Serge.

"So why aren't you parking there?"

"I am."

"But you just drove by."

"Have to get extra room so I can back in. Always back in at Florida hotels. Serge's secret travel tip number forty-two."

"Why?"

"See that police car patrolling the other side of the parking lot? What do you think he's doing?"

"Hotel security," said Coleman. "Make sure people don't break into cars and stuff."

Serge shook his head. "In Minnesota they patrol for guest safety. In Florida, they're *looking* for guests."

"What are you talking about?"

"Notice the device he's pointing out the window?"

"Yeah?"

"Checking for fugitive license plates. That's an optical reader, which transmits plate numbers back to headquarters and the national crime computer. You wouldn't believe the ridiculous amount of warrants they turn up."

"And that's why you always back into hotel parking slots?"

"The haul of criminals is so robust they don't have the man-hours to get out of their patrol cars and check plates backed up against shrubs."

"Will you hurry up and just park," said Story. "I have to pee."

"Another second." Serge threw the Javelin into reverse and cut the wheel. The car backed into the slot. Serge pulled out of the slot, then backed in again. Then pulled out, backed in. He opened the door and looked down. Shook his head. Pulled out of the slot, backed in again, pulled out . . .

"Told you I have to go to the bathroom!" yelled Story. "What the hell are you doing?"

"Respecting the community. It's a heavy rudeness guilt-cross not to park in the middle of your slot." Serge grabbed a tape measure out of the glove compartment, opened the door again and bent down. "Eleven inches to the line." He handed the tape to Coleman. "Check your side."

Coleman leaned out the door. "Thirteen."

"Fuck." Serge shifted back into drive. "Not courteous enough."

Story threw open her door. "I'm out of this boob-mobile."

Serge aligned the car one more time. The lot was quiet and empty as they stepped onto a sidewalk. A statuesque brunette abruptly materialized in front of them. "Just get in from the airport?"

Serge jerked a thumb over his shoulder. "Be gone, industrious hotel hooker. I'm onto your high-end business-traveler vagina ways." They brushed past her on the narrow walkway.

"Serge," said Coleman. "How do you know that was a hooker?"

"First, a hot-looking woman striking up idle chat with us in a parking lot. Better odds finding a woodchuck doing card tricks. Second, ever been diving in the Keys?"

"On purpose?"

"Barracudas can be unnerving at times."

"No shit. Once I was at the aquarium. Those sharp, scraggly teeth freaked me out, and I ran into a wall. I was really stoned."

"Any experienced diver knows a 'cuda will never go after an animal as large as a human, unless the water's cloudy and you're wearing something shiny, like a watch or bracelet, which they mistake for tiny bait fish." Serge felt for his wallet to confirm he hadn't been pickpocketed. "No, what's really unnerving is their blinding speed. One second you're all alone grooving on brain coral and the next, a barracuda is suddenly just *there,* right in front of you."

"So anytime a chick suddenly appears outside a hotel? . . ."

Serge nodded. "Barracuda hooker."

The hotel reception desk was dark wood with a polished black marble top. The desk was empty except for a lone woman in a smartly pressed blazer with a plastic name tag that was supposed to look like brass: JESSICA. Corporate fever charts determined business increased proportionately to marble surface area. Insufficient data on real brass name tags.

Arriving customers tended to bunch up at the official three P.M. check-in time and, much later in the evening, after businessmen and -women finished their business. This was that in-between limbo part of the day when but a single employee was required. Only three customers in the last hour. Jessica mainly answered the phone about ice machine location and whether the names of adult movies would show up on expense account receipts.

The phone rang again. She answered professionally. It was the same customer from last week who'd been calling all day to complain about the sneaking-a-pet-in-the-room penalty charge on his credit card.

Jessica maintained training-seminar poise. "Sir, I completely sympathize, but I spoke with my manager and you'll have to call our corporate office. Would you like that number again? . . . I understand your position that the barking was from a TV show about dogs . . . No, I can't change anything in the computer 'just between you and

me' . . . I'm sorry, I couldn't make out that last thing you said because of the barking in the background . . . Okay, I'll wait while you turn the volume down on the Dog Channel . . ."

Automatic front doors opened. A woman in cutoffs veered urgently for the restrooms. Moments later, the doors hissed open again. Two more entered.

"You carry that clipboard everywhere?" asked Coleman.

"Million and one uses," said Serge.

"What's it for this time?"

"To get a free upgrade."

They approached the front desk.

"Excuse me," Jessica said in the phone. "I have to put you on hold."

"Don't put me on hold—"

Serge arrived with purpose and plopped folded hands on the counter. "Reservation, Storms."

"One moment." She smiled and tapped computer keys.

Serge pulled the clipboard from under his arm and placed it on the counter, speaking as he wrote: "Front desk, cordial. Pressed navy blazer, no dandruff . . ."

The receptionist looked up from her screen. "You from headquarters?"

More clipboard writing. ". . . Asked nosy question . . ."

"I didn't mean—"

"Nobody does." Serge clicked his pen shut. He quickly looked left and right, then waved the woman closer. "I'm not supposed to tell you this, but you look like someone I can trust, and I'll need inside help to make the big layoff go smoothly."

"Layoff?"

"I'd like an upgrade."

"No problem . . . Seven-nineteen, the presidential suite. Here are your keys."

"The code word is *marzipan.*"

"What?"

"We'll be in the bar."

———

Just after dark, a police car drove slowly through the parking lot of Extended Comfort Express Suites USA. Up one row of vehicles and down another. Mostly intermediate-size rentals and SUVs. The officer in the passenger seat aimed a digital scanner out the window. They passed a backed-in AMC Javelin, turned the corner and circled the rear of the building.

The cruiser rolled quietly by an empty, backed-in white van from a septic tank company. The officers disappeared around another corner, and the van's driver sat up in his seat. He keyed a walkie-talkie:

"*Number two, how's dinner?*"

"*Almost ready to serve. She should be out any minute.*"

The driver turned toward the cargo area. "Move."

The side panel slid open and three men in maintenance overalls hit the ground with toolboxes. They pulled painters' caps low over their eyes and entered a service door. The first one pressed "7" on the back elevators and stared at the floor under the view of a ceiling dome camera.

Two floors above, a plump maid exited a room, dumped dirty towels in her cleaning cart and began pushing it down the hall. A fourth set of overalls stepped from a vending machine alcove. A stitched name over his pocket: GARY. He knocked hard on the door of 718. "Maintenance! . . ." No answer. He got out a magnetic card and synchronized his futile attempts with the maid's approach. Repeated red lights in the door handle. He pulled a walkie-talkie off its belt clip. "Charley, I'm at seven-eighteen. My card won't— . . . Hold it, Charley . . . Ma'am, could you help me? I can't seem to get my card to work."

The maid smiled and nodded. Then stood and did nothing.

"You don't speak English?"

She smiled and nodded.

"Excellent."

CHAPTER 10

EXTENDED COMFORT EXPRESS SUITES USA

*T*he hotel registration desk hit rush hour.

Lobby noise. Luggage carts. Lounge laughter. The automatic front doors never had a chance to fully close as a parade of off-the-clock business class rolled American Tourister over the threshold.

The spike began a half hour earlier when Jessica, the lone hotel greeter, held out as long as she could before calling in reinforcements.

Three more people in blazers emerged from a secret receptionist chamber behind the desk where, until then, they could be seen obliquely through an open door, chatting, chewing gum and ignoring the growing line at the front desk, with facial expressions suggesting brain injuries blocking the concept that they actually worked at the hotel.

Almost everyone checking in at this hour was a premium points member. Jessica staffed the last check-in station, roped off for platinum club. Gold and silver funneled into the rest of the desk. Everyone asked for drink coupons.

On the opposite side of the lobby, a statue of a dancing leprechaun held open the door to a lounge called Shenanigans.

Three tables had already been pushed together in the middle of the clover-green carpet. Cocktails, wadded-up napkins, PDAs, cell phones, business cards, sports talk. Salesmen for restaurant lighting, overstocked hair products and road-paving aggregate. A familiar face appeared in the doorway.

"What a bunch of degenerates!"

The table gang turned. "*Sh*-teve!" "Get over here you bastard!" Another table slid. "You got the nose bandage off."

Steve grabbed a chair. "The cat is back in the hunt!"

"What happened last night?"

"Had to kick her out of the room. Guy's got to get his sleep."

"Wow, a stewardess."

"Flight attendant," said Steve. " 'Stewardess' is insensitive."

"Your pickup?"

"Told her I teach autistic children."

"Someone get him a drink." Fingers snapped for the waitress.

"*Sh*-teve, did you hear about Ralph?"

Steve lowered his head. "Terrible, just terrible."

"We caught it on the news. Critical condition."

"Told him not to stay at the same hotel," said Steve. "Did he listen?"

"How many does that make now? Four?"

"Five."

"TV said police are talking to him, but he didn't see anything. Conked him on the head from behind as soon as he opened the door."

"Must have been the hallway lookout," said Steve. "That's why I never turn my back on people using vending machines."

Additional coin guys arrived. Ted, Henry. "Jesus, we just heard about Ralph!"

"It's become an epidemic. First Buffalo Nickel Bill, now this."

"But I don't understand," said a salesman named Jake, who moved a staggering amount of golf-course fertilizer. "No offense, but you guys just run hobby shows. Is there really that much money in dimes and quarters?"

"Didn't used to be," said Steve. "Quiet life. Magnifying glasses. Proof sets. Then *Florida* changed."

"How's that?"

"The value of our merch stayed the same, but the concentration of robbers in the state reached a tipping point. It was just a matter of time before they realized—like you said—it's only a hobby show: all us middle-class suburbanites with silver dollars and no security.

After that, bets were off. Now every coin expo has a shadowy band of predators hovering around the edge of the herd. They're probably here right now."

"Where?" Jake looked around, laughing. "Are they invisible?"

"Yes," said Steve. "Those early bandits gave way to polished crews. You wouldn't believe the extent of their preparations. Whose easel is this by my leg? . . ."

"Mine. I'll move it."

". . . Start surveillance the day before, noting security cameras, highway exits, even visit the show to see who has the best stuff. Then hit us as we leave. One guy got jumped right in the valet line loading his trunk."

"Don't forget Vic," said Ted.

"Vic." Steve whistled. "Followed the poor guy a hundred miles back to his house and ambushed him in the driveway."

"That's why we take evasive maneuvers," said Henry.

"You're pulling my chain," said Jake.

"All of us drive away in formation," said Ted. "Take turns rotating in and out of lanes looking for tails . . ."

". . . Get off the highway and immediately get back on at the same exit," said Henry. "Before finally arriving at our safe-house hotel."

Steve leaned back and inflated his chest. "Yes sir, the rare coin circuit is now one of the most hazardous occupations in the state. It takes a rare breed with nerves of steel."

Jake broke out laughing. "You're paranoid."

"That's what Ralph thought."

"Speaking of which, I should call the hospital." Henry opened his cell. "Uh-oh. Battery's dead."

"Use mine," said Steve.

"No . . ." Henry pushed out his chair and threw a pair of tens on the table. "I'll try my room phone. Behind on e-mail anyway. Better get back up there and check the ol' laptop."

Steve looked down at his own phone. "Reminds me, I need to make a call . . ."

He was interrupted by an elbow from Ted. "Whoa! Check that action at the bar!"

Three people sat at the bar. Coleman was on one side of Serge, and Story was on the other, sitting an extra stool down to leave an empty seat between them for peaceful textbook study.

Serge opened his laptop.

"What are you doing?" asked Coleman.

"Finding a wi-fi hot spot." Serge began tapping. "Need to check our online payment account the travel company set up to compensate us."

"How does it work?"

"Every time we file a report . . ." —Serge waved his arms and wiggled his fingers—". . . they magically zap money through the air and into our lives." He stopped and rubbed his palms together. "Let's see how rich we are!" A finger dramatically pressed a button.

Coleman leaned toward the screen. "Can we retire now?"

"Something's wrong." Serge sat back and scratched his head. "There's no money. In fact it's got a negative balance."

"What's going on?"

Serge pulled a cell phone from his pocket and punched numbers. "I intend to find out. Probably just a clerical error. The astounding brilliance of my first report must have left them in such shock they couldn't type straight. Can't wait to find out how much *extra* they're going to pay us . . ."

"I'm buying the biggest bong—"

"Shhhhh! They're coming on the line now . . . *Hello?* . . ."

On the other side of Serge, a man stepped to the bar. He grinned at Story. She turned, giving him an exquisite view of the back of her head.

". . . Bet you can't find the words," Serge said into the phone. "If my bonus is too large, we can work out an installment plan . . . What? . . . Could you repeat that? . . . There must be some kind of mistake . . ."

Story felt a tap on her shoulder. "My name's *Sh*-teve. What's yours?"

"Go away."

"Let me buy you a drink . . . *Bartender!*" He placed a twenty on the counter. Story grabbed the bill and stuck it in her pocket.

Steve unconsciously felt his nose. "Have we met before?"

"I severely hope not."

Steve climbed onto the empty stool between Serge and Story, invading her personal space with gin breath. "I have lots of rare coins in my room . . ."

Serge held the phone oddly in front of his face like it was an undiscovered swamp species with ten sphincters. He returned it to his ear. "Back up . . . What do you mean you're not going to pay me a red cent? . . . Of course I got your checklists for hotel quality . . . No, I didn't forget to fill them out . . . Because I thought it was some kind of performance test, like: 'Anyone with so little ambition as to use the checklist is not someone we want working for us.' . . . Oh, it *wasn't* a test? Well it should be. 'Window treatment appeal, scale of one to five.' I got a sixth square: 'Who gives a shit?' . . . I see . . ."

"Coin collecting is for wimps," said Story.

"That's just my hobby," said Steve. "I teach autistic children."

"How much extra are we getting?" asked Coleman.

Serge waved for him to pipe down. ". . . But I worked hard on that report. It goes on for pages. There must be something you can use . . . You're kidding . . . What about the Elvis room? . . . Not even the Skynyrd bar? . . . I disagree . . . No, it's got everything to do with travel. Don't you want to be a Freebird? . . ."

The next stool: ". . . *Bitch* . . ."

Story's head slowly rose, eyes boring another hole in the wall.

"Right," said Serge. "I coined that phrase myself, Barracuda hookers . . ." His left arm shot out to the side, grabbed the hair on the back of Steve's head and smashed his face down into the bar. ". . . Don't take this the wrong way," he continued into the phone, "but have you personally ever been to Florida? . . . Then that explains everything . . . Traveling down here demands an entirely different skill set . . . Yes, like backing into hotel parking slots . . . No, I don't think you *do* know your customers aren't fugitives . . . How'd you ever get your job? Sleep with someone?—"

Serge held the phone in front of his face again and slowly closed it.

"What happened?" asked Coleman.

"He hung up."

"How much are we getting?"

"Coleman, he hung up. In business, that's Morse code for zero."

"But you worked hard on that report."

"He said we won't get paid unless we use their checklist." Serge looked down and raised his elbows. His eyes followed a tiny river of approaching red liquid back up the bar toward the empty stool between him and Story. "Where'd all this blood come from?" He turned to his left. Story was looking back at him, but this time with a brand-new expression.

Coleman tapped Serge's shoulder. "So we're going to start using their checklist?"

"Absolutely not." said Serge. "It's a double test."

A man in maintenance overalls stood in a hotel hallway, playing a brief game of charades with the maid.

"Oh, *sí, sí.*"

She produced a card and opened the door.

"*Gracias.*" He went inside and made the usual quick check in case someone was planted on the toilet with a loud exhaust fan. The walkie-talkie on his waist squawked: "*Number two, we're getting off the elevator. How's dinner?*"

He keyed the mike. "*Ready to serve.*"

Seconds later, a barely audible knock on the door. He checked the peephole and opened up. The rest of the team rushed inside. Three men in unmarked white jumpsuits slipped hands into thin gloves. One pulled the blinds shut; others turned on lamps and went to work with slot screwdrivers. Faceplates came off all the power switches.

"Find anything?"

"No, you?"

"Nothing. Sure we got the info right?"

"'Light switch.' Couldn't be more clear."

"Maybe the guy varied his hiding routine like the one in Fort Walton . . ."

A secondary, wholesale search began. Dresser drawers, under mattresses, behind nightstands. Then into professional thoroughness:

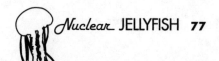

cover off the ironing board, taking apart the toilet-tank assembly. Someone stood on a chair and checked in the drop ceiling with a metal baton flashlight, which yielded three binders of nineteenth-century half-dollars and a few modest gold pieces.

The one with his head in the ceiling clicked off his flashlight and jumped down. "What do you think these are worth?"

"We're supposed to be looking for stones."

"But these look good . . ."—flipping plastic display pages—". . . we could pawn them on the side."

"Forget it," said a colleague, checking behind paintings. "First, the Jellyfish would kill you for even saying that. Second, he might do us anyway if we don't come up with the gems . . . *Where the hell are they?*"

A pillow unzipped. "What on earth were we thinking hooking up with that Jellyfish character anyway?"

"To make money."

"I just signed up to boost gems; not roll with a sociopath." The battery compartment came off the back of the TV remote. "We're facing murder charges."

"Not if we don't get caught," said the one with the coin binders. He set them aside, clicked the flashlight again and slid under the bed on his back like an auto mechanic. "Just keep looking—"

A cell phone rang. The lead maintenance man pulled it from his pocket. "Hello? . . . Oh no!" He clapped it shut.

"What is it?"

"The mark left the bar early. Everyone! Clear!"

Before they could move: the sound of someone fumbling at the door.

"Kill those lights!"

The gang dashed around the near side of the bed and bunched together in a hiding spot created by the bathroom wall. The last one leaped from view just as the door opened.

Nonchalant footsteps and whistling indicated that the pulled blinds had prevented the room's occupant from noticing the ransacked interior.

The whistling stopped. He just noticed. The two parties were still out of sight from each other, mere feet apart around respective sides of the bathroom's corner. The burglar nearest the edge pressed himself as hard as he could against the wall and clutched the baton flashlight to his chest in a two-fisted baseball bat grip.

The unseen room occupant: "Oh my God!" He took a slow step forward. Into view.

The flashlight came down.

Stars.

The crew stood over him. Business clothes, tie askew, coin-show name tag: HENRY.

"Why's he back from the bar so soon? Our guy was supposed to keep him there for at least another hour."

"What are we going to do now?"

"Call it in."

"Are you crazy?"

"You want to explain to the Jellyfish why we waited around doing nothing and *not* calling? Better to take our lumps now."

"I'm not calling it in."

"We can't just stand here until he wakes up."

"No, we can split . . ." And with that, one of the white jumpsuits ran out of the room, leaving an open door for all the world to see the gushing head wound of their prostrate victim.

"Get that fucking door before someone passes by—"

Someone passed by. A maid humming a merry tune. She stopped and looked with an initial smile at three rigid, surprised men staring back, one with a bloody flashlight by his side. The smile dissolved to terror as her eyes fell toward the unconscious man at their feet. She grabbed her head with both hands and became unhinged in Spanish, taking off down the hall.

"Shit!"

The one with the flashlight ran out the door.

The maid was already three rooms down, waddling rapidly for the elevators. She heard footsteps. *"No! Por favor!—"* She didn't hear the flashlight.

The others rushed into the hall and helped drag the maid back to the room, where they dropped her across the coin dealer, forming an X. The door slammed shut.

"Now we definitely have to call this in." The top maintenance man grabbed his walkie-talkie again. "Number one?"

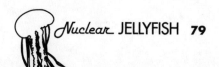

"Copy. Dinner ready for takeout?"

"Negative. We need extra table settings. Two more guests arrived."

"Did you say 'two'?"

"Affirmative."

"We copy."

The maintenance man quietly set his walkie-talkie on the bureau.

"What are we supposed to do?"

"Wait."

Six floors below, a white van remained backed into a parking slot behind the hotel. Two men in the front seat looked at each other. The one on the passenger side quietly set the walkie-talkie on the dash. "What do we do now?"

"Call it in."

The passenger began to shake.

"What are you waiting for?"

"I can't take this anymore."

"Phil, what's gotten into you? Make the goddamn call!"

"Hell with it." He jumped out the door and took off across the parking lot.

"Son of a bitch!" The driver ran around the van and closed the passenger door. Then he pulled a cell phone from his pocket.

CHAPTER 11

SHENANIGANS

*T*he bartender went through twenty napkins wiping Steve's blood off the counter. He smiled at Story because she was hot. "Sorry, ma'am, some of our customers can't hold their liquor . . ." He discarded the last napkin and looked up at the next suitor, standing patiently behind the empty stool. "I'm done. It's all yours."

A discount loan consolidator climbed on the seat and grinned. "What can I get you?"

"Solitude."

The man waved a fifty at the bartender, folded lengthwise between his index and middle fingers, indicating little-dick syndrome. "Tanqueray and tonic, and get the lady another of whatever she's having."

The bartender set two drinks and thirty-five bucks on the bar. Story stuck the bills in her pocket.

"Hey, what about my change?"

"Okay, work on not being a putz."

The loan broker slunk back to the good-natured ribbing of a gang sitting around pushed-together tables in the middle of the bar.

Serge finished his second coffee refill and nudged Coleman. "Grab your drink. I detect fertile research ground for my next report."

The pair approached the tables. Chewed stirrers, wet cardboard coasters, menu of frilly umbrella drinks in an upright Plexiglas holder. The gang's lineup kept changing as guys rotated to the restrooms and computer center. One had a rolling suitcase next to his chair with an airline tag from Baltimore. Another wore a necktie around his fore-head like a kamikaze.

"Greetings, fellow warriors of business travel!" said Serge. "Mind if me and my associate join your camaraderie of the open road?"

"More the merrier."

Serge cleared a formation of highball glasses and vigorously wiped down a swatch of personal work space. He bent over a notebook. "Just a few pointed questions. Nothing to worry about."

"You with the hotel or something?"

"Or something," said Serge. "They want me to use their checklist, but I say fuck that plastic cage. I'm in a Hendrix phase now. I march to my own checklist. How would you rate Jimi on a scale of one to mind-fuckin'-blowing?"

They stared silently.

"That concludes my Hendrix phase." Serge waved for the wait-ress. "Coffee."

The kamikaze began laughing. "You must be appearing at the comedy club?"

"That's right," said Serge. "Same one as you. It's called earth. Please cooperate. Did you back your cars into parking slots when you arrived?"

"Why?"

Serge told them.

Now the rest of the guys at the tables began laughing. Except two on the end, who got up and left quickly.

Serge turned a page of his notebook. "My revolutionary new web-site bursts with local technicolor and value-conscious travel wisdom not to be found elsewhere, like never hire a hooker who suddenly ap-pears outside your hotel."

"Why not?"

"It's usually just a foot in the door for accomplices to burst in and stick you up, because who's less likely to report a robbery than some out-of-town businessman with a wedding ring?"

The gang at the table laughed again and pointed. "Ned!"

A man who taught corporate foreign-language classes emptied a beer pitcher into his mug. "Luckily, we don't have that problem at this hotel."

"Yes you do," said Serge.

"What are you talking about?"

"Propositioned in the parking lot seconds after getting here," said Serge. "Barracuda hooker. For more on that, please visit my site. I have to leave something off the table."

"In our own parking lot?" said an independent polygraph examiner for defense attorneys who passed everyone. "That's hard to believe."

"Not just the parking lot," said Serge. "She's right here in the bar." Heads spun. "Where?"

"Over there," said Serge. "The brunette number talking to that guy in the polo shirt. Pegged her immediately as the local honey trap."

"That's not a hooker."

"To the untrained eye," said Serge. "The business suit throws most people off, but that's now the uniform for extended-stay properties. Click the special hyper-link on my site."

"No, I mean we know her. That's our district manager . . ."

". . . She's coming over here. She looks pissed."

"You didn't happened to say anything to her in the parking lot that made her angry?"

"Absolutely not. Well, maybe I mumbled the V-word."

"Oh, Jesus."

The woman arrived at the table and stared daggers at Serge.

Serge smiled back. "By vagina, I meant how well you carry it."

The woman grabbed one of the drinks from the table and dumped it on Serge's head, then stormed away.

Serge wiped his face with a napkin. "Vagina has become such a tricky word." He clicked open a wet pen. "Overall, how would you rate your stay? . . ."

Three TVs were on above the bar; four more hung from wall brackets mounted in the corners.

". . . *Police believe those responsible for the current string of Florida motel robberies are the same gang that worked the I-75 corridor from Cincinnati to Chattanooga last year . . . And now the Internet story that everyone's talking about . . .*"

One of the businessmen pointed up at the evening newscast. "Look, it's on again."

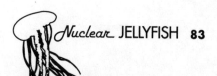

The tables became quiet. Someone asked the bartender to crank the volume.

"What's going on?" asked Serge.

"Shhhhh. You'll miss it."

"... *Investigators were initially baffled by the bodies of two young men, who appeared to have been killed by giant constrictor snakes. While reports of large exotic pets being released into the wild are well documented, no confirmed fatalities have ever been reported. Complicating matters were severe facial injuries that couldn't be explained by any known pets. Official spokesmen said the case was going nowhere until a break came, of all places, from a video anonymously posted on YouTube. The popular Internet site reported record-breaking hits until the video was taken down at the request of authorities, but not before our station was able to obtain a copy. The footage is too offensive to air, but it begins with a pair of so-called skinheads attacking a homeless man beneath an underpass near Jacksonville's picturesque St. Johns River. The video then jumps to a predawn scene where the tables have been turned and the skinheads are under attack. Meanwhile, law enforcement has requested that anyone with information please contact them, but so far all the department's anonymous tip lines have been swamped by callers registering support for the perpetrators ...*"

The TV image switched to a police captain at a podium. "*Two people are dead, and there's at least one very disturbed person out there. So if you don't have any pertinent information, please stop calling us and laughing.*"

The anchorwoman returned. "*While this station continues to stand by its policy of not airing the graphic footage, our own science editor Mary Nelson is here to explain the physics of how the young men died. Mary? ...*"

"*Jennifer, I'm standing in the outdoors section of a local Home Depot. To the stable individual, everything here appears innocent and cheerful. But to a heart filled with malice, evil lurks beneath the begonias. I'm now holding up an unassuming garden hose. This is the type with small pinholes that collapses flat and was used extensively to irrigate lawns in the nostalgic days of old Florida before built-in underground systems became the rage. It was a pair of hoses just like*

the one in my hand that police have identified as the murder weapon
and is now on sale for a limited time . . . Back to you . . ."

"*Thanks Mary . . . Later in this broadcast: It was supposed to be*
a fun outing, but in the end a bear lay dead and a father was thankful
for his son's remote-control helicopter . . ."

The kamikaze opened a laptop on the table. "Check it out. I captured the video before they took it down."

The table gang got up and crowded around the notebook's screen, showing grainy, low-light footage of two people wrapped ankle-to-shoulder in green hoses. They slowly crossed a lawn like inchworms.

"*. . . Now the Action Five business report. Brad?"*

"*Jennifer, all area home improvement stores are reporting a huge*
run on garden hoses . . ."

The loan consolidator: "Newspaper said they were in a race to get to the shut-off valve before the automatic sprinkler system came on and filled the hoses."

"So what?" said the fertilizer salesman. "How can water in those hoses hurt them?"

"Can't if they're regular hoses," said Serge. "But like the TV lady said, those are the special irrigation kind."

"Irrigation?"

"Roll up flat," Serge continued. "Hundreds of tiny holes. Stretch 'em across a lawn, turn on the water, and they expand into thick round hoses spraying a light but high-coverage mist that results in a magnificently lush tropical landscape, unless they're wrapped around skinheads, then it's a landscape of justice."

"I remember those," said a pharmaceutical salesman from Savannah. "My grandfather used them in the sixties."

"Very big in this state when I was a kid," said Serge. "Evokes idyllic childhood memories, getting goose bumps stroking the hose's sleek rubber skin the other night. I mean decades ago."

Someone pointed at the screen. "They made it to the valve. They're trying to switch the lever with their noses."

"They're bashing each other's faces!"

"Look at 'em go!"

"This is too sick to watch. Can you enlarge it?"

"The sprinklers just came on! The hoses are expanding!"

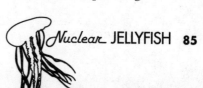

"They're seizing up! . . . Ooooo . . ."

"Jesus! Look at the blood flow from those head wounds!"

"Why is it spurting so much?"

"Fun fact," said Serge. "Most people think constrictor snakes—and now irrigation hoses—kill prey through strangulation, when death actually comes from high blood pressure. CNN's Dr. Sanjay Gupta calls it the silent killer."

The hotel robbery crew was divided into two groups: talent and muscle. Talent was thinning out. The muscle took the form of the Jellyfish/Eel's personal bodyguards, who were required when the gang locked horns with another crew in a turf dispute and won a messy, decisive victory. There was little chance of the rival faction reconstituting, and they weren't very tough anyway, but why take the chance?

Muscle had the stomach—and voracious appetite—for violence. Talent didn't. Several had been shanghaied from the remnants of the capitulated gang. Their hallmarks were tedious preparation, stealth and intel, which helped avoid any contact with the marks, who were never harmed. Consummate gentleman bandits.

Muscle had a more inelegant approach.

Talent wore overalls, and right now four of them stared down at the precedent-setting deviation of an unconscious salesman and maid on the room's tiled entryway.

A light knock at a door. Everyone knew who it was.

"Answer it."

"I'm not going to answer it."

Another quiet knock.

"Someone has to answer it."

"So you answer it."

"Damn." The one with the false GARY stitched over his pocket forced himself toward the door on licorice legs. He checked the peephole from habit and undid the chain.

Two massive bodyguards pushed their way inside, followed by a taller, thinner person in a brown leather jacket. A glowing blob peeked out the neckline of his dark T-shirt.

Two trailing bodyguards covered the flank. They made a last visual recon of the hall before coming inside and bolting the door.

The Eel squatted and felt the victims' wrists. Weak pulses.

He stood back up. He never spoke loudly, never had to. "They get a look?"

"No, I mean, the guy. We jumped him immediately. I don't know. He— . . . I think the maid can identify us."

Moaning from the floor.

Without fanfare or urgency, the Eel slowly slipped his hands into leather riding gloves that matched his jacket. Then he grabbed a lamp off the dresser, snapping the plug out of the wall, and brought the base down hard, over and over, striking both heads with a series of stomach-churning thuds that started with a thick resonance and eventually became squishy. One of the overalls ran in the bathroom and hugged the toilet.

The Eel set the lamp back. "Where are the stones?"

"C-c-couldn't find them."

"Check the light switches?"

Energetic nodding. "Just like you said."

An intimidating pause. He held out a palm. "Screwdriver."

One of the gang practically fell over himself fishing a slot-head from a toolbox and slapping it into a gloved hand. The Eel went to the wall. "Check this one?"

More nodding.

He unscrewed the faceplate. Nothing there. Then he unscrewed the switch itself, carefully removing the mechanism and letting it hang from two copper wires. He reached into the back of the junction box and retrieved a small white envelope. The contents emptied into a leather palm. The gang stood stunned at the sight of a dozen near-flawless Peruzzi-cut diamonds in the two-to-four-carat range. He gently poured them back into the envelope.

"How'd you know those were there?"

"Our inside source," said the Eel. "Same info I gave you."

"But we just thought you meant the faceplates, not behind the switch."

"That's the problem. You thought."

"I'm really sorry. I'll do anything to make it up—"

The Eel raised a hand that received prompt silence. "Mistakes happen. We got the diamonds so no harm done . . . Get your shit . . ."

"Oh, thank you! It'll never happen again!" The maintenance man with the stitched name turned and closed the lid on his toolbox. He was so unnerved by the roller-coaster events that he never realized what came out of his mouth next: "You won't be sorry, Jellyfish . . ."

The lamp came off the dresser again.

Wham, wham, wham, wham . . .

The others jumped back.

Seemed like it would go on forever . . . *Wham, wham, wham . . .*

Finally, the Eel was done. A previously white maintenance uniform was now red. A bodyguard stepped forward with Kleenex and wiped specks from his boss's cheeks.

The Eel looked at the remaining trio of overalls, frozen in the realization that they were next. Instead, the lamp flew into a corner. "Now clean all this up. And next time follow instructions."

A bodyguard opened the door and held out his arm for them to wait as he made another visual sweep. All clear. They filed out and headed up the hall, passing room after room. On the other side of one door: rapid, clipped conversation.

"Who's your favorite astronaut?"

"Frank Borman. His first lunar circumnavigation healed national wounds of 1968," said Serge. "Yours?"

"John Young."

"Good choice. He and Story Musgrave co-hold the record of six space flights."

"Except Musgrave's were all shuttle. Young did it the hard way . . ."

"Two Geminis . . ."

"And two Apollos," said Story. "*Oh yes!* Including a moon walk. *Fuck me! Faster! Fuck the shit out of me!*"

Serge thrust like a jackhammer. "Where have you been all my life?"

"*Don't stop! Oh God! Don't stop!*"

"Okay, original Mercury astronaut Deke Slayton finally made it into space on 1975's joint Soyuz mission . . ."

"Harder! Faster! I'm coming! . . ."

Serge increased his rhythm. "What made you change your mind about me?"

"Back at the bar, you defended my honor. No man's ever done that . . . *Oh God! I'm coming again! I'm coming again! . . ."*

Coleman cracked a beer in a dark corner. "I had the G.I. Joe with the space capsule, but I blew it up with firecrackers."

Story panted and raised her head. "What the hell's he doing in here?"

"You know how some guys think of baseball players to prolong ejaculation?"

"Yeah?"

Coleman crashed into the sliding glass balcony door. "Sorry . . ."

Serge thrust again. "That's why he's here."

"Make him leave."

"Coleman . . ." said Serge.

Coleman grabbed a joint from over his ear. "I'll be on the balcony."

Fifteen minutes later, Serge rolled off her in utter exhaustion.

Story fought to catch breath and wiped sweat off her face with a bedsheet. "That was incredible. I've never been with anyone like you! Must have had a dozen."

Serge stared at the ceiling in a religious trance.

"You okay?"

He spoke in a flat robotic monotone. "I can't believe it. I actually came twice. There is a God."

"You've never come twice before?"

"No, I've come more than that, but it took a long night of love-making with extended intermissions to reload the howitzer. But this time they were three minutes apart without stopping. Until now I thought the cosmos had sentenced me without parole to The Guy's Curse of One."

"Yeah, I thought you were losing it a little there in the middle."

"That was after the first. But I didn't want to say anything because you seemed to be having such a good time."

"What made the difference?"

"Guess our space conversation. Whew! After sex like that, there's one thing I love to do!" He rolled over and reached for the drawer on the nightstand.

"I didn't know you smoked . . . Well, I guess if you're ever going to smoke, it's after sex . . ."

"Oh, I don't smoke." Serge removed a small plastic device from the drawer and held it to his eyes.

Story got a puzzled look. "You like to look at View-Masters after sex?"

Serge hit the lever. "I actually like to look at them *during* sex, but it's been met with near-universal criticism."

"Let me see that . . ."

He handed it to her. She clicked the lever through black-and-white stereographic images of the Overseas Highway. "Wow! These are fantastic! Must be sixty years old!" Click, click, click. "I hope you have more . . ." Click, click . . .

Serge stared at the ceiling again. "Love has come to town."

"And here's a super-early one of Sloppy Joe's." Click. Click. Click.

Serge looked sideways on the pillow. "If I'd only known, I'd have been smashing all kinds of noses into bars."

Click, click. Story kept her eyes to the viewer and held out a hand. "Another reel!"

CHAPTER 12

NEXT MORNING

*A*n AMC Javelin raced down A1A and took a small, low bridge across the Tolomato River. It turned south on San Marco Avenue. Serge alternately glanced out the windows and down at his cluttered lap: glossy eight-by-ten satellite photos, View-Master reels, vintage postcards in protective plastic cases.

"Holy cow," said Coleman. "Look at all those shoppers at that big freakin' mall made of old stones."

"How many times do I have to tell you to keep the joints down!" said Serge. "And it's not a mall. It's Castillo de San Marcos, the massive four-hundred-year-old masonry fort—"

"—to protect St. Augustine inlet as part of Spain's early coastal defense." Story looked back down at her history text. "Coquina rock quarried from Anastasia Island. And it's three hundred years old, not four. The first century they used a series of wooden battlements."

Serge's heart went pitter-pat.

Coleman exhaled another huge hit out the window. "You know all those new malls that are made to look old? And how instead of inside, all the store entrances are outside, and everyone walks around fake brick courtyards getting sweaty, and you can't find a place to park for shit unless it's a mile away, and by then you forgot what you came to buy and now just want a taco, but have to settle for elephant ears at the county fair until the guards smell your weed behind the Tilt-A-Whirl, and you're exhausted by the time you escape back to the parking lot and decide to go to the mall. I am really, really high."

"Just keep that joint down."

"I want to buy something," said Coleman. "You sure it's not a mall?"

"Fairly certain." Serge held an encased, circa 1960 postcard up to the windshield for roadside comparison. "Ever seen that commercial about your brain on drugs?"

"I *love* that commercial." Coleman fired up another number. "It's a scream if you're toasted. 'Look, my brain's an egg!' I'm hungry. Do we have any eggs?"

"I'm trying to concentrate," said Serge.

"I'm trying to study," said Story.

"I'll look for eggs," said Coleman.

The riverfront road swung south onto Avenida Menendez. Tourists jammed sidewalks and narrow alleys. A horse pulled a carriage of Norwegians with disposable cameras. Coleman toked; Story highlighted her textbook; Serge held up a postcard. Nothing matched. He checked the satellite photo and clicked through a View-Master reel. No hits. "I could swear it's around here somewhere."

"We just passed a place with eggs."

"I've definitely driven too far." Serge made a U, retracing his route north.

Coleman pointed out the window again. "Now I know where we are. There are those giant cats that scared the piss out of me last time."

"The Bridge of Lions," said Serge.

"But they're just statues made of stone. Why was I so scared?"

"You were on mescaline."

"That would do it," said Coleman. "Once the phone rang and it was after dark before I came out from under the bed."

"Coleman!" snapped Story, gesturing with annoyance at the book she was trying to read.

"Sorry." He turned to Serge. "What are you looking for?"

"Site of the famous Monson Motor Lodge."

"What's that?"

Story clapped her book shut in frustration. "Martin Luther King Jr. was arrested during a sit-in at the Monson." She reached for her organizer and a term-paper rough draft. "June 11, 1964."

"Resulting publicity broke a House filibuster," said Serge. "Paving the way for passage of the historic Civil Rights Act."

"*Senate* filibuster," said Story.

Serge adjusted his underwear to accommodate the growing bulge.

Coleman tapped an ash. "So what's with the postcard and photos?"

"The Monson was demolished, but I was able to get this old postcard of the motel off eBay, which I triangulated to within a three-block range with my vintage View-Master collection. Then I went on Google Earth at the library and hovered over the resulting target zone looking for landmarks."

"Find anything?"

Serge unscrewed the top of a thermos. "They razed the motel, and never in a million years would I have recognized the new one. Except they kept the original pool and built around it. Must have been cost prohibitive to rip it out." He tapped a kidney-shaped spot on the satellite photo. "The configuration is distinctive, and it's the only pool on the strip that sits up against the sidewalk, just off the west end of the last palm tree-lined median strip."

"So why can't you find it?"

Serge chugged straight from his thermos and threw up the other hand. "That's what I don't understand."

"We're passing the fort again," said Coleman.

Serge pounded the steering wheel with his forehead. "This is bullshit!" He made a skidding U-turn and headed back. "I triple-checked all my calculations and sources, so the only possible answer is enemy action."

"Dear God," said Coleman. "Who do you think's behind it?"

"Someone who's going to pay." Serge killed the rest of his thermos, pulled a 9mm automatic from under the driver's seat and racked the slide.

Story looked up from the backseat. "Want me to tell you where it is?"

"No!"

"It'll save you all this silly driving back-and-forth."

"Please," Serge said patronizingly, holding a gun in one hand, looking through a View-Master and driving with his elbows. "Doesn't it look like I know what I'm doing?"

Story shrugged and turned a page.

The Javelin drove up and down the strip five more times, Serge punching the dashboard, clawing upholstery and ripping down ceiling fabric.

"Fuck it," said Story. "I can't take this stupidness anymore. It's the Hilton. They put up a tall cement privacy wall. That's why you could see the pool in the aerial photo but not from the street."

Serge stopped at a red light, wiping bloody knuckles on a towel and squinting into the rearview. "You just couldn't stand to see me having fun."

Mahoney had gone bloodhound.

The smell was all Serge.

The agent currently hunkered in a dark corner of a mangy old roadhouse near the ocean just east of Jacksonville. The tavern spoke to Mahoney. It said: The farther north you drive in the state, the more south you get. Definitely Florida, but no mistaking this for Madonna's Miami Beach. Longnecks replaced mojitos, dark wood paneling, framed photos of Bobby Bowden and Bo Jackson, pool tables, yellowed stuffed fish over bottles of budget whiskey for package sale, handwritten liquor license, signs giving the heads up for loose women. The doors remained propped open to bright light and warm salt air. It was noon. They didn't take plastic.

Mahoney wouldn't have been caught dead with a laptop, except he thought the just-out-of-the-box Toshiba on the table in front of him was a 1932 Smith-Corona with a "magic screen." He found Serge's travel website. Fingers hit six keys: PETE'S.

Up popped a dispatch dated twelve hours earlier: "117 First Street, Neptune Beach, converted from Pete Jensen's Market at the end of Prohibition. John Grisham used the joint as a setting in one of his novels, and you can sit beneath a charred oak barrel hanging from the ceiling that marks the spot where the Mississippi scribe sat while doing research, and—you're not going to fuckin' believe this!—the commemorative plaque on the barrel misspelled the book's title. Finding that golden footnote made my whole week . . ."

Mahoney looked up and read the side of a barrel. ". . . *The Bretheren.*"

He nodded gravely. Serge was close, real close.

Mahoney tapped down to the bottom of the website. The last item was a thumbnail of the state flag over words: *"This is my e-mail button. Serge really wants to hear from you! I promise to write back. In fact, you may have trouble getting me to stop writing back. Change your life forever: Click now!"*

Mahoney clicked the button, hit an invisible carriage return and began typing with one finger.

The Javelin angled up the steep, cobbled drive of the St. Augustine Hilton and parked by the office.

Serge hit the bell ten times at the front desk. Someone appeared. He kept hitting the bell.

"You can stop ringing now."

"Sorry. Surplus excitement about my life. One regular room please. And don't think a free upgrade to your top suite will get you excellent marks in my travel company's widely viewed website, even though it will."

"I can upgrade you anyway. It's pretty dead."

Serge winked. "Of course it is."

The trio checked into their suite and dropped bags. Coleman went in the bathroom. Serge meticulously stowed and restowed his gear, then cleared the dresser, nightstands and all other horizontal surfaces of ubiquitous welcoming literature, local guidebooks, stand-up cardboard advertisements and cable channel guides, stuffing them all in a bottom drawer "to preempt optical confusion."

Story climbed into a one-piece swimsuit, and knocked on the bathroom door.

From inside. "Who is it?"

"I need a towel. I'm going to lay out by the pool."

"Almost done." Humming.

"You've been in there forever."

Coleman eventually opened the door. "Serge, look at all these cute little bottles. What's this stuff called 'conditioner'?"

"In your world, background noise."

"Jesus," said Story. "Close the door!"

"Thought you wanted a towel."

"That smell! It's like a slaughterhouse. What have you been eating?"

"Stuff."

She pinched her nose. "Screw it, I'll air-dry."

Serge slipped into his own trunks and grabbed a small, flexible cooler. "I'll join you."

Coleman came out of the bathroom with toilet paper trailing from his pants. "Wait for me . . ."

Story led the way across the parking lot and pushed open the safety gate. A small pool sat empty in the middle of a tiny patio with a narrow walkway between the far edge and the high concrete wall buffering the racket of unseen traffic. Story settled into a lounger with sunscreen and textbook.

"Look!" yelled Serge. "A bronze plaque!" He raced to the wall and delicately ran fingers over the lettering. "It commemorates Dr. King's achievement! And I never would have found it without all my expert research skills!"

Story looked up with raised eyebrows.

"I was just about to find it when you blurted it out!"

She smiled and looked back down.

Serge grabbed a notebook from the side pocket of his cooler. "This is incredible. When corporations tear down all the special places, they usually don't give a hoot about leaving plaques I can touch and make rubbings." He held one of his book's pages to the plaque and lightly brushed it with the angled tip of a pencil. "This gets the hotel Serge's highest seal of approval, plus a personal thank-you note to Paris Hilton."

Coleman climbed down into the pool with a six-pack and street clothes. Serge joined him and waded over with his cooler. He placed it at the side of the pool, removed three bologna sandwiches and began ramming them in his mouth as fast as he could, accelerating the process with swigs of bottled water. His cheeks bulged like a squirrel stowing nuts.

"That's disgusting," said Story.

"I normally have excellent table manners." Serge crammed another bite. "But I'm field-testing a travel tip. This is about science."

"Science?"

"I'm going to swim without waiting an hour after eating." He pushed the rest of a sandwich in and finished the water bottle. "Nobody's ever considered challenging the prevailing wisdom—nobody's ever dared!"

"That's ridiculous."

"You think it's just one hour, but the loss in job efficiency becomes astronomical over an entire career." Serge donned swim goggles. "Time management is critical for Fortune 500 travelers on the go. If my hunch is correct, the labor-saving windfall could rock the international exchange rate . . . Coleman, what's that on your head?"

"My new hat. I found it with those little bottles in the bathroom."

"Coleman, that's a disposable shower cap."

"How do I look?"

"Like Coleman, except . . . what's that look on your face?"

"What look?"

Serge felt the water around his legs grow warm. "Damn it, Coleman! Not in the pool! And not right before my big swim!"

"At least you're wearing goggles."

"You always do this."

"I do not."

"Coleman, one time you even did a number two."

"That was in the ocean."

"We're not finished discussing this." Serge took a deep breath and dove into the water. His lack of properly coached, hydrodrag mechanics was compensated for by manic, wild-man splashing. He reached the end of the short pool in seconds, executing an Olympic flip-kick against the wall. He splashed a few more seconds and flipped at the other wall. Then another lap, and another. Coleman covered his beer each time Serge thrashed by. Story shook her head.

He continued for a solid, twenty-minute calorie burn, then popped up in the shallow end and whipped off his goggles. "Just as I thought! Come on, Coleman, we have to get back to the room and alert Wall Street. Story?"

"I have more studying."

The guys took off. She exhaled a breath of relief and uncapped a yellow high-lighter. "Finally . . ."

The hot Florida sun tacked across a clear azure sky until afternoon clouds rolled in from the peninsula. Story looked up and checked her watch. "Wow, four already?"

She gathered belongings, strolled back to the room and opened the door to horrible screams.

"What the hell's going on in here?"

Serge was doubled up on the bed as Coleman applied a wet wash-cloth to his forehead.

". . . Cramps! Bad! Ooooooo! . . ."

"You idiot."

Serge writhed and moaned in agony. He finally managed to lift his chin. "Coleman . . ."

Coleman cradled his head. "What is it, buddy?"

"Can you leave Story and me alone for a half hour. We're going to have sex."

"What!" said Story. "Have you lost your fucking mind?"

"But last night . . . Don't you like me anymore?"

"You have cramps!"

Serge shook his head. "The key to life is pushing on through cramps. I do it all the time when field-testing how long you can keep convenience store sandwiches on the road without refrigeration. General rule of thumb, two days, except tuna fish, which is one with absolutely no wiggle room. *Ooooooooooo! God it hurts! Ahhhhh!* . . . You may be right. Just give me a blow job."

"That's it. I'm going for a walk." She changed out of her wet suit in record time. The door slammed.

"What a bitch," said Coleman.

"She's not a bitch," said Serge. "Women can't help their mood swings. Try to be more sensitive like me."

CHAPTER 13

Sun baked.

Tall swamp grass. Dragonflies.

The Javelin sat at a rest stop off Interstate 95 along a wetland slough.

Serge distractedly unwrapped a Cuban sandwich while staring at Coleman. "You're mixing tequila with Yoo-hoo?"

"I'll try anything once."

Serge took a bite. "I absolutely love rest stops! Could stay here for days!"

"What's so special about rest stops?"

"People! The entire spectrum of lives in motion. Vacation, business, ill intentions. Rest stops are the great equalizer, bringing together a population cross-section that would never otherwise allow themselves to be found in the same place."

"Yuck." Coleman poured his cup out the window. "How long is Story going to take?"

"Who knows what goes on in their bathrooms?"

"I heard they have meetings."

"That would explain why us men think we're in charge, but from time to time have a paranormal sensation that our free will is fatefully controlled by invisible puppet strings. Predestination is just another word for sex."

"Wish she'd hurry."

"No harm. The whole key to life is utilizing downtime, like envisioning a utopia without downtime."

Coleman pointed at the building. "The door's opening. The meeting's getting out."

"Puppet time."

Story walked toward the car. Serge pushed a last bite in his mouth and crumpled the sandwich wrapper.

She climbed in the backseat. "Okay, let's go."

"Not yet. My field study needs more data."

"What kind of dumbness now?"

"Rest stops! I love them!" He opened his notebook. "Just a few more observations, like that amber warning sign by the picnic tables: VENOMOUS SNAKES IN AREA. Plus I haven't found the felon yet."

"Felon?"

"As I was telling Coleman: Rest stops are the great equalizer. All kinds of wanted felons and escaped cons traveling up and down the state—they have to go to the bathroom, too." Serge scribbled on a page. "Most of these law-abiding travelers will never know it, but there's always at least one dangerous criminal parked at each rest stop at the same time."

"Start the car!"

Serge leaning toward the windshield. "I found him."

"Who?"

"The felon. Over at the line of Winnebagos. Keep an eye on that last job with Minnesota plates where the retired couple is off-loading trash."

"You're insane," said Story. "Those old people aren't criminals."

"Not them. That dude walking over from his pickup. He's saying something and pointing under the RV. One of the oldest Florida scams in the book."

Coleman popped a beer. "We know about the meetings."

"It's started," said Serge. "He's telling them they have a transmission leak. That's what the pointing was about. Now he's shaking his head: 'Bad one. Probably won't make it another fifty miles.' They're beginning to panic, asking if he's sure. Says he could be wrong, so now he's crawling under the Winnebago." Serge opened the driver's door and got down on the pavement for ground-level view. "He's crawling back out, showing them a greasy, discolored hand. Leak's worse than he thought. If the couple can get the RV back in gear, they must head straight to the nearest transmission shop. Luckily, he knows one back at the last exit that does excellent discount work. Most likely a seal that can be fixed for under a hundred bucks, which will turn into a complete rebuilding job for two thousand."

"Dang," said Coleman. "You can tell what's wrong with the RV from way over here?"

"There's nothing wrong with the RV."

"But what about the transmission fluid on the guy's hands?"

"Bronze tanning lotion or some other gunk. Didn't have a good line of sight, but he probably applied it from a tube while under the chassis. Now he's wishing them good luck and says he has to get going the other way for Atlanta so they don't suspect he's connected to the shop." He reached for the door handle. "Serge's travel service to the rescue!"

Story grabbed his shoulder. "No! Don't get out of the car!"

"Society needs me."

"For the sake of argument," said Story. "What if they really have a leak and you get them stranded on the side of the highway?"

"Distinct possibility." He grabbed a roll of duct tape from under the seat. "That's why I need to run a blind test."

"No!—"

But Serge was already running across the parking lot.

The couple began climbing back into an RV with every factory option.

"Excuse me!"

They turned as Serge jogged up. "Did that guy just say you had a transmission leak?"

"Yeah," said the man in bib overalls and a Korean vet baseball cap.

"That was awfully neighborly of him," said Serge, "but these things can be tricky. Want a second opinion?"

"I—"

"Just be a second." Serge dropped to the ground and scurried out of view. He popped back up a moment later.

"Well?" asked the man.

"Not sure. Thought I could save you some money, but it looks like the other guy might know more about these things. Wish you the best."

"Thanks. Gee, so far we've only met two people in Florida. Is everyone down here this nice?"

"Pretty much."

One bit of inside knowledge from the hospitality industry is that a certain percentage of guests don't check out; they simply leave. This was a problem in the old days with brass room keys, but the new magnetic ones cost next to nothing. The front desk simply charges the remaining balance of phone calls, room service and pay-movies to the credit card—"signature on file"—that the occupant presented at check-in.

Just such a room in a south Jacksonville extended-stay was number 303. The third-floor maid got clearance to turn it around for the next guest.

Her housekeeping cart rolled up to the room later than usual because the other maid who worked the floor had failed to show without notice, and the overflow fell on her shoulders. Just after opening the door, she realized she'd caught a break with 303. The room looked hardly used, almost as if nobody had stayed there. The towel count in the bathroom matched her checklist—all hanging exactly as they'd been placed the day before by the other maid. Soap still in wrappers; tiny shampoo, conditioner and mouthwash unmoved from their perfect triangular formation on the little plastic tray. Even the end of the toilet paper retained its original folded point.

She left the bathroom to discover more non-use, everything in its proper spot, including the dresser lamp with a wiped-down base. The state of the unit lulled her into less scrutiny than normal: no notice of the few stray flecks of blood that had been missed when the tiled entryway was mopped. But most important of all to saving housekeeper time, the beds remained perfectly made, as if no one had slept in them. Because the guest, a coin-dealer-turned-diamond-courier, had never been on his bed. He was under it. The bodies of the missing maid and a man in maintenance overalls were beneath the other one.

The maid locked up the room and informed the front desk that 303 was ready for occupancy.

A two-tone Javelin sat across the street from a mechanic's garage.

"*Now* what are we doing?" asked Story.

"Staking out a dishonest transmission shop." Serge rocked enthusiastically like a child. "This is going to be the most excellent travel service ever!"

"Dammit! Take me to the hotel!"

"Please hang with us on this one," said Serge. "This isn't about me. It's those poor folks from Minnesota."

"I don't even see their RV."

"If it's the scam I think, the Winnebago is behind one of those closed garage bay doors on the end, so nobody can see the expensive work not taking place."

Story inhaled deeply for patience and looked back down at school work. "Okay, but only because I feel sorry for them, too. Just make it snappy."

"It'll be over before you know it." Serge pointed. "See? Here they come now, walking back from the Intergalactic House of Pancakes."

Fifteen minutes later, a 2005 Winnebago with blue trim eased down the driveway of the transmission shop and slowly accelerated up a service road parallel to the interstate. The Javelin fell in behind.

"Coleman, remember what I told you?"

"What?"

"Coleman!"

"Oh, that. Thought you were talking to Story."

She looked up from her reading. "You said this would be over soon."

"Blink and you'll miss it," said Serge.

The RV approached the entrance ramp. The Javelin suddenly accelerated in fugitive-stop maneuver, whipping around the side of the Winnebago. Coleman waved urgently up at the driver. "Pull over! Now!"

The driver let off the gas and rolled down his window. "You guys cops?"

"No," yelled Serge, leaning across his passenger. "But I work for the state. Just pull over—it's very important."

Soon, both vehicles sat quietly on the shoulder. Serge's voice echoed from under the RV. "Just as I suspected!" He crawled out and held up a strip of duct tape.

The man took off his VFW cap and wiped his forehead. "You think we were ripped off?"

"I don't think; I know. One of the oldest scams. Started with that guy at the rest stop."

"But he was so helpful. And he drove off in the other direction toward Atlanta. There's no way he was connected to the garage."

"That's exactly why he *said* he was heading north. Wanted to allay suspicion and make you think he was providing unbiased testimonial for the shop. But he couldn't fool Serge. I was on moral patrol at the rest stop and saw what was happening. So when I checked under your RV back there, I wasn't really checking. I sealed the edge of the transmission pan with tape."

"But I paid to have it completely rebuilt."

Serge held up the tape again. "They never even cracked the pan. Just hid your vehicle behind a garage door for the appropriate amount of time. I'm afraid you've been the victim of a 'Hollywood repair.'"

"What's that?"

"Variation on the 'Hollywood resuscitation,' where doctors in the emergency room tell immediate relatives of a hopeless goner that they'll do everything they can. Then they go inside and pull the curtains tight around the patient and just stand around until the monitors flat-line."

The man's head snapped toward his wife. "My father!"

"Sorry for your loss," said Serge. "But try to stay on point." He snapped fingers in front of the man's eyes. "Back to me . . . How much they take you for? Two grand?"

"Three."

Serge whistled. "They're growing bolder."

The woman looked at her husband in distress. "We can't afford to lose three thousand dollars. What are we going to do?"

"It'll be okay," said the man. "This guy will get it back for us. He works for the state."

"It's not exactly the kind of job you think," said Serge. "Keep this under your hat, but down here we have the highest concentration of sociopaths in the nation. You never know what kind of lunatic might be standing right next to you. And that's where my job comes in, making the daily rounds, providing comfort, safety and trivia, ensuring everyone's having a pleasant stay . . ." He lifted his gaze to the sky. ". . . Moving from town to town, following the road wherever it may lead, righting wrongs, never asking for thanks—"

"Damn it!" Story jumped from the Javelin and stomped toward them. "This was supposed to be fast!"

". . . Although a little common courtesy would be greatly appreciated."

The man glanced at the gray strip in Serge's hand. "So you can't get our money back?"

"Didn't say that either. But I'll need your help."

"Us?"

"Not to worry: You won't be directly involved," said Serge. "As long as you stay hidden in the back of the vehicle and don't make a peep."

"We won't be in any danger, will we?"

"Haven't lost anyone yet." Serge retrieved a brown paper sack from the Javelin's trunk, then returned and grabbed the RV's door handle. "I'll drive, Coleman's shotgun. Story: You follow in the trail vehicle."

CHAPTER 14

*T*he Winnebago reversed direction and sped north. A rest stop approached. A blinker went on. Serge handed Coleman the brown paper bag.

Coleman looked inside. "What are you doing with a sack of sugar?"

"Always keep a supply tucked in the trunk," said Serge. "Part of my roadside emergency jerk kit. Now here's what you're going to do . . ."

The RV pulled into a generous parking space near the restrooms. Serge turned around in the driver's seat and faced the huddled retired couple. "Remember to stay completely hidden. Any deviation from my plan and I can't guarantee anything."

"But—"

"Coleman, let's rock!"

They jumped down from opposite sides of the RV and headed for the vending machines. Serge looked back at the vehicle. He stopped and scratched his head. He bent down.

A man from a nearby pickup truck ambled over. "Problem?"

"Think I'm dripping something." Serge straightened and shrugged. "Probably just radiator fluid."

"Maybe," said the man. "But you don't want to take chances with a leak. Not on these roads. Get stranded at night and, well, most likely nothing will happen."

Serge placed a hand on his heart. "Sex slaves? Heavens, what can I do?"

"I'm pretty good with vehicles. Want me to take a look?"

"You'd do something that kind for a complete stranger?"

"Bet you've never been to Florida before." The man began walking toward the RV. "Extremely friendly state."

"And I'd heard otherwise," said Serge. "Here, come around the far side. Think you can see the leak better from there." Serge turned and tugged his ear.

Coleman stared off with a paper sack hanging by his side.

Serge tugged his ear harder.

Coleman picked his nose.

"Coleman! I'm tugging my ear!"

"Oh! The signal! Right!"

"Signal?" said the pickup driver.

"Has the mind of a first-grader. It's this eye-hand coordination game we play."

The man crawled under the RV and reappeared a minute later. "Not good news."

"Pray tell?"

The man stood and displayed a brown hand. "Transmission fluid. Real bad leak, probably won't last another fifty miles."

"Sounds expensive!"

The pickup driver shook his head. "Hundred bucks tops if it's what I think. I know this garage . . ."

Coleman walked over to the pickup truck, glanced around and opened the gas cap.

"Gee mister," said Serge. "Thanks a heap."

"My pleasure." He tipped his camo baseball cap. "Well, have to get a leg up on Atlanta."

"Wait!" said Serge.

"What is it?"

"We haven't been properly introduced. I'm Serge!" He extended a hand.

"Elliot . . . Take it easy now."

"Wait!"

Elliot sighed and forced himself to smile. "Yes?"

Coleman walked back around the RV with a crumpled paper bag in his hand. He nodded.

Serge turned toward the man. "Did I remember to say thanks?"

Elliot laughed and headed for his pickup. "Good luck."

"You might need it more."

SHENANIGANS LOUNGE

Pushed-together tables ran the length of the room. A mechanical slot sucked in a dollar bill. Music began.

"... *Night moves* ..."

A nutritional-supplement salesman walked back from the juke.

"You always play this stupid song," said Steve.

"Thought you liked Seger."

"Until you came along."

"I know the real reason you're sore."

Actually, just about everyone at the tables was sore. The reason sat at the bar, a dashing man in a tailored silk suit and thick, sexy black hair to the collar. On each side, flight attendants based out of Denver, over-laughing at his every remark. Two more attendants stood behind his stool, trying to wedge in on the hunk, who reeked of nonstop intercourse because of his aftershave, Nonstop Intercourse.

The gang around the tables shook their heads.

"What's he got that I don't?" asked self-esteem-seminar Ken.

"You never seen Johnny?"

Ken shook his head.

"The guy's practically a legend," said Ted. "Seen him in action at least twenty times, always leaves with the hottest chick in the bar."

"What's he do?"

"Nothing but live off a trust fund, troll hotel bars and get laid like nobody's business. More tail falls off his truck than we'll ever see."

Steve took out his wallet and threw a ten-spot next to the beer pitcher. "Who's in?"

The pot grew as more bills landed in the middle of the table. "I say the blonde." "Brunette for variety." "Redhead." "Asian fox ..."

Finally, the betting window closed. They turned toward the bar and waited. Every last one of the salesmen would have killed to be in Johnny's shoes. But only because they'd never walked in them. The actual truth was something none of the gang would have imagined.

Johnny attracted willing partners in such waves he had to fight them off. But sealing the deal was another matter entirely. Some calamity always interrupted the precise moment of penetration. Literally, his entire life. No possible way to overstate the phenomenon. It was such a numbing string of misfortune that General Custer, Al Gore and the captain of the *Titanic* would all have said the same thing. Man, have *you* got bad luck.

He was Johnny Vegas, the Accidental Virgin.

Back at the tables: "Looks like the blonde . . . no wait, he's getting up. He's turning to his right . . . Damn . . ."

Three guys raked bills from the middle of the table as Johnny strolled for the elevators with an effervescent redhead in an airline scarf.

A Winnebago with blue trim pulled into a transmission shop. The manager came out.

Serge jumped down from the driver's seat and gave him a giant hug, weeping on his shoulder. "Thank Jesus you're so conveniently close to the rest stop and that nice man just happened to be there. I cringe to imagine breaking down after midnight between exits and living out my days wearing a dog collar in a sex dungeon . . ."

"Easy now." The manager gently grabbed Serge's arms and calmly pushed him back. "What seems to be the problem?"

"Transmission leak! Geyser!"

The manager rubbed his chin. "That's the problem with this model. Seen quite a few lately, but it shouldn't cost much. Why don't we go—"

"—write up a work order?" said Serge.

The manager stopped. "Uh, exactly."

They went inside, and the manager grabbed a triplicate sheet with sprocket holes. He scribbled quickly and turned the paperwork around to face Serge. "Sign at the bottom."

Serge picked up a pen. "What am I signing?"

"Just says you want us to check out your transmission."

"But that's not what I want at all."

"It isn't?"

"Not even close." Serge set the pen down.

"Then why'd you come here?"

Serge held out his palm. "Three thousand dollars please."

"What?"

"That's how much you got from the retired couple who was just in here."

"Oh, them."

"I'm a close personal friend."

"I get it: You think we overcharged." He nodded with practiced sympathy. "Most people have no idea what transmission work runs. Sticker shock. But three grand is the going rate to completely rebuild those giant gear boxes on the larger RVs."

"And zero is the going rate for hiding it behind a closed garage door and doing nothing."

"I don't think I like what you're implying."

"I don't like that my hand doesn't have three thousand dollars in it."

"Hey, asshole. They came to me."

"Because you had an accomplice at the rest stop."

"I don't have no fucking accomplice! Get the hell off my property!"

The phone beside the cash register rang. A mechanic answered. He covered the receiver and called to the manager. "Elliot needs a tow from the rest stop."

Serge placed the back of a hand to his forehead and closed his eyes. "The spirits tell me that will be a highly profitable repair."

The manager stepped up nose to nose with Serge, deliberately underscoring his size advantage. "Deaf or something? I said get the fuck out!"

Serge shook his head. "Can't let you do this to yourself."

"Do what?"

"Miss out on my ground-floor opportunity!" said Serge. "Three thousand is an absolute steal for us to go our separate ways."

"Out!"

"It's a win-win! You break even and live to enjoy a brighter tomorrow."

"Fuck you!" The manager gave Serge a hard, two-handed shove in the chest.

Serge stumbled backward and caught his balance. "Investors are lining up fast! Price is now four thousand!"

The manager shoved him again.

Serge stumbled again. "You obviously don't know what the price of *regret* is running these days. But because I like you, special new deal: five thousand!"

The manager saved his most vicious shove for last. Serge crashed backward into the glass door and crumpled on the ground. The manager pointed threateningly in his face. "You've fucked with the wrong guy! Those friends with the RV? They just bought them a world of shit. I have their address on the work order. I know people in Minnesota. And when my associates pay a visit, they're going to tell them it's all because of you!"

"Sorry," said Serge. "Investment deadline just passed." He stood and opened the door. Ting-a-ling.

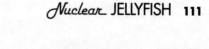

CHAPTER 15

SERGE'S SUITE

*F*renetic tapping on a laptop keyboard.

A beer can popped. "Whatcha doin'?"

"Uploading the daily addendum to my renegade travel website. Today's nuggets: avoiding transmission ripoffs and the best place to spot John Travolta."

"Travolta?"

"Coleman, you were with me there yesterday." Typing rate increased. "That old Holiday Inn across from Silver Springs."

"Now I remember."

"Travolta's an aviation fiend. Got a giant spread out in the country north of here, two jets in the driveway, including a Boeing 707, and his own airstrip, but I'm not going to reveal the location on my site because I respect his privacy."

"Is that why we kept circling his property?"

"Those were public roads—plus I wanted to make sure no unstable people were bothering him."

"What's Holiday Inn got to do with it?"

"Staff told me he's a night owl . . ." Tap, tap, tap, tap. ". . . In wee hours, he likes to eat at the Denny's attached to the motel because it's about the only thing still open in the middle of nowhere . . ." Tap, tap. ". . . Imagine that: The *Pulp Fiction* assassin frequenting this funky little place in our own fine state. Apparently a real nice guy, too. Next to the motel's reception desk are some cool photos of him on the wall posing with staff and a night watchman."

"What are you doing now?"

"I took photos of the Travolta photos, which I'm just about finished posting . . ." Tap, tap, tap. Serge stood. "There, done." He looked around. "Where's Story?"

"Still down at the pool," said Coleman, opening the suite's refrigerator to store remaining beers dangling from their plastic six-pack ring.

Serge began pacing. And pacing, wearing a rut in the motel carpet.

"What's the matter, buddy?"

Serge reached a wall and paced back the other way. "Nothing on the to-do list until my project later tonight." He came to another wall and turned. "You know how I can't stand not to have a fixation target." Another wall . . .

Coleman idly looked around the room. "Is it my dope, or did we get a bigger place than usual?"

"It's a suite." He spun at the windows. "What to do? What to do? . . ."

Coleman investigated the kitchenette, opening and closing all the drawers. "It even has a dishwasher."

Serge trudged toward the window. "I usually have the opposite problem of choice shock. Too many diversions . . ."

The microwave opened and closed. "This is the coolest place I've ever stayed." Another drawer. "I remember loving to go to motels when I was a kid."

Serge stopped in his sneaker tracks. "Coleman! That's it! You're brilliant!"

"I am?"

"How could I be so stupid? I've been thinking like a middle-aged person."

"You are middle-aged."

"Of all people I should know better." Serge ran into the kitchenette, rapidly opening and closing drawers. "Life was invented for kids. But then we all grow up, and society imposes filters that block the joy of silliness and sponging up pointless little things that make childhood the magic time for which it is widely known." He stuck his face in an overhead cabinet.

Coleman bent down and opened double doors. "Look at all this space under the sink."

"Much work at hand!" He dashed over to a bed and yanked off the sheets. "Coleman, grab those chairs."

"What are we doing?"

"It's like riding a bicycle. You never forget how."

DOWN THE HALL

Johnny Vegas couldn't miss.

The flight attendant had said she was hungry, so he'd bought her dinner and even dessert. Now, time to pay up. What's fair was fair.

The elevator opened on the third floor. The attendant had a little trouble holding her liquor. She began kissing Johnny and unbuttoning his shirt before he could get the magnetic card in the door. They tumbled inside.

She began ripping off her clothes. Johnny hurried to keep up, breaking his zipper in the rush. She slammed into him for a sloppy kiss, still disrobing in a clumsy, stumbling march across the spacious room. Sensual moaning, items of apparel randomly jettisoned. They reached the back of the suite in front of a magnificent waterfront view from the giant, floor-to-ceiling windows. Night strollers on the beach stopped and pointed up at the northeast corner of the hotel.

Johnny hopped past the TV, yanking off socks. She grabbed him around the neck, tripping backward with feet tangled in panties and pulling Johnny down on top of her. They landed hard on the carpet next to the bed.

Beach strollers sagged as the show disappeared from view.

The flight attendant closed her eyes and panted with shallow breaths. "Hurry . . ." —reaching down to help accelerate the process. Louder moaning. "Baby, now! . . ." Johnny positioned himself for the plunge. Finally! After all these years! Goodbye virginity!

More moaning. "Put it in!" Her head fell to the side. She opened her eyes. Staring back from under the bed was the blue, lifeless face of a coin dealer named Henry.

Beach people looked up again toward the source of hysterical shrieking from room 303.

Two men stood in front of a hotel room door. They whispered and glanced suspiciously up and down the hall.

One opened a brown paper bag. "Hurry up! Before someone sees us!"

The other reached in his fanny pack and removed a can of shaving cream. He squeezed the top, foaming the entire contents into the sack.

The first one pressed the end of the bag flat, and quietly slipped it under the door.

An elevator at the end of the hall opened. Story got off, wrapped in a towel from the pool. A dozen rooms ahead, two men seemed to be having trouble getting into their room. As she grew nearer, one leaned toward the door. "Stamp-collecting wussies!"

The other stomped on the paper bag.

They ran past her giggling.

She reached her own room and opened the door. "I'm back . . ."

No answer.

"Anyone here?" She checked the bathroom. "That's odd."

Then something odder caught her eye: on the other side of the room, an ad hoc tent fashioned from bedsheets and two chairs. She walked over and lifted the edge of a sheet. Souvenir matchbooks, pins and postcards scattered on the floor, next to a stack of hotel stationery covered with tic-tac-toes. And a scorecard: Serge 50, Coleman 0. Her face pinched with puzzlement.

Story began walking back across the suite. She stopped. Some kind of faint noise, like people talking. Except it had a strange electronic sound like a police scanner. Where was it coming from? She resumed walking, more slowly this time, stopping by the dresser to reach silently into her purse. Out came a shiny .25-caliber chick gun. She held it outstretched in both hands, sliding her feet across the carpet. The voices grew louder. They were coming from the kitchenette.

Story rounded the breakfast nook, gun leading the way. The mechanical voices became even louder. But still no sign of their source. Weird. A few more steps. Even louder. It seemed to be coming from the sink. She slipped closer. Actually, *beneath* the sink.

Story gripped the pistol tight in her right hand, carefully reaching for a cabinet handle with her left. She quickly jerked it open, jumped back and took aim.

Serge and Coleman sat bunched under the sink with potato chips, flashlights and walkie-talkies, a pile of playing cards between them.

"Hey, Story," said Serge.

Coleman raised his walkie-talkie "Go fish."

Serge grabbed a card and looked up. "Would you mind closing the door?"

CHAPTER 16

SILVER SPRINGS

gent Mahoney unfolded three pages of printouts from the Internet. One had pictures. He held it up to a Holiday Inn lobby wall for comparison. Perfect match. He entered Denny's.

The waitress arrived. Mahoney waved off the menu. "Just a cup of joe." She left him seated in the last booth at the back of the restaurant, facing the door. He removed his fedora and placed it on the table next to a paper placemat.

Coffee arrived. Then a thin old man in checkered slacks. He stopped in the doorway and raised his stubbled chin to acknowledge the agent.

They were soon sitting across from each other.

"Mickey, how's my favorite bartender?"

"Lumbago. You got my message?"

"No, it's a big coincidence I'm sitting here."

"Still interested in this Serge business?"

Mahoney stuck a wooden matchstick in his mouth.

The bartender looked around, then bent over the table. "Why don't you just drop it. I have a bad feeling."

"You seen Serge or not?"

Mickey shook his head. "I don't even know what he looks like."

"Then what was that message about?"

"Some wiseguy came around the bar asking about him, and I don't think it was to send a birthday card."

Mahoney angled his head to look around Mickey. "Who's the suspicious mug sitting up front that keeps glancing back here."

"Just John Travolta. Listen, I'm not kidding about walking away from this. In all our years, I've never had a feeling like this before."

"What's the lowdown on this snoop?"

"That's what's got me worried. No matter how bad this Serge character is, he can't be anything like the guy who came around. You just get a vibe off some people."

Mahoney fit his hat back on his head and stood. "Thanks, Mickey." He opened his wallet and removed a twenty.

The bartender shook his head. "This one's on the house."

Mahoney put a hand on his shoulder—"They broke the mold, Mickey"—and walked out into the night.

3 A.M.

Story was propped up in bed with three pillows, editing a composition.

A door under the sink opened, and Serge spilled onto the tiles. He and Coleman headed for the door, flashlights in hand.

Story looked up from her paper. "Where are you going?"

"To work." The door closed behind them.

A half hour later, Serge jiggled a bent paperclip, easily popping the flimsy lock. He and Coleman crept through a rusty double-wide trailer on the edge of a cow pasture just west of I-95.

They reached a bedroom. Serge clicked on his flashlight and aimed it at a sleeping face. "Wake up."

Snoring.

Serge reached out with the flashlight and bonked a forehead.

"Ow!" A man shot up in bed. He turned and shielded his eyes against the blinding halogen beam. "What the fuck?"

"I'm the ghost of Christmas past."

"Who?"

"Should have accepted my three-thousand-dollar offer," said Serge. "It will soon look like the bargain of a lifetime."

"Wait, I remember you. You're so fucking dead!"

"Goodnight," said Serge. The flashlight came down again, this time strategically harder. The transmission-shop owner went back to sleep.

One hour later, the shop owner awoke again with a splash of water in the face. He was lying down, but not on anything comfortable like a bed. In fact—his head looked side to side—where was he?

"You're in the Ocala National Forest," said Serge. "What a treat! So peaceful."

The mechanic conducted a clockwise assessment of his various limbs, spread eagle. He began struggling furiously, but the wrist and ankle restraints didn't budge a millimeter.

"That's because I used hurricane tie-downs. Had one guy almost get free, so I decided to spring for the best remedy money could buy." He reached inside a bag. "Sometimes it's expensive to be cheap."

"What are you planning?"

"Take you back to transmission school. If you're going to hang a shingle, at some point you need to actually start doing the work. Let's see what we've got here . . ." Serge's hand came out of the bag. It held a thick, three-foot-long corkscrew with a giant eye loop at the top. "Bought an extra tie-down to show you because visual aids always help my students retain their lessons." Serge got on his knees and twisted the device into the ground. "Home Depot again. Love that place! People buy these to anchor their sheds and whatnot so hurricanes don't turn them into aircraft, which means you might as well stop that flopping around . . ." Serge looked up at the Big Dipper. ". . . Found a nice, remote clearing. No trees for a hundred yards, which means you'll have full sunlight tomorrow. The weatherman says it's going to be a scorcher."

"You're going to leave me out here to die of exposure?"

"That would be sick." Serge reached in his bag again and came out with duct tape. "What kind of person do you think I am?"

"Please, I'm begging you! I'll pay the money!"

He peeled an edge of the tape from the roll. "Sorry, you threatened a family."

"I won't do anything to them! I swear!"

"Really?"

"Word of honor!"

"Hmmmm . . ." Serge tapped his chin, then ripped a long strip from the roll. "Don't believe you."

"Wait, I'll—"

Tape covered the man's mouth and wrapped several times around his head.

Serge stood over him and smiled. "Took the liberty of having Coleman follow us in your car. It would be incredibly impolite to leave you stranded way out here with no transportation." He pulled a set of keys from his pocket. "Stay put. I'll just be a sec."

The mechanic heard a familiar car start. The engine grew louder: My God! He's going to run over me!

The hostage closed his eyes and soiled himself. The engine reached a roar. Then it suddenly stopped. The shop owner opened his eyes and stared up at the undercarriage of his car a few inches from his face. He heard a voice from the side. Serge was lying on his stomach next to the vehicle, chin propped jauntily in his hands.

"See? I positioned it for total shade cover from tomorrow's sun. And for the sake of irony—which tickles me pink—the transmission is right over you so you'll have plenty of opportunity to study it. Well, at least the outside, which is about as close as you've gotten so far."

Serge stood again. The mechanic watched sneakers walk around to the other side of the car.

"Coleman, I need to borrow your disposable lighter."

"What for?"

"Just give it!"

Coleman tossed it over the roof. Serge snatched it out of the air and opened the driver's door.

"If this was a movie, the camera angle would be somewhere near the floor of the car, looking up at Serge's hand . . ."

"Serge," said Coleman. "You're doing it again."

"Doing what?"

"Talking to yourself."

"I was? What was I saying?"

"Something about a movie camera."

"I thought the narration was just playing inside my head. Oh well . . . Serge's hand reached, slow motion, as the camera zoomed on the 69-cent butane lighter being placed gently in the middle of the dashboard. Then the film sped back up as Serge slammed the door, and he and Coleman drove away in their 1971 AMC Javelin . . . Cut! Print!"

CHAPTER 17

ROUTE A1A

A two-tone Javelin sped south on the part of the highway below St. Augustine that ran against the shore. The sky was gray, extra-choppy surf. Serge grooved on the perpetual rhythm of large, rolling waves that began doming hundreds of yards out and crashed into the beach with bursts of foam and salty mist. Ahead, a disciplined line of eight pelicans rode the stout wind, gliding along the edge of the road at a velocity only slightly slower than traffic. Serge passed them at window level, saluting eight times. They crossed the Matanzas River.

"Oh my God!" said Serge. "Look!"

A compound of white buildings appeared on the sea side of the road, like a small campus or research institute.

"Coleman!" Serge reached over and shook his shoulder. "Are you looking?"

"Yeah, buildings." Coleman stared back down, diagnosing the engineering flaw in his makeshift, toilet-paper-tube bong that was flaking apart in a bowl of water. "All that work for one shitty hit." He pulled limp pieces of cardboard from his mouth.

"Someone's fixing up Marineland!" Serge let off the gas. "She's saved from the executioner! Where's a parking space?"

Story punched the back of his seat. "You're not stopping!"

"Of course we're stopping. It's Marineland, the world's first oceanarium, 1938." He hit a turn signal for the parking lot and grabbed his camera.

She hit the seat again. "Keep driving! I told you I have an appointment at the dance club. Someone in this car has to make money."

"You can strip anytime—"

Swat.

"Ow!"

"I am *not* stripping."

"Okaaaaay, we'll keep going. But just this once because I hate people who miss appointments." Serge stepped on the gas and snapped a quick photo as they went by. "But hit me one more time . . ."

"And you'll what?"

"I'll . . . stop someplace and take lots and lots of pictures."

The Javelin continued south. Beverly Beach, Flagler Beach, Ormond-by-the-Sea. Sparsely populated miles of unruined view. More waves, fried-fish shacks, sea oats, and an old beach shop with colorful, inflatable rafts stacked out front, except today they were lashed tightly to a post, flapping in the near gale.

The sky grew darker. Coleman switched to joints. "Thought this was the Sunshine State."

"Point?" said Serge.

"It's been an odd-looking week. First all that smoke from those forest fires in Georgia. Then cloudy every other day."

"I dig it," said Serge. "These rare gray afternoons evoke a sweet, childhood melancholy in my soul, like when it rained in kindergarten and we had to stay inside and do crafts with library paste and pipe cleaners and buttons, and I made the best project in the whole class, an ultra-powerful rubber-band zip gun, but the teacher gave me a zero because I got her in the eye with a button."

The road entered a strip of vintage seaside amusement. Arcades, gondola rides, short space needle, tunnel under the boardwalk for people to drive out onto the sand. And a sign:

WELCOME TO DAYTONA BEACH

Serge looked up the road and hit his blinker. "I have to make a stop."

"No!" shouted Story.

"It'll be lickety-split. Already know what I want."

Just past the 7-Eleven stood a large building with racing flags. The Javelin pulled into the parking lot of a NASCAR souvenir superstore.

Serge worked quickly through the aisles, avoiding usual knick-knack distraction by holding palms to the sides of his eyes like blinders. He bypassed officially licensed key chains, bobble-heads and Zippo lighters, finally arriving at a giant display of full-size magnetic door signs with the stock-car numbers and fonts of all the most popular drivers. He grabbed a pair with the giant number "2."

The cashier rang him up. "You're a Kurt Busch fan?"

"No, I came twice."

Serge returned to the parking lot and slapped his magnets on the sides of the Javelin. They continued down A1A.

"What's that place over there?" asked Coleman. "Looks like a giant ship."

"Supposed to." Serge grabbed his camera. "The venerable Streamline Hotel, grande dame of old Daytona, where people lined the rooftop to watch auto races when they used to hold them down here on the beach." Click, click, click. "I've often toyed with the idea of living there."

"Don't you mean 'stay'?"

Serge shook his head. "I'm fascinated by the concept of people who live in hotels. Like Howard Hughes's top-floor place in Vegas, or that rich old woman who spent years in a suite at The Breakers."

They stopped at a red light. A carload of race fans pulled up beside them. Someone from the other vehicle noticed the magnetic sign on the Javelin and pumped a fist out the window. "Wooooooo! Kurt Busch!"

Serge pumped his own fist. "Wooooooo! I came twice!"

Coleman looked back at the hotel. "What's that smokestack-looking thing on top?"

"The bar."

"Can we stop?"

"No!" yelled Story.

Serge looked in the rearview at the hotel lobby's original wraparound glass. "After the races moved out to the speedway on the other side of town, people forgot about the Streamline. Now the rooms are bargain rate, even though it's a priceless opportunity to live in the magnificent 1940s."

"Then why don't they charge more?" asked Coleman.

"Because who besides me wants to live in the forties?"

In one of the Streamline's upstairs windows, a guest stood with a coffee mug of Irish whiskey. He stared across the ocean with narrow eyes beneath the brim of a rumpled fedora. His tie had a pattern of dice and roulette wheels. Agent Mahoney's gaze went from the sea down to traffic below on A1A. A two-tone Javelin sat at a traffic light. Mahoney looked back up at the Atlantic and raised his mug. "Where can he be? . . ."

TWO MILES AWAY

Sea fog was thick as an unusually dim sun set over the ocean. Tide rolled in with a frothy chop. Couples bundled in sweaters against the nippy breeze and strolled along the mean-high-water mark. Hovering gulls cawed. Seaweed tangled around a row of PVC tubes anchoring an array of unattended surf-casting rods. Someone in headphones swept a metal detector over the sand. He stopped and dug up a rusty bicycle chain, studied it curiously, then reburied it.

North of the boardwalk, a column of upscale hotels and resorts had begun a ferocious sprout, but someone had thought to save the historic band shell. In the southeast corner of the nearest hotel, a light went on in one of the upper suites. A silhouette appeared behind the drapes. Below on the beach, a man in headphones rested the metal detector against his leg and raised a pair of binoculars.

The shadow moved back and forth behind the curtains. The man on the beach counted floors up the side of the hotel. The shadow disappeared from the window. The light went out.

The man with the metal detector grabbed a small Motorola two-way radio from his pocket. "Blue?"

"Blue here . . ."

"This is red. He just left. Fifteenth floor, southeast corner."

"Sure the room's clear?"

"Saw it with my own eyes. I'll be in the bar to make sure he doesn't come back up."

Five minutes later the lighted numbers over the elevator ticked up to "15." Doors opened. Men in maintenance overalls walked quickly down the empty hall, followed by a cluster of bodyguards around a taller man in a leather jacket.

Normally, the Eel would never let himself be caught within ten miles of a job, but there had been a recent pandemic of screw-ups. They neared the suite at the southeast corner. The first to reach the door set his toolbox on the ground. He removed a small electrical device the size of a garage opener and plugged a wire into the side. The wire's other end attached to a thin strip of metal that he ran through the room's magnetic card scanner. They went inside.

The search was silent and swift. At least in the beginning. They went straight for the bottom left dresser drawer and flipped it over on the bed. That's where their inside information said the courier always taped his packets of stones.

They stared at bare wood.

"Maybe he changed drawers."

Out came the rest.

"Well?" said the Eel.

The maintenance men shook their heads and slowly stepped backward.

The Eel's eye-bulging face turned deep crimson. "What kind of ignorant fuckheads do I have working for me?"

"But that's every drawer. You're here. You saw it—"

"Son of a bitch!" The Eel marched forward and flicked open a ridiculously large switchblade.

"Please! No!—"

A two-way radio squawked.

The Eel punched a wall. "What now?"

"Blue? Are you there? This is red. Come in . . ."

The Eel's eyes signaled a temporary reprieve. One of the maintenance men grabbed the radio. "Blue here. We copy."

"There's trouble . . ."

CHAPTER 18

MEANWHILE . . .

The Javelin rolled past a drive-in church and turned onto Van Avenue. Serge parked at the curb in front of a quaint ranch house, tastefully landscaped. He raised his camera.

"Dammit!" said Story. "You're going to make me late!"

"Relax." Click, click, click. "A travel professional always builds in a time cushion."

"That's what you said up the road at the other place. I only agreed because I thought it was going to be your only photo stop."

"That's right, it was. Seabreeze High School, where they played their first gigs. But this is the Allman Brothers childhood home." Click, click, click. "It's your fault."

"Mine?"

"You know what kind of person I am. How could you expect me to be so close to the cradle of southern rock and not get sucked into its gravity well? Gregg and 'Sky Dog' Duane probably skateboarded right on this very street."

"But I have a job!"

"I do, too." Click, click. "Recovering the credit that Florida so richly deserves. And Duane not only grew up here but laid down the most historic guitar licks ever recorded in the state, teaming with Eric Clapton on 'Layla' at Miami's Criteria Studios, 1970."

Coleman lowered a flask. "Isn't that the place we went during that hurricane?"

"The same."

"Damn you!" said Story.

"Please." Serge pointed at the house. "Respect the Sky Dog."

"I just better be there by eight o'clock."

"*Nooooooo* problem." Click, click, click.

Thirty seconds before eight, Serge skidded into a parking lot at the corner of A1A and International Speedway. "Told you we'd make it."

Story jumped out and slammed the door. "Asshole."

The guys exited the vehicle at a more leisurely pace and approached a small building with EXOTIC DANCERS in glaring neon. Over the front doors sat a large fish and another sign: SHARK LOUNGE.

The place wasn't yet open to the public. For now, it remained empty except for Story, another woman on the far side of the lounge, and Serge and Coleman, seated at the unstaffed bar. A half hour passed. Coleman swigged from a bottle of sour mash that he'd commandeered from the adjoining liquor store. "This is easily the most bizarre strip club I've ever been in."

"That's why I love the Shark Lounge!"

"You've been here before?"

"Many, many times."

"But I thought you didn't like strip clubs, except when we're lining up marks."

"The Shark is different." Serge gestured across the room. "See that tall rectangle of steel bars?"

"Looks like one of those things scuba divers use on TV."

"Girls actually dance in a shark cage." Serge's arm swung another direction. "And the main catwalk with the poles is on top of a giant aquarium."

"They strip on a real aquarium?"

"Something for everyone," said Serge. "The only negative is I go through a ton of cash tipping the dancers *not* to stick their muffs in my face while I'm trying to look at fish."

"Speaking of which . . ." Coleman's head turned the other way. "Can't believe Story's still hanging with us. Thought she'd just use us for a ride and dash at the first chance."

"I'm starting to wish she *would* dash."

"How can you say that?" asked Coleman. "She lets you fuck her."

"Coleman, have you still not learned there's more to a relationship than that?"

"Is this some kind of trick question?"

"Let you in on the big secret about chicks. It starts with intercourse . . ."

"I like that start. Go on."

"But they universally possess the same prehistoric genetic memory. Doesn't matter where you find them—Miami, Budapest, the mountains of Peru, those remote islands off New Zealand where they just discovered a tribe that's never seen a wheel—the women are all hardwired with the identical life drive."

"Which is?"

"To change you."

"How?"

Serge made a fisherman's spin-casting motion with his hands. "First, they set the hook with mind-bending kinky shit. Then a year later you're living in a Talking Heads song, dressed like Teddy Ruxpin, living with a strange woman in a big house full of frilly throw pillows, experiencing a frequency of sex that can only be charted by Halley's comet. And you're wondering: How did I get here?"

"These ways that they want to change us," said Coleman. "Are they for the better?"

"Of course," said Serge. "But that's not the point."

The Eel's head was about to explode. The walkie-talkie crackled again in the hotel room.

"Blue? You there?"

"I'm here. What kind of trouble are you talking about?"

"The mark is heading back up early."

"Roger, we'll clear the zone."

"No, I don't think you'll have enough time. He left a few minutes ago. I thought he was just going to the bathroom, but then I noticed he'd paid his tab and his coat was gone. He could be opening the door any second."

They scrambled to turn off lights. The Eel motioned with his knife for everyone to clear toward the blind side of the room from the door. Then they waited.

And waited.

The Eel telegraphed a look to the crew member with the radio, who keyed the mike. "Red, do you copy?"

"This is red, over."

"He's not here. Did he return to the bar?"

"Negative. I'm out on the beach again."

"What are you doing on the—?"

"Hold it. Something's happening. The light just came back on in the suite. You see him?"

The crew exchanged confused glances in the dark room. The one with the radio: "Uh . . . no."

"Now I see his shadow. He's walking by the curtains."

The crew heard footsteps. They looked up at the ceiling.

The Eel punched another wall. "Jesus Christ! Give me that radio!" He ran to the window and looked down at a tiny man on the beach with a metal detector. "Red, how do you know he was staying on the fifteenth floor?"

"I counted."

"You counted?"

"Three times. From right here on the beach."

"You do know that some hotels don't have thirteenth floors."

"What?"

A two-way radio smashed against the wall. A lamp flew. An ashtray shattered the TV tube with a flicker of dying sparks. The Eel stormed out of the room, and the others followed.

SHARK LOUNGE

Coleman stared across the club's dim interior. "I thought when Story said she needed to get here to make money, it was by stripping."

"Me, too," said Serge. "Live long enough and you see everything."

On the other side of the room, Story sat on a stool next to the shark cage. Inside was a naked woman with a trigonometry textbook. "So after the hypotenuse, then what?"

"Add the squares of the adjacent sides and solve for X."

"Who thought of this?"

"Subject to argument, but it at least dates to the reign of Hammurabi."

Serge faced the bar again. "Tutoring colleagues stripping their way through school. Very admirable."

"Still don't understand why she's hanging with us."

"Because she's damaged."

"Looks fine to me."

"I'm not judging," said Serge. "We're all damaged. It's a universal component of the human condition, like the stages of grief, déja vu and expired coupons."

"Am I damaged?"

Serge placed a hand on his pal's shoulder. "Coleman, there are three—and only three—kinds of people in this world: Those who don't know they're damaged and blame others; those who realize they're damaged and blame others; and then people like you and me, who wear damage like comfortable pajamas."

Coleman swigged from his pint bottle. "Mine are the ones with the little feet."

"The problem is the word *damage*. Sounds negative. But it's just another facet of higher spiritual consciousness that separates us from lower orders of life. You think some animal that doesn't even possess object permanence is whimpering about dysfunction from materially focused parents?"

"Object what?"

"Permanence. One of the things that separates humans . . . Forget it. In your case, it's easier to just demonstrate." He grabbed Coleman's pint bottle.

"Be careful with that!"

"Don't worry. Only using it to make a point." Serge held the bottle in front of Coleman's face. "Got a good look?"

"Yeah."

Serge whipped it behind his back.

"Hey! What happened to my bottle?"

"Coleman—"

"It's gone forever!"

"Okay, bad example." Serge returned the pint to Coleman.

"My bottle's here forever!"

Serge swiveled around on his stool and leaned against the bar. "This is one of my favorite Florida landmarks. And there's something I've always wanted to do here to complete the experience, but the time's never been right." He furtively glanced around. "Until now . . . Coleman, cover me . . ."

On the other side of the lounge, a woman in a shark cage looked up from her textbook. "Your friend over there's kind of cute."

"A freakin' lunatic is what he is." Story turned a page in her own book. "Wearing out my last nerve."

"Then why do you still hang with him?"

"He's damaged. Guess it brings out the maternal instinct. Plus I need transpo."

"Admit it. You think he's cute."

"I will say this: Incredibly annoying as he is, there are at least three or four times a day I have to strain with all my might not to burst out laughing."

"Don't give me that old garbage: 'He makes me laugh.'"

"He does."

"You think he's cute."

"Trust me. They don't make a strong enough dose of cute to compensate for the crap I have to put up with."

"What kind of crap."

"Wait long enough and you get a chance to see—"

The woman in the cage pointed. "Holy mother!"

Story jumped up. "Serge! What the hell do you think you're doing?"

"I'm dancing."

"Get the fuck off the aquarium!"

"But I always wanted to—"

"Get off!"

"*Allllllll* right."

Story plopped back down on her stool. "See what I'm talking about?"

"I have to go to the bathroom."

"I'll go with you."

A door of metal bars creaked open. "I'll bet I could change him."

CHAPTER 19

AFTER MIDNIGHT

*M*ahoney was going with his instincts, playing a hunch, had a gut feeling. He squeezed his way through the crowd in a dark room. Dance beat throbbed. He arrived at a woman gyrating inside a shark cage.

"I'm playing a hunch." The agent held a photo to the bars. "Seen this mug?"

"You some kind of cop?"

"Yes."

She appraised the rumpled wardrobe. His necktie had a pattern of Route 66 signs. "You don't look like a cop."

"Seen him or not?"

She continued dancing to .38 Special. "Prove you're a cop."

"Doesn't it usually work the other way in strip clubs?" He reached inside his coat pocket.

". . . *Wild-eyed southern boys! Wild-eyed boys!* . . ."

A badge went through the bars.

She studied it, then resumed dancing, eyes turned defiantly in another direction that sent an economic telegram.

Mahoney passed an Andrew Jackson through the bars.

She stuck it in her garter. "Yeah, I saw him. Just this afternoon. No way you could miss that guy."

"How so?"

"He took like a million photos. And we had to chase him off the aquarium."

"Fink to his skip?"

"What?"

"Did he give any indication where he might be going?"

She grabbed the bars on the opposite side of the cage, bent over and wiggled her ass. Mahoney stuck another twenty in the crack. She turned back around. "Just that they were heading down the coast doing research."

"They?"

"Traveling with a dancer friend of mine and some drunken idiot. That's all I know."

Mahoney began walking away. "Thanks Blondie."

"I'm a brunette."

Coleman had a laptop on his knees. Serge read a newspaper. They were driving.

"This is a pretty cool travel site you made."

"Nothing but the best." The Javelin blew south on U.S. 1. Serge checked his watch. Four A.M. "I love driving in the middle of the night! No traffic, the rhythm of the dotted fluorescent centerline, occasional diner with a guy alone in a corner booth, all the traffic lights set to flashing yellow, my heart charged with spiritual ecstasy from the approaching dawn! But the best part is the silence, especially with Story asleep in the backseat—a rare chance to take a break from the hectic modern world and relax alone with your thoughts . . . hmmm, hmmhmm, hmmm . . . now my thoughts are too fucking loud. We need some noise in this car." He reached for the radio.

". . . *Still time to save fifty! Sixty! Seventy percent at Mattress Warehouse! . . . Save a horse, ride a cowboy! . . . All weekend long at the monster truck rally! . . .*"

Serge turned a page in the metro section.

"How can you read a newspaper in the dark?"

"Just a sentence at a time as each streetlight passes. But that only makes it better: Gives every story cliff-hangers, like this one . . ." He folded the paper over. A streetlight approached. ". . . About an eccentric dude who liked to drive around with pet snakes hanging over his shoulders . . ."

The light faded.

"What happened?"

"I can hardly wait to find out!"

Another streetlight.

"Ooooo, six-car pileup in Naples."

Coleman returned to the laptop. "So we're just going to keep driving around working on your travel stuff?"

"I'm also implementing a secret plan."

"What plan?"

"It's a secret."

"Can't you tell me?"

"No. You drink too much and blab in bars."

"Sorry."

"Don't be. I've worked that into the plan."

"So I can keep doing it?"

"Absolutely."

"Had me worried for a second."

Serge reached in his pocket and pulled out a clear plastic tube that coin collectors use to store dimes.

"Isn't that one of the things you filled with dirt at famous places?"

"Correct."

Coleman looked closer. "Doesn't look like dirt."

"My toenail clippings."

"What are you collecting those for?"

"Number twenty-three on my to-do list. I've been getting strange sensations from the universe, like, who knows how much longer I've got on this rock?"

"You're not that old."

"Pushing the edge of caveman life expectancy. Of course they didn't have health insurance, but they also didn't have my lifestyle, except the one at Kubrick's monolith who figured out the club. Here . . ." Serge passed the tube to Coleman. "I want you to have this."

"What for?"

"To bury at my funeral. I'm hedging bets with that tube in case the end leaves no recognizable remains. I want people to have a place to visit and picnic."

"Serge, please stop talking like this."

"I have no regrets. Life's been good." He slapped Coleman on the knee and gestured at the surrounding landscape in general. "Someday all this will be yours."

"Cool." Coleman hit the return key on the laptop. "Hey, Serge, your mailbox is completely full."

"It's all Mahoney."

"Aren't you at least going to read what he has to say?"

Serge shook his head. "My life is now completely dedicated to positive thoughts. Rainbows, unicorns, singing flowers, cheerful elves who grant wishes frowned on elsewhere. If I open even one of Mahoney's e-mails, it could drop a turd on an elf."

"*. . . This is NPR. The life of a chimney sweep in nineteenth-century Liverpool might have seemed unglamorous . . . Rocky Mountain Way, couldn't get much higher! . . . Tom Bodette here . . .*"

"Serge, you accidentally set the radio on scan again."

"That's deliberate. I have to stay abreast of culture, and a few seconds on each station is all I need. It's also all I can stand before I lose interest. Plus, scan mode gives you the added bonus of picking up pirate radio stations, like Da Streetz, whose signal was so strong it interfered with air traffic at Miami International. And if you're really lucky, you might even pick up a numbers station."

"Never heard of that."

"Most people haven't, but they're all over the place in Florida, jumping around the dial, popping up at random times, only broadcasting a few minutes a day from a safe house with an illegally powerful shortwave."

"What do they broadcast?"

"Numbers."

"That's it?"

"Coleman, it's all code, most frequently used by the Castro regime communicating with agents stationed in Florida to keep tabs on exile dissidents. They found one guy transmitting from a grimy apartment on South Dale Mabry in Tampa. But they're also used by coke smugglers and other nefarious enterprises."

"Who runs the stations?"

"That's the best part!" said Serge. "Almost always some chick with a super-sultry voice—probably to keep the spies' attention. I've always wanted to hear a numbers station! That would be the best!"

"You mean you haven't?"

"There's always hope," said Serge. "And that's why I need scan mode. In the meantime, I must find contentment peppering myself with fractured Top Forty and advertising persuasion. I'd prefer the scan mode had shorter bursts, but the intervals are set at the factory."

"I've seen you listen to music. Ten seconds a song max."

"Because I love music so much and life is so short! That's why the iPod is the invention of the century. I've tapped mine into the car radio with this special RF transmitting cradle. Let's listen to the Stones!"

The opening hook of "Satisfaction" filled the car.

"I always listen to the Stones," said Serge, spinning the click wheel. "What else is in here? . . . Springsteen! . . . New Jersey's too depressing . . . Steely Dan! They rule! . . . I still don't know what these fucking lyrics mean . . . Floyd! I love the Floyd! . . . But I don't do drugs. . . . Creedence! . . . Bayou, bayou, swamp, bayou, I get it . . . What haven't I heard in a while? . . . The Stones! . . ."

Their Javelin continued down the dark, pensive highway, through Edgewater, along the Canaveral National Seashore and into Mims, before the road zigged out to the rim of the mainland at Titusville. Serge unplugged the iPod, restoring standard radio broadcast. NASA's mammoth Vehicle Assembly Building appeared in the distance, across the Indian River, and farther back on one of the pads, a tiny space shuttle glowing in a ring of spotlights.

"*. . . No money down! No reasonable offer will be refused! . . . Like a Bridge over Troubled Water . . . And now, page two . . .*"

Coleman tapped through the website's mailbox. "You're right. All the messages are from Mahoney."

"That guy's got obsession issues."

A cell phone rang.

Coleman looked around. "That doesn't sound like yours."

"Story's purse," said Serge. "Get it for me."

Coleman turned and reached in the backseat. He handed the phone to Serge, who flipped it open.

"Serge's Florida Experience. How may I assist with your offbeat travel needs?...Story's asleep...Of course I remember you: that chick in the shark cage doing the Pythagorean Twist...Some cop was asking about us?...Wearing a rumpled fedora? Yeah, I have a good guess... No, you did the right thing...How are your classes coming?..."

"...*Along with the Hooters girls, this Saturday under three big tents!...Take home a pound of Tennessee Pride...Buenos...*"

"...Keep studying." Serge closed the phone.

Coleman tapped some more. "What was that?"

"Mahoney's hot on our tail. He was showing my picture around the Shark Lounge."

"Maybe he's just following the stuff you've been putting up on your website."

"Not this time," said Serge. "Haven't posted the Shark yet, which is what really worries me."

"Why?"

"He's the only person who comes anywhere near my passion for the state, and his instincts are getting sharper. There's a good chance he could even show up ahead of us at our next stop. He'll never rest until he catches me."

They pushed on into the world of 5 A.M., now joined by a skeleton traffic of delivery trucks with fresh seafood, baked goods and celebrity magazines. Serge passed an off-brand convenience store, where a man yanked bundles of newspapers out the back of a panel van.

Coleman had a joint in his lips as he continued toying with the laptop. An ash fell onto the keyboard.

"I saw that."

"Sorry."

"Just watch your beer. It's the natural enemy of the laptop."

The Javelin rolled on. Bonaventure, Eau Gallie, Melbourne—sky slipping from black to dark blue, flashing traffic lights returning to standard green-yellow-red rotation—Malabar, Sebastian, Wabasso. Coleman tapped more keys and read the glowing screen.

"Hey, Serge, check this out: I don't think Mahoney wants to catch you."

"Of course he does."

"I just opened his latest message."

"Didn't I say not to open his e-mail? Now you've done it! The hex is on. And you don't trifle with a hex. It's worse than a pox. Luckily I'm protected by my magic cloaking tropical shirt."

"You mean like Harry Potter?"

"Coleman, don't be a stooge," said Serge. "That's make-believe book fiction."

"But Serge, the e-mail—"

"Don't read it!"

"He's trying to warn that someone's after you."

"Yeah, him."

"No, it says a snitch told him some hit men have been sent to take you out."

"It's a trick."

"What if it's not?"

". . . In the book of Deuteronomy the Lord smote . . ."

"Turn off the laptop before you further anger the gods."

"If you say so." He closed the lid and popped a beer. "Where are we heading?"

"I'm on the trail of the Highwaymen. The country needs to know."

"Who are the highwaymen?"

"You'll find out soon enough." Serge grabbed a coffee-table book from under his seat and opened it in his lap. "The big problem is that Mahoney digs Florida almost as much as me. If he's heard of the Highwaymen, we could be heading straight into an ambush. But wait, I'm needlessly worrying myself. There's so much other history in the area. I mean, what are the odds Mahoney would pick the Highwaymen?"

Thirty miles farther south, Agent Mahoney sat in a parked Crown Vic, blowing steam off the top of a Styrofoam cup of coffee.

The car was the only one in the lot, two blocks east of U.S. 1 on Avenue D. Across the inlet, predawn activity aboard a few boats at a marina with Spanish barrel tiles. A verdigris statue of two entwined sailfish stood at the corner of the seawall. Mahoney looked toward the water and watched the sun peek over the horizon at Fort Pierce. The agent checked his Green Hornet watch and shifted his eyes to the front doors of a building, still hours from its 10 A.M. opening. The A.E. "Bean" Backus Gallery and Museum.

Mahoney was under strict orders to the contrary, but he had called in a marker and received the latest law enforcement dossier on Serge. It lay open in his lap. There was the clichéd, long-as-your-arm rap sheet, plus copies of countless fan letters Serge had written to top political and cultural leaders. Mahoney glanced at an old letter to the president, which he now knew by heart, then flipped to a more recent correspondence to the administration that had been intercepted while Mahoney was officially off the case. He began reading:

Ex-Vice President Dick Cheney, aka the *real* 43rd president
Washington, D.C. (Your initials!)

Dear Dick,

Go fuck yourself! Ha! Remember that one? And you said it on the floor of Congress no less. When I first heard about it, milk came out my nose—and I wasn't even drinking milk! That's how funny you are!

Yes, you've coined the catchphrase for the millennium. Pithy, introspective. Plus it translates well. Unfortunately all the president can manage is a hayseed "shit" at a summit lunch when he leaves the mike on, chews with his mouth open and makes Tony Blair hover obsequiously over his shoulder like a trained parakeet. Don't get me wrong: George was an effective deterrent for a while, proclaiming America was on "a crusade," like he missed school that day and didn't realize it was the most brainless thing he could have said. Meanwhile, his finger's on the button of the largest arsenal in the history of the world, and he pretends he can't even fucking pronounce it. "Nucular." Genius! (Your idea, right?) Because while George had his moments ("Mission Accomplished" pops to mind), you, on the other hand, understand *real* deterrence. I'll never forget when insurgents were setting off all those car bombs, so you responded by outing one of *our own* CIA agents, and the insurgents went, "Not too shabby, but we've seen better," and you said, "Oh yeah? Check this out, motherfuckers," and then you shot your own friend in the face! And the insurgents went, "God*damn!*" Now that's the Cheney magic I'm talking about! I say crank it all the way up! We're facing an illogical foe, and you of all people appreciate the value of fighting crazy with crazy. So here's my plan: Now that you're out of office, move into a cave and start making underground videos, wearing a ski mask and carrying an RPG launcher. Maybe even fire the thing. (Just remember to yell "duck" this time.)

I've been your biggest fan ever since hearing you at a Tampa campaign rally in 2000. Maybe you remember me: I was the guy in back chanting "Hal-li-bur-ton! Hal-li-bur-ton!" until the Secret Service made me run. (Sorry, didn't realize that was a secret.) The administration's just drawn to a close, and history will judge harshly, but don't think for a second that it applies to you. True Americans in the fly-over states appreciate your brilliance. I'll bet you'll even get a stamp! They've got antique sewing machines and "Lady and the Tramp," so it's only right. The post office could even hold a vote, like fat Elvis or thin Elvis (Cheney classic, or ski mask).

Now *that's* a legacy! Of course, nothing like "Go fuck yourself."

You crack me up!
Serge A. Storms

Mahoney finished the letter and stuck the dossier back in his briefcase. Then he pulled a coffee-table book from under his seat.

The agent took a tentative sip of still-too-hot coffee and opened the book in his lap, refreshing himself on the history of the Highwaymen.

CHAPTER 20

FORT PIERCE

*T*he Javelin cruised down U.S. 1 and reached the city at first light.

"Here we are!" said Serge. "Birthplace of Florida's Highwaymen. The air is electric! I must roll the window down!"

"Sunrise!" said Coleman. "That calls for a beer!"

"You already have one going."

"It's not the sunrise beer." Coleman popped a second Schlitz for his other hand and plowed into the new day with his signature two-fisted zeal to beat back agenda.

"Coleman, I'm trying to teach you a little culture."

"I'm listening. They were some kind of painters, right?"

"Not just any painters. Florida's seminal landscape artists of the fifties and sixties, a loose collection of twenty-six African Americans who used their talent to escape the period's low-pay citrus fields."

Coleman finished the first can. "Why were they called the Highwaymen?"

"Not known as such in their day, but the spot-on name was bestowed in 1994 by art lover Jim Finch. They cranked out pieces at a prodigious rate, selling them door-to-door or roadside out of trunks, hence the name. Fame was elusive, and their efforts were originally dismissed as so-called motel art, referring to the typically cheesy stuff hanging in such rooms."

"Like dogs playing poker?"

"Except the Highwaymen were ahead of the postcard curve in

appreciating the state's natural beauty. You've no doubt seen their work without even realizing it: seaside vistas with coconut palms, royal poinciana and glowing, turquoise waves rolling ashore, moon-lit rivers, graceful herons, stalking egrets, stunning marshes, sunsets in a bold, reddish light that made the sky look like it was on fire."

"I like clowns and superfat ladies on the beach."

"The Highwaymen couldn't afford canvas, so they painted on cheap epson board, which required extraaggressive brushstrokes that defined their genre. It's what strikes you at the Backus Gallery that you can't pick up from a book: distinctive wood grain under the paint. Without texture, what's the point of life? From now on you are only to refer to me as 'Epson Board' Storms, like a southpaw from Pascagoula who pitched for the Dodgers in '38 but was killed midseason in a freak beekeeping mishap, or maybe third-base coach Mush-Head McGee, who delighted fans with uncontrollable facial tics, or the aptly named adult-film star Gooseneck Johnson . . ." Serge stopped and slapped himself on both cheeks. "Sorry, had to reboot. Go back to calling me Serge."

"Serge, what's an Epson board?"

"Who knows? I press a lot of people I meet for answers, but they all say the same thing: 'Please, don't hurt me.'"

"What's that building by the water?"

"The Backus Gallery I just mentioned, dedicated to this white dude who nurtured a robust, artistic hang-out scene at his house, regardless of race: packs of jazz musicians, other painters and unpopular thinkers, always welcome because of Backus's Left Bank leanings. Not the Seine, the Kissimmee."

"We're going to a gallery?"

"No, been there a hundred times." Serge flipped through the coffee-table book in his lap. "Galleries are great, but they're like churches: offsite worship. For the true spiritual experience, you must follow the brightest star to the manger."

"Manger?"

"An old juke joint called Eddie's Place."

AT THAT VERY MOMENT . . .

Two tire wholesalers entered a motel lounge called Mulligans. The rest of the day, the bar served drinks. But just before sunrise, the staff laid out free continental breakfast.

Toasters popped. Coffee poured. Plastic cups went under orange juice spigots. The salesmen slid styrene trays along the bar, loading up on croissants. Nobody touched the giant, see-through bins dispensing Special K and Froot Loops.

A TV was on in the corner. *". . . Authorities have yet to identify the charred remains tied beneath a burning vehicle in the Ocala National Forest. However, officials have traced the source of the blaze to the dashboard and an ordinary disposable lighter . . ."* The picture changed to a fire inspector interviewed on the scene. *". . . Most Floridians understand the danger of leaving children or pets in cars with the windows rolled up, where midday temperatures can reach a hundred and fifty degrees or more. But few give a second thought to cheap, throwaway lighters, which are butane under pressure and can easily explode at those temperatures, spraying flammable liquid all over the interior . . ."* He looked back as firefighters continued hosing down the car's smoldering shell. *". . . Whoever did this knew his physics. Simple but effective . . ."*

The broadcast switched back to the anchorwoman. *"In other news, police were called to the Convention Center earlier today when fighting broke out between rival unity conferences . . ."*

Another tray slid down the bar.

"Steve!" said one of the tire guys. "How'd it go last night?"

"Regular tiger." He placed a jelly doughnut on his tray. "Barely got a wink."

"Details!"

"Well, first she . . ."

A looming shadow fell over Steve like a rolling thunderhead. He turned around. "Oh no."

Five massive bodyguards. "Someone would like a word with you."

"Sure, right after breakfast."

A giant hand grabbed the doughnut and squished it into a tiny ball, jelly squirting between his fingers. "Now."

"Uh, guys, be right back," said Steve, dragged away by large hands under his armpits.

They shoved him into the men's room and up against a wall. One braced the door against accidental interruption.

Someone was washing his hands at the sink. He dried them on a blower without rush, then calmly walked over to Steve.

"Good morning."

"Eel, I was going to call you! I swear!"

"Now I'm here."

"That thirteenth-floor business—could happen to anyone."

"Of course it could."

"Thanks for understanding."

"Only one problem. Ted checked out of the hotel before we could get the stones. He already made the delivery."

"You win some, you lose some is what I always say."

"I want *your* diamonds."

"Now wait a minute," said Steve. "That wasn't part of the deal. My shipments go untouched, otherwise it'll attract attention to the information I'm feeding you."

"The diamonds."

"Let me make it up some other way. Anything but that. It'll look way too suspicious if I report a theft."

The Eel placed a chummy arm around Steve's shoulders. "You know, you're right. We wouldn't want to place our trusted associate in that kind of position."

"Glad you agree."

Wham. A jackhammer punch to the stomach. Steve doubled over.

The Eel bent down for eye contact. "You stupid motherfucker! How difficult is counting floors?" He twisted the hand-drying vent upward, then mashed the large chrome button with his fist and pressed Steve's right cheek over the opening.

"Ahhhhh! It burns! It burns! . . ."

The Eel kept Steve's face jammed against the machine and turned to his goons. "Our friend is worried about appearing suspicious."

The gang closed in with a swarm of fists. Thirty seconds later, they stepped back revealing a bloody, crying coin dealer crumpled on the ceramic floor. One of the guards snatched Steve's torn coat and felt along the silk lining. "Here they are, sewn inside." He tossed a tiny sack to the Eel, who gave Steve a final kick in the ribs. "Now you look very convincing."

Serge turned right onto Avenue D and cruised west through Fort Pierce.

"Coleman, look here . . ." He tapped a spot in his oversized pictorial book. "This magnificent painting was created by one of the Highwaymen's two founders, Harold Newton, whose brother Sam now tends his own gallery in Cocoa's thriving historic district . . ."

Coleman saw a pastel green juke joint surrounded by palm trees. A handful of people milled in the unpaved road. One leaned against a red coupe. Long shadows from telephone poles said it was late afternoon. The sky moody.

"Looks nice."

"It's Eddie's Place, the yin-yang of the Highwaymen's saga: subject of one of their most beautiful paintings, yet also site of the saddest day in their history. The movement's other founder, Alfred Hair, was the only Highwayman to study formally under A.E. Backus."

"That art gallery dude?"

"As the story goes, a stray bullet fatally felled Hair in Eddie's Place on August 9, 1970. Until now, all I've had to go on was this painting, driving up and down Avenue D over the years looking for Eddie's, but much has changed. The road's paved, fresh paint, many upgrades. Plus there's always the constant threat that the building had simply been demolished or burned down."

"What changed?"

"The Internet." Serge slowed and scanned the south side of the road. "Found some informative articles. Like the Pastime in Jacksonville, Eddie's Place lives on under a new name, now the Reno Motel."

Coleman completed his second sunrise beverage as they crossed Eleventh Street. A hard slap from the driver sent the can flying. "There she is! There she is!"

"Where?" asked Coleman.

"Up there." Serge pulled over and parked on the opposite side of the street. He ran to the trunk. "Coleman, give me a hand."

Coleman fell out of the car like a medicine ball and rolled to the curb. He got up, rubbing skinned palms. Serge handed him equipment.

"Aren't you going to take a bunch of pictures like you usually do?"

"Something more relevant first." Serge handed him a large rectangle.

"What's this?"

"Canvas." Serge grabbed a second one.

"You're going to paint?"

"You, too."

"But I've never painted before."

"Neither have I. But what if I'm a natural who can paint like a photograph and don't know it because I've never tried?"

Coleman grabbed a brush. "I thought you did try painting about ten years ago in Tampa. Remember? You set up an easel on the bay, saying the overwhelming beauty was suffocating, then went berserk with three brushes in each hand."

"That was different. I was working in acrylics."

"You ended up covered head to toe in paint with a shredded canvas hanging around your neck."

"Acrylics are a much more difficult medium."

Coleman uncapped a squeeze bottle. "How do I start?"

"First, get rid of the brush. Everyone uses them. The key to making a living as an artist is volume. I learned that from Hair. See how I'm slathering the entire painting at once—background to final detail—with nothing but my bare hands."

"Just looks like a big mess."

"It's called a primitive. Or post-modern. Depending on the market."

"I think it needs something more."

"Maybe you're right." Serge scratched the canvas with a fingernail. "I'll add a stick man for scale. Now you try."

Coleman began swirling his hands on the other canvas. "What about Story?"

"Should stay asleep in the backseat for at least another half hour, long enough for us to whip off two or three masterpieces before she awakens and becomes an art critic."

"Look." Coleman pointed with a blue hand. "A bunch of people are staring at us."

"I knew it! We're already attracting the attention of the art crowd. They detect our homage to the Highwaymen."

"An art crowd in front of a barbecue shack?"

"Another thing I love about Avenue D: all barbecue all the time!" Serge inhaled deeply. "I love the smell of oil paint and babybacks in the morning."

"Some of them are coming over."

"Perfect." Serge lifted his canvas off the hood of the Javelin. "Just in time for our first sale."

An older man with white hair approached on the sidewalk. "You guys painters?"

"Painting consumes my entire existence!" said Serge. "Ever since I discovered the Highwaymen."

"Oh yeah," said the old man. "I met Newton. Gibson, too. Both great guys. How do you know about them?"

"I studied under the Highwaymen."

The old man's brow furrowed. "*You* studied under the Highwaymen."

"Yes, except it was years later and they didn't know about it. I'm always making up stuff like that. It's my life's motto: If you're not willing to invent cool-sounding bullshit about yourself, don't expect others to. Are you with me? Do we have a communication?"

Others from the barbecue hut joined the old man, forming a semicircle around the Javelin. "What's going on?"

"Not sure," said the old man. "These guys *say* they're some kind of painters."

Serge winked at Coleman, then faced the onlookers. "See you all have a keen eye for art." He turned his canvas toward them. "I call it *Eddie's Place, Redux*. Who wants to make the first bid?"

"But it's just a blob."

Serge reached his arm around and tapped the middle of the canvas. "There's a stick man."

The old man pointed at Coleman's canvas. "What's that Y with a black triangle in the fork?"

"A twat."

One mile away, Agent Mahoney was out of coffee. He looked at the front entrance. The museum's ten o'clock opening had come and gone. How could his hunch about Serge have been wrong? He looked back down, turning pages of the book in his lap. Spanish moss, cypress swamp, hibiscus, rotted fishing pier, another hibiscus, a pastel green building. Mahoney slapped the book. Eddie's Place! Of course!

Mahoney tossed a chewed toothpick out the window, and a Crown Vic with blackwall tires squealed out of the parking lot.

The agent raced a dozen blocks, past Miracle Ribs, Soul Fighters for Jesus, a youth outreach center with murals, the Fried Rice Hut, a combination bail bond-private eye office, and the Buffalo Soldier Caribbean Restaurant. It skidded to a stop in front of the Reno Motel. A stunned crowd stared at the street, which appeared to have been the site where two armies had waged a fierce paintball battle.

Agent Mahoney jumped out, flashing a badge and a photo. "Anyone seen this mug?"

"That crazy son of a gun?" said the old man. "He was just here. None of us will ever forget *him*."

"How so?"

"We were laughing at his butt-ugly painting when he said it was just his warm-up exercise and that he was now going to paint the most fantastic piece of art anyone had ever seen. Then he got out a new canvas and went completely apeshit! We thought he was having a seizure."

Mahoney pointed at the canvas in the old man's hands. "Don't tell me you actually bought a painting from him."

"No, the other guy." He turned his canvas around. "Excellent primitive erotica."

"See which way they went?"

The old man pointed south. "Look for the guy driving with a canvas around his neck."

CHAPTER 21

www.sergeastorms.com

$\mathcal{S}$erge's Blog. Star date 937.473.

Today's topic is traveling with Coleman. Just substitute that one friend we all have whose level of partying can create its own weather system. But Coleman and I have an understanding. I do my travel thing, and he does his. I'm on a fact-finding mission; he's on the Booza-palooza Tour. But he never nags, no matter how many photos I take of historic markers. The perfect traveling companion. Not like Story, who's put me on a two-picture limit, which I grudgingly accept because travel is the art of compromise. But then she demands that Coleman stop throwing up out the passenger window. Now she's messing with a decade of tradition. Against that benchmark, Coleman's a treat. Plus he's value conscious. Once we had to fly somewhere and he checked half a pizza through in his luggage. The downside is motel room damage, which could quickly add up to thousands on the guy's credit card we're using.

Today's Tip #1: Fixing Coleman's damage. Last week I left him unsupervised, and when I returned, the mini bar was empty and he'd locked himself in the bathroom, screaming about pygmies. By the time I jimmied the door open, he was unconscious in the tub with the snapped-off towel rod across his chest. Solution: Wet squares of toilet paper and wrap them around the anchor-bolts of the ripped-out rod holder. Then, gently push the complete assembly back into the wall. And if you don't breathe hard, it should stay put until after checkout, when the maid knocks it loose hanging new towels, and hopefully she's undocumented and pushes it back in herself.

Tip #2: Refilling the mini bar. The next morning I tell Coleman he racked up a three-hundred-dollar mini-bar tab. He says there must be some mistake. I say, it's simple economics. Mortgage companies build into their rates for potential inflation. Mini bars build in for a cataclysmic meteor strike. So we make a supply run. Liquor miniatures are a snap, but mixers are the real killer. Hotels know we're refilling the mini bars, so they deliberately use short, fat eight-ounce soda bottles that you can't get anywhere except other hotels. Solution: Fish empties out of the trash and refill with 99-cent generic two-liter soda bottles. Screw the caps on tight and hide in the back row, and the mini-bar guy won't notice the seals are broken because the fridge's handle just came off in his hand.

Tip #3: What ever happened to the Shell No-Pest Strip? Not a tip, just been thinking about it a lot lately. I'd kill to have sat in on the corporate meeting that gave birth to that feel-good product. "What would be an irresistible status symbol to hang over the dining room table?" "I know: a box full of dead flies on a sticky piece of cardboard."

News from Serge World!

When my collected travel knowledge is finally published as a bestselling book, I've decided to simultaneously release a special children's edition. It's almost completely finished. I've only got the first page, but that's the hardest part. It's called *Shrimp Boat Surprise*. Coleman asked what the title means, and I said life is like traveling on one big, happy shrimp boat. He asked what the surprise was, and I said you grow up and learn that life bones you up the ass ten ways to Tuesday. He started reading what I'd written and asked if a children's book should have the word *motherfucker* eight times on the first page. I said, absolutely. They're little kids after all. If you want a lesson to stick, you have to hammer it home through repetition.

To the Mailbag!

Let's see what's here . . . "Mahoney, Mahoney, Mahoney, Cialis soft-tabs, Mahoney, Mahoney, Tiny size is killing your woman's interest, Mahoney, Mahoney, Cialis, Irish Lottery, Mahoney . . . I know I shouldn't open this, but the curiosity is killing me . . .

The Javelin continued south along the coast. Serge took A1A out of Fort Pierce, and roadsides quickly thinned. Gas stations, mom-and-pop diners, retro sign of a smiling alligator bowling. The Javelin swung inland and picked up U.S. 1 below Port Salerno.

Serge's window was down, an ocean breeze mussing his hair. "What a magnificent day to be alive in this state! God has once again fulfilled my definition of happiness: Florida, a full tank of gas and no appointments."

Coleman held up a beer and a joint. "My definition, too."

"Crank the radio! Scan mode!"

"Aye-aye!"

". . . *Life is a highway! I'm going to ride it . . . Fifty-two, forty-one, seven, thirteen . . .*"

"Oh my God!" Serge dove for the dash and hit a button, knocking the radio out of scan.

"What is it?" asked Coleman.

"A numbers station! I finally found one!"

". . . *Ninety-nine, eighty-six . . .*"

"Serge, that babe really sounds hot!"

"Told you." Serge wrote as fast as he could in a notebook.

"What are you doing?"

"Trying to crack the code."

The numbers broadcast soon ended and Serge stowed his notebook. They entered the Hobe Sound area. Blowing rocks and turtle egg-laying country. Sparse development ceased altogether, Serge copping a natural buzz on white sand dunes running down both sides of the highway.

An intersection approached in the distance.

Serge looked at Coleman. "Meet Mahoney or not?"

"You're actually thinking of going through with that?"

Serge shrugged. "He's pretty insistent with all those e-mails."

"But you said you didn't believe that someone was out to whack you."

"I don't. But Mahoney's up to something. I'm dying to find out."

In the backseat, Story looked up from a French lit textbook. "Who's Mahoney?"

"My nemesis."

She rolled her eyes again and looked back down. *Madame Bovary, c'est moi.*

"But Serge," said Coleman. "What if it's a trick?"

"That's the thing about Mahoney. He's one of the few people left like me who still lives by a code. If he says it isn't a trick, you can bet the farm on it." Serge handed something across the seat to Coleman.

"What do I need your gun for?"

"In case it's a trick. You got my back."

"But Serge, I'm royally baked. Remember last time you gave me the gun?"

"Yeah, it accidentally went off eight times."

"Then I dropped it and another bullet went through the end of my shoe. Lost a toenail."

"Grew back, didn't it?"

"I liked the first one better."

"I'll unload it, all right? Just the threat should be enough . . . Here comes the intersection. A1A or U.S. 1. Which direction?"

"Sounds like an appointment."

"Shit, you're right." Serge got over in the far lane and began hanging a left. Midintersection, he suddenly cut the wheel, weaving expertly through oncoming, honking traffic.

Coleman puffed his joint and looked back at the spun-out cars. "What changed your mind?"

"Mahoney picked the perfect place. Been forever since I visited Harry and the Natives."

"Who?"

"Let the magic begin."

Minutes later, the Javelin parked in front of a rustic greasy spoon splashed in lively Jamaican colors. A Crown Vic was already there.

Serge looked at the rearview. "Story, for your own good I suggest you stay in the car. Don't want you up on charges of accessory before, during and after the fact."

She closed the textbook and grabbed her purse. "No way I'm sitting in some hot parking lot while you play fort."

"Story—"

"I'm hungry!"

"Okay, but don't take this personally. Could you sit at another table and pretend like you don't know us?"

"My pleasure."

"Then here's the plan. Coleman and I go in first. Story: Lie on the backseat and wait five minutes until I can distract Mahoney. You silently exit the car so he won't have the slightest inkling we all came together."

She got out and slammed the door hard.

"Or that," said Serge.

He and Coleman approached the eatery's front door.

Coleman stopped and looked through the windows. "Serge, I think I took too many pills."

"And that's different how?"

"Everything's weird. Look at all that crazy stuff inside. Cans of Spam in the cigarette rack."

"It's not pills. It's Harry and the Natives! A half-century of Florida I-don't-give-a-shit and ticky-tack covering the walls. 'Waterfront dining, when it rains.' Everybody comes to Harry and the Natives!"

"It's in the middle of nowhere."

"Now it is. But back when they first opened in 1941—Pearl Harbor Day for those playing along at home—this was the perfect, high-traffic commercial spot. Those dunes we passed earlier formed an ideal ridge for the federal highway, and Harry's was a convenient pull-over for the tin-can tourists. Then they built the Turnpike and I-95, spelling doom for roadside funk. But not Harry's! Loyal customers wouldn't hear of it, and kept coming in droves to ensure its survival." Serge opened the door and instantly spotted the rumpled fedora. Mahoney had his usual aces-and-eights seat, back corner facing the entrance. "Coleman, stand by the bar and look like you're armed." He took a deep breath. "Here goes nothing . . ."

Mahoney saw him coming. He sat back and wiggled a wooden matchstick in his teeth.

Serge grabbed the opposite chair and took a seat at the table with yellowed ephemera lacquered into the gnarled wooden surface. Both sat rigid and motionless, squaring off with squinty eyes.

Mahoney theatrically removed the matchstick like Clint Eastwood. "Originally the Cypress Cabins and restaurant."

"Fashioned from tidewater pecky cypress," said Serge. "Chopped at Kitchen Creek."

Mahoney leaned in challengingly. "Rockin' juke joint for the jungle warfare soldiers training at Jonathan Dickinson."

Serge matched the lean. "Michigan MacArthurs bought the spread in 1952."

Mahoney angled closer. "Native son Harry born here."

Serge, nose to nose. "Reopened under present name, 1989."

Mahoney settled back into his chair with a wry smile. "Wondering if you still had it."

"It was you I was worried about." Serge opened his menu. "What looks good today?"

"Smoked fish dip, venison burger."

"Fried oyster po' boy has my name on it." Serge slid the menu toward the center of the table. "What's with all the crazy e-mails? Have you finally gone 'round the bend?"

"Mattress time. Uptown boys rolled a mystery joker. Snooping for a dime drop from the Georgia line to St. Lucie . . ."

"What's it to you if someone takes me out? Isn't that what you want?"

"What I want is to take you down myself. Can't do that if some button man gets to the party first. But you already knew that or you'd never have darkened this door."

"We live by the same code, you and me. If you said it wasn't a trick, I take you at your word."

Mahoney nodded toward Coleman.

"What's with the second banana?"

"In case it was a trick," said Serge. "So don't try anything. Coleman's a crack shot, and his ability to remain absolutely focused on the target . . ." Serge turned around and pointed. ". . . Crap . . ." Coleman was over at the gift counter, slipping his head through a Harry's bar T-shirt: "Give me what the guy on the floor is having."

Serge turned back to Mahoney. "You're wasting your time. There is no assassin. You've been trying to get inside my head so long you've gone battier than me."

"Gut's never been stronger," said Mahoney. "Remember the psychology article I wrote for that law enforcement magazine about profiling you?"

"My feelings are still hurt."

"Ultra-intense mugs burn out twice as fast."

"What are you saying?"

"Your mental state."

"I know. Isn't it great?"

"Short money on your mind slipping. Might even fragment soon, different personalities, blackouts, memory loss, losing your edge, not picking up approaching threats like you would have in earlier times because your noodle's tuned between channels."

"Not a chance."

"Give me the lowdown: Anything out of the routine lately?"

"*Everything*," said Serge. "That's how I like my life, kicking Routine's ass around the block."

"I mean hook up with any new accomplices?"

"No one comes to mind."

"Think hard. Recently meet anyone by so-called chance? Somebody you might even be traveling with?"

"Nope." Serge's eye glanced involuntarily toward Story's table.

Part Two

THREE
WEEKS EARLIER

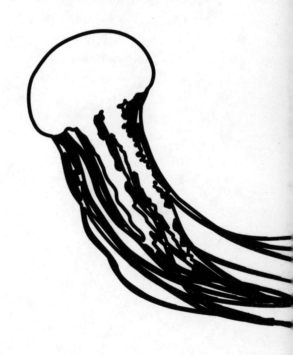

erge's Blog. Star date 574.385.

Holy Cow! How could I have forgotten? A whole bunch of stuff happened before this. It all started three weeks ago. I *knew* I had a feeling something wasn't kosher—because it wasn't! Turns out Mahoney's right about my memory. Here I am bopping along, seeing this chain of events a certain way. But then I just recalled all this other earlier jazz that explains everything! Sorry about that. My mind tends to jump around a bit. Usually it's from subject to subject. But sometimes it hops around in time. And it can be especially challenging if the time dislocation is fractured, like when part of me ended up in the Bronze Age, and another part in a rerun of *She's the Sheriff*. And I'm congratulating these bearded dudes on their spears and helmets, but they just point and say, "Who's that?" And I say, "She's the sheriff." And time's definitely tricky if you get pulled over by a cop who never studied Einstein. This was years ago, before they wanted to question me for all those, well, you know. Anyway, the officer is writing me a ticket, saying I ran a red light *and* was speeding. I said, Exactly! That's why it's only fair you let me off with a warning. I explained that matter and energy bend the universe, and the closer an object gets to the speed of light, the more time slows down. So by speeding, I was actually trying to *obey* the law, accelerating in order to stretch out the yellow light. Of course, for it to work, you need to be traveling 186,000 miles a second, and I was driving an old car. Wouldn't listen. Cost me $200. I digress again. See what I mean? But I think I've got this memory glitch ironed out: Everything that's happened up to now on this trip—let's call it Part One. And all the crazy stuff I just remembered that went on three weeks before, we'll call Part Two, which is a superlong flashback that takes place entirely before Part One. Then, when we're back up to speed, we'll return to the present in Part Three. Got it? *Comprende?* . . . Good, because that cop wouldn't be able to. I'm still pissed. But no sense dwelling on the past. Time's a-wastin'. Tick-tock, tick-tock . . .

CHAPTER 22

AMELIA ISLAND

A two-tone Javelin sat in an empty motel parking lot at the northeastern corner of the state. Only one occupant.

Coleman reached over from the passenger side and hit the horn.

A second-floor door opened. Serge stepped onto the balcony buttoning his tropical shirt. A woman appeared from the room. Latin bombshell, jet-black hair, beauty mark, all hips. She grabbed Serge roughly by the collar and yanked him back for a final, deep kiss.

Serge trotted down the stairs with a zippered pouch and hopped in the driver's seat. They cruised south across the island.

"Finally!" said Coleman.

"I'm here now." Serge blew through a yellow light. "What's the problem?"

"I've been bored for an hour while you were having all the fun."

"What? Back there?" Serge wiped lipstick off his mouth. "That wasn't fun. That was business."

"What kind of business?"

"Can't tell you."

"Why not?"

"Part of my secret plan."

"What's in the zippered pouch?"

"Can't tell you."

"I'm out of beer."

Serge pulled into a convenience store. "Here's your pharmacy."

Back at the just-departed motel room, a Latin bombshell opened a closet door and sat in front of a small table. She pulled the cover off a vintage 1941 Zenith Trans-Oceanic. Switches flipped. Tubes glowed inside the shortwave. The woman opened a notebook, pulled a heavy steel microphone toward that pair of full, fiery lips, and began in a melting voice: *"Ninety-seven, twelve, one-thirty-two, sixty-eight . . ."*

A couple miles up the road, Coleman ran out of the convenience store with a cardboard suitcase. "Beer, sweet beer!"

They pulled out again, two small flags flapping atop the front fenders, like it was the governor's motorcade, except . . .

"Serge," said Coleman. "I don't recognize either of those flags."

"Because I had to draw them myself. I *love* Amelia Island! Two centuries ago this was an international Dodge City." Serge fit an odd-looking baseball cap on his head and pointed at the left side of the hood. "That green cross was the flag of the creatively named free republic of the Green Cross. Can you believe there once was an independent nation right here on this island?"

Coleman ripped open the twelve-pack. "That's almost interesting."

"One of the most bizarre underdog stories in state history," said Serge. "This crazy Scottish soldier of fortune named MacGregor convinced fifty-five guys to attack Spain. It was the kind of thing frat boys concoct when only suds are left coming out of the kegs. Even stranger, it worked."

"How'd they do it?"

"MacGregor's plan was to kick the Spanish out of Florida, and he started by attacking Fort San Carlos, which was at the end of this street we're now passing. They didn't even have a strategy, just an unheard-of direct charge at the fort without cover, which never would have worked except this gang-who-couldn't-shoot-straight was getting eaten alive by insects. So they broke sprigs off local plants known to repel bugs and stuck them in their hats. The guys on the fort walls saw them advancing straight through the marsh and thought: Nobody's this stupid. Something must be up. Then they mistook the hat sprigs for plumes that only officers wore, multiplied it out by the corresponding divisions of enlisted men, and believed they were being attacked by a force of thousands. Surrendered without a fight."

Coleman pointed up at Serge's head. "Is that why you taped all those twigs to your baseball cap?"

"My adversaries will think they're facing overwhelming numbers."

Coleman crumpled an empty beer can. "Some story."

"Gets even weirder. Green Cross nation only lasted two months, until the Spanish stopped laughing and kicked them out. But then . . ." Serge pointed at the flag on the other side of the hood. ". . . Another bunch of loons led by an ex-Pennsylvania congressman and a French pirate overtook the island and briefly claimed it for Mexico. Amelia Island was a refuge where every crackpot with some lunatic notion was allowed to express himself with tiny armies, like a military version of talk radio."

They continued south. Two hours passed. They reached a shore. A line of cars was backed up ten deep. Eventually, vehicles began moving at a crawl. Then stopped again.

Gulls and herons swooped over the Javelin's roof in a brisk outgoing breeze. They began crossing the St. Johns River. The car's engine was off.

"I've never taken a ferry before," said Coleman.

"One of America's most excellent but rapidly disappearing road-trip pleasures." Serge turned the steering wheel left, then right. "I could have taken a faster route, but we'd miss the ecstasy."

Coleman was on a train schedule. He cracked his 10:15 beer. "So why aren't you in a better mood?"

"Because that jerk wouldn't let me drive the barge. Usually when I ask for something fifty times, they cave."

"Why are you turning the steering wheel if the car's stopped?"

"Pretending to drive the ferry." Serge sneered out the windshield at the barge tender. "And he thought he was dealing with a child."

Coleman sipped his grog and glanced out the window. "Sure is pretty. Never been this far north in Florida before."

"Few people have because we're way off all the major highways."

"What was that place where I regained consciousness this morning?"

"Fort Clinch State Park, just across St. Marys in Georgia." Serge cut the wheel left with the current. "The leg of A1A we just traveled is one of Florida's best-kept secrets, an uncrowded driving-tour orgy, starting with the Palace Saloon on Amelia Island, oldest bar in the state, established 1878, where I got excellent photos of the mural, tin ceiling and mahogany bar where the Rockefellers used to roll . . ."

"And you wouldn't even let me get a drink. You just stuck your camera in the door for two minutes."

"One and a half. Because time management is crucial." Serge turned the wheel right. "Then continuing south along the magnificent shoreline bluffs of the Talbot islands and salt-marsh flats at Fort George . . ."

". . . Where you spent an hour chasing butterflies and smelling plants."

"That's why time management is so important. You never know what emergency might arise." The wheel rotated left again. "It's essential to showcase crack motion-efficiency skills if I expect to land my new job."

"What does a travel guide do?"

"Provide inside tips for visitors not familiar with the area, like leaving extra space at dark intersections so you don't get boxed in by car-jackers and dismembered behind a time-share booth."

"Who doesn't know that?"

"Everyone who uses traditional travel websites," said Serge. "Those big Internet companies worry that providing grids of tourist homicides will only make people stay home, which is insane because the first rule of business is to keep your customers alive."

"Fuckin'-A."

"And they need my expertise now more than ever. Something's gone horribly wrong in paradise. There used to be an agreement among criminals that we left the most vulnerable alone."

"I think I signed that."

"It's useless paper now. Last Christmas they were jumping pregnant moms for gifts in mall parking lots, and one gang went on a rampage slashing inflatable snowmen in Clearwater."

"That's just wrong."

"Which is why I'm as good as hired today."

The barge docked on the south side of the river, and the gate came down.

"But it's your eighth Internet Job Fair," said Coleman. "Three fired you, and the rest turned you down, including two who physically threw you out on the sidewalk. How will this time be different?"

"I've learned a lot about structuring my pitch." Serge drove off the ferry. "Never lead with the tourist murder rate."

INTERSTATE 10

Truckers downshifted as they took the cloverleaf off I-75 just north of Lake City. The air had a burnt stink from the month-long forest fire in the Okefenokee Swamp that jumped the state line.

Dawn revealed a thick layer of smoke, which dropped visibility to a quarter-mile and would soon prompt officials to close the highway and tie up traffic back to Tallahassee. But not yet.

The sun continued its rise directly over the lanes for Jacksonville, the haze making it look more like a dim Alaskan morning. A young man behind the wheel of a cobalt-blue Volkswagen Beetle began another in a series of utterly content days. Because he was on the road in Florida. People called him Howard, because it was on his birth certificate.

Howard's love of travel was advertised by the space-maximizing configuration of his car's interior, which resembled a professionally organized closet: interlocking matrix of clear plastic bins and tubs and filing containers from Office Depot filled the entire backseat and cantilevered over the front passenger's; zippered, easy-reach pouches hung everywhere from hooks and Velcro straps. Contents obsessively segregated: toiletries, clothes (clean, dirty, dirtier), car maintenance, all-purpose repair tool, kitchen including complete mini pantry, coffeemaker, micro-microwave and world-class collection of condiment packets from convenience stores squirreled away in see-though fly-fishing tackle boxes. On the passenger seat sat an executive mobile organizer of maps, pamphlets, guidebooks, notepads, pens, receipts and backup sunglasses. Between the seats wedged a first-aid kit, and mounted over the dash was a quick-release fire extinguisher.

But the most important cargo was under the hood of the Beetle's trademark front-end trunk: Howard's product line.

A fast-moving high-pressure system had lifted most of the smoke by the time the Beetle rolled into downtown Cocoa Beach. A cell phone rang. He grabbed it from a hanging pocket.

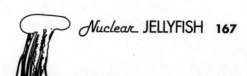 *Nuclear* JELLYFISH **167**

"Good morning, Howard Enterprises . . . Oh, hi Mom . . . I was going to call . . . I'm not just saying that . . . Mom, we talked yesterday . . . I already have a job . . . It *is* a real job . . . Mom, I have to go. I'm in the middle of something . . . Traffic . . . No, the other cars aren't more important than you . . . You asked me if I had a girlfriend yesterday . . . I know you liked Cathy . . . Mom, she broke up with *me* . . . I did try calling . . . a number of times . . . because she said 'never call me again' . . . What do you mean, 'Maybe if I didn't cry so much'? It was a tough time . . . I know she was sweet . . . And beautiful . . . And I'll never find anyone else like her . . . Mom, I've been trying for months to stop thinking about her . . . *You'll* call her? Oh, please!— . . . You already did? . . . I know her answering machine says, 'If this is Howard, I'm dead.' . . . Mom, I really have to hang up . . . I've got a call on the other line . . . No, I seriously doubt that it's Cathy . . . I really have to hang up . . . Right, I'll call . . . And visit . . . I don't know when . . . Love you! Bye!"

The Beetle turned up a commercial driveway and pulled around the side of a convention center. It parked next to a propped-open service entrance that was a nexus of unloading activity.

Howard made the regular rounds of the expos, and nobody knew what to make of it. From the Panhandle to points south, Howard presented his wares with incandescent pride. And left at the end of the day with everything he'd arrived with. His credit cards were maxed. The Beetle needed new oil.

It was a business-model problem that could have been diagnosed over the phone. Howard signed up for expos that had nothing to do with what he was selling, because there were no such markets for his wares. Didn't stop Howard. He'd just find a cheap table at any event that had surplus vendor space. So what if all the customers were there for baseball cards, lapidary supplies or *Star Wars* figures? He was on the road. He was happy.

The Javelin pulled off the highway and into the parking lot of a budget motel.

"Serge, why are we stopping here? I thought you needed to get to your job fair?"

"Need more travel research for my first report." Serge got out of the car. "First rule of job interviews: always bring a work sample." He headed for the lobby.

The whiskered motel manager had little to do since switching over from the bulletproof night check-in window and unlocking the front doors. He sat in the backroom, feet on the desk, reading a hot rod magazine with a centerfold. His free hand rustled through a bag of pork rinds. A sound from the front desk:

Ding! Ding! Ding! Ding! Ding! Ding! Ding! Ding! Ding! Ding! Ding! . . .

He popped a final rind in his mouth and furled the centerfold.

Ding! Ding! Ding! Ding! Ding! Ding! Ding! Ding! Ding! Ding! Ding! . . .

The manager appeared from the backroom, wiping pork-rind dust on a T-shirt that appeared to have been tie-dyed in motor oil. "Can I help you?"

Ding! Ding! Ding! . . . Serge stopped and stilled the bell with his hand. He removed a clipboard from a canvas shoulder bag, clicked a pen and began writing. "Response time, twenty dings."

"What's the clipboard for?"

"Pay no attention to the clipboard or it'll skew the experiment. I need to observe you in your natural habitat. Personal appearance: *The Hills Have Eyes.*"

"Are you from the home office?"

"You wish." Serge pulled a rolled-up coupon book from his back pocket. "I'd like a room."

"Check-in isn't 'til two P.M."

"I know. Wanted to get my reservation request in early enough so there'd be no misunderstanding."

"What kind of misunderstanding?"

"That I arrived too late, and you didn't have any more of the rooms I wanted."

The manager opened a reservation book. "What kind of room would you like?"

"The kind you won't allow me to have with my coupon. Any of those left not to give me?"

"I . . . What's the question?"

 Nuclear JELLYFISH **169**

Serge ripped the coupon from the book and slapped it on the counter. "One of these rooms. How many do you not have left?"

The manager picked up the torn square of recycled paper. "Oh, the coupon. Yeah, we don't have any of those rooms left."

"Bingo," said Serge. "I want one of the rooms you don't have."

"They're all full."

"Your parking lot's nearly empty."

"We have other rooms just like it that you can have for the regular price." The manager turned a wary eye to Coleman, swaying and drinking his breakfast from a paper bag. "Want one of those?"

Ding! Ding! Ding! Ding! Ding! "Look at me," said Serge. "Try to stay on message. How many of the discount rooms do you usually not have?"

"Varies."

"Is it ever a negative integer?"

"What?"

"I'll just put down zero." Serge stuck the clipboard back in his shoulder bag. He pulled out a can of spray paint and rattled the metal ball. "Well, that just about does it."

Coleman reached for the counter. *Ding! Ding! Ding!*

The manager turned. "Can I help you?"

Ding! Ding! Ding! . . .

Serge grabbed Coleman's arm and grinned at the manager. "I'm his caregiver. He just likes to ring bells and play with cat toys."

The pair left the office. The manager returned to the backroom and picked up a magazine.

CHAPTER 23

COCOA BEACH

ables lined the walls of hotel conference room number one. Most were vacant.

Steve completed his setup procedure, straightening a locked glass display case of Liberty dimes. He felt a presence and turned, expecting his first customer of the day.

"Uh-oh."

A hulking, sunburned man with long stringy hair.

"Jesus! What are you doing?" Steve's head whipped side to side. "Nobody can see us together at the shows!"

"We need to talk."

"Not here. In the hall."

Steve rushed out and darted into a nook by the restrooms. "What's so important to risk everything?"

"Nice job last night. Excellent stones."

"That's what you came to tell me?"

"The Eel wants more couriers."

"Like I told you on the phone, I don't know any more."

"So recruit some new ones like you always do."

"We need to cool it." Steve glanced around again. "Every coin guy I've brought in has been hit. It's just a matter of time until the cops figure out it's me."

"You've been very useful. Do you want to become useless?"

"What are you implying?"

The bodyguard smiled with missing teeth.

"Okay, listen, see what I can do. But I'll need some time."

The goon smiled again and slapped his shoulder. "That's all I wanted to hear."

Steve went back inside conference room number one as four people came out of conference room number two. Three of them had Serge by the arms. "But I buried the part about the tourist murder rate . . ."

They threw him to the ground. Coleman got off a bench in the hall and came over. "Did you get the job?"

"Economic philosophy differences." Serge checked his tropical shirt for rips. "I'm a supply-side Keynesian, and they're pricks. Come on."

"Where are we going?"

"I passed another door when we first arrived. Took all my powers to resist going in, but the job search came first."

They entered conference room number one.

Coleman pulled a flask from his back pocket. "What is this place?"

"Coin and stamp show," said Serge. "I love coin and stamp shows!"

They approached the first table. Two dealers in deep conversation:

". . . Great opportunity," said Steve. "Few hundred dollars for practically no work. You're already driving down the coast—just make an extra stop for the delivery."

"I don't know," said the other. "Sounds dangerous."

"Howdy!" said Serge.

They turned. "Can we help you?"

An hour later, Serge was still bent over a table, scanning pages of a tenth album with a magnifying glass. He closed the three-ring binder. "Just remembered I hate Mercury dimes. Too many hard dates to fill my Whitman binder when I was a kid. Let me see the pennies again."

"Sir," said Steve. "Do you plan to buy anything?"

"Tons of stuff! I've got such a giant shopping list in my head from the other binders that I now need to look at them all again and reallocate my budget."

Steve displayed obvious annoyance as he retrieved the first album Serge had looked at.

"Ooooo. The 1909-SVDB. Coleman, that's the Cadillac of Lincoln pennies. The guy who did the engraving snuck his tiny initials onto the back, and when the government found out, they removed them, making the early ones extra rare, especially with the San Francisco mint mark. Wanted it ever since I was a kid!"

Steve pulled out his cash box. "So you'd like to buy it?"

"Hell no!" Serge slammed the album shut. "I stared at that empty hole in my penny book every day after school until it represented all issues of emotional rejection. I despise that coin with every cell in my body." Serge stood and dabbed his eyes. "Sorry, can't buy anything today. Don't need that kind of negative energy in my life. Let's go, Coleman . . ."

They continued around the room, long lines of display tables with initially smiling salesmen. Serge walked briskly, glancing in glass cases as he passed. ". . . Coins that suck . . . More coins that suck . . . Fuck half-dollars . . . Quarters will only break your heart . . ."

They reached the back of the room and a stretch of folding tables that were all oddly empty except for a single exhibitor in the middle with no customers.

"Wait. What's this?" said Serge. "It can't be . . ."

"What is it?"

Serge raced over and fell to his knees. "It's . . . too good to be true. Coleman, am I awake?"

Howard straightened and smiled at his first and only customers of the day. "How ya doin'?"

Serge stood with sparkling eyes. "Excellent! Where'd you get all this great stuff?"

"Mainly estate sales and flea markets."

Serge stepped back to catch his breath. Spread before him was an immense, eclectic feast of Floridiana. "And I thought *I* had a collection . . ." His eyes didn't know where to start. They went from the hundred-year-old 3-D stereoscopics, to vintage sterling spoons with pineapple handles, to faded felt pennants—Gatorland, Cape Kennedy, Sunken Gardens. "Look at all these lapel pins! And license plates! And salt and pepper shakers!" He picked up an ashtray from the Algiers. He set it down carefully, then lunged against the table. "How much for all of it? Wait, get a grip—there's no way I can

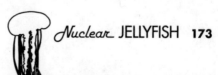

afford—Wow!" He grabbed a matchbook from the Collonades. "You must make a fortune selling these things."

"Actually, I'm barely getting by."

"You're kidding!" Serge stopped and appraised the young man for the first time. Not very tall, way too thin, the wormy type who was probably picked on relentlessly as a child and undermined as an adult. Howard seemed okay with the arrangement.

"I don't understand," said Serge. "You've got the best stuff I've ever seen. How can you not be raking it in?"

"Doesn't seem to be much of a market. But at least I get to do what I like—"

"Oh my God! Coleman, check it out!"

"What is it?"

Serge looked up with begging eyes. "Can I touch?"

"Be my guest."

He gingerly picked up a slender protective sleeve. "Coleman, this is one of the highly sought-after Lansdorf alligator-border postcards, circa 1910. And it's from Tampa! Henry Plant's old railroad hotel and staging ground for the Spanish-American War."

"Really know your Florida souvenirs," said Howard.

"You don't have any idea." Serge opened his wallet. "Damn. I'll need to find some cash. Actually, I need to earn some."

"Take it."

"What?"

"You're the first person I've met who loves this stuff like me," said Howard. "If it means that much, then you should definitely have it."

Serge went mute.

"What is it?" asked Howard. "Are you okay?"

Serge just stood with an open-mouth expression as if Howard had just removed a thorn from his paw.

The whiskered manager of a budget motel tore open a bag of red-hot pub fries with a picture of Andy Capp on the front. Morning became early afternoon. The manager had his feet up again, watching a bounty hunter show. Then an odd feeling. He hadn't noticed it until then, but something was different.

The manager got up and walked to the reception desk. Business was always slow at this location, which was fine by him. But today, except for checkouts, there hadn't been any. Literally.

He crossed the lobby and looked out the front window. A van with Indiana plates rolled onto the lot. Here we go: a customer. Must be imagining things.

He waited for them to come in, but the van kept rolling past the office before speeding away.

Oh well, lots of people didn't like the looks of the place when they got up close. Seen it hundreds of times. The manager was about to return to the backroom when he saw a station wagon from Tennessee pull off the highway. He waited at the desk. The vehicle drove up to the office and screeched out the exit. Then an SUV. And a Chrysler.

Curiosity was killing him as the scene repeated over and over, all kinds of high-mileage family vehicles approaching the office, slowing down as the occupants strained for some kind of view, then fleeing at escape rate.

The manager scratched a scab. He pushed open the front door and stepped out into the parking lot as a Monte Carlo took off. He looked up at the side of the building. In giant, spray-painted letters: COUPON RIP-OFF MOTEL (AND CRABS IN THE SHEETS).

Serge couldn't take his eyes off the magnificent Landsdorf postcard. "Howard, I seriously owe you. Promise to make this up in a big way."

"Forget about it."

"I insist." Serge slipped the card into his canvas shoulder bag. "You going to more shows?"

Howard handed him a flyer; Serge scanned the dates and cities. "You're heading south just like we are. I'll definitely try to make some of these, drumming up huge crowds of customers requiring police to direct traffic. Or I might come alone."

A cell rang. Howard pulled it from his pocket and held up a finger.

"Coleman, hear that personalized ringtone?" said Serge. " 'Gimme Back My Bullets.' Another Skynyrd fan!"

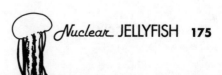

Nuclear JELLYFISH **175**

Howard turned around for privacy. ". . . Mom, slow down. You're talking too fast . . . When did you find out? . . . No, that doesn't sound fair . . . I'll see what I can do . . . I don't know yet . . . I have to ask around . . . And I'll call . . . I don't know when . . . Mom, I have customers . . . I do so care about your problem . . . I'll call . . . I really have to go. Bye."

Howard hung up and set the ringer to vibrate. He turned back around.

Serge's face was grave. "Couldn't help but hear. Is your mother all right?"

"It's nothing. I'll take care of it."

"Maybe I can help."

Howard stared at the floor. "No . . ."

"Look at me," said Serge. "What's going on?"

"Well, after my dad passed last year, mom's been looking for a smaller place . . ."

"Smart financial move."

". . . Just closed this morning on a cozy little cottage. Especially loved the kitchen."

"Problem?"

"All the appliances were brand new, but when they went to the house after the closing, the refrigerator had been switched with an old rusty one that buzzes and the door won't even shut all the way. I'm thinking of calling an attorney."

"Won't do any good."

"Why not?"

"I know this scam inside out. The contract lists all nonpermanent fixtures that are supposed to come with the house. When dealing with reputable people, it's enough to just write 'refrigerator, stove, washer, dryer,' but it's not airtight. If the seller and agent aren't scrupulous, you need to put the make, model and even serial number into the contract, or they can swap 'em out with any old pieces of crap, and it's totally legal."

"So there's nothing I can do?"

"Didn't say that. What's the name of this real estate agent?"

CHAPTER 24

BACK STORY

There was a scandal a little time ago at one of south Florida's less prestigious colleges. It stayed behind closed doors.

Sexual harassment. Ho-hum. At least as far as the administration went. Young women disgruntled about poor marks were always threatening trumped-up charges to get a grade bump. Others with father complexes took revenge when their crushes went unrequited.

The rest of the allegations, the wide majority, were simply true.

One case was different from all the others.

Rape.

But that's not what set it apart.

Sure, the test kit came back positive. DNA matched the professor, and bleeding from soft-tissue lacerations in the expected location ruled out consent. Not to mention a pattern of fingertip-sized bruises around the neck from forced fellatio.

No, what separated this case was that the professor also ended up at the hospital, and in distinctly different shape than his victim. The young woman was soon up and walking, while the teacher had a concussion, three broken ribs and a punctured lung—all while a team of surgeons labored into the fourth hour to reattach his half-bitten-off member.

The school's board of directors freaked. No hiding from this one. Until, that is, a king-size gift fell in their lap. The lawyers pounced. They visited the D.A., who called in the victim and broke the news.

"What do you mean, *they're* not going to press charges against *me*?"

The prosecutor laid out the unpleasant political realities of modern jurisprudence.

"But that's got nothing to do with it!"

Sorry, said the D.A., but his office had to allocate resources based upon odds of prevailing at trial. And strippers don't win rape cases.

"But he—" She cut herself off, as she had throughout her life. Then composed: "That's why he attacked in the first place. Called me up for an office conference and said he was surprised I was failing, which was impossible because I'd aced every test. Then he mentioned a friend had seen me at the club, and that a private lap dance would go a long way. I said I'd rather fuckin' fail, and tried to leave his office. You know the rest."

This was the part of his job the prosecutor hated.

He explained that normally, with a victim in her profession, they plea bargain out with greenhorn defense attorneys who don't know they've got a winner with the jury. But the college's legal team was top notch. And they'd be sure to mention the woman's criminal record for aggravated assault: in her second trimester, beating the snot out of an abortion protester blocking the clinic entrance.

Oh, and more bad news. She was expelled.

The now ex-student went numb in the face.

The prosecutor offered to call the victims' assistance unit, even drive her over.

She refused.

Did she have family?

No.

Need any money?

She got up and left.

Every stripper, before she was a stripper, was a little girl.

Story Long wanted to be a teacher, astronaut, veterinarian. And to stop the beatings from her alcoholic mother's boyfriends.

Most children who are dealt such hands withdraw and wither. Some lash out antisocially. A rare few, like Story, overachieve. Straight A's, clawing for every crumb, hiding the shame of her welts with makeup or long sleeves. No dances or proms. Just a one-in-a-thousand thermonuclear survivor's drive. If you stepped in front of her dreams, prepare to get run over.

By the time she was kicked out of the house, it became an instant calculation of math and desensitization. Stripping was the best way to make it through college.

Her first job lasted a week.

"What do you mean I'm fired?"

"You kicked that guy in the nuts!"

"He tried to grope me."

"It's a fuckin' strip club!"

That was eight jobs ago, all ending more or less the same.

The evening after the expulsion and leaving the D.A.'s office, Story arrived for work at her ninth gig, a high-roller Fort Lauderdale lounge. The bouncer shook his head and barred the door with a thick forearm.

"What?"

"Owner says you can't dance here anymore."

"Why not?"

"Lawyers came around."

"What lawyers?"

"The college. Threatened to sue."

"But you didn't have anything to do with this."

"Doesn't matter. Owner said we can't afford the legal bills."

Another wave of numbness. Then she raised her chin, turned and walked back to her car.

The bouncer had been one of her best friends at the club. Tutored him for his G.E.D at no charge. He wanted to say something but instead just watched her ten-year-old Taurus leave a trail of Valvoline as it disappeared down Old Dixie Highway.

Nothing left but to drive back home to Jacksonville. At least there were a few old friends where she might bunk a night or two before regaining her footing. No money for the Turnpike, so it was I-95. She reached Lantana by midnight. The engine block cracked by Tequesta.

She began walking.

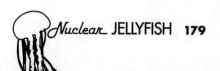

Another sweaty day on U.S. 1.

Below Daytona Beach, a small bridge crosses picturesque Rose Bay, and a little north of that sits a tiny brick building pressed up against the sidewalk, somewhat alone on a sparse stretch of highway featuring traffic intent on getting anywhere else. Many of the building's bricks were painted with people's names. A cinder block propped open the front door. Inside: darkness and the vague outline of clientele. On the roof, a plywood sign: THE LAST RESORT BAR.

Coleman sat on the penultimate stool of the infamous biker dive, staring up at bras hanging from electrical conduit. Bloodshot eyes drifted to layers of ever-present graffiti representing mankind's existential yearning to write on shit while drinking: The Hedz, Slut Puppies, T-Fox, Deap (sic) Dick, Zippo, Kroakerhead, Bike Week, Total Eclipse, "1500 miles to get here!" then doodling of boobs, a rodent and a pentagram.

Serge came running through the bright doorway, sweating rivers. He hopped aboard the stool next to Coleman.

"Hey, Serge, how'd it go at the Fairview Motel?"

"Excellent. We're booked into room 9 on the north shore of the bay, where Aileen Wuornos—America's so-called first female serial killer—holed up with her lover while picking off johns. Then I traced Aileen's footsteps up the side of U.S. 1, where she stumbled each night from the Fairview to this bar . . ." He pulled out his trusty digital camera. ". . . Documenting her route every ten yards."

The bartender came over. "What'll it be?"

"Bottled water. And one of every souvenir you've got, including that T-shirt, 'Home of ice cold beer and killer women.'" Serge turned on his camera. "I need to document this with total photographic coverage."

"But you already took a bunch of pictures this morning."

Serge aimed the camera at a wall. "No I didn't." Click.

"Yes you did," said Coleman. "Must have shot hundreds."

"You're messing with me." Click. "I wasn't even here this morning."

"If you don't believe me, just ask the bartender."

Click. "Why?"

"Because you talked to him for a long time, bunch of questions like you always do."

The bartender arrived with water and a pile of keepsakes.

"Thanks," said Serge. "Maybe you can help settle something. My friend says I spoke to you this morning."

"Quite a while."

"Really? What did I say?"

The bartender smiled diplomatically. "Don't take this wrong, but it was pretty weird."

"Then it must have been me."

"Told you," said Coleman.

"If I did take a load of pictures, they got to be in here." Serge hit the review button on his camera and scrolled through a massive file of photos from the bar: movie poster for *Monster,* framed newspaper articles, every inch of wall scribbling, plastic pig. Then more from outside. The colorful patron bricks, including Wuornos's, a fence of small, sheet-metal tombstone plaques remembering fallen riders.

Coleman leaned for a better look at Serge's tiny digital screen. "What's that big tree with all those motorcycles hanging from it?"

"The motorcycle tree," said Serge. "Out behind the bar. Ashes from riders on those tombstone plaques spread under it."

"I've been noticing a lot of biker bars lately," said Coleman.

"Because we're in the Biker Trapezoid."

"The what?"

"You know the Bermuda Triangle?" Serge clicked through more photos. "Florida has what I've dubbed the Biker Trapezoid. St. Augustine to New Smyrna Beach, then over to Kissimmee and Leesburg. Extends farther, but that's roughly the core. Magnificent back-road scenic tours for the two-wheel crowd, which is now welcomed everywhere."

"I remember when police would fuck with bikers."

"Until the financial statements came in. Ask any Daytona Beach merchant who used to bank on spring break. College students eat and drink on the cheap, pack ten to a room and trash the place. Then they

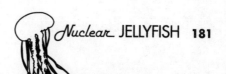

had a couple motorcycle fests and couldn't believe the contrast. Bikers spend a fortune. Not only that, but they behave better than the kids and leave rooms in one piece."

"They don't still party like maniacs?"

"More than ever," said Serge. "Which is a bigger plus. Capitalism's favorite son is anyone getting hammered on a full wallet. The cash infusion to the local economy is so ridiculous that chambers of commerce persuaded police departments to go on flex-mode during motorcycle migrations. Instead of arresting rambunctious bikers, they now politely steer them from trouble so they can live to spend another day." Serge looked at the floor next to Coleman's stool. "What's in the bag?"

"Oh, almost forgot." He bent down and handed it to Serge. "Howard asked me to give this to you."

"When?" Serge reached inside.

"I don't know. Couple days ago at one of the hotels."

"And you're just now getting around to it?"

"Sorry."

Serge pulled out his hand. "Oh my God!"

"What is it?"

He slowly rotated the white plastic dolphin. "Carolina Snowball! The famous albino dolphin from the sixties at the Miami Seaquarium." Serge held it right to his eyes. "This came from one of those vintage, glass dome injection-mold vending machines. And it's just like the one I got as a kid when my grandfather took me to the aquarium, except I lost mine years ago."

"That was awfully thoughtful of him."

"But how'd he know?"

"You told him all about it."

"I did?"

"Went on and on . . ."

Serge hopped from his stool. "Watch my souvenirs." He ran out the door to their car and returned in a flash, opening a laptop on the bar.

"What are you doing now?"

"That reminded me about my promise to Howard." He typed nonstop on the stolen computer with wireless Internet access. "Here we go . . ." Serge found a website for the hometown newspaper where Howard's mother lived. Serge clicked into the classified section and read down a column of homes for sale. "Here's one . . . Here's another . . . and another . . ."

"Another what?"

"Homes listed with the agent who ripped off Howard's mom. If my hunch is correct . . ." He flipped open his cell and dialed the number from the ads.

Coleman turned. "But how are you going to—"

"Shhhhh! It's ringing . . . Hello? Mr. Miller? My name is Tom Gifford with the *Clarion-Ledger-Beacon*. I'm in the classified department, and I apologize for the inconvenience, but one of my new employees incorrectly entered the credit card information when you placed some recent home ads. No, I can't get it from the last time: Database is down for maintenance . . . Yes, I have a pen . . . Uh-huh . . . uh-huh . . . uh-huh . . . and the expiration date? . . . and the three-digit security code on the back? . . . and your billing address . . . Got it. Again, I'm awfully sorry for the trouble . . ."

Serge hung up and surfed the Internet until he found another phone number. He dialed again. "Hello, Appliance King? What's your most expensive refrigerator? . . . Sounds perfect . . . That'll be delivery . . . Yes, I have my credit card ready . . ."

Minutes later, another phone call. "Eduardo, Serge here. Remember the favor you owe me? . . . That abandoned gas station next to your shop is about to get a delivery, and I need you to sign for it . . . No, not your name. T.A. Miller . . . Real estate agent . . . Right, then I need you to deliver and install it at another address. Got something to write with? . . ."

Serge finished the call and closed his laptop. "The Justice League triumphs again."

CHAPTER 25

COCOA BEACH

*M*ahoney walked across a parking lot, unfolding a flyer and reading it for the tenth time: "Howard Enterprises. Floridiana from all eras. Estates appraised." The agent returned it to his pocket and entered the only conference room in a modest beach motel.

Against the back wall, a young man boxed up pins and buttons and citrus-packing labels. It had been a slow day, as in nothing. Howard decided to bag it early.

"Excuse me."

Howard looked up. "Yes."

Mahoney pulled a brown leather holder from his tweed jacket and flashed a badge.

"Wow!" said Howard. "That's a Dade sheriff, 1942. I'll give you fifty."

Mahoney turned the shield around. "Shoot, grabbed the wrong one." He returned it to his jacket. "Genuine article's back on my dresser."

"You're a cop?"

Mahoney answered by whipping out a mug shot. "Seen this man?"

Howard instantly recognized it. "Has he done something wrong?"

"Just answer the question."

"I gave him a postcard the other day."

Mahoney stuck a matchstick in his mouth. "Which way'd he hoof?"

"South, I think."

"Anything else?"

"Seemed real nice."

Mahoney pulled the matchstick out. "Fits his M.O."

THE LAST RESORT BAR

An uncharacteristic mood swing. Serge jumped and reflexively glanced behind his stool. Nothing there.

Coleman killed another longneck and slammed the empty on the bar. "What's the matter?"

"Not sure. You know how you sometimes get the feeling you're being followed?"

"No."

Serge took a swig of spring water. "I've been having them more and more lately, and I don't understand why. Well, actually I do."

"Really?"

"Hasn't it ever struck you odd that, given my lifestyle all these years, I've never been caught or clipped? I'm good, but not *that* good."

"What are you saying?"

"Everyone's luck runs out sometime."

"Serge! Don't talk like that!"

"It's okay." He placed a consoling hand on his buddy's shoulder. "Life's already rained an abundance of blessings on me."

"But you've always had a wild imagination. Nobody's following us."

"Probably right." He raised the water again. "Must be all in my head . . ."

A new customer appeared in the doorway, slowly scanning the dim room before taking sideways steps along the wall. He clutched a folded newspaper to his chest like it concealed a grenade.

"Still," said Serge. "There eventually has to be a time. Everyone's got a bullet with their name on it."

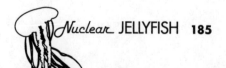

"I thought you didn't believe in that fate stuff."

"I don't," said Serge. "I'm more afraid of bad ratings."

"What do you mean?"

The new customer tiptoed around the near wall, clandestinely sliding behind Serge's chair.

"My life's so weird, it's like I've been walking through the script of a sit-com." Serge drained his water. "I'm just worried the universe will grow tired of my character and write me off the show. That's why I chose this seat."

"Why *did* you choose it?"

"Got views of all three assault ports: entrance, side door and bartender's service exit. If the script guy comes in here . . ." —he patted the gun butt under his tropical shirt—". . . I'm doing some rewrites."

"Maybe I can help," said Coleman. "I'll stay alert for anyone suspicious who might come in here lookin' for you."

"Someone already has."

"Where?"

"Right behind me. Don't look—"

Coleman looked.

"Thanks."

"Serge, he's got something hidden in his newspaper."

"I picked up on that." Serge slowly slipped his hand off the bar and down to the bulge under his shirt.

"Think it's a hit?"

"No," Serge said sarcastically. "He just popped in to give a complete stranger a whole bunch of money."

"Serge, he's coming toward you! He's lifting the newspaper!"

Serge simultaneously spun on his stool and whipped out the pistol, aiming it sideways, low in his lap, so only the new customer could see.

The man froze and took quick, shallow breaths. He looked at the empty stool on the other side of Serge from Coleman. "May I?"

"Knock yourself out."

The man sat and placed the folded paper on the bar in front of him. "Are you Scagnetti?"

"Nope."

"Never mind. It's better I don't know your real name." He glanced at his watch. "You're early."

"Why put things off?"

The stranger's eyes shifted a final time before surreptitiously sliding the folded paper to his right.

"*News-Journal*," said Serge, keeping aim from below bar level. "Excellent paper."

"Thought you'd be more muscular."

"I make up for it with deceptive speed, Zen-like mental toughness and champion bird calls." Serge's free hand lifted the newspaper's front edge, revealing a bulky brown envelope tucked inside. He lifted the flap and peeked like a poker player. Thick wad of bills.

"It's all there," said the man. "Two grand."

Serge reached under the money, pulling out a Polaroid, a scrap of paper and a house key.

"My wife and the address."

"I guessed that." Serge slipped the photo back inside. "How'd you know it was me?"

"That tropical shirt." He pointed down. "And the particular stool you're on, just like Vince said."

"Vince?"

The man covered his mouth. "I wasn't supposed to use his name."

"What else did Vince say?"

"That you could make it look like an accident."

"Anything else?"

"Make her suffer."

"That I don't do. You want her to suffer, grow some balls and handle it yourself."

"I'll pay an extra grand."

"How much screaming do you want?"

"This isn't a joke!"

"See me laughing?" Serge stood with the newspaper. "Consider it done. But you need to do a few things."

"Like what?"

"You know that other bar south of the crossroads?"

"Yeah?"

"Make yourself visible. Have a few pops, talk to everyone. Keep asking if the clock over the bar is right and all that police-show alibi shit. And don't leave the bar for anything, especially the bathroom, even if you have to piss like a racehorse. Some asshole will always say 'Yeah, he left to take a leak,' and the three minutes you took will later balloon into a half hour when the cops grill him, long enough to get back and forth from your house. Last question: Any kids?"

"Two. They're staying out of town with my mother." The man looked down; his voice became tentative: "When will I know?"

"I'll find you. Now git!"

The man scurried out of the bar.

Serge slid over a stool. He reached inside the brown envelope, removed some of the cash and stuck it in his hip pocket.

Five minutes passed.

A muscular man in a tropical shirt stepped through the doorway. Gaunt, sun-dried face like a walnut. He headed directly for the bar and climbed on the stool Serge had just vacated.

Serge turned. "Scagnetti?"

"Got something for me?"

Serge slid the newspaper over.

The man peeked inside. "Looks light."

Serge shook his head. "It's all there. A grand."

"A grand? It's supposed to be two."

"That's not what Vince said. I give two to him and one to you."

"You were supposed to give *me* the two! Fuckin' Vince, holding out."

"Does this mean it's off?"

"No," snarled the man, pulling out the photo and address. "I'll deal with Vince later. How do you want it done?"

"Double tap to the back of the head."

"But that'll draw attention your way. Sure you don't want me to make it look like an accident? The latest thing is getting run over by your own car in the driveway."

Serge shook his head. "Even make it easy for you. I'm going home to play with the whore first. You'll find her tied up and gagged in a closet."

"You're one sick bastard! Why not just finish it if you're going that far?"

"Need to establish my alibi when the forensic team pegs time of death. Give me four hours to reach Miami, well outside the margin of error."

"That puts us at five-thirty." He looked up from his watch. "Which closet?"

"Uh . . ."

"You don't know your own house?"

"Of course I know my house! The front closet. You'll probably hear muffled screams."

The man left abruptly.

"Serge," said Coleman. "I have no idea what's going on."

"We're driving over to the address."

"But you only kill jerks."

"I'm not going to kill her. I'm going to save her."

"Shouldn't you go to the police?"

"Are you listening to yourself? Go to the police? *Me?*"

"I meant call anonymously on one of those tip lines."

"There's no guarantee they'll nail him. And even if they do, he'll still eventually get out because it's only *attempted* murder. You saw that level of rage—'make her suffer'—she'll always be in danger unless I tie a bow on this. Luckily, her husband mistakenly came to an undercover citizen. Guys like that turn my stomach."

"Then why are you smiling?"

Serge broke into a skip as he headed out the door. "Because this is going to be so much fun!"

CHAPTER 26

PORT ORANGE

A Kenworth semi took the Atlantic detour from I-95 to avoid state weighing stations. It crossed the bridge over Rose Bay. The driver had been the consummate gentleman, as had all the other truckers, who recognized one of their own social class in need and helped pass a hitchhiker named Story up the coast like a relay baton.

Brake hydraulics wheezed as the rig pulled up to the Fairview Motel. "This is as far as I'm going."

"But it's only two in the afternoon."

"I've been running thirty of the last thirty-four hours."

"Your log books?"

"Fiction."

"Amphetamines?"

He just smiled. "I need to take the edge off if I'm ever going to get to sleep. There's this spot up the road if you want to join me. Coldest beer you'd ever want."

Story knew men well enough to know it wasn't a come-on. The driver had been talking nonstop about his wife and kids since Titusville, showing wallet pictures.

"Sure," said Story.

The two walked through a blazing sun up the side of U.S. 1. They stood on the sidewalk along the east side of the street, locally known as Ridgewood Avenue, waited for a dump truck to pass, then scampered across the highway toward the inviting doorway of The Last Resort. Story wiped sweat off her face with her tank top.

She was almost to the entrance when two men ran out, paired physically like Abbot and Costello—"Woooo!" "We're rockin' now!"—and sped off in a Javelin.

Story looked back. "What's with them?"

"It's The Last Resort," said the driver.

They went inside to the coldest beer anyone could want.

The Javelin sped up a dirt road in Port Orange. Ahead: old cracker house with sagging porch. A woman heard the over-revving engine and came to the screen door. Serge jumped out, bounding up the steps. "Mrs. Milford?"

"Stop right there! Who are you?"

"Your husband—"

"No!" She slammed the wooden door behind the screen and ran to call the cops. Serge knocked it in with his shoulder. He ripped the wire from the wall before she could dial.

"I'm begging you!" She crumpled into a ball below the cuckoo clock and shielded her face.

"It's okay," said Serge. "We're here to help you."

She looked up. "You aren't his friends?"

"Hell no. Now listen carefully: You're in great danger from your husband."

"But I just got a restraining order last week. He's not allowed near me."

"Afraid 'allowed' isn't part of it."

"You're not saying . . ." She began sobbing uncontrollably.

"My partner and I need this place for a stakeout. Have relatives nearby?"

She gulped back tears. "Sister. Let me get some things."

"No time." Serge grabbed her arm. "Get moving. And whatever you or your sister do, don't talk to anyone for four hours, especially the police."

"But I thought you were the police."

"Elite undercover unit." He led her down the porch and into the driveway. "But if you call regular cops, they could show up in marked cars and blow the whole takedown before we have enough evidence.

And next time he might approach a *real* hit man instead of us."

"Oh my God!"

"Don't lose it now." Serge opened the driver's door of her Camaro. She got in and looked back out the window. "How will I know when it's safe?"

"It already is."

ANOTHER EXTENDED COMFORT EXPRESS SUITES USA

Steve sat alone in the motel's glassed-in business center, leaning back in an ergonomic chair and tapping a keyboard.

The door opened. Steve quickly hit a key, switching the computer screen from porn to spreadsheet. He swiveled to see who it was.

"Uh-oh."

A bodyguard pulled up another leather seat.

Steve scooted his chair backward on casters. "We have to stop being seen together."

"Just take a minute. Who's your next courier?"

"There aren't any more."

"Recruit one."

"No, I mean, literally, I've gone through every last coin dealer," said Steve. "When you took down Paul last night, that was it."

"So recruit one of the stamp guys."

Steve shook his head. "There's a war on."

"Then come up with someone else."

"Aren't you listening? There isn't anybody."

"Then I guess I'll just have to tell that to the Eel. Probably throw you a retirement party."

"No! Wait, I'll come up with something."

"Great." The bodyguard stood. "You can go back to your porn."

THE CROSSROADS

Just south of where two rural routes met, a building that looked more like an abandoned farmhouse sat framed by oak and moss. Serge burst through double saloon doors. A man at the end of the bar jumped up and swallowed a deep breath. Serge nodded. The man exhaled.

They both walked outside. Serge turned at the bottom of the steps and held out an expectant hand.

"What?" said the man.

"Where's the back end?"

"Vince said I don't have to pay the rest until I get proof. You were supposed to take a picture."

"What picture?" Serge's hand stayed out. "Vince didn't say anything."

"Can I wait for the morning paper?"

"You're really starting to piss me off!"

"Sorry, it's just that Vince promised—"

"Fuck Vince! And fuck you! I smell where this is going. I'm heading out of town, and on the way I'm dropping a little something in the mailbox to the police."

"No! Jesus! Don't!"

Serge swished the toe of a sneaker in the dirt. He looked up. "Sorry, got a little heated. If I was in your position, I'd demand proof, too. When you're right, you're right." He opened the door of the Javelin. "Get in the car."

"What for?"

"We're driving to Proof City."

"I'll take your word." He reached for his wallet with a trembling hand.

Serge grabbed him by the arm and shoved him into the backseat. "Wouldn't hear of it."

They sped inland.

The man recognized the way. "We're not going back to the house, are we?"

"Oh, no, no, no, no, no!" said Serge. "This other place is around the corner."

Cows watched through barbed wire. The Javelin continued across the hot, Florida pastureland and turned up an unmarked dirt road.

"We *are* going to my house!"

"Okay, I lied," said Serge. "Because I can't wait for the money. I doubled down on football last Sunday and have to meet these bookies by midnight or I'll end up in more pieces than your wife."

"I told you, I'll pay without proof!"

"But not seeing the pieces wouldn't be fair to you. Except I hope you don't mind: Not all the pieces are still there. You never told me you have the new Brahman gas grill! Your tastebuds don't know they're alive until they've met a Brahman! . . . I got a great idea! We'll celebrate over dinner!"

The husband turned green and lunged for a door handle. Serge hit the brakes, cracking him across the face with his pistol. Then he jammed the barrel in a bloody ear. "You *are* going in the house."

CHAPTER 27

The Javelin parked at the front porch, and the husband was forced into the house at gunpoint.

The man clenched his eyes shut. "I can't look."

Serge jabbed him in the back. "Look!"

The man opened his eyes to a slit. Thoughts of dread turned to puzzlement. Eyelids went up the rest of the way. No trace of his wife, no expected blood trails, not the least sign of a struggle. In fact, the whole house looked in perfect order. The only thing out of place were two brand-name shopping bags on the coffee table. Hardware and toy store. "What's going on?"

Serge shoved him into the middle of the room. "I didn't do your wife."

"Oh, so this was a ripoff . . . Well, that's fine. I'll give you the rest of the money. Just don't hurt me."

"This isn't a ripoff."

The man's confusion returned. "Then what is it?"

"I came to protect your wife." Serge pulled handcuffs from his back pocket.

The man's legs began to buckle. "You're an undercover cop?"

"Worse," said Serge, fastening the bracelets behind the man's back. "Undercover citizen."

"Yeah," said Coleman. "Like that song 'Undercover Angel.'"

"Not like that song," said Serge. "I hate that song. And now it's playing in my head."

"Sorry."

Serge seized the man by an arm and dragged him toward a spacious closet. "I took the liberty of doing a little remodeling while I was here." He opened the door.

The man looked inside. Now he was totally baffled. Two wooden chairs faced each other, both reinforced to the floor with aluminum bracket-straps used for roofing trusses. Must have been a hundred penny nails and galvanized screws. Atop the chair nearest the door was some kind of unidentifiable customized mount fashioned from a miter box and bench vise.

"It was a tight fit, but I knew it would work," said Serge. "'Measure twice, cut once,' save yourself a world of headaches."

"What's it for?"

"You!" said Serge. "I put in a lot of work, always treat my clients right. . . . 'Undercover Angel'! Coleman, it's still playing!"

"Said I was sorry."

"That's okay. I'll just switch channels in my head to the Rock Vault."

"What's the Rock Vault?" asked Coleman.

"When most people don't have a sound system, they go: 'Shit, no sound system.'"

"Not you?"

Serge tapped his temple. "Every song already stored for easy access. Let's listen to something!"

The horn from a Florida East Coast locomotive blared in the distance as it clacked down tracks along the Old Dixie corridor.

"I know," said Coleman. "How about 'Train, Train'?"

"Blackfoot." Serge nodded his approval. "Another excellent band of Florida's native sons."

They began bobbing their heads in silence. The husband thrashed in wild panic as the extent of his captor's insanity became clear. He was bound securely in the chair at the back of the closet.

"And you have two kids!" Serge grabbed a thick roll of duct tape off the opposing seat. "You were going to take away their mom."

"I was just about to call it off. I swear! Praying at the bar that you'd come back and say something went wrong so I could—"

Serge sealed yet another in a long career of taped mouths. It was a toss-up: whether the man was more or less terrified by not having any idea what was in store.

"Here's what's in store . . ." Serge slowly pulled a long string from his hip pocket like a magician. "The gravy on my project is this special mount atop the other chair. That's where the gun goes. I'll tie this string to the trigger, then the other end goes around the closet's inside door-knob, which I'll tighten from the outside with the door a few inches ajar, giving it just enough slack for a quick, ten-pound pull when someone opens it. Hold still—be right back!" The door closed.

The man desperately wiggled in the darkness, muted screams under the tape. Light hit his face as the door opened again. He got a brief glimpse of a black handgun before Serge leaned around the front of the opposing chair, blocking his view. Finally the pistol was clamped firmly in the vise, string around the trigger. Serge stepped back with a big smile. "What do you think?"

The husband's hysteria went off the scale, but the roof brackets more than held. Then he suddenly became still as he stared at the vise. It didn't look like a regular gun. And it had an orange plastic safety tip, like a toy. He leaned for a closer view. It was a . . . *cap gun*? He stared up at Serge with knotted eyebrows.

"What?" said Serge. "You didn't think I was actually going to use a real gun? I just wanted to teach you a lesson . . ." He looked down at a puddle around the man's feet.

". . . Which I believe you've learned in spades. Excellent student!" Serge grabbed the edge of the duct tape.

The man yelled in brief pain as the strip ripped free. "You almost gave me a heart attack."

"Sorry about that," said Serge. "But those are the lessons that stick best . . ." He noticed his watch: 5:15. "Wow, that late? Don't mean to be rude and dash off, but I have to get somewhere." He tore another long stretch of tape and held it in front of the man's mouth.

"What are you doing? I learned my lesson."

"Remedial tutoring." Serge wrapped the mouth again. "Be right back." The door closed.

The man listened. Quiet. Then heavy footsteps and Serge talking to himself: *"Damn, this thing weighs more than it looks."*

The door opened. "You've got great taste. I am definitely going to have to get me one of those Brahman grills first chance I get!" He reached down and hoisted a squat, roundish metal tank, placing it on the empty chair facing the man. "Hope you don't mind if I borrow your propane. Hear they're pretty cheap to refill." Serge twisted the tank's valve all the way open. A quiet hiss. He started closing the door, leaving a three-inch gap with the frame. He reached inside for the string hanging from the trigger of the cap gun and tied it around the inside doorknob.

"Toodles!"

The closet door closed.

EXTENDED COMFORT EXPRESS SUITES USA

Howard had called it another early day. He sat alone in the corner of the hotel bar, enjoying a dinner of free happy-hour finger food.

"Howard! Old pal!"

He turned around. *"Steve?"*

Steve slapped him hard on the back. "How you doin'?"

"Uh, fine?"

"Mind if I join you?"—dragging a chair.

"What do you want?"

Steve grabbed a cheese cube off Howard's plate and popped it in his mouth. "Have I ever mentioned how much I admire you?"

"I thought you didn't even like me."

"Why do you say that?"

"Because you said you didn't like me. And you're always making fun of me whenever we're at the same hotel. And you tried to trip me in front of the guys. And—"

"You got the wrong idea."

"I do?"

"That's how I treat all my friends."

"You don't do it to anyone else."

"I don't like them," said Steve. "Plus, I'm completely blown away by this whole thing you're doing with souvenirs. Total genius."

"I'm broke."

"Because you're way out in front of the trend. Just wait 'til the country wakes up!"

"That's what you came to tell me?"

Steve took a hot wing from Howard's plate. "Except you'll never get the chance to succeed if you go under first from lack of funds. And I'm not about to let that happen!"

"You're giving me money?"

"Even better." He grabbed one of Howard's napkins and dabbed mouth corners. "Great business proposition for you."

"I already have a business."

"And a fine business it is. But every venture needs capitalization, and that's where I come in."

"What's the proposition?"

"Straight to the point! That's what I like about you, kid." He slid his chair closer for added privacy. "The other guys are okay, but not the sharpest knives in the drawer. That's why I've come to you. This has to be just between us. Do I have your word?"

"Okay."

Steve sat back smugly. "Diamonds." He winked.

"What about them?"

"Big money as a courier. You'll start tonight."

"Courier?"

"Teach you everything you need to know."

"I don't think so." Howard's fork speared a marinated meatball. "I'd have to give up the souvenir thing."

"No, you see that's the beauty of it. You keep doing souvenirs. It's the perfect cover. All couriers need one."

"Cover? Sounds dangerous."

"Absolutely not. You take a bigger risk every time you step in the shower."

"Your coins? Is that also a cover?"

"About a year ago I was at this big show in Pensacola where a gem expo was also being held. And that night over drinks in the hotel bar, the top diamond guy at the place said he needed more couriers for his distributorship." Steve left out the part where the distributor was in on the whole robbery thing with the gang, for the insurance and fencing angles.

 JELLYFISH **199**

"Don't they use armed guards and stuff?"

"That's what everyone assumes. But there's over a thousand jewelry stores across the state, and nowhere near the available security. They have to get product from somewhere. So there's a giant invisible army out there making deliveries, hiding in plain sight, some even carrying stones around in crumpled bags that look like trash they want to throw away."

"I don't think I have the nerves."

"And that's why you'll be perfect." Steve gestured up and down at Howard. "Who'd ever suspect someone like you?"

"What's that supposed to mean?"

CHAPTER 28

*S*erge drove back down the dirt driveway and turned onto a country road. The Javelin made a skidding U-turn and pulled onto the shoulder next to flat pasture with a clear view of the house.

"What are you doing?" asked Coleman.

"Waiting for our surprise guest."

It was peaceful. Two cattle egrets picked at cows by the drinking hole.

Coleman cracked a beer. "Sorry about 'Undercover Angel.'"

"Dang it. And I'd just gotten that out of my mind."

"See what else is in the Rock Vault."

Serge concentrated, then began tapping the steering wheel.

"Can I listen?" asked Coleman.

"Outlaws. 'Green Grass and High Tides.'"

Coleman swayed to the rhythm. "Another Florida band?"

Serge nodded and tapped faster with the growing tempo. "Formed 1972 in Tampa."

One of the cows turned its head. A mile up the country road, an older-model Ford pickup with bad mufflers crested a low hill. It raced toward them, getting larger.

"Duck," said Serge.

A roar passed. Serge slowly raised his head above the dash. The pickup turned at the dirt driveway and bounded toward the house. It parked sideways at the porch. A muscular man in a tropical shirt got out and circled the residence, scoping for anything that didn't feel right.

"Hey," said Coleman. "That's the other guy from the bar. Now I get it."

"Two for one," said Serge. "Took me a while to think this up, because they're equally wrong. And his wife would never be safe until both are out of the picture."

"You're my hero."

"This is going to be so much fun!"

They stopped talking and watched. Coleman noticed Serge had a rare frown.

"What's the matter, buddy?"

"I thought this was going to be fun."

"I'm having fun."

"I'm not. Something's wrong." He opened a cell phone and punched buttons. On the other side of the state, a phone rang in a psychiatrist's office. *"Hello? . . ."*

"It's me, Serge . . . No, I'm out of town. That's why I'm calling instead of just popping in . . . I'm sure you *are* busy . . . You have a patient waiting? But this is an emergency. I read where psychiatrists are always on call for clients in crisis . . . Okay, I'll tell you. I'm not having fun . . . That is so an emergency . . . All right, I'm bored, too . . . You think I might be coming down with depression? . . . No, I don't feel depressed, just not having fun . . ."

"Serge . . ." Coleman pointed at the house. Scagnetti reappeared from the far side, satisfied that everything was in order. He trotted up the front steps and stuck a key in the door.

". . . Wait! Don't hang up!" said Serge. "Listen, I read a psychiatric article: manically enthusiastic people like me burn twice as bright and half as long. The first symptom is uncontrolled rage, but who knows if it's true since the article was written by that Mahoney shit-sucking asswipe should-have-cut-his-goddamn-head-off-when-I-had-the-chance motherfucker! The second symptom is disinterest, but what do I care? . . . No, see, that's why I'm calling. I've been getting this weird feeling lately, like I'm reaching the end of the line and might do something crazy . . . Crazier than that . . . Crazier than that . . . You've made your point . . . But this time it's different . . ."

Scagnetti scanned the living room. His eyes locked on a door. He gently pulled the pistol from his waistband and screwed on a silencer.

". . . Plus, paranoia, just like in that article," said Serge. "I've never been paranoid a day in my life . . . No, that time the Trilateral Commission really was trying to silence my international call to arms . . ."

Scagnetti quietly stepped across the living room and up to the closet. He raised the pistol and grabbed the knob. The door quickly jerked open. Nothing. Unless he wanted to shoot winter coats and boots.

". . . Like right now," said Serge. "I'm doing one of my absolute favorite things in the whole world . . . Can't tell you that . . . Why would you think someone's tied up? . . . The point is that I should be having the time of my life with a little snack tray. Instead, emptiness . . ."

Scagnetti closed the door and looked around. Another closet. He headed across the room. Something stopped him. He sniffed the air. What was that funky smell? He looked at the bottom of the door, where a tiny trickle of urine rolled out. A wicked grin. "Yoo-hoo! Anyone in there?"

Muffled screams from the other side. Scagnetti grabbed the doorknob.

"But Doc," said Serge, "I really think there's something wrong with me . . . You agree? Good . . . You know 'Tears of a Clown'? . . . Because I'd always thought it was just a cleverly contrived song targeting the self-pity dork market . . ."

A giant fireball exploded out the west side of the farmhouse. A smoldering arm landed fifty yards away in the pasture.

A wide smile spread across Serge's face. "That was excellent! . . . And look: Here comes a foot!"

A loud bang on the Javelin's hood.

"I feel like a snack."

"Serge," said Coleman. "The phone."

"Oh, right." He placed it to his head. "You still there? . . . Sorry, false alarm . . . I said I was sorry . . . Yelling never helps . . . Maybe *you* should do something about *your* anger problem . . ." Serge winced and held the phone away from his head. He brought it back to his ear. "I have to go. The cows are stampeding."

THAT NIGHT

A motel room door opened. Howard stepped inside.

He turned on the TV and sat at the end of the bed. *SportsCenter.* Howard opened his wallet and thumbed through the three hundred dollars of advance money for his first delivery to Miami.

He stopped for a moment to whistle at the most cash he'd seen in forever. Yes, he had been skeptical, thinking Steve was setting him up for some kind of scam, maybe looking to boost his whole souvenir collection. But then the meeting an hour later in the hotel restaurant where Steve introduced him to the distributor and the initial payment was made. No scams came to mind where the victim got a bunch of cash.

The billfold went back in his pocket. From another pocket came a small, padded brown envelope. He glanced around: Where to hide it? Steve had given him a few ideas. Howard got up to check behind a mirror.

A sound at the door. A magnetic key. Howard turned.

The door opened. Two massive men with long, stringy hair.

"I think you have the wrong room."

"We have the right room."

CHAPTER 29

VERO BEACH

*T*he motel room's decor was a bit on the blue side.

The property sat, as it had for decades, just north of State Road 60 between the municipal airport and a configuration of manicured baseball fields.

When Coleman first stepped into the room a few hours earlier: "It's kind of blue in here."

Serge followed with a suitcase in each hands. "Because it's Dodgertown! I've been waiting my whole life to stay here!"

"Dodger-what?"

"You've *got* to get into sports more, even if just from the couch." Serge dropped luggage and pressed the side of his face to a wall. "Brooklyn Dodgers began spring training here in 1948, one of the first teams to make Florida their preseason home. And one of the few to construct their own accommodations for the players."

"That's where we are?"

Serge ran and leaped onto one of the beds. "Yet another hidden jewel. Most people don't know it, but after spring training ends, they rent out the players' rooms, and you get to sleep in Brooklyn-blue history. No true Florida-phile can die before staying at Dodgertown." He rolled onto his back, sweeping his arms and legs across the bed's covers like he was making snow angels. "Wonder who slept in this room? *Roy Campanella? Duke Snyder, Gil Hodges,* maybe even *Jackie Robinson!*"

"Serge." Coleman had picked something up from the dresser.

"Says in this pamphlet that players used to stay in a refurbished navy barracks until they built these villa-style quarters in 1974."

Serge stopped and glared angrily at Coleman, then suddenly smiled and began swinging his arms and legs again. *"Steve Garvey, Ron Cey, Don Sutton, Fernando Valenzuela . . ."*

Hours passed. ". . . You know that tiny airport we saw on the way in? Filmed as a Nicaraguan airport during the Somoza overthrow in the 1983 Jan Michael Vincent classic *Last Plane Out*. The entire city was the star, townspeople flocking to be extras . . ."—Serge shook Coleman to stay awake—". . . and they didn't even have to film Latin American rebel scenes out-of-country; just shot the bad parts of Vero, jeeps full of guerrillas driving past American stop signs . . ."

Today became tomorrow. Dark in the room with the TV off. Coleman's eyes were closed tight as he lay tucked snugly under a bed-spread with a pattern that made people subconsciously want to buy baseball tickets.

As he slept, Coleman smiled the smile of children. A pleasant dream was playing. He was standing in a field of nachos. The smile grew bigger. His eyeballs moved back and forth, making his eyelids poke around disconcertingly like a small animal trying to find its way out from under a collapsed circus tent. Coleman's smile fell, then an open-mouthed silent scream. He was being chased by the nacho monkeys. He ran as hard as he could, faster and faster, but his legs just spun in place like a cartoon. He suddenly sprang up in bed with a cold sweat.

Someone was standing over him.

"Oh, hi Serge."

No answer.

"Serge?"

Still nothing.

Coleman noticed Serge's right hand. "What's the gun for?"

Serge just stared down at him.

"Serge! You're scaring me!"

Serge blinked a few times. "Hey, Coleman." He looked around. "What the hell am I doing here?"

"Must have been sleepwalking again."

"What do you mean 'again'?"

"You've been doing it a lot lately."

"No, I haven't."

Coleman nodded. "Usually pacing and mumbling. Or tonight standing over me with a gun. I got the strange feeling you were going to kill me."

"Not a chance."

Coleman pointed.

Serge looked down at the pistol in his hand. "How'd that get there?" He tossed it on his own bed. "Have I been doing anything else while sleepwalking?"

"Yeah, but it's kind of weird."

"Coleman, we're way past the turnstiles at that theme park."

"You'll be in the bathroom talking to yourself in the mirror."

"What am I saying?"

"Hard to make out, but it sounds like you're saying good-bye."

"To whom?"

"Yourself."

"Saying good-bye to myself? That's weird."

"Told you."

"Did I mention why?"

"Just that you had a gnawing sixth sense your luck might be running out and wanted yourself to know there weren't any regrets."

"Maybe Mahoney's right about unraveling." Serge sat down on the edge of the bed next to Coleman and placed his face in his hands. "I could always at least bank on my own stability—relatively speaking—but now I'm turning into a mumbling freak who somnambulates."

"And sleepwalks." Coleman grabbed an ashtray and lighter off the nightstand.

"This is worrisome. If I'm blacking out and don't know what I'm doing, you may no longer be safe around me."

"Don't feel bad," said Coleman. "When I go to bed really trashed, I sleepwalk, too."

"Yeah, but at least there's no gun in your hand. You just wake up covered in pizza."

"That's the best part. Breakfast in bed."

A cell phone rang. Serge reached for the dresser.

Coleman reached for a joint. "Who could it be at this hour?"

"Probably one of the big travel websites wanting to apologize." Serge flipped the phone open. "Hello? . . . This is he . . . Yes, I know him . . . He asked you to call me? . . . But why couldn't he just call himself— What! . . . When did this happen? . . . I'll be right there!"

Serge jumped up and grabbed his gun.

"What's the matter? Are you starting to cry?"

But Serge just ran out the door.

JACKSONVILLE

Story Long had found a place to stay with one of her scattered old high school friends—"just a few days until I get some money." The classmate's live-in boyfriend didn't like the idea, but too bad. He didn't have a job, either.

The boyfriend was currently at a bar around the corner under protest. Fine by the gals. It was after midnight. Empty wineglasses. Story's busted lip was almost healed.

"You should sue," said the friend, named Beth.

"Better to just forget it and move on."

"*I* wouldn't forget it." Beth poured the dregs of a $3.99 bottle of Zinfandel. "Want me to open another?"

"No." Story stretched and yawned. "Already started online registration at the community college. My grades will transfer—"

A cell phone rang. Story reached for her purse.

Beth reached for a pack of cigarettes. "Who could it be at this hour?"

Story shrugged and flipped the phone open. "Hello? . . . Yes, this is she . . . The hospital? . . . I don't understand . . . What! . . . When did this happen? . . . I'll be right there!"

She jumped up and grabbed her purse.

"What's the matter?"

"I need a ride."

MEMORIAL HOSPITAL

The Javelin skidded into a parking space. Serge and Coleman jumped out and ran through the emergency room's automatic doors.

"There's the admissions desk!" Serge practically dove over it demanding information.

"Take it easy." The nurse behind the counter flipped pages on a clipboard. "Room three-twelve. But he's only seeing immediate relatives. Are you . . ." She looked up from the clipboard.

Serge and Coleman had already taken off.

The nurse leaned over the desk. "Wait! Your visitors' passes! . . ."

The pair took the elevator and arrived at the open door of the appointed room. Serge caught one look inside and gasped. He'd never seen so many bandages and tubes and wires.

A doctor came down the hall carrying an X-ray folder. Serge grabbed him by the arm. "That kid in there . . ."

The physician noticed Serge's welling eyes and placed other thoughts on hold. "Everything's going to be fine. He's through the worst of it. Just needs his sleep."

"Thanks, Doc."

The physician continued down the hall. They slipped quietly into Howard's room. The young man looked up at Serge, and his own eyes became glassy. The slight movement of his mouth indicated he wanted to say something but was too weak.

"Rest," said Serge, pulling a chair bedside. "We can talk later."

"Serge," said Coleman. "What's this tube here?"

"Looks like a morphine drip."

Coleman's face lit up. "Really?"

"Fuckin' touch it and you'll be sharing the next bed."

Coleman dropped his hand and sulked.

Howard tried to speak again.

Serge placed his hand across the young man's fingers, just below the IV port. "Whatever it is, it can wait."

He made a slight shaking motion with his head, indicating it couldn't.

"Okay," said Serge. "What is it?" He leaned over the bed with his ear an inch from Howard's mouth. The young man whispered.

A minute later, Serge stood back up, his head throbbing with rage.

"Uh-oh," said Coleman. "I've seen that look before."

A woman's voice from behind. Quiet but angry. The nurse from the desk. "You didn't get your passes! You have to leave!"

Serge raced past her. "I'm going to get them! I'm going to get them all! . . ."

The elevators opened on the first floor.

Serge and Coleman sprinted out the emergency room entrance, dodging a red Firebird as it screeched up the circular drive. Story and Beth hopped out and ran for the automatic doors.

An ambulance driver on smoke break: "Ma'am, you can't park there!"

Story nearly crashed into the reception desk. She stuck her head through the sliding glass window. "Anyone here?"

The nurse returned from shooing off two rule-breakers. "Can I help you?"

"Howard Long, what room?"

The nurse checked a log again. "Three-twelve, but he's only seeing immediate relatives."

"I'm his sister."

"You'll have fill out a visitor's pass," said the nurse. "What about her?"

Story scribbled quickly. "Beth's a close friend."

"I'm sorry . . ."

"It's okay," said Beth. "I'll wait here."

Story stuck the adhesive label on her shirt and ran for the elevators. She was half out of her mind as she ran past rooms, counting numbers, 302, 303, 304 . . .

Two detectives and a uniformed officer approached just as quickly from the opposite direction and arrived first.

"Stay right there by the door," one of the investigators directed the uniform. "Don't let anyone inside unless personally cleared by me."

"What's going on?" asked Story.

"Who are you?"

"The sister of the patient in there."

"Can I see some identification?"

She opened her wallet. The detective studied a student ID and handed it back. "Your brother was the victim of a robbery."

"Robbery?" said Story. "What? For souvenirs?"

"Businessmen traveling alone are common targets at motels."

The other detective stepped forward. "Miss Long, did your brother ever mention anything about diamonds?"

"Diamonds? Why? No."

"Maybe he didn't tell you for your own safety."

"He told me everything. What's the guard for?"

The detective glanced briefly at the uniform. "Just got word. Nothing definite, but he may have been hit by the same people responsible for a string of similar crimes over the last month."

"So again, why the guard?"

The detective bit his lip.

"Whatever it is," said Story. "I can take it."

The detective knew people—knew she could. "You might want to have a seat."

"I'll stand."

"Okay, two of the other victims didn't make it. We think your brother got a good look, which is why they left him . . ." The detective stopped.

"For dead?" said Story.

"If it is the same people, your brother may be the only living witness."

"Are you saying they'll come back?"

"This is just a precaution."

Story took an extra-deep breath. "Can I see him now?"

"We'll have to pat you down."

"But you saw my ID."

"Sorry, ma'am, but I'm sure you'd want us to take every safeguard."

"You're right."

"It'll only take a few minutes for a female officer to arrive."

"Can't *you* pat me down?"

"Against the rules . . ." He felt the emotion in her face. "Hell with it: Go on in."

She involuntarily froze at the doorway. There he was, her baby brother, all gauze and beeping machines, face unrecognizably swollen, one leg hanging from a pulley. She walked quietly to the side of the bed. Crying would only upset him. She used her strength to smile.

Howard looked back up and parted his mouth slightly, but nothing came out.

"Shhhhh." Story gently patted his arm. "Don't talk now. Just rest."

He opened his mouth again, the sound of a weak breath. Then, in the quietest possible voice. "Ser . . ."

"Ser . . .?"

His eyes went to a bedside table and a Ziploc bag of personal possessions. Story opened it and went through his wallet, finding an oddly handwritten business card with a Web address. She turned it toward her brother. "Is that what you're trying to tell me?"

The slightest nod from Howard. Another weak breath and finally the full word. "Serge . . ."

"Serge?" said Story. "Who's Serge? Is he the one who did this to you?!"

Howard strained to say something, but lost consciousness first.

Part Three

BACK TO THE PRESENT

CHAPTER 30

U.S. HIGHWAY 1

*S*erge's Blog. Star date 574.385.

I'm writing this entry in my mind while driving for efficient time management. But there should be no problem transcribing this tonight back at the hotel because I have an excellent memory. Or at least used to. Been forgetting things lately, like at The Last Resort Bar and Dodgertown. Is my mind slipping? Here I am again, tooling down my beloved Florida on another fabulous morning, exactly what I love to do most in the world, watching scenery go by: palmettos, petticoat palms, some guy living in a wheelless Airstream, roadwork ahead, another town, another sign at the city limits telling me the Kiwanis and Moose Lodge are glad I'm here, old billboards, fresh-squeezed orange juice, pecan logs, Jesus knows what's ailin' me, that cop pulling over a speeder with a pair of checkered flags flapping from the windows of his sports car. Ain't life wacky? So why aren't I happy? Look at Coleman over there, blissfully content. Maybe *I* should do drugs. And how do I explain that nagging feeling I've been having lately that won't go away? What if Mahoney's right? Or what if it's all a trick? Of course! He's trying to rattle me into a fatal mistake by getting inside my head. Well, good luck Mahoney! But how do I explain the sleepwalking? I've never done that before. And I'm not even taking those new medications from the TV commercials that CNN says have side effects of people sleepwalking to the fridge at night or waking up behind the wheel of a car going seventy. What's happening to our republic? We used to be tougher than that. But today the pharmaceutical companies encourage us to whine like babies and take a bunch of pills that aren't supposed to be handled by women who are pregnant or may become pregnant: My bad cholesterol's too high, my good cholesterol's too low, sometimes I'm sad, I pee a lot, I can't nod off, my legs are restless, my acid refluxes, diarrhea interrupts my active life-style, uninvited relatives show up right after I've taken a pill to bang my wife, which is why we're sitting in separate bathtubs on a bluff overlooking a cornfield. But they never consult me. The problem's obvious; everyone's too tired to fuck from lugging bathtubs. I know what you're thinking: Coleman and I have sat in our share of hilltop tubs, but that's something else. I just see things on TV and want to participate in my times. Like right now I'm applying something directly to my forehead. Had to buy a new stick of that stuff because I wasn't about to put it back on my forehead after catching Coleman rubbing it on his dick. I said, 'Coleman, why are you rubbing that on your dick?' He said, 'What have I got to lose?' What indeed. Here's another city line, Elks and Optimists thrilled to see me. But it all comes back to Mahoney and sleepwalking. One minute I'm closing my eyes on the pillow, the next I'm standing over Coleman. With a gun no less! That's what really scares me. What could I have been thinking? Hope it wasn't a murder-suicide. I don't *feel* suicidal, but who knows what's going on in my subconscious? I mean, yeah, I've given a lot of thought to suicide. Who hasn't? But it's within the normal psychological range where everyone else thinks about it on a daily basis, like, remember to pick up some milk at the store and take the trash down to the curb and don't forget not to blow your brains out. It would be totally against my nature—unless Mahoney's onto something. What if he and my sub-conscious know something I don't? Maybe my pre-amphibian brain sees fate just around the corner, and it would be better to end it myself instead of what *they* have in mind. Then it would only be logical to take Coleman out first. Because if I'm gone, who would handle his care and feeding? At that point, it would be an airtight mercy killing. Actually, it would be at any time. But I'm not one to play God. I have from time to time, but only when God's running late. I don't schedule the killing urge. Society does, like when I buy a new DVD that won't let me skip through the ads for other DVDs. It's not even a rental; I own the goddamn thing, and *then* I have to sit through a fucking Interpol warning until I'm ready to grab the next European I see and shove a bumbershoot up his ass. Hmmm, maybe I *should* warn Coleman. He could be in great danger. Tell him before he goes to sleep to surround his bed with peanut shells or bubble wrap. No, he sleeps too soundly to hear me. What about mousetraps? No, that would hurt too much. Dang, missed an exit. Isn't it odd how you can hear your own voice inside your head? My mouth will be completely shut, like now, and I'm hearing these words perfectly pronounced. I can even turn up the VOLUME FOR EMPHASIS. Or yell: AHHHH! AHHH! Yet, outside my head, perfectly quiet. Or like when you're reading a book and hear the character talking inside *your* noggin with a voice you give him. Hey, I just thought of something: If it's internal dialogue in the book, is it doubled for the reader? You know: a character talking inside his brain, who's also talking inside *your* brain. Is that why I usually get an echo, *echo, echo*? What about you, *you, you*? Missed another exit. Then there are the other voices in my head: Mahoney, regretfully, and God, who's mainly silent, and the devil, who sounds like Henry Kissinger: "Serge, do it, do it, do it. You won't get caught. Do it. And while you're at it, kill Coleman." I sure hope I'm not planning a murder-suicide . . . Uh-oh, Coleman's staring at me . . .

"Coleman, was I just talking to myself?"

He shook his head.

"You didn't hear a word?"

"No, what's the matter?"

"Nothing." Serge reached for the sun visor and pulled down some kind of yellow styrene implement.

"What's that?" asked Coleman.

"Florida device nobody up north would ever recognize: canal-survival tool."

"Never heard of it."

"You know how in Michigan they have windshield ice scrapers? This is the Sunshine State's counterpart. Down here we don't have ice; we have drainage canals. Friggin' deep too, often running right alongside the road. Some of the ones south of Lake Okeechobee go down twenty feet or more. Combine that with south Florida's well-earned 'Most Reckless Drivers in America' crown, and you've got pimped-out whips constantly spinning off roads and diving into the drink. Miami-Dade actually has police vans that say, 'Submerged-Vehicle Response Unit.'"

"That little tool thing keeps you from going off the road?"

"No, it gets you out of the car." Serge tapped the end of the tool on the side of his head. "Ow . . . Lots of people were drowning from not being able to get their electric windows open. Became so common in south Florida that it barely warranted a paragraph on page twelve of the metro section. Luckily some corporations took notice of grieving relatives at the funerals and said, Hey, I see a way to make a buck here."

"How's it work?"

"The windows are safety glass, so smacking it with your elbow won't make the grade. These survival tools don't look particularly threatening, being small and plastic, but it's the brilliance of elemental engineering that turns them into lifesaving super-hammers. The metal head is tapered to a fine point, concentrating the pounds-per-square-inch force at impact."

"Can I see?"

"Sure." Serge passed it across the front seat.

Coleman turned the tool over and ran his finger along a sharp strip of metal indented in the side. "What's this razor thing halfway down?"

"Second challenge of canal submersion. Seat belts. People panic or the buckle jams in the crash. And tearing the strap with your bare hands is even less possible than breaking windows. So just slip the edge of the strap in this indentation, give it a yank, and the razor edge slices like butter. Out of the car you go."

Coleman reached into his lap and pulled. "You're right."

"Coleman, you fucked up the seat belt. You're supposed to be underwater first."

"But that would be harder."

"Gimme that thing." He jerked it from Coleman's hands. "Now I'm going to have to tie you to the seat with a boat-trailer strap."

"When do you think we can use it for real?"

"Never. I rarely drive by canals."

"Then why'd you get it?"

"Coolest gadget by the cash register. It was this or the tire gauge, but I decided to be practical." Serge slid it into his hip pocket. "It's my new good-luck charm. From now on I'm carrying it everywhere."

YET ANOTHER EXTENDED COMFORT EXPRESS SUITES USA

"Serge," said Coleman. "All these motel lounges look the same. Why don't we go to a cool bar?"

"Because I'm working on my travel service . . ." Serge twisted his stool toward a group of pushed-together tables. ". . . And keeping Steve under surveillance."

"Still?"

"The Master Plan takes patience."

"But we've seen him in like ten hotels now where you could have nailed him. I thought you were in a hurry to take revenge for Howard."

"Steve's a minnow," said Serge. "But he's also the sole person that Howard ever met who was connected to the robbery crew. It was the only name he could give me."

"When you talked to him in the hospital?"

Serge nodded. "I've been waiting for Steve to make personal contact with the gang and lead me to bigger fish, but so far just cell phone calls."

Coleman turned and looked toward the far end of the bar, where Story sat with militant disinterest as a storm-shutter salesman chatted her up.

"What's she doing?" asked Coleman.

"Working on her twenty-dollar-bill collection."

"Let's go to a cool bar."

"Hold everything." Serge suddenly perked. "I think our luck just changed."

"What is it?"

"Those two goons with stringy hair talking to Steve."

"He looks scared."

"Now one grabbed his arm and is pulling him toward the lobby." Serge tossed currency on the bar. "We're rolling."

Serge and Coleman shadowed the bodyguards as they hustled Steve into an alcove where pay phones had been removed.

"What do you think they're talking about?"

"If my hunch is correct, Steve's been tardy with inside dope on their next mark."

Steve gestured excitedly.

"Looks like he's making up for lost time."

"Act inconspicuous," said Serge. "Whatever you do, don't attract the least bit of attention."

"How do I do that?"

"Like me. Pretend you're looking at this rack of tourist pamphlets . . ."

Crash. The goons looked.

". . . Or knock the whole thing over."

"Don't worry." Coleman got on his knees. "I'll pick 'em all up."

"No time. They're on the move."

The goons left Steve behind. Serge and Coleman followed them to the fifth floor.

"Think that's their room?" asked Coleman.

"Not the way they're buttering up the maid and patting their pockets in the universal lost-key signal."

"She's letting them in."

"Must be the next mark," said Serge, picking up the pace. "Keep walking by the room or they'll get suspicious."

"Is this the beginning of your revenge?"

"Remember the end of the first *Godfather* movie during the baptism?"

"It ruled! All those guys killed in a row. My favorite was the dude who got a bullet through his glasses."

"What I've got planned will make that look like *The Bridges of Madison County*."

FIFTEEN MINUTES LATER

The burglary "talent" had thinned to the point that bodyguards were pressed into service, and the art of the silent search gave way to Attila the Hun.

"Find anything?" asked one of the goons, smashing a phone on the nightstand.

"Not yet," said the other, flinging a dresser drawer against a wall.

"The stones have to be here somewhere." Smash. Numbered phone buttons flew.

Knock-knock.

They spun.

"Who the hell's that?"

"Maybe the guy came back early."

"You idiot. He's not going to knock on his own door." He set the phone chassis down. "Just be quiet and whoever it is will go away."

Knock-knock-knock.

They stood still.

Knock-knock-knock.

A whisper: "He's not going away."

Knock-knock-knock.

"He will."

Knock-knock-knock.

"Dammit."

"You better check the peephole."

Knock-knock-knock.

A goon's eye went to the small glass hole.

"See anyone?"

The man at the door shook his head. He pressed his eye closer for a wider field of vision, not noticing the flattened end of a brown paper bag sliding under the door.

"See anyone now?"

"Nope."

Suddenly, a muffled pop outside the door. The man looked down, pants leg splattered with shaving cream. "Son of a bitch!" He opened the door and lunged, expecting the prankster to be hightailing it down the hall.

Instead, the end of an emergency canal-survival tool landed between his eyes.

He reeled backward, hands over his bloody face. "Fuck!"

Serge's other hand held a chrome automatic. "Down on the floor! Both of you! Hands behind your back!"

The two-tone Javelin sped through Indiantown on the Bee Line Highway. Deeper into the state, into the night. They were riding the new moon. No illumination but stars and the Javelin's high beams, occasionally reflecting off mystery wildlife eyes in dense thickets of cabbage palms.

Coleman strained to see above the beams. "Serge, there's nothing out here."

"*Everything's* out here," said Serge. "Nature's what it's all about, but our people have been brainwashed into thinking that life is a cell phone against your head and the TV on a beer commercial with hot chicks."

"It isn't?"

Serge reached over and lightly tapped the top of Coleman's head with the window punch.

"Ow!" He rubbed his skull. "What was that for?"

"Debriefing you."

Two lights appeared in the distance. Serge grabbed a lever on the steering column, popping down to low beams.

"Serge?"

"That's me."

"I don't like being tied to my seat with a boat-trailer strap."

"I say this with complete sincerity: It's you."

An oncoming poultry truck passed precariously close on the narrow two-laner that slanted across the state, connecting West Palm Beach with Lake Okeechobee. Serge clicked back to high beams. "When you say Florida, everyone thinks the coasts. But inland, there's an entire 'nother world to appreciate. The Highwaymen picked up on this, and before them the Tin Can Tourists."

"Who were they?"

"Started as a loose movement of noble people from up north, who appreciated the state for its intrinsic magnificence and began driving down way before all the motels and tourist attractions. Many slept roadside in tents and bathed in rivers. Others soon began towing small aluminum campers. The first official group coalesced in 1919 at Tampa's DeSoto Park."

"What's the name mean?"

"Subject to debate. Some consider it a sobriquet for those shiny campers, while others think it's because many of the original visitors cooked soup in tin cans placed on radiator caps."

Coleman turned around in his seat. "There's that banging sound again."

"Note to self: soundproof trunk."

"What are you going to do with those two dudes we grabbed in the motel room?"

"Serve up a feast of inland Florida splendor. With a side order of revenge."

The Javelin's red taillights blew through a junction at the county line. A vulture took flight. Coleman's joint glowed. "So, like, if there weren't any theme parks, then these Tin Can guys drove down here just to hang around doing nothing?"

"Coleman, that's my whole point. They came purely for spiritual communion with our rapidly diminishing natural beauty, perfectly happy to just sit out among pristine tributaries, marshes, prairie vistas, upland hammocks. To enjoy it today, people think they need Mickey's Upland Hammock Flume of Terror and Alligator Jug Band Jamboree." Serge grabbed a slender book off the dash.

"What's that?"

"Audubon field guide to identify flora and fauna. A must if you're going to dig inland Florida," said Serge. "People have no idea all the critters that roam these parts."

Bang, bang, bang, bang.

Coleman turned around again. "I think they want out."

"Their wish will soon come true." Serge stuck his head through the driver's open window and looked up at constellations. "Let's see how many I can name. There's Gemini, Pegasus, Ursa Major and Minor, Benny the Truculent Dry Cleaner." He brought his wind-blown head back inside. "Couldn't have picked a better night to reenact the Tin Can lifestyle."

"Serge! Watch out!"

But Serge had already seen it. A husky dark form dashed across the road. Serge swerved right.

From miles of back-road experience, he knew its mate could be right behind. Sure enough, a second, smaller form exploded from the underbrush. Serge slalomed the other way.

"Jesus!" said Coleman. "What the hell was that?"

Serge handed Coleman the field guide. "Page three-seventy-four."

"You know it by heart?"

Bang, bang, bang.

Serge glanced back at the trunk, then the field guide in Coleman's hands. "That gives me an idea."

CHAPTER 31

OKEECHOBEE COUNTY

*S*erge leaned into the Javelin's open trunk with a tape measure. "Stop flopping around or I won't get your right size. Trust me: You definitely don't want the *wrong* size . . ."

"Serge," said Coleman. "I'm getting tired."

"Just keep digging." Serge slammed the trunk and let the tape measure zip itself shut. He grabbed his own shovel and opened a low, rickety wooden gate in a barbed-wire fence. They began digging side by side. Every few minutes, Serge stopped and extended his tape measure into each of the two holes. All around them: nothing but peaceful darkness, trees bending in the wind. The only sign of human life nearly a mile away.

Coleman leaned against the end of his shovel for breath. "What if the farmer sees us?"

Serge stood chest deep in his own hole. A spade of dirt flew over his shoulder. "Too far away and probably asleep. Plus, his view is obstructed."

Coleman looked up through a line of trees, where a porch light from a very distant farmhouse flickered in the branches. "Hope you're right." He resumed digging. A continuous grunting sound. Some of it was Coleman; some wasn't. "Those things give me the creeps."

On the far side of the fenced-in pen, dark forms milled about with guttural communication. "They're totally harmless," said Serge. "At least to us."

A half hour later, another check with the tape measure. Serge was satisfied with his own hole. He walked over to Coleman's and extended the metal strip. Not even close.

"Coleman, climb out and let me finish or we'll be here all night."

The edge of the second hole was at Coleman's bellybutton. He tried to pull himself out. He fell six inches back down. He tried again. Same results. He panicked and attempted to scramble up the side, sneakers digging into the soil wall.

"Coleman, stop that. You're just pulling dirt back down into the hole."

"I'm going to die!"

Serge yanked Coleman up by the armpits. Then he jumped in the second hole and quickly finished the task with a flurry of shovel action. One last measure with the tape. He nodded. "Time to welcome today's lucky contestants."

Serge went back to the trunk, pulled out the first hostage and slammed the hood. The man's hands were bound behind his back, but his feet were free. Serge ordered him at gunpoint through the squeaky gate. The man saw the holes. Terror. About to be buried alive! He took off running, but Serge quickly tackled him in the mud.

"Listen to him trying to scream," said Coleman.

"That's why I love duct tape." Serge dragged the squirming man by the ankles and reached the edge of a hole. He pushed him in feet first. A horrified scream from behind the mouth tape. Until the man's shoes hit bottom. Confusion replaced dread. The man looked around, the hole's edge only up to his neck.

Serge grabbed a shovel and began filling dirt in around their guest.

"Putting the dirt back around a guy looks easier," said Coleman.

"That's always been my experience."

Minutes later, Serge was done. He stomped in a circle around the man's head, packing ground firmly.

"What now?" asked Coleman.

"Like shampoo. Repeat as needed." He went back to the trunk for the second hostage. Into the other hole. Dirt shoveled in. Serge's soil-packing dance again.

Two heads looked up with wide, puzzled eyes.

Serge smiled back. "Inland Florida is such a hoot!"

Time passed. An invisible moon tacked across the sky. The Javelin's engine was running with the front hood up. A metal can rested on the radiator cap.

"Can you dig it?" Serge swept an arm across the dim panorama. "We're blessed with a rare opportunity to soak in the pure, untainted natural essence of Florida exactly as the original Tin Can Tourists found her almost a century ago."

"Even wiggling heads sticking out of the ground?"

"Especially wiggling heads. Florida's changed, but people haven't." Serge dipped a spoon into the can and tested a sip. "Still too cold."

"Can I try?"

"Go for it."

Coleman ladled a spoon into his mouth. "Ow. That's pretty hot."

"Not for me," said Serge. "I demand all my soup be tongue-blistering."

"Then how do you eat it?"

"I don't. It's way too hot. I have to blow on it awhile. That's why I love soup! Anticipation building while I blow until I lose interest and dump it out."

Coleman peered back through the barbed wire at what looked like two bowling balls in the darkness. "I still don't get what you have planned for those dudes."

"Plan's complete." Serge wrapped a towel around the tin can and removed it from the radiator. "Mechanism's already in motion, totally self-contained and under its own renewable, earth-friendly power."

Coleman pointed at the radiator. "May I?"

"Be my guest."

Coleman stepped forward with his own can. It was empty and dry. He set it on the radiator cap, then began breaking up pot buds and dropping them inside.

Serge rubbed his chin. "I'm not sure I want to ask."

"Old party technique, but you have to know someone who's no Bogart." Coleman meticulously disassembled another bud. "Fill an aluminum can with a two-finger bag, stick it on a hot plate in a bathroom, then cram as many people as you can inside and hyperventilate. You want to talk about *high*."

"What made you think of trying it here?"

"All your history talk." Coleman turned his Baggie upside down, emptying residual shake into the can. "Dope goes way back. Bet anything those Tin Can guys were getting righteously ripped."

Serge dumped chicken noodle on the ground. "Why do you say that?"

"You're kidding, right?" Coleman looked at the surrounding fields and woods and marshland. "No TV out here. And back before TV, dope *was* TV. All the heads understand this." Tendrils of smoke began snaking out of Coleman's can. He bent over and inhaled deeply. "Like you know how one of my favorite TV shows will be coming on, and I'll fix myself a plate of Cheetos and torch a mondo fattie?" Coleman leaned for another deep breath. "Then I'll get so stoned I forget to turn on the TV and just watch my reflection in the blank tube for a half hour? Still a good show."

A chorus of grunting in the background. Serge turned toward the fenced pen. "Speaking of show . . ."

On the other side of the gate, the gathering of dark forms began to emerge from shadows.

"Hey," said Coleman. "Those pigs don't have those things."

"That's pretty specific."

"You know what I mean," said Coleman, wiggling an index finger on each side of his nose. "The pointy deals on the wild pigs we saw run in front of the car."

"Tusks."

"I thought when you handed me your field guide and said the pigs gave you an idea, we were going to bury these guys so they could get stabbed in the head with tusks."

"That would be gross."

"I was looking forward to it."

"Those were wild boar, but they gave me the idea because people all around these parts raise livestock pigs," said Serge. "Most people don't realize how extremely intelligent they are because of their poor hygiene. But pigs roll in the mud to cool off because they don't have sweat glands."

"What are they doing now?"

"Sniffing the heads." Serge walked over and leaned on one of the fence posts like a ranch hand. "Incredible sense of smell. That's how they find truffles. Another thing about pigs is they're omnivorous. Nature's garbage disposal. Devour absolutely anything, I mean *anything*."

"Eat their own poop?"

"Coleman, you ask me that same question every day, except this is the first time it's in context. Yes, they do."

"What about attack?"

"No, just your friendly foragers. But if something's conveniently left on their plate, like a dead or injured animal that can't move much, they won't send it back to the kitchen. And afterward, nothing left, no hair, not even the smallest bone."

"Like piranha?"

"No. Well, yes. Well, maybe super-slow-motion piranha. They just kind of gently nibble at their own relaxed pace. It's actually kinda cute."

"Like what that first pig is doing to the top of that guy's scalp?"

"Field guides are worth every penny."

Four hours later, the sun rose on foggy, dew-covered fields. The farmer had been making his rounds since well before first light. He left the chicken coop for a short tractor drive down the hill to his pigpen, where he hoisted a hefty burlap sack and began scattering feed to the swine herd. Nothing out of the ordinary, just like every other morning—except for a pair of barely noticeable reddish-brown circles in the mud at ground level.

CHAPTER 32

BIG WATER

End of another day in paradise. The atmospheric conditions were Serge's favorite. Cirrus clouds refracted the setting sun into chromatic brilliance, while a distant storm front sent flaming shafts across some of the most wide-open ranch and wetlands in all of central Florida. Nearer to his vantage, waning light peeked through palms and danced off a tiny nest of silver mobile homes.

Serge and Coleman had binoculars. Serge scanned the horizon. Coleman uncapped an eyepiece on his nonfunctioning pair and swigged from the hidden flask inside. Serge panned to the south. "Absolutely beautiful. I can never get enough of the lake."

"Lake?" said Coleman. "Thought that was the ocean."

"Coleman, we're in the middle of the state."

"Are you sure? I can't see the other side."

"Because it's Lake Okeechobee. *Big Water* in the Native-American tongue."

"What's that smell?"

"Baked muck. Never seen the lake level so low." Binoculars panned the eastern shore. "Down at least eight feet from the drought, killing the local sportsmen economy. Probably finding all kinds of bodies and weapons and stolen cars at receded banks. On the bright side, it's the perfect opportunity to *add* bodies." Serge pulled out a pen and pad. "Note to self: . . ."

Coleman looked over a railing, got dizzy and stumbled back. "How high up are we?"

"Five-story viewing platform. I'm helpless to resist viewing platforms, and my life record is still intact: never passed one without stopping and climbing to the top, or at least being told to get off the fence if the gate is locked."

"What's that giant grass wall in front of the shore?"

"Massive berm. Runs all the way around the lake. That's why we have to be up here to see the water."

Coleman chugged his binoculars. "What's the berm for?"

"To prevent a repeat of the '28 hurricane, which literally pushed the lake onto the surrounding countryside, killing hundreds."

Coleman walked across the platform and looked over the opposite railing at a flat tar roof. "I've never seen a viewing platform on top of a motel before."

"It's the Pier 2 Resort." Serge jotted in the notebook. "That's why they're getting extra-high marks in my report. They didn't have to, but the owners spared no expense for the enjoyment of their paying guests."

"So this is our hotel tonight?"

"No, we snuck up here." Serge slipped his notepad in a pocket. "Let's go to the bar."

They climbed down and started across the parking lot. Coleman poked Serge. "The hotel's back there. Where are you going?"

"To the bar."

Serge headed away from civilization and toward the lake. Just outside the berm, the lake was surrounded by a man-made access waterway, which shallowed into a dense swamp that stretched the last couple hundred yards to shore. Serge reached the edge of land and stopped at a sign: NO SWIMMING. BEWARE OF ALLIGATORS.

Coleman caught up. "*That's* the bar?"

"One of the finest in all of Florida."

They strolled a lengthy boardwalk. Ahead: a small building on stilts in the middle of the swamp. Serge circled its wraparound porch until they reached another boardwalk that extended from the pub's screened-in back deck, farther toward the lake.

"Serge, we just passed the bar."

"Exactly. I'm checking all escape routes. Then we enter from the rear. They won't expect that."

"Who won't?"

But Serge just kept walking. Even though the planks were elevated a good six feet, the surrounding reeds and cattails reached above their heads and, with the growing darkness, came alive in a racket of nightlife.

Coleman clutched Serge's sleeve with both hands. "What's all that eerie noise?"

"Bullfrogs and insects."

"What?"

"*Bullfrogs and insects!*"

"It's freakin' loud!"

"That's the thing about inland Florida. The coasts deceive us into thinking we humans are running things, but out here you realize nature's the true boss and can swallow you in a blink."

"Serge, I'm scared."

"We're perfectly safe up here, just stay on the boardwalk. Whatever else you do, keep telling yourself: Never get off the boardwalk."

Serge eventually came to the end of the pier. The water's surface was, as they say, like glass, reflecting the last twilight, perfect for picking out ominous, drifting bumps.

"There's an alligator," said Serge. "And another. And another. Man, they're everywhere! Coleman, let's see how many we can count. Five, ten, fifteen . . . Coleman? . . ."

Serge turned around. Empty boardwalk.

"Coleman!" His eyes shot left and right. Off to the side, a cluster of nearby reeds shook wildly. Serge ran over. "Coleman! What are you doing down there?"

"I found this big dope plant!" More shaking vegetation. "I can't get it loose. Come help me."

"Coleman, it's just a swamp reed."

"Are you sure?"

"I'm sure you're an idiot. Give me your hand!"

Serge reeled him up just as unseen reptilian jaws snapped below his feet.

Coleman rubbed scratched-up palms on his pants. "*Now* can we go to the bar for that meeting of yours?"

"Sure, he's here."

"You just saw him arrive?"

"No, he's been here the whole time."

"Then why weren't we in the bar?"

"Had to give the alcohol time to take effect."

They entered through the back deck. Tables pushed together again in the middle of the room. The Okeechobee Coin & Stamp Show.

Serge and Coleman proceeded directly to a pair of empty stools at the bar. A draft and bottled water arrived.

Coleman toasted his buddy. "Pretty cool joint."

"One of the coolest." Serge pointed above rows of bottles behind the bartender, where three-sided bay windows provided a panorama of the darkening swamp. "That's my number one rule for bars: All the best have views behind the bottles, like the revolving lounge at Tampa International or the top of La Concha in Key West. Except those have views *over* stuff. This is even better, looking out from *inside* the swamp."

Coleman signaled for a refill. "Where's Story? I almost forgot about her."

"Studying back at the motel."

"I didn't see her at the motel, either."

"Got her a separate room."

"What for?"

"Our relationship is progressing more rapidly than I'd anticipated. We're getting on each other's nerves."

"How do you know it's the relationship? Men and women do that anyway."

"You're right," said Serge. "But she's also started using sex as a weapon."

"What's that?"

"Remember how the Romans built their empire by laying siege to a city? Think of that with guest towels."

"Can I use sex as a weapon?"

"You already do, except in your case it's a nuclear deterrent."

"But she's still hanging with us, right?"

"She's still with us, just won't be around as often now that classes are about to start at the college."

Coleman turned toward the crowd at the tables. "Where's Steve?"

"Over there on the end."

"Why didn't you meet with him before, right after we saw him talking with those guys you left in the pigpen?"

"Because the Master Plan has to evolve and constantly change its approach, or the gang will scatter before I have a chance to pick off a satisfying number."

"So how'd you convince Steve to meet?"

"Oh, he doesn't know we're meeting. That's why this has to be handled very delicately. My gambit must be completely . . ."

Coleman stuck two fingers in his mouth and made a shrill whistle. "Yo! Steve!" Big waving motion with his arm. "Over here!"

". . . subtle. Thanks, Coleman."

Steve came over and gave the pair a look of non-recognition. "Do I know you?"

"Met a bunch of times," said Serge. "Hotel bars."

Steve didn't like the vibe. "Sorry, you got the wrong guy. I don't know you."

"Let me buy you a drink."

"I remember you now." He grabbed a stool. "Bart?"

"Serge."

Steve raised a finger to the bartender. "Double Chivas on the rocks, his tab." He turned to Serge. "So how's business been?"

"Business is wonderful! Couldn't be better! So good, in fact, that I have a proposition for you."

Steve laughed. "I've heard this come-on before. Should have known: There's no such thing as a free drink."

"Seriously," said Serge. "My business is taking off."

"It's on the tip of my tongue," said Steve. "Your business was . . ."

Serge leaned and lowered his voice. "I fix problems. Heard you have a big one."

Steve cocked his head back with a new expression. "Who are you, really?"

"Close friend of Howard Long."

"Howard?"

"The guy who sold vintage Florida souvenirs at your shows."

"*Ohhhhh.*" Steve began nodding. "I remember him. Great kid.

Just terrible what happened to him. Absolute shame, the decline of this state."

"Interesting perspective since you were in on it."

"Huh? Me? . . ."—pointing over-innocently at his own chest—". . . What are you talking about. I barely knew the guy."

"You recruited him to be a courier. He told me in the hospital," said Serge. "But I could always be wrong. I'll check with the police—"

"Okay, okay, look . . ." Steve glanced around, then scooted closer. "I lied about not knowing him because the whole courier thing is very confidential and I don't know who you guys are. But if you say he told you at the hospital . . . I mean, you understand my position."

"I understand your position. Ten percent."

"What?"

"More or less. But ten would be the standard cut for fingering Howard."

"I have no idea what you're—"

"You recruited him, and he gets hit on the first run. What are the odds? Nobody knew where he was staying or that he was holding. Except you."

Steve shook his head and got off his stool. "Thanks for the drink."

Serge raised the edge of his tropical shirt, revealing a pistol butt. "Don't be rude."

Steve sat back down and became verbally incontinent. ". . . I'm so sorry. It was all a mistake. He wasn't even supposed to be in the room. These guys are crazy. They'll kill me. I just want to sell coins. You're not going to kill me, are you? I'm so sorry . . ."

"Get a grip. And stop crying—you're attracting attention."

He sniffled and wiped his eyes.

"That's better." Serge handed him a napkin. "Nobody's going to kill you. At least I'm not. But you have to do me a favor."

Steve blew his nose. "What is it?"

"I'm guessing right about now the gang is pretty pissed at you for the two guys they lost going after your last target."

"You know about that?"

Serge smiled.

"Oh my God!"

"Keep your shit together," said Serge. "I told you: I fix problems. If you go back to them with a new courier, it could go a long way toward smoothing ruffled feathers."

"But I don't have a new courier."

"I do. The perfect guy."

"Who?"

Serge beamed and thumped his chest. "Me!"

"*You?*"

"I know. Isn't it great?" Serge slapped Steve on the back. "We're going to be partners! Spending all kinds of time together, barbecuing in each other's backyards . . ."

Tears returned. "I can't take this anymore."

"I'm afraid you're between a rock and a hard place. Of course I'm the one who put you there. Sometimes I'm the rock, sometimes the hard place, sometimes both if there's enough elbow room."

"You're insane."

"Just plug me into your network, and I'll handle the rest."

"Can't do that."

"You don't have a choice."

"No, I mean my distributor will never go for it. He'll smell this a mile away."

"Look, I'm not going to be a real courier. So there won't be any gems to worry about."

"I don't understand."

"I'm asking you to plug me into the gang, not your distributor," said Serge. "You just *tell* the crew I'm your new recruit."

"Why on earth would you want me to do that?"

"It's better you don't know. I'm watching out for your safety. They can beat you stupid for days, and what can you tell them?"

Sobbing again.

Serge pulled a scrap of paper from his wallet and slid it along the bar. "Here's where we'll meet tomorrow night."

Steve studied the address. "What's this place?"

"Excellent joint. I've been dying to go there. If you survive long enough, we'll get to see all kinds of Florida funk together. It'll be a gas, right, Coleman?"

"All party, all the time . . . You do weed?"

"What?"

"Just meet us there at seven," said Serge. "I'll give you all the details to feed the gang so they can take me down."

"Take you down?" said Steve. "You really *are* insane."

"Going to play ball?"

"Forget it. Those guys will kill me for sure if they ever find out."

"Then I'm afraid I'll just have to go to the gang myself and tell them you've been blabbing. Sorry, I don't make the rock-and-hard-place rules."

"Dear God . . ."

"Let you in on the big secret," said Serge. "They're already going to kill you. My guess is sooner rather than later."

"But we're in business together."

"You're a tool. When you finally want out, you think they're just going to let you walk away: 'Hey guys, it's been a load of yuks.' Then you'll go to another routine meeting to get your final cut, and the Coast Guard will find your torso in a shipping channel. Your torso doesn't have any tattoos, does it?"

Steve shook his head.

"Then it'll be your torso."

"But why would they do that?"

"Because you're a schmuck. One of the biggest risks they have right now is you eventually turning state's evidence, and that's a risk they'll never take."

"Dear Jesus, what am I going to do?"

"You're in luck!" Serge grinned and put an arm around Steve's quivering shoulders. "I'm your only hope."

CHAPTER 33

THE NEXT EVENING

*A*nother multi-hued sunset over Okeechobee. An orange-and-green Javelin rolled slowly along the edge of the lake. It turned onto a gravel drive in front of a massive aluminum building with no doors or windows.

Coleman bent toward the windshield. "What in the hell is that?"

Half the letters were missing on the side of the structure, and passers-by had to play *Wheel of Fortune* to make out the name.

"Stardust Lanes!" said Serge, driving slowly around the west side of the building. "I love bowling alleys! Along with pool halls, they're among the last museums of the old ways."

"What's it doing out here in the middle of the swamp?"

"That's why I love this place so much," said Serge. "Nobody expects it here. It's a complete geographical non sequitur, like when that NASA probe beamed back photos of Elvis's face on the surface of Mars."

"We're going to bowl?"

Serge shook his head. "You can, but my unorthodox style always invites conflict with the management."

"What's your style?"

"You know when a bowler releases the ball, it travels a short distance before landing in the lane and rolling the rest of the way to the pins?"

"Yeah, that's how everyone plays."

"Because they don't have the kind of imagination that gives me total advantage. I've never seen any rule that says how far down the lane the ball must land. My patented style exploits this loophole. I twirl three times like an Olympic hammer throw and release in a forty-degree arc. If the ceiling's high enough, it hits the pins on the fly. Unbeatable technique. The rest of the competition weeps from inadequacy and pawns their equipment."

"You can actually hit the pins on the fly?"

"In theory. But bowling balls are fucking heavy. Plus, with all my twirling, there's no telling what direction the ball will go. I tried explaining to the last owners that this is precisely the kind of excitement the sport needs to fill those empty lanes, but they wouldn't stop yelling."

"Why were they yelling?"

"In my first frame, I got excellent hang time and the ball made it most of the way down the lane. Except it was the third lane over. Landed a few feet in front of the pins and stuck, just the top half of the ball poking out of the wood. They wouldn't even let me pick up the spare."

The Javelin curled around the back of the building, which was the front. Serge and Coleman trotted up steps and went inside. Serge stopped by the front desk, closed his eyes and took a deep breath. An irrepressible smile crept across his face. "Coleman, listen to that symphony: baritone of balls rolling in staggered sequence, clattering of pins, guy across the desk from me spraying disinfectant in rental shoes that you'd never think of wearing if you saw the last guy."

"Sir, are you okay?"

Serge opened his eyes and looked across the desk at the manager. "I'm freakin' great! Hope you are, too!"

"Do you want to bowl?"

"Oh, I want to bowl all right, but I don't know what kind of insurance you have."

"What?"

"Coleman, come on!"

"Serge, wait up! You're running away from the lanes."

"We're going to the bar."

"They have a bar?"

"Remember when we were talking in the car about how strange this place was? That was only the tip of the berg. Its bizarreness quotient is about to go off scale."

They reached a pair of double doors. Serge pointed at a sign: THE ORBIT LOUNGE. "Even if they bring nothing else to the table, any joint called The Orbit Lounge is priceless. But wait, there's more! The stage over there is for stand-up night. That's the weirdness trifecta: a bowling alley in the middle of a swamp with a space-age lounge hosting comedians catering to bass fishermen."

Coleman grabbed a stool on the end of the bar. "How do you find these places?"

"It's my job. Except no employers recognize the position, unless they're just saying that and filling all the open slots with no-talent nephews."

Coleman waved for the bartender. Serge checked his watch: 7:01. "Steve's late."

"I don't think he's coming," said Coleman. "He looked pretty shook."

"He'll come."

Coleman was soon into his fourth draft. It was 7:25. "He's not coming."

"He just arrived."

They turned toward the doorway. Steve stood frozen. He jumped at the sound of a ball hitting pins. He took a timid step forward, then back, then jumped again, head jerking in all directions.

"Steve!" Serge yelled with hands cupped around his mouth. "The coast is clear! None of the robbery gang is here!"

Steve sprinted past rows of people feverishly playing casino-style arcade games. "Keep your voice down!" He looked around again. "Are you crazy?"

"Have a seat."

"Let's make this fast."

Steve slid half his butt on the stool, keeping a foot on the ground.

Serge pushed a scrap of paper along the bar. "I've listed the carats, clarity and cuts of all the stones I'm supposedly carrying—they won't be able to resist—along with the time we'll be out of the room and where the stash is hidden. For convenience, I'm staying at the same hotel you are up by the rodeo arena."

"How'd you know what hotel I'm staying at?"

Serge gave him a stupid-question look.

"Are we done here?"

"Unless you want to stay for the comedian."

Steve bolted out of the bar.

"Serge, how long do we have to stay in the closet?"

"Shhhhh! We can't let the robbers hear us when they enter the room." Serge raised a pistol next to his head. He checked the glowing hands on his diver's wristwatch. "What's taking them so long?"

"Can I get a beer?"

"No!" Serge looked at his wrist again, then smacked himself in the forehead. "Shoot! I *knew* I forgot to tell Steve something! Our room number."

"Steve knows what room we're in."

"He should, but he's Steve." Serge jumped out of the closet and started down the hall.

Coleman jogged to catch up. He stopped. "Ow. Serge, something just got me in the eye."

Serge turned around and laughed.

Coleman rubbed his face. "What's so funny."

Serge pointed at a tastefully unobtrusive beige plastic container attached to the wall. "Automatic air-freshener. Battery powered. Sprays a fragrant blast of chick-magazine goodness every half hour or so. They're usually mounted higher, but this hotel's got low ceilings. And you just happened to be walking by."

"Son of a bitch."

"On the positive side, you're the new, improved Coleman, now in jasmine potpourri."

Coleman stopped rubbing and held the hand to his nose. "It stinks."

"Women have a completely different sense of smell, highly sensitive to flowers or when guys are up to something sneaky."

They resumed walking down the hall and came to a door. Serge knocked lightly. "Pssst! Steve, it's me, Serge."

Coleman wiped his palm on the wall. "Maybe he's not in."

"Steve!" Serge knocked harder. The door was unlatched and creaked open. Serge stuck his head inside. "Steve?"

"I don't think he's in."

Serge silently padded into the room. "Steve?"

"I told you he's not here."

Serge stopped by the dresser and drew his gun. "You're half right."

"What do you mean?"

He pointed at the floor between the double beds. Steve, facedown, three entry wounds in the back of the skull. Serge's shoulders sagged. "We're screwed."

"Steve's the one who looks screwed."

"He was my 'in.' I worked hard on surveillance, intelligence and counterintelligence. Now I'm on the outside again."

"Who do you think did it?"

"Who else? The gang."

"Think they found out about your plan?"

"Hard to say." Serge grabbed the deceased's cell phone off the dresser. "When you're a fuck-up like Steve, you could get whacked over any number of things. Still, the timing so close to our meeting at the Orbit is a bit too coincidental . . . We better get out of here. Don't touch anything . . ."

Serge tucked the pistol back in his waistband and opened the door. He took one step into the hall, then jumped back, crashing into Coleman.

"What's the matter?"

"I don't believe it." Serge peeked his right eye around the door-frame. "Down the hall, telephone repair uniforms. Long, stringy hair. They're going in our room."

"We're back on?"

"Dang it. We were only gone five minutes. There goes our ambush."

"What do we do now?"

"Plan B."

"What's that?"

"The anti-plan."

They headed quietly down the hallway. Coleman ducked under an air freshener. Serge reached the room first and placed his ear to the door.

"Hear anything?" asked Coleman.

"Just rummaging." Serge removed a small black tube from his pocket.

"Where'd you get that?"

"Off a law enforcement website. Used by police extraction teams before they charge in." Serge placed one end of the tube over the outside of the door's peephole. "Series of lenses reverse optics so you can see everything going on inside a hotel room." Serge put his right eye to the other end of the tube. "Also picked up a bunch of plastic wrist straps, cheaper by the dozen."

"What's going on?"

"The painting's off the wall with back ripped open—right where I said the stones would be."

"Guess Steve had the room number after all."

"They're busy taking the place apart, the perfect diversion." Serge stuck the tube back in his pocket and pulled a gun from his waistband. "Extraction team ready?"

"Ready."

Serge silently slipped his magnetic room key in the slot. A green light came on. He burst through the door. "Freeze."

They stopped where they stood. "We're here to fix the phone."

Serge pulled a pair of wrist straps from his back pocket and handed them to Coleman. "Both of you: Turn around and put your hands behind your back."

"We want a lawyer."

Coleman finished and stepped away. Serge walked up to test the tightness of the straps. "Lawyer? Why? Drawing up a will?"

"You're not cops?"

"You wish. I mean that earnestly."

"So you're really a courier?"

"Strike two."

"Then who are you?"

"Very close personal friend of Howard Long."

"Howard?"

"Florida souvenir guy. Intensive care thanks to you."

The hostages shot each other a knowing look, then over their shoulders to Serge: "That was never supposed to happen . . ."

"It's our boss . . ."

"He's crazy!"

"Bet I can give him a run for his money." Serge opened the lower dresser drawer and removed an empty yellow legal pad. He clicked open a pen. "I'm going to need the names and addresses of everyone in the gang, your fences, where you're currently staying, everyone you've hit in the last six months, who you're planning to hit next, the location of all stashed gems, and personal preference: Ginger or Mary Ann?"

"What?"

"Threw that in to see if you're listening." Serge leaned over the pad with his pen. "Ready when you are . . ."

"He'll kill us . . ."

"We're not telling you shit . . ."

Serge dragged a pair of chairs in front of the entertainment center. "Wilma or Betty?"

"You're crazy."

"Told you. Time's up." Serge waved his gun toward the chairs. "Have a seat. We now proceed to the consolation round." He opened the drawer again and removed a second legal pad. This one covered with crude drawings. Serge rapidly flipped pages: deep pits full of snakes, vats of acid, catapults, homemade guillotine, jugs of poison with skulls on the side, mad scientist giant laser, large pool with circling shark fins—all containing bloody stick figures, some in pieces, others with flames or electricity bolts. Serge tapped his chin with the pen. "What will it be? . . ."

Water was running in the bathroom sink. Coleman's voice: "I can't get the stink off."

Serge stopped tapping his chin and looked up with big eyes. "Coleman! That's it! You've done it again!" He tossed the legal pad back in the drawer and kicked it closed with a foot. "This way I don't have to use up any of my ideas. They'll all still remain eligible for the play-offs." He ran to a suitcase, pulling out several coils of rope and rolls of gray adhesive. "Duct tape again—I should buy voting stock . . . Hold still. This won't take long."

"What are you planning?"

"Ever watch *Flip That House*?"

"What?"

Serge worked industriously with the rope and tape. Repeated loops and triple knots, between their legs, around chest and necks, up behind their backs, threaded under arms, circling chair legs and ankles, until little of them was left showing. "Fairness is very big with me. Give everyone a chance, I always say. So if you can get free from your bindings by morning, before my plan has a chance to fully bloom, you're free to go. My word of honor. Except the odds are against it. You never want to get tied up by an obsessive-compulsive. We over-engineer *everything*." Serge finished the last knot, fastening them securely to the chairs, which in turn were rigidly held in place with ten large loops around the giant TV cabinet. Then mouths were finally silenced with another excessive amount of duct-tape head wrapping. "Stay here. Have to make a quick trip to the hardware store." He ran out the door.

Coleman returned from the bathroom and sat on the edge of a bed with a beer. He smiled at the men, then turned on the TV with the remote. *Three's Company*. "Could you move your heads?"

A half hour later, Serge burst back through the door with shopping bags, two large cardboard boxes and overflowing zest. "You're in luck: found everything I needed." He dumped the bags on the bed, grabbed a pair of scissors and the cardboard.

Serge's ensuing labor was dedicated, furious and made no obvious sense. Soon, the captives found their heads resting inside the boxes, poking up through round holes in the bottom Serge had cut, their necks sealed to the openings with tape. Then more tape held the boxes fast against the entertainment cabinet. The men looked straight up through the open cardboard tops. Serge looked back down. Something was in each hand, which he enthusiastically thrust in their faces. "Know what these are? Bet you do, if you think hard. Take a guess! Coleman knows. People usually don't even notice—and now the people on the top floors of this hotel can't, because I snatched all the automatic air-fresheners from the walls. Internal timer triggers an actuator that presses the button on top of an aerosol can at olfactory intervals predetermined by focus groups." Serge gave them each a manual squirt. "Lilac." He popped covers off the dispensers and discarded the cans of freshener. "Have to modify these so my replacement cans fit. Be right back." He disappeared from view. The hostages heard a high-pitched buzzing sound and struggled without result.

"Dremel hobby tool if you're curious," said an unseen Serge. "Sands, polishes, drills, cuts. Million and one uses. Now, million and two." More buzzing. Then, abruptly, quiet.

Serge appeared again at the top of the boxes, literally bouncing. He held up a prototype of his new device, which had been sliced in half and reassembled with a cardboard stent to accommodate the new, taller cans.

"And I replaced the batteries with the super-alkaline ones in those commercials that show someone narrowly averting a horrible death, and tearful loved ones say, 'Thank God for these batteries!' Don't want an operational failure at the crucial moment." The device was stuck in their faces again. "Recognize the product? It's great stuff. That's really its name: Great Stuff."

Serge pulled the dispenser back. "Revolutionary breakthrough for the do-it-yourself home improvement crowd! Seals wall fittings around pipes so roaches and rats can't squeeze through, insulates voids in walls and under baseboards. But you ask, Serge, how on earth can such a reasonably priced product do all that? I'll tell you! Revolutionary chemical breakthrough! These cans slowly squirt an innocuous gooey liquid foam, like whipped cream except yellow. If whipped cream ever comes out yellow, take shortcake off the menu that night. Where was I? The foam! When it first dispenses from the pump, it appears useless—and you look questioningly at the can: I got fucked! But then something miraculous happens. The yellow slurry eventually expands until it's ten times original size! And after reaching full volume, the foam begins to cure until a few hours later it's hard as a rock. I see the question in your eyes. I don't know how it works either. But I don't understand cathode rays, and I still watch TV."

Serge went back to the bed and returned with an armload of his newly customized air-freshening dispensers. "Figured three per customer should do the trick." He taped them around the lips of the boxes.

"One for you, and one for you. Another one for you, and another . . . hey, look, one of the timers already went off and squirted."

The captive on the right felt something wet against his neck and strained to look down. A small worm of goo expanded into a giant, thick snake. Frantic eyes shot up toward his captor.

"I know exactly what you're thinking," said Serge. "Next renovation, I gotta get me a case of this shit. Hides a multitude of sins . . . Coleman, you ready?"

"Where are we going?"

He looked back at the vibrating boxes. "We need to respect their privacy. No telling how people react under these circumstances. Probably be embarrassed if we saw them cry."

Another dispenser squirted.

"That one's already crying," said Coleman.

"It's our cue." Serge leaned over the boxes a final time. "I'll put out the DO NOT DISTURB sign so the maid won't see you. That would really be embarrassing. Women *say* it's okay for men to cry, but forget any more nookie if you do. And forget any more nookie if you even use the word *nookie*. Except with hotel maids, because there's often a language barrier. So, in summation, if for some reason the maid *does* come in here: A. Don't cry. B. It's your call whether to use the word *nookie* . . ." Serge patted down their pants pockets. The first guy only had a wallet, but the second produced a cell phone. "Excellent."

They headed out the door.

Coleman suddenly turned and ran back inside.

"Coleman," Serge yelled from the hall. "What the hell are you doing?"

"Forgot something." He uncapped a Magic Marker and leaned toward the wall next to the TV cabinet. "Just be a sec."

"Come on!"

"Okay." Coleman capped the marker and ran out of the room.

The door closed.

Squirt.

CHAPTER 34

THE NEXT MORNING

A two-tone Javelin sat next to a boat ramp on the causeway over the Intracoastal. The day had that deep-purple overcast. Then lightning laced the sky, sending smaller fishing boats back to shore.

Serge was in the driver's seat, messing with a pair of cell phones.

Coleman poured from a pint of vodka with a vulture on the label. "Where are we?"

"Phil Foster Park," said Serge, trial-and-erroring his way through the phones' menus. "Between mainland Riviera Beach and Singer Island." He looked across the water at a forty-foot sailboat cruising under the giant, modern bridge arcing high into the sky before sloping back to Blue Heron Boulevard. "I *love* this place! Spent many a childhood afternoon here. I hate that fucking bridge."

"Why?"

"Horrible development of the New Sunshine State. Many barrier islands have replaced their gloriously historic drawbridges with these towering new spans so people don't have wait for boats. But the old bridge still lives in my heart. I'd ride my banana bike out here with my fishing pole, a barefoot Florida Huck Finn, tackle-box-of-hope sitting in the handlebar basket, which I got for my newspaper route."

"You were a paperboy?"

"Another tragic turn of culture: No more paperboys because it's now too dangerous for kids to ride around throwing papers before dawn, or collect weekly payment after sunset . . ." Serge navigated the phones' on-screen displays. ". . . I fondly recall delivering the award-winning *Palm Beach Post*. Only lasted three days, even though you're looking at one of the best paperboys who ever pedaled a Schwinn."

Coleman stirred his drink with a finger. "What happened?"

"Should have seen me in action, zooming down the sidewalk as fast as my legs could churn, slinging papers like nobody's business. I could hit nine out of ten roofs blindfolded. Then it turns out they didn't want roofs. I said, what about doors? They said doors were good. And could I hit doors! Wham! Nobody had any doubt when their paper arrived. But as I said, this was all before sunrise. I figured they needed to start getting up earlier anyway. To compound the growing ungratefulness, I went for style points and tried throwing while doing a wheelie. You break *one* picture window, and that's all they want to talk about."

"So you used to fish around here?"

"I wasn't fishing. I was playing with sharks."

Coleman chugged half the drink and clenched his face. Then drank some more.

Serge punched phone buttons.

"What are you doing?"

"Steve was our only connection with the gang who attacked Howard. Since that's off the table, I'm correlating recent calls made by the respective phones I took from Steve and the bandits in that room yesterday."

Coleman finished the rest of his drink and involuntarily shivered from the aftertaste. "You said something about sharks?"

"Excellent topic retention, Coleman. People swim around here all the time with no clue. We're at the mouth of Lake Worth Inlet, incredible tidal flows, all kinds of giant fish. I'd hang out at the base of the bridge by the Crab Pot, where my granddad always took me for fried catfish before it was torn down by heritage-phobes. That's where older dudes cast-net and spilled junk fish all over the ground, then sliced 'em up for bait, the bloodier the better. They knew me—was like their mascot—so I'd always get a chunk, which I hooked to my line, go out on the bridge and throw it over the side."

"You caught sharks?"

"Hell no. I was a puny nine-year-old and my tackle was too light. I just played with them, jerking bait chunks up and down, slapping the surface of the water to get a scent trail going. Once I had this giant hammerhead a good three feet out of the water, those freaky prehistoric eye-pods whipping back and forth, ripping the bloody hell out of my fish. All in all, excellent childhood." He held the cell phones side by side. "Here we go. Last calls from both phones to the same number. Better use Steve's instead of the foam-heads' or they might get the idea I had something to do with that."

"You did."

"Why invite conflict?" Serge hit the call-back button. It began ringing.

A voice on the other end: "Steve?"

"Steve's not here. This is Serge."

"Who's Serge?"

"Steve's silent partner. I've taken over his operation."

Pause. "My caller ID says you're using Steve's phone."

"A rocket scientist."

"What . . . uh, *happened* to Steve?"

"Don't play dumb," said Serge. "We both know what happened to Steve."

"*We* didn't do that."

"Whatever. Listen: Since we're going to be doing a lot of business together, I thought I'd introduce myself. I'm Serge."

"You already said that."

"This was the formal introduction. We need to build trust. What are your feelings about a blood oath? I'll even let you pick the finger."

"Buddy, I don't know who the fuck you are."

"The guy who's going to get you out of a jam. Steve's gone—your information stream's fucked. I'm guessing your boss will want to make an example out of someone."

"How do you know I'm not the boss?"

"You answered the phone?"

"Yeah?"

"You're not the boss."

"This is bullshit. You don't have any information."

"Where do you think Steve got his?"

"I really don't—"

"And I'm going to have to tax you for Steve, which you're free to continue denying. An extra ten percent on the gross haul."

"Ten percent! The Jellyfish will kill us both."

"Jellyfish?"

"Shit. I wasn't supposed to say that."

"You have my number."

Click.

"What now?" asked Coleman.

"My daily tradition." Serge started the car and headed back to the mainland. "Read the local paper."

"Why are you always reading newspapers when we could be having fun?"

"Coleman, that *is* fun, one of the biggest joys of travel. Most people just visit a place like tourists and only skim the surface. But reading the daily paper lets you see through the eyes of a local. Plus this is my old hometown—I *have* to read the paper."

The Javelin came off the crest of the bridge and approached the intersection of Blue Heron and Broadway.

"Serge, what if that guy doesn't call you back?"

"He'll call." Serge searched the sides of the road. "He's scared to death of this Jellyfish character, and screwed without Steve."

"So he needs you."

"I always try to put myself in the position of helping others . . . There's a news box . . ." He pulled over. "I love this intersection!"

"It just looks like a million others."

"The pawnshop's still here—and the Dairy Belle! We used to walk there from my house when I was a kid and get ice cream. It's just about all that's left to remind me of my childhood . . ." He pointed toward the other side of the street. ". . . Those Mayan ruins used to be a Publix supermarket with the old chevron logo where I'd ride in the shopping-cart kiddie seat, back when they still had mechanical cash registers."

"What happened to it?"

"Probably the same thing that doomed the venerable Spanish Courts motel and the Bazaar market with the trilon sightseeing tower—my old Riviera Beach got too dicey a proposition after it became a crack flea market. I'm getting the paper now."

"Rip it up."

Serge returned and flipped through sections, gleaning the meat of articles. ". . . Missing person's body found in bedroom after six weeks; relatives thought the smell was dead Norwegian rats in the wall . . . Members accuse condo association of holding secret meetings in Canada . . . Superhot teacher has sex with her student . . ."

"That makes fifty-one now."

"Fifty-two . . . Cuban refugees land in middle of coastal defense exercise . . . Immigration uncovers plot to smuggle Eastern Europeans into Orlando as circus performers . . ." Serge turned another page. "Oh my gosh!"

"What is it?" asked Coleman.

"This is a great day!" Serge held the page toward Coleman. "Look who's giving a lecture."

"Don't know him."

"Coleman, he's a Florida legend! I've wanted to meet him my whole life and now I get the chance. All because I read the local paper." Serge looked at his watch. "Shit."

"What's the matter?"

"Looks like we missed it. But if I hurry, maybe we can catch him on the way out." Serge threw the car in gear.

"But what about those people you want to kill?"

"I know this is irresponsible, but sometimes you have to treat yourself."

The Javelin made record time across West Palm Beach, turned onto Okeechobee Boulevard and skidded up to the curb in front of a giant modern building with glistening glass facade. A crowd walked down the front steps.

"We're in time," said Serge. "They're just getting out."

"What is this place?"

"The fabulous Kravis Center for the Performing Arts." Serge pointed with a quivering arm. "And there he is!"

In the middle of the exiting audience, people shook hands with a distinguished older gentleman in a cowboy hat.

"Come on!" Serge jumped from the car and sprinted across the lawn. He was out of breath by the time he'd pushed his way through the crowd and finally reached the cowboy hat. He thrust out an enthusiastic hand. "Howdy! I'm Serge! Honor to meet you! Missed your talk—bet it was a doozy! I'm Serge!"

The man graciously shook the hand. "You okay?"

"Couldn't be better now that I've met you!"

The man laughed. "Not everyone feels that way."

"Give me their names!"

Serge suddenly stumbled forward as someone crashed into him from behind.

"Coleman! Behave!" Serge turned back around. "Sorry about that. This is my associate, Coleman. Coleman, this is Claude Kirk, the oldest living governor of Florida, elected 1966, also known as Claudius Maximus for how he shook the good-ol'-boy power structure to its knees and sent rascals scampering back under their rocks. I'm Serge!"

"You mentioned that," said the governor, shaking other hands.

"So what are you doing after this? Fighting crime?"

"Going home."

"Got a ride?"

"Someone's supposed to pick me up."

"We'll give you a lift!"

"Appreciate the gesture." The governor looked at his watch, then scanned the edge of the street.

"Coleman," said Serge. "You'll love this. A few years back, the governor was being questioned on the witness stand in some court case by F. Lee Bailey, who asked Kirk to identify himself, and state for the record what he used to do. And he said he was a former governor of Florida. And Bailey asked what he was now, and Kirk said, 'A has-been, just like you.'"

The governor laughed. "That really pissed him off."

"Coleman, why I really admire this guy is his unbridled passion for Florida, or at least what it could become if they'd only listen to him. After all these years, still battling the dark side."

The governor glanced at his watch again. "Sounds like you really care about this state."

"You have no idea!"

The governor took off his cowboy hat and wiped his forehead as he stared at the street again. "Damn hot out here in the sun. Maybe I will take you up on that ride."

"Let's rock!"

"Shotgun!" said Coleman.

"Have manners," said Serge. "Shotgun goes to our special guest."

The Javelin headed north on I-95.

"Tell me son, are you a Republican?" asked the governor.

"No, a Whig. I'm leading the comeback." Serge turned sideways, photographing the governor with his digital camera.

"Shouldn't you be watching the road?"

"It's okay." Click, click, click. "I do this all the time."

"I'd rather you watch the road."

"Got enough pictures anyway." Serge faced forward. "So what's on the governor's mind these days?"

"Sugar industry."

"What about it?"

"I want to sink 'em."

"Why?"

"Special-interest lobbyists control all the politicians and keep price supports in place. If it wasn't for that, Americans would have more affordable sugar."

Serge punched the dashboard. "Sugar prices!"

"Even worse," said the governor. "In the process of raising the cane, they've altered the flow of the Everglades, killing what's left with fertilizer runoff. Then they leave town before having to clean it up."

"I'm on board!" said Serge. "We'll get some bricks and clubs and kung fu throwing stars . . ."

"Absolutely not!"

"But I thought you wanted to sink the sugar daddies."

"*Within* the system. That's always been my philosophy. Work within the system for change."

"Can I start my own system?"

"No."

"*Allllll* right." Serge reached under his seat and pulled out a yellow legal pad. He handed it back over his shoulder to Coleman: "Start a to-

do list. Action Item Number One: Sink big sugar within the system."
He turned to his right. "What next, governor?"

"It's all about water. Between thousands of new residents moving into the state and the decline of the Everglades, we're running out . . ."

"Dear God!"

". . . Nobody's thinking ahead," continued Kirk, "and it'll be too late when the people start screaming. It's already started."

Serge grabbed his chest. "Tell me, governor, what can we possibly do to thank you for caring."

"Well, I do have one wish. I'd like to be buried on the capitol grounds."

"Coleman," Serge said over his shoulder. "Action Item Number Two: Bury the governor on the capitol grounds."

"Now?"

"No, you idiot! After he dies . . . Sorry about that, governor . . ."

The drive continued into a residential neighborhood west of the interstate, next to a canal with familiar reptilian eye-knots poking out of the water.

"Coleman," said Serge. "The governor almost single-handedly saved the Florida alligator from extinction." He turned toward the passenger seat. "They were down to less than three hundred, right?"

"Poaching was out of control," said Kirk. "And you know the importance of alligators?"

"Females dig alligator holes."

"You really know your stuff. The life cycle of the Everglades. And when droughts come, those holes are the only place for the rest of the animals to get water. So people said, well, we got to get a bunch of people out at night to catch the poachers. I said that's bullshit. You can't catch a poacher if he doesn't want to be caught. What we need to do is go after demand. All those stores in New York selling alligator purses. Stop making purses, you'd be surprised at how fast they stop poaching alligators. But they wouldn't listen."

"Holy mother!" said Serge. "What did you do?"

"Some guys came down from the Department of Interior, and to prove it was pointless going at it from the poacher end, I took them down to Punta Gorda, and *I* was going to be a poacher. Went out alone after dark in an airboat, and they had everyone in the world looking, but they couldn't find me for anything."

"Coleman, you listening?" said Serge. "He was like a superhero, sneaking around the swamp at night in an airboat and shit. Now *that's* how you govern."

CHAPTER 35

HOMESTEAD

*F*orty miles south of Miami, a clapboard hacienda sat on the outskirts of the outskirts, hidden behind a thriving palm tree farm. Inside, a robbery crew lieutenant ate breakfast with his assistant. Over-easy eggs, cheese grits, Canadian bacon, white grapefruit juice and vodka.

A white van screeched up in a cloud of arid dust. The Eel and three goons jumped out and stormed up steps.

A door crashed open. "What the fuck's the story about this goddamn phone call?"

The pair jumped up and quivered. "Eel," said the lieutenant. "The guy called me out of the blue. I just passed along what he said."

The goons surrounded them. Anxious eyes darted. The Eel advanced on the lieutenant, nose to nose. "And how the hell did he get your number?"

"S-s-said it was in Steve's cell phone—"

"You worthless piece of shit!" yelled the Eel. "Another thing. How'd you let our best informant get killed?"

"I-I-I . . . Steve— . . . I don't know . . ."

The Eel nodded toward one of the goons in the background. The lieutenant spun to see a steel strangulation ligature stretched between beefy hands.

"*Noooooooo!!!!!!*"

The goon suddenly lunged sideways, wrapping the wire around the neck of the lieutenant's assistant. Twitching feet left the floor. The goon used a wooden dowel to twist the cord tighter. Thirty seconds of silent horror. Then it was over with a lifeless thud on the pine floor.

The lieutenant's eyes whipped back toward the Eel. "Jesus Christ! What'd you do that for?"

"Because we're going to give this new informant of yours named 'Serge' a trial run." The Eel headed for the door. "And that was to reinforce what will happen if anything goes wrong."

WEST PALM BEACH

Serge sped south, bobbing in the driver's seat. "Governor, tell the story about the rat bait. Please?"

"You *do* know your history."

"Coleman," said Serge. "This is a quintessential Kirk story kicking over the money changers' tables in the temple. There used to be this big state contract for rat bait, and the governor wanted to make sure it was actually being used. So he went to Gainesville, where there were a lot of abandoned properties, and a bunch of hardworking low-economic citizens were living in unacceptable conditions. Take it from there, gov . . ."

"Big politicians were always coming back to watch University of Florida football games and would drive right by these neighborhoods, not giving a damn. So I went to the local health officials and said, 'How many rat baits have we put out here?' And the top guy said, 'I don't know.' I said, 'Go get a rat. Logically if you've put rat baits out, you've killed a rat. Show me how many damn rats you've killed. Bring a couple in here. And let's weigh 'em. And next time we have a meeting, you'll bring some more rats in and weigh *them*. Now if we've done our job, the rats have to get smaller, because they're younger and they're not eatin' good.' The issue got across . . ."

A cell phone rang. "Sorry," Serge told the governor. "I need to take this. Would you mind grabbing the wheel?"

"What?"

"The key to Florida road-tripping is a dependable travel companion who's good at steering from the passenger side so the driver can tend to other tasks."

"Don't let go of the wheel!"

Serge let go.

The governor's left arm swung out and gripped it. "What's wrong with you?"

Serge held up a finger for quiet, opening a notebook and holding the cell to his head. "Had a feeling you'd call back . . . No, my terms are unnegotiable . . . Want the diamonds or not? . . . Is that a threat? . . . Oh yeah? Well, *I* make the threats around here . . ." Serge pulled a gun from under the seat and waved it around the car. ". . . You want to fuck with me, motherfucker? . . ." He pulled up to a curb and turned to the governor. "That's your house. You can let go of the wheel now." Then into the phone: ". . . Is that so? I should smash your fucking skull in just for saying that! . . . Call me back when you calm down [click]."

The governor got out and slowly backed away from the car, watching silently as the Javelin sped off, gun waving out the window.

OKEECHOBEE

Police held back a growing crowd of the curious in a hotel hallway. Forensic techs came and went with boxes and clear, sealed bags.

Inside the room, the hotel manager stood next to a homicide detective. Behind them, medical examiners peeled cardboard off a pair of hardened foam blocks encasing the victims' heads.

The manager turned and looked across the room at a uniformed officer taking a statement from the hysterical maid who'd discovered the scene.

"She's pretty hot," said the detective. "Is that the one you were close to nailing?"

The manager sighed. "Speaks perfect English."

The detective placed a consoling hand on the manager's shoulder, and they both looked back at the wall, where someone had written in thick Magic Marker: NOOKIE.

DANIA

Serge led the way across a debris-strewn parking lot toward the last room on the end of a budget motel. "Coleman, did the governor seem a little jumpy to you?"

"Maybe he's on the pipe."

"Probably the economy."

"Hey, Serge, just had an idea. Can I help with your travel advice thing?"

"Dying to hear your insight."

"Got a great one. Like, at every budget motel, there are at least three or four rooms where people are staying just to hole up and drug binge. Or deal."

"That's no tip—it's just Florida."

"But I can find them."

"Are you already drunk?"

"Of course. Here's the deal: Observe the parking lot, plug into its rhythms, and after a few minutes, you just *know*."

"You're wrecked."

"Time me."

Serge held up his wristwatch. Coleman squinted in concentration. People coming and going, crossing the parking lot, stopping to chat, walking dogs, getting ice, feeding quarters into vending machines, taking unbolted TVs from rooms, driving up in the kind of pitiful, hanging-together car that would soon be pulled with a rope by another car. Coleman pointed. "That room. One-forty-seven. How long?"

"Ninety seconds." Serge looked up from his wrist. "But you just pointed at a room. That doesn't mean anything."

"I'll prove it." He took a step forward. Then stopped. "Oh my God."

"What is it?"

Six police cars whipped up the motel's drive and parked, hidden behind the office. "They've found us! We're going to jail!"

"Not this time."

"How do you know?"

Serge gestured at a red van with TV antennas following the police cars around the backside of the office. "That's the film crew from *COPS*."

"And?"

"It's so widely known it's a running joke: On *COPS*, they only arrest the guys not wearing shirts."

Coleman looked down to make sure he was wearing one. "I'll be right back." He headed across the lot to room 147, then knocked three times in slow cadence. Someone with a mullet opened. They spoke briefly. The man glanced over Coleman's shoulders and waved him in. The door closed.

Serge shook his head. "Unbelievable." He went inside his own room. A cell rang. He flipped it open. "Serge here. Fulfill my dreams."

"Still want to sell that information?"

"Hey, buddy, long time! Great to hear from you! Calm now?"

"There's no way we'll go the extra ten percent."

"That was just my initial offer. You have to open a business dialogue somewhere. Make me a counter."

"My boss will cut your fucking head off."

"See? We've established trust. How much to keep my head?"

"Five."

"Done," said Serge. "Let's meet. I don't like to conduct this kind of transaction over the phone."

"Where?"

Serge told him.

"I know the place. Five o'clock."

"It's a date."

"How will I know you?"

"Trust me, you'll know." Serge hung up, then punched numbers.

Coleman came in the room. "Hey, Serge . . ."

"We got a meet at five." Serge listened to the phone and jotted something. "I lucked out. Guy messed up and phoned from a landline instead of his cell. Called reverse directory and got the address."

"We're going to surprise him at that place and not make the meet?"

"No, we're still going to the meet." He closed the notebook. "This is for the post-meet follow-up sales call. In business it's important to reinforce relationships."

Coleman smiled and held up a Baggie. "They're running an excellent deal on sensimilla. And I got a free bump of coke, just for being a member."

"Of what?"

"The Partying Brotherhood."

"But how did they, I mean, you're a total stranger . . ."

"We can smell each other." Coleman sat on the bed and sniffed a pungent bud.

"Stow that." Serge pulled the strap of a canvas bag over his shoulder. "We're rolling."

They went out the door and headed for the Javelin. A film crew ran behind them as police pulled a shirtless man from room 147.

CHAPTER 36

erge's Blog. Star date 937.473.

So much to tell! So little time!

Tip One: Not a tip, just weird shit I saw today. From the only-in-Florida file: a hooker with a walker on the side of U.S. 1. At some point your heart just isn't in it anymore.

Tip Two: Capture the memories! You can never have enough extra tapes for home movies, especially around Coleman. I ran out yesterday and discovered Coleman had been using my camcorder to bootleg in-room movies off the TV. I said, Coleman, you can make a perfect copy with the VCR on top of the TV. But he said "the street" won't respect you.

Tip Three: Dealing with loud drunks in the next room who stumble in after closing time and disturb your sleep: At daybreak, start calling their room every fifteen minutes. Hangovers will take it from there.

Tip Four: Best travel tool: those twelve-foot-long telescoping letter-grabbers that hospitality employees use to change messages on tall marquees. Got one in my trunk. Guests at the last place I stayed woke up this morning to: "Welcome Hotel Emergency Delousing Team." The fun ship never docks!

Closing word for the day: Postcards! Don't forget about the loved ones back home who missed the love-cutoff to come with you. And don't be trite by purchasing the usual cards from spinning metal racks. Instead, schedule a virtual postcard. What's that, you ask? I'll tell you! E-mail those second-tier relatives with a preordained time and

Internet site. Then, when they log in, they'll find one of the many live Web cams positioned around the state. And they'll see you standing in streaming-video splendor, holding up a personalized greeting sign. The key is finding the right cam. The long-range skyline jobs atop Doppler radar towers aren't good unless you want to hold up a billboard. But there are plenty others: Sloppy Joe's, the Cocowalk and Pier 60. Let's pull one up now! Here's the sidewalk cam from A1A in Fort Lauderdale, showing happy visitors walking the beach and cool convertibles in the background cruising the strip and . . . hold it, what's this?

A man in a rumpled fedora stepped into view and held up a sign: SERGE, WE HAVE TO MEET AGAIN.

FORT LAUDERDALE

The Javelin took exit 31 off I-95 and sped east on Oakland Park Boulevard.

Serge looked ahead at a roadside bench. "There's Story now."

"Just got out of class?"

"Took the bus to meet us." Serge pulled over.

Story climbed in. "You're late!"

"No time like the present."

Onward east. The coast grew near. A high-end neighborhood extensively laced with finger canals.

Yachts.

"Trivia flash," said Serge. "Fort Lauderdale has more miles of canals than Venice."

They crossed a tiny hump bridge at one of the narrowest points over the Intracoastal Waterway. A wall of exclusive high-rises blocked the sea. A half-century ago it would have screamed spring break. Now it said: Go away.

Serge found a metered spot on the side of A1A. "We're here!"

Story looked around. "Where's our hotel?"

Serge pointed out the windshield. "Right there."

"That's not a hotel," said Story. "It's a condo."

"Bingo! Now L'Hermitage." Serge grabbed his beach bag and

threw a camera inside. "But back in the day it was the fabulous Galt Ocean Mile. I can see it all now . . ."

"Idiot!" said Story. "You promised there'd be a great swimming pool where I could get some sun."

"There is," said Serge. "One of the most historic. Famous wire photos from forty years ago seared into the nation's collective consciousness. Let's go dig it!"

"Didn't you hear me?" said Story. "You can't just waltz right in a condo."

"You *have* to waltz right in," said Serge. "Otherwise they'll get suspicious that you're up to something. So when you're up to something, dress proper and stroll confidently like you own the place because it's the last thing they'll expect. And if some guard or factotum in a blazer gets nosy and starts coming toward you, you head their way even faster and badger them with difficult questions until *they* want to get away from *you*. Never fails. I get at least fifteen minutes to sponge up history before they throw me out."

Story angrily hoisted her beach bag. "You owe me big-time."

"I forgot what a treat it was when you were off studying."

The condo theory held. They marched through the lobby—Serge smiling and waving aggressively at everyone—and right out back to the pool.

Serge reached in the breast pocket of his tropical shirt and unfolded a library microfilm printout. An old AP newspaper photo. He held it up to the patio and gauged layout. His eyes narrowed on a particular patio lounger by the ocean. He couldn't run fast enough.

Story went the other way, for maximum separation.

Serge stopped next to the lounger and disrobed down to plaid swim trunks he was wearing underneath: the too-short, too-tight style fashionable in the sixties. He lay down, reached in his beach bag and handed Coleman a notepad and pen. "Write."

"What do I write?"

"Just look like you're writing." Serge snuggled into a comfortable position on the hot plastic straps and raised his voice. "The Jets will win! I guarantee it! . . ."

A heavily perspiring man in a tweed jacket emerged from the back

 Nuclear JELLYFISH **265**

of the condo. Mahoney quickly acquired the target and walked around the pool. The agent pretended not to know Serge as he reclined on the adjacent lounger and placed a rumpled fedora on his stomach.

Serge turned his head sideways. "Hope your money's not on the Colts."

"This is too conspicuous," said Mahoney. "I can't be seen with you."

"That's why I picked it. I knew you couldn't resist coming here."

"Poolside press conference," said Mahoney. "Friday, January 10, 1969."

"New York quarterback Joe Namath repeats his historic guarantee of victory in Super Bowl Three that he'd boldly made the night before . . ."

". . . At the Miami Touchdown Club banquet," said Mahoney. "Bad news: The hit's still on."

"You're losing it. There is no hit."

Mahoney shook his head. "Someone's still asking around."

"Must be my Internet travel service. It's outrageously popular."

"You're being shadowed straight down the coast, stop for stop. At first they were a couple days behind, now just hours. It's almost as if they have someone on the inside." Mahoney gazed across the pool as Story applied lotion. "Nice gams."

Someone in a blazer walked up to the end of Serge's lounger. "Excuse me, sir. Do you live here?"

"No." A big smile.

"Then what's going on?"

"A press conference."

Serge checked his watch: 4:45.

"Why can't I sit at the bar?" asked Coleman.

"I already went over this. I need you for my backup." He handed Coleman his piece.

"But I don't know how to shoot a gun."

"You won't have to. Just sit in this booth while I'm at the bar. In the absolute worst-case, I'll give a nod, and all you have to do is stand, look mean and briefly raise the edge of your shirt to expose the pistol butt."

"But don't you need the gun?"

Serge patted a bulge under his tropical shirt. "Have something better."

Coleman plopped down in the booth beneath brass portholes and hanging maritime lanterns. "Why do I feel like I'm on a ship?"

"Because you're supposed to. It's the incredible Wreck Lounge in Fort Lauderdale's Yankee Clipper hotel." Serge swept an arm across the ultra-dark interior and up at thick, aged timbers. "I *love* the Wreck. Designed to look like the cargo hold of a nineteenth-century schooner." He pointed another direction, toward the source of a dim turquoise glow that seeped through the lounge as its primary light source. "Best feature of all! Remember my number one rule for grading bars?"

"The view behind the bottles?"

Serge nodded. "Those thick windows framed with nautical rope provide a magnificent underwater vantage of the hotel's pool."

Someone came off the diving board and knifed through the water behind the Bacardi.

Coleman waved for a waitress.

Serge grabbed his arm and lowered it. "Stop drinking."

"But it's a bar."

"Coleman, you're already halfway in the bag. You need to stay on your toes."

"I'll be fine." He raised his arm again.

Serge lowered it again. "I'm just asking for a half hour. Until the meeting's over, whatever you do, don't drink. Then you can do whatever you want."

Coleman folded his arms. "This sucks."

Serge glanced at his watch again. "Better take our positions. And I'll need to ask that guy to get up."

"Why?"

"Because that's where Robert DeNiro sat in *Analyze This*."

Serge left Coleman in the booth. He reached the bar and tapped a designer shoulder. A low-grade golf pro turned around and looked Serge over. "What's your problem, loser?"

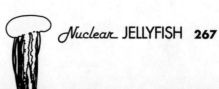

"DeNiro sat there."

"So?"

"I have to sit there."

"Fuck off."

Moments later, hotel staff rushed in to aid a customer twitching on the floor.

"He was just fine a minute ago," said Serge, buoyant atop the DeNiro stool, making sure his tropical shirt covered the stun gun.

A ship's clock ticked. A stretcher rolled out of the lounge. Serge sat with his back to the bar, facing the entrance. Coleman ordered two drinks. Bikini babes dove into the pool. Tension grew.

5:01. Four men entered the lounge: a scrawny accountant type flanked by three bodybuilders. They looked around.

Serge held up a chauffeur-type sign: HOTEL ROBBERY GANG.

The quartet rushed over. "Put that damn thing down!"

Serge folded the cardboard. "I'm on the DeNiro chair."

"You wanted to meet, so meet."

"You the one I talked to on the phone?"

He nodded.

"We probably should use names."

"Dick."

"Dick, what's with the goon squad?"

"In case of a double-cross. Then you'll be taking a little ride."

"Sorry fellas, not today." Serge leaned smugly against the bar. "I've got a crack backup man. Best in the business. He's sitting anonymously somewhere in this bar, but you'd never guess who until it's too late. Won't ever hear the bullet. Yes sir, the consummate pro."

The goons looked around the lounge, including the rear booth. No Coleman.

Suddenly, a splash and small explosion of bubbles. They all turned and looked through the underwater pool windows. A fully clothed man dog-paddled toward the surface. A pistol drifted down to the drain.

Serge closed his eyes and placed his forehead on the bar. He raised his head. "Would you believe I have two backups?"

"You're wasting my time."

"Okay, here's the deal." Serge slipped Dick a matchbook. "Hotel, room, time."

"What's the take?"

"Opals, small but decent quantity. The big catch is a twenty-carat flawless ruby."

"How do you know?"

"If I told you, I'd be out of a job."

"Better not be a trick or *you* won't hear the bullet."

A Javelin flew out of Miami on South Dixie Highway. Blistering afternoon. Mercury flirted with a hundred. Even hotter in the car since Serge had the heater up all the way. Sweat sheeted down their heads.

Coleman wiped his face. "My eyes are stinging."

Serge grabbed a handle. "Roll down your window."

Coleman cranked the knob on his own door. "Why'd you turn the heater on full blast?"

"Because the car's overheating at this temperature."

Coleman stuck his head out the window like a cocker spaniel. "I don't understand."

"Most people don't. Serge's travel tip number 739: When a radiator gets too hot, some drivers know to turn off the air conditioner, because the law of thermodynamics adds heat to the engine inversely proportional to the cooling of the passenger compartment. But the real trick in averting a boil-over is to turn on the *heater*. There is no real heater in most cars. It just sucks hot air off the engine and blows it in here. See?" He tapped the dash's temperature gauge.

Coleman came back inside and looked at the instrument dial. "It's working. The needle's dropping out of the red zone."

"The radiator was about to blow, but we successfully improvised to continue the mission. I should have been on *Apollo 13*."

"So what's the mission?"

"Perimeter sweep."

They reached Homestead at the bottom of the state and took a small county road to the western outskirts. Low, flat agricultural fields with tomato pickers in wide-brimmed straw hats. "I'm driving

out to the address I got off that phone call. We need daylight to assess the layout for our counter-offensive against the gang tonight."

"I thought we were going to double-cross them at that hotel room on the matchbook."

"Correct. Two sets of targets today, so timing will be tight. My Master Plan to take out most of the gang requires an intricate sequence of perfectly ordered strikes or we risk picking off only a few. After the ambush tonight, we'll need to get back here toot-sweet before word of the betrayal leaks out."

"But won't they already suspect us from the foam-heads?"

"Probably not, because that was based on Steve's tip—and before my phone call. But after tonight, there'll be no doubt. And as soon as they find out, they'll come after us with everything they've got."

"What'll we do then?"

"Beat 'em to the punch."

Farther west. Limestone quarry, dump trucks, abandoned airstrip and, finally, an isolated hacienda on the back side of a palm tree farm. Serge rechecked his notebook. "I think that's the place now."

Moments later, Serge and Coleman crept through rows of coconut palms. They reached the edge of the trees and a clearing that led to the front porch. A van and a pickup. Buzzing crickets. Pesticide odor. A screen door opened. Serge raised binoculars. Three men came out: two strapped with weapons, the other holding a walkie-talkie. There was a short conversation at the foot of the porch, then the smallest raised the two-way radio to his mouth. They headed for the vehicles.

Coleman peeked over Serge's shoulder. "What do you see?"

"Just as I thought. Two goons and 'Dick' from the Wreck Lounge." He lowered the binoculars and swatted a mosquito on his neck. "Some kind of stash house, nice and secluded, just how I like it."

The gang pulled out of the driveway and sped down a dusty road along the edge of the palms.

"Quick," said Serge. "Behind a tree."

The vehicles shot past them.

CHAPTER 37

THAT NIGHT

*T*wo burly goons in electricians' uniforms stood in a motel hallway. One had a toolbox and the other a universal magnetic card key bribed from one of the motel's staff. They looked both ways, then jumped inside.

The first burglar abruptly pulled up after two steps. Their informant had said nobody was supposed to be inside. He was wrong, except in this case it was better: no need to search for the hiding place.

On the other end of the room, Coleman sat at a desk with a jeweler's magnifying loupe in his right eye, examining a large tray full of real-looking fake gems. He glanced up when he heard the men; the loupe fell from his eye and bounced across the desk.

The one with the toolbox smiled at the other. "This is too easy."

The second pulled a gun and moved quickly across the room. "Step away from the tray and you won't get hurt."

Coleman got up and stumbled backward until he was pressed against a wall.

"Now stay there and don't move a muscle."

The armed electrician kept him covered while the other dumped the tray's contents into his toolbox. He closed the lid and latched it. "Got it. Let's go."

The one with the gun: "We have a witness."

"Didn't you hear me? We got the stones."

"He can identify us."

"We don't need the heat."

"You want to explain that to the Jellyfish? He was very specific:

Never leave a witness. We can't take the chance now that they can pin those two murders."

"Why don't we just split and say the room was empty."

"Jellyfish will kill us." He raised his shooting arm.

Suddenly, Serge rolled out from under the bed. He laid on his back and braced a pistol between his knees. "Drop it!"

The man glanced down at Serge, but kept his gun on Coleman.

"You're not that fast," said Serge, slowly standing up.

The man took a step backward toward the door. "Let's call it a draw."

"Let's not," said Serge. "We want our stones back. Then we'll let you leave."

"Fuck off." The man took another retreat step, gun still trained between Coleman's eyes.

"Don't move another inch."

"There's no way you can shoot me before I take out your friend."

"So what?" said Serge. "I've never seen him before in my life."

"Serge!" yelled Coleman.

"You're bluffing."

"Am I?" He grabbed a pillow off the bed, placed it in front of the barrel and fired.

The electrician heard the bullet whiz by. He placed a hand to his arm, then looked at it. Blood. He dropped the gun.

"That's better." Serge walked over and kicked the pistol under the bed. "Take a seat in that chair. And you . . ."—waving the gun at the other intruder—". . . grab that other chair."

"What for?"

"We going to play a little parlor game."

Minutes later, Serge was giddy with excitement. The electricians sat back-to-back in the pair of rigid motel room chairs, hands bound behind their backs with plastic wrist cuffs. Ankles wrapped with rope to the chairs' legs.

Serge then tied another plastic cuff around each of their necks, leaving them slightly loose.

Both captives struggled vainly against their bindings. "Whatever you're planning, you won't get away with it."

"I already have," said Serge. "Now here's the fun part . . ." He displayed a roll of sturdy nylon twine, then unrolled two short lengths and cut them.

"We'll yell," said one of the bandits.

"No you won't." Serge tied loops of twine around each of their foreheads and held them in place with his coveted duct tape. "You want to escape without getting arrested, and I'm giving you the perfect opportunity." Each loop of forehead twine left a two-foot-long tail behind each of their backs. Serge tugged them. "What I'm doing now is attaching the twine from each of your heads to the end of the plastic cuff around your friend's neck."

"But Serge . . ." said Coleman.

"Shhhhh!" He threaded both lengths of nylon through the top slats of the opposing chairs and back to the ends of the straps around their necks. "Coleman, your lighter . . ." Serge caught it on the fly and flicked it between the heads. They couldn't see the action but smelled burning plastic. Serge began blowing to cool the welded joints between the melted nylon and straps. He stepped aside and smiled. "There. Done. And not a shabby job if I do say so."

Coleman came over. "Seems like we've been leaving a lot of guys in chairs."

"My life is now completely about chairs and things that remind me of chairs."

The hostages looked up at him without a hint.

"I'll give you a hint," said Serge. "I'm sure you're familiar with those plastic cuffs. When you pull them, they notch progressively tighter, but don't loosen. I'm conducting a behavioral test."

"What kind of test?"

"Moral dilemma. If you work as a loyal team and remain calm, you'll survive until the maid comes in the morning. Of course you'll get arrested when they realize you're not legitimate electricians working for the hotel. If you turn state's evidence and testify against the Jellyfish or Eel or whatever, you can dodge the death penalty. Still go to jail for a long time, but at least you'll be alive."

"You said we had a chance to escape."

"That's the dilemma part," said Serge. "If you pull forward with your heads, the twine will tighten the notched strap around your colleague's neck. Those things are ten times strong enough to effect

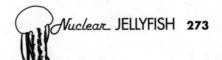

strangulation." Serge reached with both hands and tugged. They each heard a notch click and felt the straps tighten slightly against windpipes.

They gulped.

The one on the left looked up. "How does that help us escape?"

"I'll be back in an hour. If only one of you is still alive, I'll let you go. If you're both still kicking, I'll leave you for the maid. And there's the big moral choice: Sacrifice a jail sentence to save your friend's life, or betray him for your freedom."

"You're sick!"

"I can see you'd like a little privacy to discuss it. Come on, Coleman . . ."

They left the room and closed the door.

Coleman stopped at a vending machine for a rum mixer. "I still don't understand what's going on in there. You didn't attach the twine to the other guy's neck strap."

"That's right. I lied." Serge fed quarters into the machine for his own bottle of spring water. "I looped each piece of twine through the other guy's chair slat and back to his own neck cuff. So if he pulls to strangle his pal, he's only tightening his own strap. Then, of course, he'll think the other guy's doing it, and he'll pull harder to try to kill his friend before the guy can kill him first, and so forth. Whoever coined 'vicious circle' had no idea."

"I'm still not getting it."

"When I come back in an hour, the one who survives and gets to go free will actually be the guy who was loyal to his friend. I like to reward those who live by an ethical code."

"You're always helping people."

"Yet for some reason they never say thank you."

Coleman felt his pockets. "I forgot my lighter."

"You'd forget your head . . ." They went back to the room and Serge opened the door.

Coleman grabbed his Bic off the dresser, next to a pair of blue heads slumped lifelessly to their chests. "That was fast."

"Again, no thank-you."

CHAPTER 38

HOMESTEAD

*S*erge squinted up as wispy clouds parted around a crescent moon. "Still more light than I'd like. But no going back now. We'll wait for the next cloud."

Coleman peered out from the edge of the palm tree farm. "Where's Story?"

"Auditioning."

"Another strip club?"

"Not exactly." Serge kept his eyes on the hacienda. "At least she's out of our hair. Women don't approve of guys' habits."

The pickup and van had returned to the driveway. Lamps glowed through slits in hurricane shutters on the back of the house.

Serge held a travel thermos that had risen above all others in function, value and personality statement. He clicked open the drip-proof sipping spout, raised it straight up and sucked a good fifteen seconds. Then he tucked the half-empty bottle into the shopping bag at his feet. Next to the bag were a pair of hefty black machines with molded rubber grips, the size of small suitcases. Serge reached down and grabbed one in each hand. "Here's the next cloud. Coleman, get that shopping bag."

"What's in it?"

"You'll find out soon enough. So will they. I *love* surprises! The expressions are priceless."

They slipped quickly across the clearing.

"Hope we're in time," said Serge.

"For what?"

"If my suspicions are correct, once the Eel finds out 'Dick' hooked the gang up with a double-cross, he won't have the life expectancy of a lottery-winning heroin addict."

They slid along the side of the hacienda and reached a side door.

"You don't want anything to happen to 'Dick'?"

"Not before I get him." Serge set his cargo on the ground and tried the knob. Locked. He pressed an ear to the door. Loud TV and louder voices. "Perfect." He picked the lock with a pair of thin metal tools and slowly opened the jalousie door. A rusty creak. They tiptoed into a small utility hall with hooks for rain gear. Voices grew louder. Light in the next room. Serge pulled his pistol and peeked around the corner. The goons were rolling up a Persian rug, two feet sticking out the end. Serge stepped back.

"What is it?" asked Coleman.

" 'Dick' won the lottery."

"What now?"

"They're distracted." Serge sprang from the hall and spread his legs in police academy shooting stance. The thugs looked up, unimpressed.

"Turn around!" yelled Serge. "Against the wall, hands high!"

They bitterly complied.

Serge ran over and pressed his pistol to the back of a skull.

The goon turned his head sideways. "You've just written your own death warrant. I can't wait to be there. It won't be quick—"

"Shut up!" Serge's free hand slammed the man's head, smashing his face into the wall. He jerked the goon's right arm behind his back and pulled out the plastic wrist cuffs. "Coleman, coffee me!"

Coleman reached into the shopping bag, opened the thermos and held it to Serge's mouth . . .

Moments later, another typical scene of increasing frequency. Two bound hostages. With one crucial distinction.

"Hey, Serge, how come you're not using chairs this time. You don't like them anymore?"

Serge looked down at the floor. "Chairs are out."

"What about songs?"

"No more chair songs either. Especially instrumentals."

On the side of the room lay Dick's broken, lifeless body, where it had rolled to a stop against the baseboard after Serge had grabbed the edge of the Persian rug and unspooled him. Now in Dick's place were his two killers, only their gagged heads visible, wrapped back-to-back in six layers of carpet that were secured with a hundred feet of thick hemp rope and almost as much reinforced packing tape.

Coleman fired up a joint. "You like that rug?"

Serge looked down at the wiggling hostages. "It brings the room together."

"Rugs are now in?"

"And rug songs."

Coleman took a deep hit. "Can we go to the Rock Vault?"

"Lead the way."

"'Magic Carpet Ride'?"

"Good choice."

The goons looked up in terror as their clearly off-kilter captors swayed to silent music inside their heads.

The music ended. Swaying stopped. Serge stood directly over the captives. "And now we've come to the Q-and-A portion of the program. Most of the other guys have tons of questions when they reach this point. That's why I like people: We're adorably curious. So, what's on your minds?"

Muted desperation under mouth tape.

"Oh, right. Your particular procedure means you can't ask questions at this time. No problem. It's come up before. We'll just go to Serge's Florida Experience F.A.Q. And if you don't know what F.A.Q. stands for, that's actually the first question in my F.A.Q. None of the other travel service F.A.Q.s think of that. Accept no substitutes!" Serge squatted low for intimate conversation. "Second question: What kind of incredible learning curve of jollies is old Serge about to take me on? The answer is in that shopping bag! Shall we go to the shopping bag?"

Coleman took a triple hit off his roach clip. "Whoa! Good weed! Serge, can we go over to the shopping bag with out-loud music this time?"

"I don't see why not."

"Cool." Coleman stubbed out the roach and joined Serge, singing and jitterbugging across the room: *"Let's go over to the shopping*

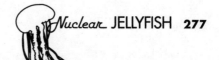

bag! Let's go over to the shopping bag! Let's go over to the shopping baaaaaaaggggggggg! . . . And see what fun's inside!"

Serge grabbed the sack, and they began dancing back across the room to piercing whines of desperation.

Serge: *"And see what fun's inside!"*

Coleman: *"And see what fun's inside!"*

Serge: *"Ohhhhhhhhh! Let's look into the shopping bag . . ."*

Coleman: *"Right on into the shopping bag . . ."*

Serge: *"What the fuck's in our shopping baaaaaaaggggggg? . . ."*

Coleman: *"Some crazy fuckin' shit!"*

Serge opened the top of the bag and began rummaging. "Let's see what we got here . . ." He extracted items one by one. "Doorbell, extension cord, vegetable peeler, post office overnight express envelope . . ."

Coleman, pianissimo in the background: *". . . Some crazy fuckin' shit, some crazy fuckin' shit . . ."*

". . . Bicycle inner tubes, soldering iron, model railroad tracks, tiny envelope of fake diamonds. That's about it . . . Oh, and those two other big things on the floor with the molded rubber grips. Travel tip two-fifty-four: Always have a portable, self-powered five-in-one roadside auto emergency center. Heavy as hell, but worth every ounce. That's because of the giant internal electric cell you charge up at home. But you ask, Serge, what are the five uses? To the F.A.Q.! One, fluorescent lamp for engine work; two, cell-phone recharger; three, battery jump-starter; four, flashing highway-shoulder warning light; five, air compressor with over-pressure cutoff to fill tires after using Fix-a-Flat . . . And for today's lucky contestants, a sixth additional use chosen especially for you!"

"They fainted," said Coleman.

Serge lightly tapped cheeks. "Wake up, you don't want to sleep through the additional use or you'll kick yourselves." Tapping turned to slaps. "Wake up! . . . That's better. Pay attention because I'm only going to say this once. My intricate plan begins with this doorbell. Houses are so much bigger today! Who can hear the doorbell from the Jacuzzi? So they came up with a new remote broadcasting system. See this little ringer?" Serge turned it around. "Wireless. Takes a single double-A battery. Adhesive back that sticks permanently to the out-

side doorframe and transmits a hundred feet to electric chimes . . ."
—he held up a small white speaker in the other hand—". . . that you
plug into a wall socket in the back of the house . . . Again, I read in-
quisitiveness in your eyes: How on earth did you dream this up? Home
Depot! Whenever I'm suffering a creative block, I wander the aisles
and ideas flood! . . . Now just sit back and enjoy the show."

Serge turned on the soldering iron and grabbed the vegetable
peeler. He dove into his science project with usual speed and obsessive
attention. Covers were unscrewed on the doorbell chimes and roadside emergency units. Wires pulled out and stripped with the peeler,
circuits rerouted. Tendrils of smoke rose from fused electrical posts.
He gripped each of their heads. "Hold still. This won't hurt." More
plugs went into sockets. Rubber tubes clamped onto male fittings.

Serge stood. "And that about does it . . . Brilliant, eh?"

They looked up with vacant eyes.

"I keep getting that expression," said Serge. "You don't get it? It's
so obvious!"

Still no flicker in their stares.

"Okay. Guess I have to explain *everything*. I'll start at the back
end with a little diamond-courier inside dope."

Coleman's head snapped up. "Dope?"

"Knowledge."

"Ick."

"Live human couriers are still the preferred method, but believe
it or not, some expensive gems are simply sent through the U.S. mail
in small, unassuming packages like this one." Serge held up the express pouch. "Heavily insured. Back in the day, this was unheard of,
because when you purchased insurance, the amount of the surcharge
was stamped on the package. And they didn't have computers to track
packages back then. So all that any postal employees in the transit
stream had to do was multiply the surcharge stamps to get the value of
a package's contents. Not too good a procedure. But then came laser
scanners! The insurance amount was concealed inside bar codes. The
package could contain a Ginsu knife for all they knew. Then, upon
hitting its final destination, the last bar scan triggered a code sum-
moning a top local post office manager, who had to personally accept
and sign for the package. Imagine that! Every day, millions in gems

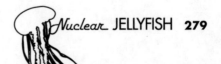

flying all around us, mixed up with Publishers Clearing House."

Serge grabbed a small brown envelope, stuck it in the express package and sealed the flap. "These are just fake diamonds, though still a nice present for someone's girlfriend if you don't think it'll last. And since they're not real, I won't need insurance. But don't underestimate the importance of the package! Its value in the domino chain is essential! In this case, the dominos are a series of electrical circuits that need to be competed." He set the parcel aside.

"Now, on to the heavy lifting. You've probably noticed that I've wrapped deflated bicycle inner tubes around your necks, and their inflation stems are connected to the rubber hoses of the roadside emergency air compressors. This button on top of the unit turns on the compressor by, as everyone knows, completing the circuit of the two wires attached inside. That's why I removed the back panel and snipped the wires off the switch, which unfairly voided the warranty. Then I soldered the 'on button' wires to the model railroad tracks. But not any model railroad tracks! This piece here is called the switch. It's one of those Y-connections where you can let the choo-choo go straight or divert it off into the mountain tunnel. The switches are complex to wire because they're controlled by solenoids, but I rigged tons of them in parallel circuits on my train set when I was ten, then took little plastic people off the depot platform and put them on the tracks and—Oh my God! Here comes the Atchison Topeka & Santa Fe! I can't watch! . . . Throwing the switch at the last second. Whew! . . . But wait, what are those other crazy people doing up on that trestle? Hours of endless fun!"

Serge grabbed the stretch of railroad track and its magnetic controller. "The beauty of a solenoid is that, in order to throw the switch, it requires but a single pulse of electricity, which can be supplied by . . ."—he grabbed another pair of wires leading to the wall—". . . say, door chimes. And there you have all the dominos: If someone comes to this house and presses the doorbell, which I took the liberty of installing on your porch, it transmits a small frequency to this wall unit. The chimes will ring, but they'll also supply power to the train tracks, which will switch, turning on the air compressor, filling the inner tubes around your neck and cutting off your oxygen. If it was a regular compressor and nobody was around to monitor, the tubes would simply keep expanding until they exploded and you'd be in the clear. But as I said, the roadside unit has an over-inflation cutoff. You wouldn't want me rigging you to something unsafe."

Now that the entire picture had taken shape, the goons fought to free themselves like never before.

"Whoa!" said Serge. "Hold on. You don't have much to worry about. Given unlimited time, there's a hypothetical point where people can wiggle themselves out of even the most complex restraints. Or someone else in your gang could drop by and stumble upon you. Just as long as nobody rings that doorbell. And what are the odds, way out here in the middle of a palm tree farm?"

Struggling continued unabated.

Coleman checked the fridge for beer. "You really thought this up in Home Depot?"

Serge nodded. "Had this plan in my back pocket ever since I bought those garden hoses in Jacksonville. It's the perfect complementary bookend to those skinheads, whom I only wrapped to their shoulders—blood pressure, remember?—and now I've wrapped the rest of the way, completing the spiritual cycle of life, or, well . . ." He faced the goons again. "I always like my science projects to have a relevant theme. In this case we're dealing with the transportation of diamonds." He picked up the overnight express package. "Hey, look, it already has an address on it." He held it to his face. "Well what do you know? It's *this* place. Isn't that an amazing coincidence? Better get it to the post office right away because, if you're anything like me, you can't wait to get a surprise in the mail!"

Serge collected three cell phones from around the room and started walking for the front door. He stopped and looked again at the express mailer in his hand. "Whoops, almost forgot to check this box on the form." He turned it toward the goons and smiled.

Signature required.

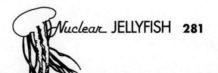

CHAPTER 39

Serge leaned back in a bamboo chair. Another dark room. Tiered wooden serving bowls sat on the table in front of him, next to a pineapple with a lampshade.

A man in a tweed coat and rumpled fedora grabbed the chair on the other side of the table. His necktie had a pattern of tiki gods, similar to the giant, carved versions guarding the entrance. He set a briefcase on the ground.

Serge pointed at the bowls. "I ordered the pupu platter. Try the crab Rangoon."

"Serge, I have something important—"

"Bet you're impressed I picked the Mai-Kai." Serge glanced around at decorative coconuts, wicker and ceremonial face masks. "Since 1956, Polynesian splendor on the side of Federal Highway, recently mentioned by a Colombian hit man as a rendezvous point in the excellent documentary *Cocaine Cowboys*, now out on DVD."

"This is serious!"

Serge opened a leatherbound menu. "I'm leaning toward the Singapore prawns."

"Forget food! I need to tell you something—"

He was interrupted by loudness at the front of the room.

"Hold that thought." Serge bent over to sip iced coffee through a straw from a hollowed-out souvenir fertility statue. "Stage show's starting."

A feverish beat of South Pacific drums filled the room as men in authentic loincloths twirled flaming batons. In the middle, five women, sensuous hips and grass skirts, gyrating at an astounding rate.

"Serge—"

"Isn't Story great?" He took another sip. "Thought I was immune to exotic dancing, but this hula business is an entirely different proposition."

"Serge! It's Story I want to talk about!"

Still watching the stage: "What about her? . . . Hold it . . ." He turned to Mahoney in alarm. "You're not speaking noir."

"Back on my meds."

Serge slumped in his chair. "Now why'd you go and do that? We had a thing, you and me."

"I know what you've been into."

"Enlighten."

"Picking off the Eel's gang."

"Why would I do something like that?"

"Your code. They beat Howard pretty good. But not good enough. Left a living witness. There's a contract out on him, which I'm guessing you already knew."

"If I cared."

"Serge, you don't have to play coy. I gave you my word, so I can't take you in on this. But let us handle it. They moved Howard to another hospital under an assumed name, and he's got around-the-clock police protection."

"President Kennedy had protection."

"There's more. A contract on you, too. The mess at those motels, not to mention down Homestead way."

"Me?"

"Damn it! What do I have to say?"

"That you'll stop taking your meds."

Mahoney looked toward the stage. "Remember when I asked if you'd met anyone new, possibly even traveling with them? Someone who might be feeding info on your movements to whoever wants you dead?"

"Yeah, back at Harry and the Natives."

"I was wrong."

Nuclear JELLYFISH **283**

"This is a first."

"It's Story."

"What about her?"

"She's not passing info. She's after you herself."

"That's crazy."

"I would have thought so too, until I found out she's Howard's sister."

Serge's head snapped back. "You're shitting me."

"Been using you to lead her to the gang. Steve ring a bell?"

"I didn't kill Steve."

"I know."

"Another first."

"Don't get all happy. I'd have bet anything it was you until I saw the tape."

"Tape?"

Mahoney reached down for his briefcase and opened a laptop on the table. "Security camera at the end of the motel hallway. I downloaded the digitized footage."

The agent turned the computer toward Serge. On the grainy screen, a woman walked down the hall. Stiletto heels, mini skirt, big hair. She stopped in front of a door and knocked.

"That's Steve's room," said Mahoney.

"I get it now. Barracuda hooker. One of the oldest scams," said Serge. "Getting her foot in the door to let the Eel's hit men in."

"There are no hit men."

"What are you talking about?"

Mahoney fast-forwarded the video. The woman came back out and closed the door.

"*She's* the killer?" said Serge.

"Keep watching."

The woman walked back down the hall toward the elevators. As she grew closer to the camera, facial features became recognizable.

"It's Story!" Serge smacked himself in the forehead. "Of course. Said she was studying."

"Believe me now?"

"I believe she wants revenge for Howard. But there's no way she'd whack me."

"Howard was pretty incoherent by the time she got to the hospital. The police guard overheard him mention your name before going back under."

"But I'm Howard's friend. If she's using me to get to the gang, she must know I want the same thing she does."

"Serge, she's not using you to lead her to the gang because she thinks you're after them. It's because she thinks you're *one* of them."

"What!"

"At first she wasn't sure. Just had your name mumbled from her brother's lips. So she went to the convention center show where Howard was supposed to appear next, figuring you'd be there, which you were, then followed you to the Skynyrd bar."

"That *is* a big coincidence," said Serge. "But it still doesn't explain why she thinks I'm with the crew who attacked her brother."

"Think about it," said Mahoney. "All your cloak-and-dagger to infiltrate the gang, meeting with Steve, the guys at the Wreck Lounge . . ."

"You know about that?"

". . . Surreptitious phone calls, feeding disinformation on nonexistent couriers—everything you did was designed to fool the gang into thinking you were a legit and let you in. Meanwhile, she's been observing the whole time. Your plan worked too well. It also fooled her."

Serge looked back toward the stage. Tahitian drums beat louder. Story's hips reached blinding speed. "I don't know . . ."

"Okay, if nothing else," said Mahoney. "Doesn't it seem a bit odd she's still hanging with you?"

"We're an item."

"Please!"

Serge's head sagged. "I thought it was too good to be true, View-Master and all."

"How are you going to handle it?" asked Mahoney.

"Ambush."

"You're going to kill her just for being mistaken?"

Serge shook his head. "The Benevolent Ambush. If I wait for her to come to me, it might not turn out too well. I need to get the drop when she least expects it so I can explain everything without having to dodge bullets."

"Isn't she staying with you?"

"No. Packed everything up before her audition earlier today and moved in with roommates at her new school."

"That fits with everything I just told you."

"When you're right, you're right."

"Serge, I know how stubborn you are, so you're not going to like what I'm about to say next, but I want you to leave town, the whole state would be even better. Just until this blows over. I promise I'll take care of the gang."

"No can do."

"Damn it, Serge! A crew is after you, Story's after you and . . . I shouldn't be telling you this but I'm way past the point of caring about whatever's left of my career: State agents are closing in. They've been homing off your laptop's wi-fi connection. You've been lucky because you move around so much, but it's just a matter of time."

"Have to stay. It's a question of character, my loyalty to Howard."

"Can't you be reasonable this one time? I don't have a good feeling."

"Neither do I," said Serge. "But nobody lives forever. Had a good run." He reached down in his lap and placed a large, lumpy envelope on the table. He slid it across to Mahoney.

"What's this?"

"Addresses and keys. Various storage lockers around the state."

"Please tell me you're not keeping bodies in refrigerators."

"My Floridiana collection. If anything happens to me, I want you to be my executor—split it with Howard. That second page is the request for my funeral arrangements."

"Serge, you're scaring me. Don't talk like that."

"In return for the treasure trove, a small favor."

"What's that?"

"Adopt Coleman."

"Huh?"

"He's already an adult, so you won't get to take him on Cub Scout trips. And he's 'special' on multiple levels, but they say those are the most loving."

"Serge!"

He pushed out his chair and stood.

"What are you doing?"

"I gotta be me!"

He sprinted out of the restaurant.

The Eel's cell phone rang. He opened it.

"Talk."

"Hello, worm."

"You must have the wrong number."

"I don't have the wrong number," said Serge. "I know most people call you Eel, but I think worm is a better name, or sea slug. What do you think?"

"Who are you?"

"Serge, the guy who's been messing up your operation. You should never have touched that kid."

"What are you talking about? Where'd you get this number?"

"From the cell phones I collected at your Homestead stash house, *Jellyfish*!"

A prolonged moment of steaming silence on the other end of the line. Then: "Why don't we meet somewhere and discuss this?"

"We will," said Serge. "Wait, I just thought of a better name for you. Dead Man."

"You do realize what you've just done."

"See you in hell." Click.

A goon came over. "Who was that?"

The Eel studied the display screen on his cell. "Someone who just seriously fucked up. He called from a hotel phone and told us where he's staying."

"I know that place," said the goon. "It's in Miami Beach."

"Get Frankie. Take the van."

Serge walked away from a courtesy phone in the lobby of a Miami Beach hotel.

"Serge," said Coleman. "Why'd you use that phone when you got your cell?"

"To tell him where I'm staying."

"Why would you want to do that?"

"Make myself bait."

CHAPTER 40

MIAMI BEACH

*T*wo bulging men with long, stringy hair glanced down the length of the hotel bar.

"That's him."

"You sure?"

"Inside source got us a name on our witness."

"That kid we put in the hospital?"

"Police moved him to an undisclosed location. But we lucked out and got his sister's name. Tracked her to a local college."

"So how does the guy over there fit in?"

"I tailed the sister from the school this afternoon. She came to this bar and met that guy. They seemed to know each other *real* well."

"And this guy's going to tell us the new hospital where the witness is?"

The first bodyguard shook his head. "We have a new problem. Just got briefed. Looks like the kid's sent some people after us."

"Who'd have ever thought he had muscle behind him?"

"They even threatened the Eel on his own phone."

"Jesus, the balls."

"And I thought it was just a big coincidence."

"What? All the guys in the crew we've lost lately? . . . You're saying someone's on a revenge spree?"

"Starting to look that way."

"Even the Homestead stash house?"

"Especially the Homestead stash house. And we could be next."

"Let's make our move." He looked down the bar again. "Guy's alone. Perfect chance."

"Why's it perfect?"

"He's stewed."

Coleman slipped off his stool and clawed vainly for the edge of the bar before he went down.

Large hands grabbed him from behind—"Easy there, fella"—and propped Coleman back onto his seat.

"Gee, thanks."

The bodyguards took a stool on each side. "What are you drinking?"

"Whiskey."

A muscular arm went up. "Bartender, double Jack over here for our new friend . . ."

"So," said the thug on the other side. "What brings you to town?"

"I'm not supposed to tell you."

"Drink up."

A half hour later: ". . . Then we started tracking this band of hotel robbers who beat the hell out of this kid."

"Sounds like an interesting job. Is the girl working with you?"

Coleman shook his head. "Completely in the dark."

One goon looked at the other. "Think he's lying about the chick?"

"He's too drunk to lie." Then, back to Coleman: "What do you think of this hotel?"

"Great place. Free liquor."

"We're not that happy with our room."

"You're kidding," said Coleman. "Ours is great!"

"Sometimes the quality differs floor to floor," said the thug on the other side. "What room are you in?"

"Three-twelve."

The larger of the goons got off his stool and glanced back at the other. "Stay here with our new friend and make sure he doesn't come up. I don't want to be disturbed."

———

Serge opened the motel room door. "Coleman, I'm home!"

No answer.

"Coleman?" He checked the bathroom. Then looked across the suite. "That's funny. Could have sworn I turned the TV off." He walked toward it.

Someone jumped from the shadows, looping a strong, thin cord around Serge's neck from behind.

Serge heard him at the last second, but only enough time to get two fingers up under the cord. It wouldn't be enough. The assailant possessed brute force, and the ligature was like a razor. Serge's fingers began to bleed as he choked and gasped for breath. He twisted and jumped. They slammed into one wall, then another, crashing into the television cabinet. The much stronger assailant easily maintained his grip. Even laughed.

Serge gave it everything he had, and, with a primordial grunt, tried to double forward and flip the man over his back. They barely moved, telling Serge he was dealing with at least three hundred pounds. So back to slamming into walls, each failed attempt sapping energy from Serge's body. The man laughed again and whispered in his ear: "The Eel says, 'Hi.'"

Serge's face turned bright red. He strained with all his might, pulling the attacker forward, and they both fell onto the bed. The hit man jerked Serge back up by the cord, his feet briefly leaving the floor.

Toying time over. Another whisper: "You're really beginning to piss me off." The goon had a wooden dowel through the ends of the cord, which he twisted over and over, tightening the strangle hold. Blood ran down Serge's left arm from where his fingers were sliced clean to the knuckles. His right arm flew out desperately, swatting a lamp off the dresser. The light bulb shattered and the room went dark. Serge's arm quivered by his side. His tongue hung out, eyes rolling back in his head.

A final whisper: "Goodnight." Then the death pull on the cord. Serge's feet left the ground again. His twitching right hand found the top of a hip pocket. Out came something the attacker didn't recognize. But so what? Just a harmless piece of plastic.

Serge quickly brought it to his neck and slipped it between the two bleeding fingers of his other hand.

 JELLYFISH **291**

The attacker found himself in utter shock as he stumbled back a step, holding two pieces of cord snapped apart by the seat-belt cutter. He looked up.

Serge swung with a wicked sidewinder motion. The point of the survival tool's window punch caught the man in the temple, buried itself a good inch and stuck. Serge let go and stepped away.

Normally a person would have immediately collapsed, lights out. But every once in a while, if a foreign object enters the brain just right, there's a short period of otherwise comical short-circuiting through the nervous system, like over-voltage in a robot. The man's limbs flapped spastically, his face contorting in all kinds of crazy expressions . . . Okay, it actually was funny. The attacker briefly caught himself in the mirror, his last memory on the planet: this ridiculous-looking hazard-yellow gizmo sticking out the side of his head like a tiny toy ax. Then, all life ceased, and he went straight down as if someone snipped the wires on a marionette.

Serge looked at his fingers. "I got a boo-boo." He grabbed a travel first-aid kit out of his suitcase, stepped over the body and went in the bathroom. A faucet came on. Minutes later, Serge came out with fresh bandage dressing. He bent down and wiggled his lucky tool free.

CHAPTER 41

*T*he sun went down over South Beach. Topless bathers grabbed their tops. Neon came on. A Crown Vic with black-wall tires headed up Collins Avenue.

Mahoney had lost Serge. But not his scent. He'd picked up the next best thing. Story reclined against the back window of a metro bus a hundred feet in front of the agent's car.

Behind Mahoney was a windowless white van with magnetic lawn-care signs. The front passenger had long, stringy hair and bin-oculars focused on the rear window of the bus.

The bus stopped every few blocks. People got on and off. Mainly on: domestic help heading home to the mainland. Story stayed put. So did Mahoney.

To local residents, the sight of a transit bus was the signal to get over in the left lane or be stacked up, stop after frequent stop, cursing under breath. Cars that hadn't already gotten over did so. That's how Mahoney spotted the van, the only other vehicle remaining patiently in the right lane.

They left the surface flash of South Beach. At the intersection with Arthur Godfrey, two nondescript sedans with extra antennae, tinted windows and yellow government plates made a wide left, join-ing the public bus motorcade. They entered the realm of the old guard, Fontainebleau, Eden Roc. More stops. The blond hair on the back of Story's head stayed pressed against the glass. Mahoney checked his mirrors and noticed the growing population.

"Damn."

Ten blocks ahead, an orange-and-green Javelin reached the grimy north end of the strip, where people lived out of mildewed motel rooms, and old Cuban men with straw hats popped into narrow storefronts all day long for shots of espresso. Serge's favorite part of the beach.

"There's the Stardust!" he told Coleman. "Where porn star John Holmes hid out while on the lam from the Wonderland murders in the Hollywood Hills."

Serge drove a few more blocks and hid the car as far down a tight alley as he could before a discarded sofa stopped him. He got out and climbed over the couch. "Careful, Coleman, those springs are sharp."

They ended up in a parking lot on the back side of a stark cement building with black streaks from roof runoff. Cars began trickling in. Ten-year-old Camaros and Subarus and Toyotas. All the drivers were women, all tall, acutely sexual and high mileage. Torn jeans and loose jerseys, carrying gym bags like they were headed for the spa. The first knocked on a reinforced steel door. A barrel-chested man with shaved head, goatee and gold earring opened it. Four women filed inside. More cars, another knock on steel; the door opened again, etcetera.

Opposite the front of the building, a bus stopped. Story got off in torn jeans, carrying a gym bag. She jaywalked across the street and went through the building's front entrance, which was a chipped, blood-red door under a row of half-burned-out cabaret lights.

The lawn-care van parked at the corner in a parallel metered slot. Mahoney followed the bus a block past the club to avert detection. Two government sedans made a left.

Five muscle-bound men exited the landscaping van and assembled in the street outside the vehicle's side door. They made the usual visual sweep of surroundings, hands over concealed weapons. When they were satisfied of no imminent danger, the door slid open. The Eel stepped down into the middle of the gang for a circular human shield. The clot of goons moved across the street without regard for brake-screeching traffic that stopped in both directions and would have leaned on horns, but appraised the men first and thought better. Even the bouncer at the door retreated against the entryway as they marched inside. One of the bodyguards peeled off to check the building's perimeter.

The strip club was cave dark and characteristically vacant at opening time. Just three ringside hard-cores staring up at empty firehouse poles. Someone turned on the sound. A deafening dance-beat, eighties funk, extra-heavy on the bass.

The gang moved along the southern row of lap-dance booths, maintaining its security envelope around the Eel. A second guard broke away to check the restrooms.

"... *You dropped the bomb on me! Baby, baby ...*"

One of the entourage pulled out a chair for their leader, who took a seat at the edge of the catwalk. From the neckline of a shirt, a jellylike blob glowed a fluorescent, toxic-waste green in the club's dim light. The rest of the gang remained standing in their protective ring, backs to the Eel, looking out toward empty seats that would soon begin filling.

A bodyguard returned. Restrooms clear.

Curtains at the back of the club parted. A malnourished peroxide-blonde with science-fiction tits strutted out in lingerie.

Another guard returned from his outside rounds. He leaned to the Eel and whispered. Bad news. Two-tone Javelin in the alley. Lingerie fell to the stage.

The Eel snapped his fingers. Others knew what to do.

A pair of the crew jumped up on the back of the catwalk. Another bouncer appeared from the curtains. He couldn't be heard above the pounding music, but his emphatic gestures said: You can't go back there!

"... *Super freak! Super freak ...*"

The bouncer recovered from a hard shove and followed the men to the dressing room. At the opposite end of the club, the front door opened again. Four G-men with white shirts and thin black ties.

Across the street, Mahoney observed the other agents enter the club. A fifth G-man spotted the Javelin in the alley and stood watch, leaning against the orange trunk. Mahoney pulled the front brim of his fedora low over his eyes, trotted across the road and went inside. He kept his head down, looking away from the starched white shirts, now luminous blue, and commandeered a seat in the darkest booth at the back of the club.

The catwalk's curtains flew open. Bodyguards jumped down from

the stage and walked quickly up the aisle toward the Eel, shaking their heads: no sign of Serge. The Eel motioned for one of his goons, whispering instructions to stand guard in the alley by the Javelin. He ran out the front door. The Eel slipped a twenty in a garter belt.

The dancer sashayed out of sight through the curtains, which opened again as quickly as they had closed. New dancer, redhead in pig-tails, cheerleader uniform. Tempo changed.

"... *You!* ... *Shook me alllllll night long!* ..."

The dispatched guard entered the west end of the alley and took up position, leaning against the Javelin's front hood. He nodded at the state agent by the trunk.

Back inside, the Eel leaned forward with another twenty and a slimy grin. The dancer stepped over the fallen pom-poms, cocked her knee forward and stretched an elastic garter.

More dancers and music. The Eel became increasingly engrossed. Patrons trickled in, and the bodyguards tightened their outward-facing semicircle around the Eel's chair, cynically evaluating each new customer.

Then the main attraction. Another theme song.

"... *Devil in a blue dress, blue dress, blue dress* ..."

Story pushed through the curtains in a long, blue bedroom gown and launched into an impressively aerobic routine on a fire pole. One of the crusty regulars sitting along the other side of the catwalk held out a dollar bill. He looked up from under a wig and fake mustache that kept having to be pressed back in place. "Pssst! Story, it's me, Serge!"

She glared back, sliding down from the pole into a split.

From the other side of the catwalk, the Eel made a slight waving motion with another twenty. Story shed the gown and swaggered over. The bill motioned her closer. She squatted right in front of him in a catcher's crouch. His eyes were not on her face.

Story began a slow, rhythmic thrusting of her pelvis. The Eel licked his lips. She grabbed the top edge of her lace panties, just below a pierced belly button, and pulled them down at a teasingly slow rate. The customers on the other side of the catwalk had a prime angle: Story's great ass and a slender, odd bulge in the backside of her underwear.

The Eel extended his arm with the twenty. Music pounded louder. Story reached a hand behind her back.

"*. . . Devil in a blue dress, blue dress . . .*"

Serge cupped his hands around his mouth: "*Jellyfish!*"

The Eel barely heard it above the music, but heard it nonetheless. He tilted his head and peeked around Story's left leg for the source of the insult.

The split second of distraction was all she needed to grab the straight razor from her panties, flip it open and swing with a firm crossing motion.

The bodyguards scrutinized a rambunctious new group of customers. Conventioneers. Dismissed as minimal threat. One of the goons felt dampness on his arm. "What the hell—"

A second guard got hit with jugular spurts. He wiped his cheek and turned. The Eel slumped facedown on the edge of the catwalk, gurgling. The gang looked up, where a man in a wig had jumped onto the stage, taken Story by the hand and was racing her back through the curtains.

"Get them!"

Instantly, the catwalk was a traffic jam of bodyguards and state agents, all fighting for position to get through the curtains.

The back door of the club flew open and slammed against the concrete wall. "This way!" said Serge, pulling Story around the side of the building.

Seconds later, the others poured out, making a hard right and racing toward the alley with the stashed Javelin. They found an agent and a bodyguard casually leaning against the car.

"Shit!"

On the other side of the building, Serge and Story piled into a second car, where Coleman had been waiting with the engine running.

Mahoney stood on the corner and did nothing as they sped off.

CHAPTER 42

NEXT DAY

*T*he Crown Vic turned down a side street off Ocean Drive for a rare chance to escape South Beach glitz. Mahoney parked in an alley and headed for the entrance of Ted's Hideaway.

It was noon. Empty.

"Babs, the regular."

"You got it." A veteran female bartender grabbed a bottle of Boodle's. She looked up from her mixing. "Still interested in the guy asking around about that Serge character?"

Mahoney pulled over a glass ashtray for his spent toothpick. "Thanks for the help, Babs, but all the loose ends got tied up yesterday. I'm officially on vacation."

"Good to hear." She set a drink in front of him. "So another agent's assigned to the case?"

"No, why would you think that?"

"You said 'yesterday.'"

"Yeah?"

"Because the guy was back in here asking about Serge this morning."

"You must be mistaken."

"No, I'm positive. He just left a few minutes before you got here." The bartender began wiping a glass. "Seemed like it was really urgent. Split in a big hurry."

Mahoney jumped up and pulled a mug shot from his jacket. "Recognize him?"

"Yeah." The bartender tossed a towel over her shoulder and looked closer. "Definitely."

"Thought you said you'd never seen Serge."

"I haven't." The bartender turned to grab another glass. "Who's that guy?"

When she looked back, a ten-spot lay on the bar in front an empty seat.

Mahoney dove in the Crown Vic. "Dear God, I hope I'm not too late!"

He grabbed his briefcase off the passenger seat and rapidly thumbed manila folders. The tabs had names of recent victims. He stopped at a late coin dealer named Steve. On a hunch, he flipped through pages of personal data until his finger found the number of a cell that was reported missing from the deceased's motel room.

Mahoney flipped open his own phone and dialed.

"Hello?"

"Who's this?" asked the agent.

"Coleman."

Mahoney heard potato chips crunching. "Coleman, where's Serge?"

"Taking pictures." Crunch, crunch, crunch . . .

"No, I mean where physically? What's the address?"

Crunch. "I'm not supposed to tell you that."

"Coleman! It's important!"

"Serge was very clear. He said, 'Coleman, if Mahoney calls, don't let him trick you into telling him where I am. He'll probably even say it's an emergency.'"

"It's an emergency!"

"Okay." Crunch, crunch. "Hotel Franklin. It's just past—"

"I know the address." Mahoney tossed his phone aside and screeched out of the alley. Less than a minute later, he skidded into a fire lane on the 800 block of Collins, jumped out and ran through a stucco Mediterranean arch.

The agent spun around in the lobby and spotted Coleman at the bar.

"Coleman, where's Serge?"

"Back in the room changing camera batteries."

"What room?"

"He might get mad at me."

"The room!"

"Five."

Mahoney thrust out an arm. "Key!"

Coleman reached in his pocket.

Mahoney snatched it and galloped down a historic wooden hallway. He stuck the key in the knob and burst inside. "Serge! Don't do it!"

"*Mmsdfgkdd* . . ."

"I can't understand you with that gun in your mouth."

Serge removed it. "I said I'm busy." He stuck the barrel back in.

"Serge!"

He pulled the gun out. "What!"

"I don't care how bad it may seem. Talk to me. We can work through depression."

"But I'm not depressed. Couldn't be happier." He swallowed the barrel again.

"I don't understand. If you're not depressed, why kill yourself?"

Serge rolled his eyes and removed the gun again. "Because we live by a code. Two things I hate most in life are bullies and hypocrites. And in my time I've taken care of many in both categories who violated that code. But then I got to thinking, hey, *I'm* a hypocrite, too. If I give myself a free pass for everything I've done, my life is all a big lie. But if I'm consistent and take care of myself as well, then I'm not a hypocrite anymore."

"Serge, it's not your fault."

"Of course it's my fault. I'm always preaching about people assuming responsibility for themselves, and now I'm following my own advice . . . But I have to hand it to you. Someone was after me. *Me.* How'd you know?"

"Didn't until this morning. But then it snapped into place: way too huge a coincidence that someone could follow you step for step down the coast."

"That's another reason I need to do this. Up to now, I've always been confident that I'd never harm someone who didn't deserve it. But then I found out I've been blacking out during the day, asking about myself, and sleepwalking at night, babbling in the mirror. For heaven's sake, I nearly killed Coleman!"

"Let me get you help."

"You've helped enough," said Serge. "Made me face the truth about myself. You were right back during those hurricanes when you thought my personality was splitting. Just took a couple more years." Serge looked down at the gun in his hand. "No, I can't subject society to that kind of risk."

"Listen to me," said the agent. "Done a lot of study on your case. There's all kinds of new breakthroughs for your condition."

"Really?" Serge smiled and relaxed. "Thanks, Mahoney."

"Glad you're starting to think straight."

"I am."

Serge stuck the gun back in his mouth and pulled the trigger.

EPILOGUE

THE FLORIDA KEYS

erge's funeral was held at one of his favorite places on earth.
Mahoney had made the arrangements, faithful to the request on a sheet of paper Serge had given him at the Mai-Kai.

The sun was high and strong, humidity brutal. Mahoney stood in the concealment of a nest of banana trees on Big Pine Key, fedora in hand, wiping his forehead with a silk handkerchief. It had flamingos. To the east, a small bridge arced over Bogie Channel to No Name Key. In the middle of the span, Coleman stood with a plastic tube. He was joined by a collection of diehard regulars from the venerable No Name Pub, along with members of a Keys twelve-step cult deprogramming group who had become devoted disciples of Serge's a few years earlier, all wearing identical T-shirts with their guru's face over his motto: I FOLLOW NOBODY.

Mahoney's mind raced back through the events of the last forty-eight hours:

Standing in that hotel room, Serge suddenly sticking the gun back in his mouth, Mahoney yelling, "Noooooo!" Lunging forward, a step too late. Serge pulling the trigger.

Then Mahoney, freezing in shock. "What the hell?"

And Serge, smiling. "You didn't really think the gun was loaded?" He tossed it on the bed.

Bang.

A mirror shattered.

Mahoney's mind sped back up to the present. He stared at the top of the Bogie Channel Bridge and wiped his face again, then turned to the person standing next to him in the trees. "You almost gave me a heart attack."

"Got you good, didn't I?" said Serge.

"I should turn you in."

"Thanks for the funeral."

"Least I could do." Mahoney looked across the channel at a pair of sedans on the opposite bank. Men in white shirts, thin black ties, aviator sunglasses. One aimed a telephoto lens at the mourners on the top of the bridge. "Gave my word, but then I unintentionally brought all that state heat down on you with my crazy chasing around."

"You're a good man," said Serge.

Mahoney peeked through the trees again at the other agents in the distance. "This ruse should give you a couple days head start."

"They actually put you on indefinite suspension for meeting with me?"

"No, they don't know about the meetings. But I violated about a thousand regulations conducting my own private investigation without filing reports. They frown on that."

"I've seen the police shows. What now?"

"Bought a fishing pole."

"Why don't you come over to our side? You're practically there already."

"Criminals?"

"No, freelance law enforcement. We have lots of fun."

"I don't approve of vigilantes."

"We can take care of them, too."

Mahoney shook his head. "Hear the bonefish are biting off Boca Chica."

"That's hard to compete with. If you change your mind . . ."

"So what are you going to do now?"

"Have some business to tidy up in Miami."

"Story?"

Serge nodded.

"You had me completely fooled. Can't believe she was in on it the whole time."

"I'm not saying anything."

"I know: You want to protect her. I guess Howard wasn't as incoherent in the hospital as I thought when he met with his sister and mentioned you. She needed an ally going after the gang."

Serge just smiled.

"How's the kid doing, anyway?"

"Just released from the hospital. Story said he still looks like shit and has to wear that wrap around his chest for the ribs."

Mahoney looked back at the bridge. Coleman twisted the lid off the plastic tube. "He really thinks you're dead?"

Serge shook his head. "Just gets weepy at sentimental gatherings."

"Got to admit, he played his part surprisingly well."

"He wasn't playing," said Serge. "We had to keep him in the dark and put on a show—for everyone's safety."

"So he really didn't know about your plan with Story?"

"Talks too much in bars. Which I was able to put into play for our benefit."

They both stared back at the gathering. Coleman dumped the plastic tube over the side of the bridge, and a collection of toenail clippings scattered on a light breeze as they fluttered down into the channel. The disciples in Serge T-shirts respectfully bowed their heads and raised fists to the sky: *"Shula!"*

Mahoney lifted his chin. "They're coming."

Serge and the agent retreated deeper into the tropical vegetation. People dabbing eyes filed by on the isolated road and headed for the pub. Coleman brought up the rear, turning off the road and thrashing into the brush. "Serge! Where are you?"

Serge grabbed him by the arm and jerked him into cover. "Quiet! I'm supposed to be dead." He pushed Coleman's head down, and the three crouched. A small convoy of government sedans drove by.

Coleman stood back up. "Does this mean we can't go in the pub?"

Serge turned to Mahoney. "See?"

The agent looked across the street. A white-and-aqua '72 Plymouth Fury sat on the shoulder. "Moving up in the world?"

"Gave myself a promotion." Serge peered through banana leaves, scanning the empty, lazy surroundings. All clear. "Later! . . ."

He and Coleman dashed to the car and jumped in.

"Be safe," called Mahoney.

"When am I not?"

Serge patched out.

Mahoney stepped into the middle of the road and watched the Plymouth disappear around the corner, back toward the Overseas Highway.

MIAMI

Rush-hour traffic on Biscayne Boulevard.

The downtown skyline had gone condo. But there were still enough office workers to jam the streets at five o'clock. BMWs and Jaguars racing for the suburbs and chain-store comfort. They sped past an old strip of retail shops tended by the faithful.

One particular enterprise had recently relocated from the beach, now occupying the slightly larger retail footage of Dade One-Hour Cleaners. It was run by a legend from the sixties that none of the current residents had ever heard of. Roy the Pawn King. The dry-cleaning sign over the door now read: ROY AND SONS DIAMONDS FOR LESS.

A Plymouth Fury skidded to a parking meter. Doorbells jingled.

Roy looked up from the *Herald*. "Serge!"

Big reunion hug. Serge held him out by the arms. "Still have that thick head of white hair."

"Still a hyper son of a gun." He looked around. "Thought Coleman was with you."

"He's busy passed out in the backseat." Serge pulled a strap off his shoulder and set an aged leather case on the glass counter. From it came a vintage View-Master.

"I remember those when I was a kid," said Roy.

"This was the original model, before there was even a slot to slip in reels. You had to open the back."

Serge opened the back. No reel. Instead, a folded rectangle of slick white paper. He handed it to Roy, who peeled the edge and carefully poured the contents onto a small tray. The Pawn King bent over with a jeweler's loupe in his eye.

"Well?" asked Serge.

Roy raised his head and slapped him on the shoulder. "Still my best courier."

"Who would ever suspect someone chasing courier bandits?"

Roy removed the loupe from his eye. "You play the edges too close." He reached under the counter and handed Serge an envelope.

Serge stuck it in his back pocket.

"Not going to count it?"

"Never have before."

Roy noticed the wall clock over Serge's shoulder. Big hand on the three, little on the six. "Excuse me a minute." He reached for a small radio on the counter and tuned it between stations. Loud static. Roy watched the second hand on the clock reach twelve. Then a woman's sultry voice: *"One-fifty-two, nine, eighteen, forty . . ."*

Roy jotted each number on a yellow legal pad until the broadcast was over. He ripped off the top sheet and handed it to Serge. "Maria has another delivery. Amelia Island. Tuesday." A sly grin broke across his face. "Latin bombshell, eh?"

"That she is."

"Great idea you had giving her a shortwave to direct shipments with all my couriers," said Roy. "I'd heard about those coded numbers pirate stations, just never dawned on me to use—"

"That's what I need to talk to you about."

"The radio station?"

"The courier gig."

"Not paying enough?"

"Plenty. But I've given this a lot of thought. I'm retiring."

"Anything wrong?"

"Too much structure in my life."

"What am I going to do without you?"

Bells jingled again. They looked toward the front door. A man and a woman.

"Roy," said Serge. "I'd like you to meet Howard and Story . . . Howard and Story, Roy the Pawn King. Last of the old gang."

Story shook his hand. "Serge speaks very highly of you."

"Me and his grandfather did great things back in the day. Rest in peace." He turned to shake Howard's hand. "Jesus, what happened to you, kid?"

"Cut himself shaving," said Serge, heading for the door.

"Where are you going?" asked Roy. "You just got here."

"The three of you have a lot to talk about."

"What do you mean?"

Serge continued walking. "Your new couriers. The best and the brightest."

"But what about you?"

"Got plans."

"What kind of plans?"

Bells jingled. Cars whipped by.

Serge turned around in the open doorway. "Florida, a full tank of gas and no appointments."

The door closed. He climbed into the Fury.

A passing race fan noticed the magnetic sign on the Plymouth's door. "Wooo! Kurt Busch!"

Serge flashed a peace sign out the window. "Wooo! I had two!" And he took off down Biscayne Boulevard.